They talked lo~~~~~~~~~~~~
against his side, a handful of hair wound around her fingers.
When she started to slide to the floor, he picked her up, laid
her out on the bed, and covered her with one of the furs.

His affection for the human grew steadily by the day.
Sometimes by the minute. And it wasn't simply her beauty,
but her utter lack of fear of everything and anything except
her brother. She didn't fear dying. She didn't fear battle. And,
most importantly, she didn't fear Fearghus. She touched him.
Ran her hands across his scales and through his mane.

But it was when he covered her up with the fur and she
sighed his name in her sleep that he lost his heart.

Dragon Kin novels from G.A. Aiken

Dragon Actually

About a Dragon

What a Dragon Should Know

Last Dragon Standing

The Dragon Who Loved Me

How to Drive a Dragon Crazy

Published by Kensington Publishing Corporation

DRAGON
ACTUALLY

G.A.
AIKEN

ZEBRA BOOKS
KENSINGTON PUBLISHING CORP.

http://www.kensingtonbooks.com

ZEBRA BOOKS are published by

Kensington Publishing Corp.
119 West 40th Street
New York, NY 10018

All Kensington titles, imprints and distributed lines are available at special quantity discounts for bulk purchases for sales promotion, premiums, fund-raising, educational or institutional use.

Special book excerpts or customized printings can also be created to fit specific needs. For details, write or phone the office of the Kensington Special Sales Manager. Attn.: Special Sales Department. Kensington Publishing Corp., 119 West 40th Street, New York, NY 10018. Phone: 1-800-221-2647.

Zebra and the Z logo Reg. U.S. Pat. & TM Off.

ISBN-13: 978-1-4201-3352-3
ISBN-10: 1-4201-3352-7

First Printing: September 2008
First Expanded-Edition Printing: November 2013

10 9

Printed in the United States of America

To Cypress B. and Terri O.,
the first fans of Fearghus the Destroyer
and his kin.

As they both know,
there is nothing like having the loyalty of dragons.

Dear Reader:

As I write this letter to all of you, the one thing I can't get over is that the first story in this book and the first story in the Dragon Kin series, "Chains & Flames," started off as a short story. Something for me to write just to pass the time.

And now, nearly ten years later, here we are. Again. With my first dragon love, Fearghus the Destroyer, and one of my absolute favorite heroines, Annwyl the Bloody. I love that I'm back here again with my dragons. I never get tired of them. First Fearghus and Annwyl, then Bercelak the Great and Dragon Queen Rhiannon. And, for the first time ever, Bercelak's brother, Addolgar the Cheerful and his future dragoness love, Braith of the Darkness.

In past books, I briefly mentioned that Addolgar had a mate and her voice makes an appearance in Bercelak and Rhiannon's story, but I've never really written about her in any detail. Until now. And I have to say, it was entertaining to discover all her foibles and issues. Of course, she's one of the few dragons willing to admit that she actually has foibles and issues.

Now one thing I wanted to point out to everyone was the reading order of this book. I haven't changed the original order of the first two stories and I've added Addolgar's story at the end, because that's how I've written them. And much of the humor builds on that. But I do know that some readers like their stories in chronological order. If that's you, then you should read the stories in this order: "A Tale of Two Dragons," "Chains & Flames," "To Challenge a Dragon."

I hope that helps. And thanks to my readers. All of you are the absolute best.

Enjoy.

—G.A. Aiken

Contents

DRAGON
ACTUALLY

Chapter 1

He'd heard the sounds of battle for quite some time. But, as always, he ignored it. The wars of men meant nothing to him. Never had. But those same sounds right outside his den? Well, that did stir him to move.

His tail unwound from around his body and he slowly moved to the entrance of his home. He didn't know what to expect and was not sure he even cared, but things were pretty boring right now and this just might prove interesting. Or, at the very least, provide dinner.

The blade entered Annwyl's side, ripping through armor and flesh and tearing through organs. Blood flowed and she knew she was dying. The soldier smiled at her cry of pain, which only brought out the telltale rage Annwyl had become famous for.

She raised her blade and, with a cry of pure bloodcurdling fury, swung it. The steel sang through the air as it swiped through the man, separating his head from his neck. His blood slashed across her face and arm. The other soldiers stopped. They had handily disposed of her small band of warriors without much trouble once they had them backed into this desolate glen. But she never allowed them an easy path to the killing blow. Until now.

Her life's blood drained from her body and she knew her

time grew short. Her vision hazy, she felt weaker and lighter. She struggled to breathe. But she'd fight as long as she had breath in her body. Annwyl raised her sword, clasping the handle in both bloody hands, and waited for the next attack.

One of the men stepped forward. She could tell by the look on his face that he wanted to be the one to take her head. Present it to her brother so he could keep it as a trophy and warning to others who would dare question his reign.

She watched him move with assured slowness. Clearly, he also knew she was dying. Knew she couldn't fight much longer.

Her legs shook as her strength fled, and her body ached to lie down for just a few minutes and sleep. Just a little nap. . . .

Annwyl's eyes snapped open and she realized the soldier was that much closer. She swung her sword and he easily parried the blow. He smiled and Annwyl would give her soul for just one last surge of strength to wipe that smug smile off his face.

The soldier looked back at his comrades, making sure they were all watching before he killed her. But he left himself open. And one thing her father always taught her . . . never let an obvious opportunity pass by. She ran him through with her blade, slamming the steel into his stomach as his head snapped back around to look at her in horror. For good measure, she twisted her sword in his gut, watching in satisfaction as he opened his mouth to scream but left the world with nothing more than a whimper.

She yanked her blade out of him and he dropped to the ground. She knew that would be her last kill, but she would still die with her blade raised. She turned to the remaining men but they, to her surprise, no longer found her of any interest. They looked past her. Into the cave she now stood in front of.

Annwyl tried to figure out what new trick this could be, but she never took her fading eyes off the men in front of her. Even as the ground shook under her. Even as they backed away from her in obvious horror. Even as the enormous shadow fell across her body, completely blocking out the sun.

It wasn't until the men screamed and began to run that she glanced up to see black scales hovering just above her. When the scales moved, as a large breath was inhaled into even larger lungs, she finally looked back at the fleeing soldiers.

The stream of fire flew across the glen, destroying trees, flowers, and, eventually, men. Using her sword now to prop herself up, she watched as the enemy soldiers were engulfed in flame, their bodies writhing as they desperately fought to put out the fires that covered them.

A small sense of satisfaction rippled through her, even with the knowledge that she would be next. As the screams died away, Annwyl again looked up to find the dragon now looking down at her. He watched her with obvious curiosity and made no move to blast her into oblivion. At least not yet.

"I'd fear you, Lord Dragon," she got out as the little strength left fled her body and she dropped to one knee, her hand still holding her blood-covered sword. "If I weren't already dying." She gave a bitter half-smile. "Sorry to deny you that tasty morsel." She coughed and blood flowed onto her chin and down her burnished steel armor.

Annwyl's body dropped to the ground. And, soon after, she felt herself moving. She didn't know whether her soul had passed over to the land of her ancestors or into the mouth of a beast, but either way she was done with this life.

Chapter 2

Annwyl heard moaning. Incessant, loud moaning. It took her several long moments to realize that she was the one making the annoying sound.

She forced her eyes open and struggled to focus. She knew that she lay in a proper bed, her naked body covered with animal furs. She could hear the crackle of a pit fire nearby and feel its warmth. Other than that, she had no idea where she was or how by the gods she got here. Last thing she remembered . . . she died. But there was a little too much pain for her to be dead.

Her eyes focused and she realized she was in a room. A room with stone walls. She blinked again and attempted to still the rising panic. These were no mere stone walls. But cave walls.

"By the gods," she whispered as she reached out and touched her hand to the cold grey stone.

"Good. You're awake."

Annwyl gulped and prayed the gods were just playing a cruel joke on her. She raised herself on her elbows when that deep, dark voice spoke again, "Careful. You don't want to tear open those stitches."

With utter and almost heart-stopping dread, Annwyl looked over her shoulder and then couldn't turn away. There he was. An enormous black dragon, his wings pressed tight against his body. The light emanating from the pit fire causing his shiny black scales to glisten. His huge horned head rested in the center of one of his claws. He looked so casual.

If she didn't know better, she'd swear he smirked at her, his black eyes searing her from across the gulf between them. A magnificent creature. But a creature nonetheless. A monster.

"Dragons can speak, then?" *Brilliant, Annwyl.* But she really didn't know what else to say.

"Aye." Scales brushed against stone and she bit the inside of her mouth to stop herself from cringing. "My name is Fearghus."

Annwyl frowned. "Fearghus?" She thought for a moment. Then dread settled over her bones, dragging her down to the pits of despair. "Fearghus . . . the Destroyer?"

"That's what they call me."

"But you haven't been seen in years. I thought you were a myth." Right now, she silently prayed he was a myth.

"Do I look like a myth?"

Annwyl stared at the enormous beast, marveling at the length and breadth of him. Black scales covered the entire length of his body, two black horns atop his mighty head. And a mane of silky black hair swept across his forehead, down his back, nearly touching the dirt floor. She cleared her throat. "No. You look real enough to my eyes."

"Good."

"I've heard stories about you. You smote whole villages."

"On occasion."

She turned away from that steady gaze as she wondered how the gods could be so cruel. Instead of letting her die in battle as a true warrior, they instead let her end up as dinner for a beast.

"And you are Annwyl of Garbhán Isle. Annwyl of the Dark Plains. And, last I heard, Annwyl the Bloody." Annwyl did cringe at that. She hated that particular title. "You take the heads of men and bathe in their blood."

"I do not!" She looked back at the dragon. "You take a man's head, there's blood. Spurting blood. But I do not bathe in anything but water."

"If you say so."

His calmness made her feel overly defensive. "And I'm not just taking men's heads. Only the enemies of Dark Plains. My brother's men."

"Ah, yes. Lorcan. The Butcher of Garbhán Isle. Seems to me if you simply took *his* head your war would be over."

Annwyl gritted her teeth. And it wasn't from the pain of her wound. "Do you think that I've not thought of that? Do you think that if I could get close enough to the little toe-rag that I would not kill him if I had the chance?" The dragon didn't answer and her rage snapped right into place.

"Well . . . *do you?*"

The dragon blinked at her sudden outburst. "Do you always get this angry at the mention of your brother?"

"*No!*" She barked. Then, "Yes!" Annwyl sighed. "Sometimes." The dragon chuckled and she fought the urge to start screaming. And to keep screaming. His laughter wasn't an unpleasant sound, but chatting up a dragon . . . well, perhaps she *was* finally going mad.

The dragon slowly moved from behind her and brought more of his enormous body into the room. He settled to her right, but she could only see half of him without turning her head. The rest remained outside the alcove. She wondered what he looked like in his entirety.

"Why, exactly, am I not . . ."

"Dead?"

She nodded.

"You would be, if I hadn't found you."

"And why did you save me?"

"I don't know. You . . . fascinate me."

Annwyl frowned. "What?" Compared to a dragon, she was nothing. Just human.

"Your bravery. It fascinates me. When you saw me you didn't try to run like those men. You stood your ground."

"I was already dying, what was the point?"

"It doesn't matter. The dragon-fear affects young and old. The dying and the strong. You should have run for your life or dropped to your knees begging for mercy."

"I drop to my knees for no man," she snapped before thinking. He laughed outright. A low, pleasant sound. Like his speaking voice. Shame it belonged to a monster.

"I'll keep that in mind." He chuckled as he carefully turned his big body, his head coming frighteningly close to her, and walked out of the chamber. She watched as his tail swung into the room, its sharp end grazing against the stone walls. She tried not to panic when she realized that his tail alone stretched the length of at least two of the tallest men in her troops. "I will send someone to help you up and get you fed."

"A man?"

"What?" The dragon slammed his large head into the ceiling.

Annwyl lowered herself back on the bed. That had just been a dream. "Nothing. I'm tired."

"Then you best get some sleep."

"Wait!" He stopped and looked over his shoulder at her. Annwyl took in a deep breath. "Thank you. For saving me."

"You're welcome, beautiful one." He started walking again. "But don't get too comfortable," he casually tossed over his shoulder. "Who knows what I'll make you do to repay me my kindness."

Annwyl leaned back against the soft bed and felt a shudder run through her. She just wished she could say that she shuddered from fear or, at the very least, revulsion. What truly worried her was that it felt like neither.

Fearghus rubbed the fresh bump on his head. He'd heard about Annwyl the Bloody's rage, but he had no idea how overwhelming it could be. Her angry bellow was damn near as powerful as a dragon's roar.

No wonder she hadn't defeated her brother yet. He terrified her. He could tell from her overzealous rage at the mere mention of the man.

If she faced Lorcan now, even if her body completely healed, he doubted she would defeat him. Either her anger or her fear would get the best of her.

And for some inexplicable reason that thought worried the hell out of him. When did he start caring about humans? Unlike some of his kin, he didn't hate humans. Yet he didn't live among them either. So his original plans for the human girl were to simply heal her wounds, then dump her near a human village. He didn't like complications. He didn't like anyone around him. He liked peace. He liked quiet. And not much else. But the mere thought of just leaving her somewhere sickened him.

He could already tell this was going to get complicated. And he hated complications.

"Good. You're awake." Annwyl looked up into the face of a woman. A witch, based on the precise, but brutal scar that marred one side of her face. All witches were marked in such a manner on order of her brother. The face behind the scar looked as if it might have been beautiful once. "You must have fallen asleep after he left." She pulled the fur covering off Annwyl's body. "Let's get you up."

Annwyl slowly swung her legs off the bed and, using one arm, pushed herself up.

"Careful now. Don't want to open up that wound again."

Annwyl nodded as she sat quietly, waiting for the nausea that suddenly descended upon her to pass.

"You're very lucky, you know."

"Am I?"

"Most other dragons would have made you a meal. Not a guest."

Annwyl nodded slowly, "I know." She looked at the witch again. "I have seen you before."

"Aye. I help at the village when I can."

"The healer. I remember now. I had no idea you befriended the dragons."

"They have my loyalty."

Annwyl looked at the woman's scars. Not surprising she risked life among the dragons rather than of men. "Did my brother do that to you?"

"He ordered it. He is not a friend to the Sisterhood." The woman wrapped a robe around Annwyl's bare shoulders.

Her brother hated all witches. Mostly because they were women. And he absolutely hated all women. "He's always been afraid of that which he does not understand."

"Does that include you?"

Annwyl laughed as she slowly pushed herself off the bed. The laugh sounded bitter even to her own ears. "My brother understands me all too well. That's why both of us have struggled to take any ground."

"I see you did not escape his punishment." The witch motioned to the wounds on the young woman's back. The raised flesh healed but still an angry red.

"That's not from him." Annwyl pulled the robe tight around her body. Velvet and lush, she loved the softness of it against her battle-hardened skin. She wondered what rich baron the dragon took this from as he tore his caravan apart and ate the occupants.

The woman put her arm around Annwyl's waist and helped her to a table laid out with food and wine. "Your name is . . . Morfyd. Yes?" Annwyl lowered herself into a sturdy chair.

"Yes."

"Did you help heal me as well?"

"Yes."

"Well, thank you for your help, Morfyd. It is greatly appreciated."

"I did it because the dragon asked. But betray him, lady—"

"Don't threaten me." Annwyl easily cut in without even looking up from the food before her. "I really hate that. And you need not remind me of my blood debt to the dragon." Annwyl sipped wine from a silver chalice and stared at the woman. "I owe him my life. I'll never betray him. And don't call me 'lady.' Annwyl will do."

Carefully placing the chalice on the wood table, she found Morfyd staring at her. "Something wrong?"

"No. I'm just very curious about you."

"Well," Annwyl grinned, "I've been told that I'm fascinating."

Morfyd pulled out the only other chair and sat across from Annwyl. "I have heard much about your brother. It amazes me you still live."

Annwyl began to eat the hearty stew, desperately trying not to think too hard about what kind of meat it contained. "It amazes me as well. Daily."

"But you saved many people. Released many from his dungeons."

Annwyl shrugged silently as she wondered whether that was gristle she currently chewed on.

"No one else would challenge him. No man would step forward to face him," Morfyd pushed.

"Well, he's my brother. He used to set fire to my hair and throw knives at my head. Facing him in combat was inevitable."

"But you lived under his roof until two years ago. We've all heard the stories about life on Garbhán Isle."

"My brother had other concerns after my father died. He wanted to make sure everyone feared him. He didn't have time to worry about his bastard sister."

"Why didn't he marry you off? He could have forged an alliance with one of the bigger kingdoms."

Annwyl briefly thought of Lord Hamish of Madron

Province and how close she came to being his bride. The thought chilled her.

"He tried. But the nobles kept changing their minds."

"And did you help them with that?"

She held up her thumb and forefinger, a little bit apart. "Just a little."

For the first time, Morfyd smiled and Annwyl found herself warming up to the witch a bit.

Annwyl pushed her nearly empty bowl away from her and drank more of the wine. It shocked her how well she ate. Shocked her that she still breathed.

"Make sure you finish off the wine. I have added herbs that will heal you and stave off infection."

Annwyl stared warily into her wine chalice. "What kind of herbs?"

Morfyd shrugged as she stood, picking up Annwyl's empty bowl. "Lots of different ones. It's my own potion. It works quite well. It can also heal rashes and gout. And prevent a woman from becoming with child. But I guess that doesn't matter to you."

Annwyl glanced up from her wine. "Why do you say that?"

"Because you're a virgin."

Annwyl froze. That couldn't be just an assumption. She'd lived with a male army for well over two years; everyone assumed she'd lost her virginity ages ago.

"How did you . . . know that?"

"He told me."

Annwyl knew the witch meant the dragon, and that's when the fury built up in her chest. A fury she never could control. "*Dragon!*" She bellowed his name so loudly, Morfyd stumbled back away from her.

The ground shook as the dragon returned to her. "What? What is it?"

Annwyl forced herself to her feet, her hand against her recent wound. "How did you know? And tell me true."

"Know what?" He looked at Morfyd who shrugged and quickly left. Almost ran.

"That I was a virgin. No one knows that. How did you?" She had no idea how long her deep sleep held her. Unable to protect herself. Unable to stop someone from . . . she shook her head. She couldn't bear to even think it.

"This is why you *demand* my presence? Because I know your deep, dark secret?"

"Not that you know. But *how* you know."

He lowered his head until they were eye to eye. But Annwyl, too angry for logic, did not flinch or back away. Considering his head was the length of her body and she towered over most men, she probably should have. Instead she let her anger wash over her. Just as she always had. "Well? *Answer me!*"

His black eyes narrowed at her angry shout, and his nostrils flared. "I can smell it on you."

Annwyl reared back from the dragon. "What?"

"I can smell it on you. That no man has been with you. That your maidenhead is still intact. That you, beautiful one, are a virgin."

Annwyl looked at the dragon in horror, her voice no more than a whisper. "Really? You can smell that on me?"

"No," he responded flatly. "But you are quite chatty in your sleep."

She rolled her eyes. "You tricky . . ." Her anger fled as quickly as it came. She leaned against the table, her strength waning.

"So, did you think I somehow took advantage of you while you slept?"

"Well. . . ." Annwyl flinched as one talon tapped impatiently on the stone floor awaiting her answer. "The thought had crossed my mind." She lowered herself into one of the other chairs surrounding the table, too weak to stand any longer. "I'm sorry. I know only what I learned from my brother . . . and he would have checked."

The great beast sighed. "I have heard tales of your brother. You do realize he should have been killed at birth?"

Annwyl smiled. "If only." She looked across the cave floor to the bed. It looked so far away and her body was still so weak.

"Here." He lowered his claw and opened it. Black talons as long as her leg glistened at Annwyl.

"You must be mad."

"How did you think you got in here?"

"Yes, but . . ." There she went again. Treating him as an animal when, in the little time she'd known him, he'd treated her with more respect than any man she'd met at her brother's castle.

She pushed herself up and took the two steps to his outstretched claw. With force of will she didn't know she possessed she stepped onto it, pushing out the vision she had of him shoving her into his mouth like a piece of steak. He lifted her up, gently moving his forearm until he had reached the bed. He carefully lowered her onto the fur coverings.

"Now, let's try not to have any more fits of anger until you get more of your strength back."

Annwyl laughed. "As you wish."

She sat down on the bed, her long legs hanging over the side. She watched his body leave the cavern. His long tail following behind. But Annwyl wondered if it had a will of its own as it whipped out and wrapped itself around her leg. For a brief moment she worried it might drag her across the room. But instead it caressed her leg, the ebony scales rubbing against her calf. Then it released her and disappeared with the dragon that wielded it.

Long after he'd gone and she slid herself back under the fur covers, Annwyl still felt where he'd touched her leg. And she wondered what insanity had begun to take over her normally sensible mind.

Lorcan of Garbhán Isle stared out over his battlements, watching the two suns lower in the west, and wondered how his sister kept slipping from his grasp.

No matter what he did or what he tried, she just wouldn't die. And the longer she lived, the more men she killed. His men. His troops. The number of headless bodies with her name carved on their chest rivaled even his own. Of course, his took thirty-one years to achieve. She'd accumulated hers in little over two.

He wished now he'd killed her when he had the chance. She was ten, he just fourteen. She had just arrived, sleeping soundly in her new bed. He held the pillow in his hands. He knew he could smother her, and no one would ever know. But she woke up, looked at him, and flew into a blinding rage. Which he returned. His father found the two of them rolling around on the floor trying to choke each other. The man had not been pleased and he made them pay for waking him out of a sound sleep.

Lorcan winced, remembering the brutality of the beating they both received. What gave him small satisfaction was that he'd expected the beating. His bastard sister apparently lived a simple life in her poor village and received little or no discipline. Her reaction to her punishment . . . well, truly reward enough for him.

He didn't know one could hate someone as much as he hated this girl. But she continued to make a fool of him. There were several surrounding kingdoms that gave her campaign gold and troops in the hopes she would do what they could not. Kill him. Take his throne.

He'd see her head on a spike outside his castle walls first. And he now had the perfect ally to assist him.

He never much liked witches. Didn't like the idea of such weak beings as females having that kind of power that they probably could not control. But he tolerated sorcerers well enough. And Hefaidd-Hen was just what he needed. Pay him well and Hefaidd-Hen would hand you the world. He'd proven himself over and over the few months they'd been allies. Although he still hadn't captured his sister.

Lorcan heard the moan of the soldier pinned to the floor beneath his boot. With a sneer, he pushed his foot down harder on his neck. The worthless little bastard had failed him. He'd come back without the bitch.

He glanced over his shoulder at his lieutenants. They watched him, trying their best to hide their fear. But he could smell it. He looked back at the lowering suns. "I want my sister." He growled the words low. "*I want my sister!*" He slammed his foot down, snapping the man's neck and crushing his jaw. "*Now get out of my sight!*"

He heard them run from the room.

They better run.

He would have his sister. He would see the bitch dead if he had to destroy half the world to get to her.

"Well, I see now why the women in the village avoid her. She's crazy."

Fearghus the Destroyer settled his enormous bulk near his lair's underground lake. "She's not crazy, little sister. She's angry."

Morfyd settled against a rock opposite her brother, wrapping her cloak tightly around her body. Her human form was constantly cold, constantly shivering. And yet, she lived freely among the humans. They all believed her to be human. Merely a powerful witch and healer. Even as Annwyl's brother ordered her face sliced open during the early days of his reign, she stayed human. Fearghus could simply never understand why.

But for the first time, Fearghus needed to call on his sister as a human. His power could only keep Annwyl alive for a short time. Morfyd and her ancient dragon Magicks actually healed the girl by mending her damaged organs. And as a human female, she could comfortably tend to the girl's needs.

Morfyd nodded. "From what I've heard she has much to be angry about. It's a well-known fact that her father was a tyrant and her brother hated her from the day she appeared."

"Do you know why?" Fearghus found himself becoming obsessively fascinated with the girl.

"I know they don't have the same mother. Annwyl's mother never married her father. You know how important that is to these humans. And Lorcan never let her forget that she was a bastard. A *poor* bastard, no less, from some little village east of Kerezik."

"Can she be trusted?"

Morfyd shrugged. "Her men are loyal to her. And as much as the village women avoid her they do respect her. They trust their men's lives with her. But whether *we* can trust her? That I do not know, brother. She's still human."

Fearghus, too, wasn't sure he could trust Annwyl. Dragons possessed powers that far outweighed most creatures. But these powers, like their ability to use flame or to shift to human, kept them alive. Humans were a treacherous and dangerous lot and made killing one of his kind as some sort of rite of passage. No. His brethren relied on secrecy. He couldn't and wouldn't betray that to a girl he knew nothing about. Just bringing her to his lair was a dangerous risk he normally would never take. There were very few who knew a dragon lived in Dark Glen. And those who stumbled upon him in the past he quickly silenced. But that hadn't been an option for Annwyl. She really did fascinate him, just as he said. Her bravery. Her strength. Her beauty. And she was beautiful. Tall. Strong. Brown hair with golden streaks that reached down past the waist of her lean body.

"I'm still impressed she challenged you like that," his sister continued. "Although it could just be more proof that she's mad."

Fearghus heard her, but barely. His mind busy recalling when he first found Annwyl. He shifted to human to easily remove her armor and get at her wound. He remembered how quickly and strongly his human body reacted to the sight of her. Naked, pale, and covered in her own blood, there was something about her that called to him. As he chanted the spell that would keep her alive until Morfyd arrived, she watched him with the darkest green eyes he'd ever seen. Over the subsequent days, while he cared for her, he kept seeing those eyes in his dreams. That long, lean body covered in many battle scars there as well. Without even trying, the girl trapped his attention and he couldn't stop thinking about her, which was unusual. Quite a few females had graced his life over the more than two hundred years he existed. All of them beautiful and cultured. Some human and some dragon. But none entranced him like this tiny girl. How tall was she anyway? Maybe six feet? He smiled; only his people would call her "tiny."

A small fireball hit him in the face. He again looked at his sister, smoke still curling out from her human nostrils.

"What, brat?"

"I said she'll want to return to her men as soon as she can."

"I know."

His sister smiled up at him. "And will you be ready for that, idiot?"

"It's Lord Idiot to you." Fearghus rested his head on his crossed forearms. "And yes, brat. I will be."

No matter how beautiful Annwyl was to him, he wouldn't

get involved with some human girl. He would simply let her heal, then send her back to her people. And that would be the end of that.

Chapter 3

Annwyl dreamed again. Ever since that bastard's sword impaled her, the same dream returned to her over and over again. Of a beautiful man with long black hair and dark brown eyes. Tall, powerful, and strong of body. Standing over her, he would wipe her brow and softly whisper that she would live. And once, in her favorite dream, he'd kissed her. The softest, sweetest kiss she'd ever received.

And every time she woke up and found him not there, the same twinge of regret tightened her chest and made her body ache. The same twinge of longing racked her waking hours.

Long ago Annwyl gave up hope that she'd ever find a man she could love and respect. The warriors at her brother's castle were brutish, rude, and often brainless. By the time she escaped and went on to lead her army, she'd become almost dead inside. Over the two years she led the rebellion a few of her men showed her some interest . . . until something made her angry. Then they all seemed to drift away. Unlike the dragon. He didn't shrink from her rage. He appeared to enjoy it. Greatly.

The strange way of man and beast. It never failed to confuse her.

She wondered where she'd created this dream lover from. Had she ever seen the man before? Perhaps in one of the towns or villages that aided her troops? Or perhaps she created him from her own imagination. She knew not. But lately she'd begun to regret having to wake up.

He sat on the edge of the bed and stared at her, as he always did. He stroked her face with his large, strong hand. She sighed contentedly and smiled. He returned it with a smile of his own. Annwyl felt bold in this dream world. Brazen. She reached out a hand and slid it around the back of his neck, drawing him down for a kiss. She liked this dream lover, he didn't resist her. Instead he let her lead him. When their lips met, her whole body responded. Intense heat from his body licked over her flesh. Her nipples tightened and grew hard, begging for the touch of those strong hands of his. Heat and moisture pulsed between her legs. She experienced things she never felt before. And she wanted more.

His tongue licked across her lips and she instinctively opened her mouth to let him in. She moaned as his tongue slid across and around hers, and her body arched as she tried to get closer to him. She wanted her dream lover. In her bed. In her.

But he pulled away from her. She grasped for him . . . and found herself facedown on the floor. Again.

"By all that's . . ." She pushed herself up as Morfyd hurried to her side.

"By the gods, lass. Are you all right?"

"Yes. Yes." She took Morfyd's arm and allowed the woman to help her sit back on the bed. "I'm fine." She couldn't keep ending up on the floor. Now it was just getting embarrassing.

"You should leave her there. She looks adorable. Like a puppy."

Annwyl turned narrowed eyes on her dragon rescuer as he sat by the entrance to this part of his lair. "Quiet, dragon," she warned playfully. She'd become used to the dragon lingering near her. Teasing her. In fact, she found she started to like it. To like him.

Morfyd examined her wound, already less painful than it was the previous day. "Why do I keep finding you on the floor," Morfyd asked with a slight mixture of annoyance and humor.

"I keep having this dream about a man. . . ." Remembering they were not alone, Annwyl stopped. She cleared her throat. "Uh . . . it's nothing though." Morfyd only glanced at her, then she turned two suddenly angry eyes on the dragon. Annwyl watched as the dragon looked up at the ceiling. Perhaps examining it for cracks.

"So, how long before I can return to my men?"

"Well—" was all Morfyd got out before the dragon cut her off.

"We need to make sure you're well first. Wouldn't want you to get caught in a battle still weak."

Annwyl shrugged. "That's fine. I just worry about my men. They need to know I'm alive. I don't want them to . . ."

"Give up hope?" Morfyd gently asked as she cleaned off the wound and placed another bandage over it.

"Aye. I can't desert them now."

"You're not. And I doubt they will give up hope." Morfyd straightened up. "But I will see what I can do."

"Thank you."

"I'll bring you some food." Morfyd left, punching the dragon in his side as she walked past him. Had the witch gone mad? Did she not see his fangs?

"Tell me, dragon, do you have anything to read?"

"Read?"

"Yes. Does your kind read?"

"Of course we read!"

"Don't yell."

The dragon growled at her and she fought her smile.

"Come on then." He headed off deep into his lair. Annwyl

wrapped the fur covering tight around her naked body and followed.

Definitely one of the stupidest things he'd ever done. He really couldn't believe he was doing it. He turned a corner and led her to the right. He could have just brought her some books. Dropped them right into her lap. Instead he led her here. He led a human to *his* treasure. *What the hell am I thinking?*

He reached the entrance and stepped in. She stopped dead in her tracks and waited.

Fearghus didn't say anything. He wanted to see her reaction. She didn't speak for several moments. Then, "I'm freezing me tits off. Where are the books?"

Fearghus blinked. "'I'm freezing me tits off,'" he mimicked back to her.

Annwyl shrugged. "I've been with my troops for over two years now," she muttered as if that explained everything.

Fearghus motioned to a corner of the room. "The books are over there." He watched her clamber over gold, jewels, and the other riches he'd claimed over many, many years. She reached the books and examined them closely.

"So do you like to read or are you desperately bored?"

"No. I'm not bored at all. I'm actually enjoying myself quite a bit. It's nice and quiet here." She grabbed two books. "And I love to read. To learn. I should have been a scholar."

"Why aren't you?"

She shrugged as she walked back over the riches as if she stepped on old stones. "My father had other plans for me. He thought I'd make a fine noble's bride."

Fearghus couldn't stop the laugh that burst from his snout. Annwyl glared at him. "Well thank you very much!"

"I mean no offense. I simply don't see you worrying about the supplies for the kitchens or whether you'll breed a son to carry on the family line."

"Really? And what do you see for me?"

"Exactly what you're doing now. Protecting your people from a tyrant."

She smiled and he felt pride for causing it. She began to head back toward where she slept.

"Wait."

"Yes?"

"Wouldn't you like some clothes?"

"You have clothes?" He motioned to several chests buried in a corner. She handed the two books to him and descended on the wooden boxes. She dug through the clothes quickly. She ignored the beautiful and richly made gowns, tossing them aside like a wench's bar dress. But when she discovered a chest filled with men's clothes, she began to take several articles for herself. Several pairs of breeches, shirts, and leather boots that she held up against her rather sizable feet to make sure they would fit.

Once she had what she needed, she took her new clothes and books, and headed out of the cave.

"Well, come on then," she barked lightly at him.

And, like some idiot human, he followed her back to her room. Once there she dropped the clothes and books on her bed and the fur covering to her feet.

Fearghus tried his best not to watch her naked body. But he sadly failed in the attempt. He couldn't help himself. She was beautiful and strong. A fierce warrior with the scars to show it. He desperately wanted to lick every one of those marks.

She pulled on a pair of breeches that were the right length for her, but a little big. When she turned around, showing her beautiful large breasts, he barely bit back his groan in time. She ripped one of the shirts into long, wide strips, her chest moving seductively in time with her actions. When done, she used the strips to wrap around her breasts, binding them in place. She pulled another plain shirt on over her head, pulled on the boots and stood before the dragon.

"Well? What do you think?"

I think you're the most amazing female I've ever met. And I would like to fuck you all night long. Bend over. "What do I think about what?"

She sighed. "Typical male."

Annwyl sat on her bed and rubbed her eyes. Her side ached. Her body cold. But she finally had clothes.

"What's wrong?" She looked up long enough to see the dragon settle down in the chamber, watching her. She found him doing that often.

"Just thinking about my men."

"You are truly worried about them?"

Annwyl nodded. She closed her eyes again and rubbed her palms against them. It helped to relieve the ache that started in her head when she fell to the floor. "They are all good, strong men. But my brother's troops . . ."

"Outnumber you?"

"Aye. Even with the help from the other kingdoms, my brother still has more troops. More supplies. More everything." She lowered her hands. "And we have. . . ." She turned her eyes to the dragon and stopped.

Then she smiled.

If Fearghus were human, he would have run from the room simply from the expression on her beautiful face. He knew what she was thinking. So he decided to end this now. "No."

"I haven't asked you anything yet."

"But you're going to, and the answer is no."

She released a frustrated little growl. "Why?"

"I don't involve myself in the petty problems of men."

"But I'm a woman." She smiled again, and he would have laughed if he weren't so annoyed.

"That you are. And the answer is still no."

She pushed herself off the bed. "We could help each other."

"Wouldn't you rather just take all my gold and jewels, kill me in my sleep, and be done with it?"

She dismissed the riches he offered with a wave of her hand. "Gold I have. I need your power, dragon."

"No." He watched her walk around the cave floor, impressed with how quickly her body was healing. She already appeared stronger, which only seemed to make her more determined.

What have I gotten myself into?

"There must be something we can offer you. Something you want or need."

He sighed dramatically and fell silent for a moment. "Well, I'm always in need of fresh virgin sacrifices."

She rolled her eyes. "Very funny."

"Annwyl, there is nothing that a human can offer me. I have everything I need. There's a reason no one has seen me in nearly seventy years."

She became so agitated he feared she might come out of her skin. "I'm not asking you to give up your life here. Help me defeat Lorcan, and then it can be like we never met. I'll leave you to your solitude."

For some reason that was the last thing he ever wanted to hear from her, but he ignored the pang of regret her statement caused.

"I can't help you defeat your brother. You must do it yourself. And you must do it alone."

"Why?"

"If you do not kill Lorcan yourself, your reign will always be in question. The other kingdoms will rise up against you and kill you and your precious troops. Is that what you want?"

"Of course not."

"Then you best take his head yourself."

Her eyes narrowed as she looked at him. "But you don't think I can." She walked toward him. "Do you?"

"No. Not really."

There went that rage. "*Why not*?"

"Because *you* don't think you can."

Her rage came and went so quickly, it was quite the sight to behold. Her whole body seemed to deflate, her hand going to her wounded side. "You're right. I don't think I can." She sat on her bed. "He's so fast. His skill with a blade . . . I couldn't even touch him."

"You give up too easily. You just need training."

"From whom? I know of no warrior as skilled as my brother."

"I do."

Annwyl looked up. "You know someone?"

"Uh . . ." Things just kept getting more and more complicated. "Yes. I do."

"Do you trust him?"

Only as much as he trusted himself. "Aye. I do."

"And he will help me prepare to kill Lorcan?" Fearghus nodded. "Then, perhaps, you could help my army against my brother's troops?"

"Annwyl . . ."

She leaned forward, wincing from the pain she caused her side. "Please, Fearghus. I know I already owe you my life. But if there's anything . . . It's just to have the power of a dragon behind us—"

"So I help you defeat your brother," he cut in churlishly. "And then what are your plans?"

Annwyl frowned. "My plans?"

"Yes. Your plans. You take your brother's head, your troops are waiting. What is the next thing that you do?"

Annwyl just stared at him. He realized in that instant that

the girl had no plans. None. No grand schemes of controlling the world. No plots to destroy any other empires. Not even the plan to have a celebratory dinner.

"Annwyl, you'll be queen. You'll have to do something."

"But I don't want to be queen." Her body shook with panic, and he could hear it in her voice.

"You take his head, you'll have little choice."

"What the hell am I supposed to do as queen?"

"Well . . . you could try *ruling*."

"That sounds awfully complicated."

"I don't understand you."

"What do you mean?"

"You command the largest rebellion known to this land. From what I understand, your troops are blindingly loyal to you. And other kingdoms send you reinforcements and gold."

"Your point?"

"You're already queen, Annwyl. You just need to take the crown."

She shook her head. "My father didn't believe in crowns. There's a throne, though."

"Then take your throne. Take it and become queen."

"I will. If you fight with me, dragon."

"Will I get any peace if I don't?"

"Sometimes queens have to do things they're not always proud of," she teased. "Including the torturing of handsome dragons, such as yourself. I could have people traipsing in and out of here all the time. *Talkative* people." She smiled as she spoke—and called him "handsome"—but he wouldn't put anything past her.

"Then you don't give me much choice, do you?"

"No. I don't."

"Then I will fight with you, Annwyl."

She grinned, and he felt pride for causing it.

Chapter 4

As the days passed and Annwyl became stronger, she began to venture out into the glen surrounding the dragon's lair. She'd never felt safer than she did at this very moment. In the middle of a dragon's territory with only a sword to protect her. And she could never be safer. He allowed her to do what she wished. Go where she wished. Which she did. Although she actively avoided the section where the smell of burned men still lingered.

Annwyl moved slowly among the trees and flowers. All so beautiful and hers to enjoy in solitude. Like everyone else in the surrounding kingdoms, she had learned to fear Dark Glen. And from the outside, it stood dark and imposing. But once inside, the dense forest created a place of tranquility and quiet. If she'd known as a child that she had nothing to fear, she would have escaped to it long ago.

She rubbed her side. Her wound still a bit tender, but nearly healed. The dragon and witch had done a brilliant job of keeping her alive.

Yet she agonized over the agreement she'd made with the dragon. Was she that desperate to defeat her brother? That desperate to see her brother's blood on her sword that she'd risk the life of the dragon who saved her? Clearly the answer was yes.

But she must be mad. She should flee. Back to her men. Back to the safety of her troops and away from the dragon. She should. But she most likely would not. The question she kept asking herself, though, was why. Why wouldn't she leave this place? Why wouldn't she leave him?

And why did he himself seem to resist the idea any time she mentioned leaving?

Annwyl smiled as she thought about how her little space within his lair kept becoming more and more furnished. First only a bed to sleep in and table for her to eat at. After that, several stuffed chairs appeared. Then a rug. Then a tapestry. Some beautiful silver candlesticks with sweet-smelling candles.

He wanted to make her feel comfortable. At home. Surprisingly, the beast's lair felt more like a home than any place she'd lived in since she was a child and sent to live with her father.

No. She could never repay the dragon for his kindness. As it was, what life she possessed already belonged to him. And yet she felt no fear. She should. He could ask her for anything in order to pay her blood debt to him. No, she felt something altogether different from fear. Anticipation.

Annwyl stopped, her silent revelry broken. She'd sensed the battle before she heard the clash of swords and the cries of dying men. She knew she didn't have all her strength back yet, but she had to see. Had to know if her brother's men had infiltrated the dragon's glen. And if they had, she'd kill them all. She wouldn't put the dragon at any more risk.

She ran quickly and silently, reassured by the weight of the blade strapped to her back and the dagger sheathed at her hip. She slipped behind a boulder and watched the brutal conflict. Her brother's men. About eight of them. All fighting one man.

The man from her dreams.

Annwyl's chest constricted as gooseflesh broke out over her skin. She watched him with wide eyes. His face was the face she saw in her dreams almost every night while she recovered her strength. That black hair the same hair she always made sure to dig her hands into. Who the hell was this? Other than remembering him from her dreams, she still didn't recognize him. A stranger. A large, gorgeous stranger who wore the crest of an army not seen for many years on the bright red surcoat worn over his chain mail.

Annwyl shook her head. She refused to believe that her dream had come to life and now brutally fought her brother's men.

And fight he did. He moved fast. Faster than she'd ever seen a man move before. His skills with a blade unparalleled. He dispatched two of the men within seconds and moved onto the remaining six.

But the blade in her back distracted her from the knight. There hadn't been eight men in the dragon's glen . . . there had been nine.

"Lady Annwyl. When I had the men scout this area, I had no idea we would actually find you."

Annwyl gritted her teeth. She recognized that voice. Desmond L'Udair. One of her brother's many lieutenants and the man who once grabbed her breast during dinner. Of course, only the remaining four fingers on his right hand currently held the blade now digging into her spine.

"Lord L'Udair. I'd really hoped you died." She looked over her shoulder at him. "So, how's the hand?"

Some thought L'Udair handsome. But she only saw the ugly side of him. Like now, when his lips twisted into an angry snarl. He seized her by the hair and snatched her to him so her back and sword slammed against his chest.

"The question, as always, my sweet, is whether I return you to your brother with or without your head?" He held the blade of his weapon against her neck. "Or perhaps we should spend a little time together before I return you at all. I still owe you for the loss of my finger."

"Lay with me, L'Udair, and you risk the rest of your . . . parts." She smiled at him and saw his leer fade.

"What amazes me," said a low voice in front of her, "is that you haven't killed him yet."

Annwyl focused on the mysterious man who had, while L'Udair made his threats, eliminated the rest of the small scouting party.

"Do you really have time for this?" he asked.

She raised an eyebrow. "You're right, of course." Annwyl unsheathed the dagger at her side and in one fluid move brought it back over her shoulder, not stopping until it tore through L'Udair's eye. As soon as he began screaming she pulled away from him before he could finish her off with his own sword. She would have taken his head, but he died quickly and she rarely removed the heads of the dead.

Annwyl heard her dream lover move. She drew the blade strapped to her back, touching the tip against his throat as he got within arm's reach of her. "Hold, knight." She stared at him, taking a deep breath to still her rapidly beating heart. *By the gods, he's beautiful.* And Annwyl didn't trust him as far as she could throw him. Which wasn't far. He had to be the biggest man she'd ever seen. All of it hard-packed muscle that radiated power and strength.

She tightened her grip on her sword. "I know you."

"And I know you."

Annwyl frowned. "Who are you?"

"Who are *you*?"

Her eyes narrowed. "You kissed me."

"And I believe *you* kissed *me*."

Annwyl's rage grew, her patience for games waning greatly. "Perhaps you failed to realize that I have a blade to your throat, knight."

"And perhaps you failed to realize"—he knocked her blade away, placing the tip of his own against her throat—"that I'm not some weak-willed toady who slaves for your brother, Annwyl the Bloody of the Dark Plains."

Annwyl glanced down at the sword and back at the man holding it. "Who the hell are you?"

"The dragon sent me." He lowered his blade. "And he was right. You are too slow. You'll never defeat Lorcan."

Her rage welled up and she slashed at him with her blade. But it wasn't one of her well-trained maneuvers. It felt awkward and messy. He blocked her easily, slamming her to the ground.

Her teeth rattled in her head. Good thing her wound had already healed, otherwise Morfyd would be sewing it up once again.

The knight stood over her. "You can do better than that, can't you?" She stared up at him and he smiled. "Or maybe not. Guess we'll just have to see."

He wandered off. Annwyl knew he expected her to follow. And, for some unknown reason, she did.

She found him by the stream that ran through the glen. It took all her strength to walk up to him. She really wanted to run back into the dragon's lair and hide under his massive wings. She wasn't afraid of this man. It was something else. Something far more dangerous.

As she approached, he turned and smiled. And Annwyl felt her stomach clench. Actually, the clenching might have been a bit lower.

She'd never known a man who made her so . . . well . . . nervous. And she'd lived on Garbhán Isle since the age of ten; all she'd ever known were men who made it their business to make women nervous, if not downright terrified.

"Well," she demanded coldly.

He moved to stand in front of her, his gorgeous smile teasing her. "Desperate are we?"

Annwyl shook her head and stepped away from him. "I thought you said something about training me for battle, knight." *For the dragon.* She would only do this because the

dragon asked her to. And she would damn well make sure he
knew it, too.

"Aye, I did, Annwyl the Bloody."

"Do stop calling me that."

"You should be proud of that name. From what I understand, you earned it."

"My brother also called me dung heap. I'm sure he thought
I earned that too, but I'd rather no one call me that."

"Fair enough."

"And do you have a name?" He opened his mouth to say
something but she stopped him. "You know what? I don't
want to know."

"Really?"

"It will make beating the hell out of you so much easier."

She wanted to throw him off. Make him uneasy. But his
smile beamed like a bright ray of sunlight in the darkened
glen. "A challenge. I like that." He growled the last sentence,
and it slithered all the way down to her toes. Part of her
wanted to panic over that statement, since it frightened her
more than the dragon himself. But she didn't have time. Not
with the blade flashing past her head, forcing her to duck and
unsheathe her own sword.

He watched her move. Drank her in. And when she took
off her shirt and continued to fight in just leather leggings,
boots, and the cloth that bound her breasts down, he had to
constantly remind himself of why he now helped her. To train
her to be a better fighter. Nothing more or less. It was *not* so
he could lick the tender spot between her shoulder and throat.

Annwyl, though, turned out to be a damn good fighter.
Strong. Powerful. Highly aggressive. She listened to direction
well and picked up combat skills quickly. But her anger definitely remained her main weakness. Anytime he blocked one
of her faster blows, anytime he moved too quickly for her to

make contact, and, especially, anytime he touched her, the girl flew into a rage. An all-consuming rage. And although he knew the soldiers of Lorcan's army would easily fall to her blade, her brother was different. He knew of that man's reputation as a warrior and, as Annwyl now stood, she didn't stand a chance. Her fear of Lorcan would stop her from making the killing blow. Her rage would make her vulnerable. The mere thought of her getting killed sent a cold wave of fear through him.

Yet if he could teach her to control her rage, she could turn it into her greatest ally. Use it to destroy any and all who dare challenge her.

The shifting sun and deepening shadows told him that the hour grew late. The expression on her face told him that exhaustion would claim her soon, although she'd never admit it. At least not to him. But he knew what would push her over the edge. He grabbed her ass.

Annwyl screeched and swung around. He knocked her blade from her hand and threw her on her back.

"How many times, exactly, do I have to tell you that your anger leaves you exposed and open to attack?"

She raised herself on her elbows. "You grabbed me," she accused. "Again!"

He leaned down so they were nose to nose. "Yes I did. And I enjoyed every second of it."

Her fist flashed out, aiming for his face. But he caught her hand, his fingers brushing across hers. "Of course, if you learned to control your rage I'd never get near you." He brought her fingers to his lips and kissed them gently. "But until that time comes, I guess your ass belongs to me."

She bared her teeth, and he didn't try to hide his smile. How could he when he knew how it irritated her so? "I think we've practiced enough for the day. At least I have. And the dragon now has a scouting party for his dinner. But I'll be back tomorrow. Be ready, Annwyl the Bloody. This won't get any easier."

Fearghus entered what he now considered her chamber, but immediately ducked the book flung at his head. Clearly she'd been waiting for him. And she was not happy.

"*He's the one supposed to be helping me?*" she roared at him.

"Did you just throw a book at me? In my own den?"

"Yes. *And I'd throw it again!*"

Fearghus scratched his head in confusion. He'd never met a human brave enough—or stupid enough, depending on your point of view—to challenge him. "But," he croaked out, amazed, "I'm a dragon."

"And I have tits. It means nothing to me!"

"What exactly is wrong with you?"

"That . . . that . . ."

"Knight?"

"Bastard!"

"Me or the knight?"

"*Both of you!*"

His anger crawled up his spine and settled itself against the back of his neck. He briefly closed his eyes, taking in a deep soothing breath. She was making him angry, and Fearghus the Destroyer didn't get angry. "I'll come back when you've calmed down." He turned to go, but she seized his tail . . . and pulled.

"Oi! Don't walk away from me!"

If Annwyl could have punched herself in the face, she would have. Anything had to be better than watching the dragon turn, oh so slowly, to face her. She had clearly angered him. *Really* angered him. And when he just as slowly walked over to her, Annwyl knew that she might finally see her ancestors waiting to welcome her home. But no matter, Annwyl planned to stand her ground. She wasn't going to let some dangerously grumpy dragon make her cower. Of course, she did let him back her up against the far cave wall. But she had no choice—he just kept coming.

Annwyl thought briefly about panicking, but that seemed about as useful as punching herself in the face. Instead she straightened her shoulders and looked directly into the dragon's dark eyes.

"You don't scare me, you know." Impressive. She almost sounded as if she meant that.

"Really?" His tail appeared and the dangerously sharp point smashed into the cave wall right beside her head. Her body tensed as bits of stone hit the side of her face. He placed the tip of one of his wings on the other side of her, effectively boxing her in. He leaned in close to her, the flaring nostrils of his snout almost touching her face. "I should scare you, beautiful one. I can turn you to ash where you stand."

The beast had a point, but no use backing down now. "Then do it if you're going to."

The dragon's eyes dragged across the entire length of her body. Then he breathed in deep, his eyes closed, as if he were sniffing a really good meal. . . . *Well, that's not a soothing thought.*

"No one's ever thrown anything at me," he finally got out as his dark eyes again focused on her.

"Well, you deserved it. You should have warned me about him."

Fearghus took a step back. She realized that she'd held her breath the entire time. She let it out as the beast took another step away from her. She guessed he'd decided not to eat her . . . today. "Was it really that bad, Annwyl?" His anger seemed to have dissipated. She wondered how he did that. Control his rage. She envied him the skill.

"Yes. It was."

"But did you learn anything?"

Damn dragon with his bloody life lessons. "That's beside the point."

"Annwyl?"

"All right. Maybe a little." He chuckled and Annwyl, without meaning to, smiled in response. "I've always been better than anyone I've ever fought." Not that she had a choice. Her father knew teaching her to fight was the only way she would ever survive her childhood. Her brother had actively tried to kill her on more than one occasion and she had a tendency to say things that caused some men to want to see her dead. She guessed, though, that none of the men—including her father—expected her to be as good or as brutal a fighter as she turned out to be. "But your knight. He made me feel like I couldn't fight off a ten-year-old boy."

Fearghus sighed. "Give it time. He's . . . uh . . . doing what I asked him to." She didn't want to give it time. Or give the knight a chance. She found him . . . disconcerting. And she didn't like that feeling one bit. And she hated him for making her feel that way. She hated him a lot.

"You sure?"

"Positive." He studied her. "All right?" She shrugged. "Annwyl. Answer me." Gods, he could be commanding. He didn't yell. He didn't have to. And it had nothing to do with the size of him. It sent a delicious little shiver throughout her entire body.

Gods, Annwyl. Get control of yourself!

"Yes. All right." She glared at him, even as her rage slipped away. "But I won't be nice!"

The dragon looked her up and down. "I don't think he'll mind much."

She rolled her eyes. "Probably not." She stepped away from the dragon. "Men are disgusting."

Fearghus couldn't believe how angry she'd made him. He didn't get angry. Annoyed? Definitely. Stern? Absolutely. But to lose his temper? He didn't do that. Ever. Until her. And it didn't help that when she was angry, she gave off that scent . . . a musk, maybe. Something that called to him. He'd smelled it before when, as the knight, he'd annoyed the hell out of her. He'd worked hard to ignore that smell. But this time he leaned in and enjoyed her scent. Let it pulsate through his veins. It gave him all sorts of visions. Things he could do to her. Things she could do to him. It didn't help his resolve.

He watched her walk away. Watched her tight rear move in those leather leggings. He couldn't help himself. He swatted that rear with his tail.

"Oi!" She jumped and turned to glare at the dragon. "What was that for?"

For having the most amazing ass I've ever seen. No. He probably shouldn't say that.

"To remind you that you're in my lair. And don't forget it."

She should have been angry, but she smirked instead. *Interesting.* "I'll bear that in mind."

They stared at each other. And, if Fearghus had been in human form, he would have kissed her and anything else he could think of. But he couldn't do that. He *wouldn't* do that. No involvement with the human. He'd made the decision. He'd stick to it. No matter how much he wanted to suck on those . . . *Dammit.* He needed to go before he did something inappropriate. Fun. But inappropriate. "Well, is there anything else?"

"No."

Good. Fearghus walked to the exit.

"But . . ."

Fearghus cringed and looked back at her. "But?"

"Well, now that"—she cleared her throat—"we have all that resolved, I was hoping we could talk."

"Talk?" That completely distracted him from sucking on anything of hers. "About what?"

"About anything."

If Fearghus had eyebrows he would have raised them. She couldn't get away from the knight, who she believed to be human, fast enough. But she wanted to sit and chat with the dragon who had, just moments before, threatened to burn her to embers. Such an odd girl.

He smoothly turned his big body around and sat back on his hind legs, his head scraping the ceiling. "Well . . . I guess I can."

"Good." She eagerly jumped up on the table, sitting cross-legged. "Should I start then?"

"Perhaps you better."

"As you wish." She fell silent as she thought, and he stared at her breasts. She'd taken the bindings off and he could see the outline of the perfectly round mounds under the cotton shirt. *Gods, Fearghus! Get control of yourself!*

"I know. How old are you?"

"Two hundred and sixty-eight."

"Years?"

"Aye."

"So dragons are immortal?"

"No."

"But legends say you are."

"They're wrong." She prompted him to continue. He wasn't used to talking so much. "The first dragons, the elders, were immortal. But a mated pair asked the gods for the gift of children. The gods agreed, but the price would be that they lose their immortality. Our line is descended from them."

Annwyl stared at him with her mouth open. "That is the sweetest story I've ever heard."

"It is?" The girl read too many books.

"Yes. It's romantic. They gave up immortality to be together and start a family."

Fearghus shrugged. "It's a tale they tell the hatchlings. I'm almost positive there was more to it than that."

"Are you always so cynical?"

"Yes."

"So you're not immortal, but your kind clearly lives a long time."

"Yes. About eight hundred years or so."

"So, compared to other dragons, you're kind of a baby?"

Fearghus grunted. "If you feel the need to put it that way."

"Any siblings?"

"Yes."

"How many?"

Fearghus sighed and settled down for what would clearly be a long and painful night. He almost missed the days when she lay unconscious and near death. "Too many. And you?"

With a frown, "Is that meant to be funny?"

Oops. He actually just meant to be polite. Of course, he'd never been very good at polite. "No. Just wondering if there was anyone else besides the demon-spawn you call kin."

"Sadly no. Or at least none that my father has claimed." She propped her elbows onto her knees and cupped her chin in the palm of her hands. "Are you close to your family?"

"Just one sister. The others I only see at family times. And that is grudgingly."

"Dragons have family times? Is that just a simple get together or are virgin sacrifices required?" Fearghus barked out a laugh and the girl smiled. "See? Got you to laugh."

"That you did."

Maybe the evening wouldn't be that painful after all.

Chapter 5

Brastias, general of the Dark Plains rebellion and Annwyl's second in command, leaned back into the hard wood chair and rubbed his tired eyes. She must be dead. She had to be dead. Annwyl would never disappear this long without word sent. He'd already sent trackers out to find her, but they came back empty-handed, losing her trail somewhere near Dark Glen, a haunted place most men dare not enter.

Of course, Annwyl was not most men. She often dared where others fled. She remained the bravest warrior Brastias knew and he'd met many men over the years who he considered brave.

But Annwyl could be foolhardy and her anger . . . formidable.

And yet every day for two years Brastias thanked the gods for his good fortune. On a whim they had attacked a heavily armed caravan coming from Garbhán Isle. Its cargo had been Annwyl. Dressed in white bridal clothes and chained to the horse she rode, her destiny to be the unwilling bride for some noble in Madron. And based on how heavily armed her procession was, dangerously unhappy about it as well. Once the attack began, one of his men released Annwyl and told her to escape. She didn't. Instead she took up a sword and fought. Fought, in fact, like a demon sent from the gods of hate and revenge. Her rage a mighty sight to behold. By the time the girl finished, she stood among the headless remains of those she killed. Her white gown completely covered in blood. On that day the men had given her the name Annwyl the Bloody and, as much as she hated it, the name stuck.

They returned with her to their encampment, but no one knew what to do with her. The women of the camp shunned her. She frightened them and she turned out to be completely useless with anything domestic. But she possessed information on her brother. She knew where to attack and when. She knew his strengths and his weaknesses. And she wanted nothing more than to destroy him. Soon she brought in the financial assistance of other regions. No one wanted Lorcan in power longer than necessary. If his sister could stop him, she would have their loyalty. She protected their borders and the rebellion's troops grew.

Eventually Annwyl took control and Brastias gave it over gratefully. She earned their loyalty and trust, and after two years the men would follow her down into the very pits of hell if she asked them.

But, if she were dead . . . Brastias didn't want to even consider it. They hadn't found her body. Perhaps they could still rescue her.

"General." Brastias's eyes shifted to the front of his tent. Danelin, his next in command, stood waiting. "There's a witch here to see you."

Brastias nodded once. She probably wanted to see Annwyl or, if his world contained any luck at all, perhaps she could tell him where to find his missing leader.

A tall woman entered his tent. An astounding beauty, tragically marked as a witch. He truly hoped that a special hell waited for men like Lorcan.

She walked toward him. Almost glided. He knew he'd seen her before. The people considered her a talented witch with healing powers. But he had no time for magic or witches. Even beautiful ones. He had a rebellion to win.

"Yes, lady?"

"You are General Brastias?"

"Aye."

The witch glanced at Danelin, refusing to speak in front of him. "Go, Danelin. I will call if you are needed."

Danelin left, closing the tent flap behind him. The woman stood before him. She didn't speak. She just stared.

"So, what is it, woman?" She raised one delicate eyebrow and he felt as if she'd dug down into his very soul.

"I have word of Annwyl of the Dark Plains."

Brastias stood quickly, grasping the woman by the arms; she stood almost as tall as he. "Tell me, witch. Where is she?"

She stared at him. "Remove your hands, or I'll make sure you don't have any." Brastias took a deep breath and released her. "She is safe and alive. But she is healing. She won't be back for another fortnight."

Brastias heaved a sigh of overwhelming relief as he sat heavily in his chair. "Thank the gods. I thought we'd lost her."

"You almost had. But the girl must have the gods smiling down on her."

"Can I see her?"

The woman watched him carefully. "No. But I will get any messages you may have to her."

"Give me a few moments, I need to write something." He grabbed quill and paper and wrote Annwyl a brief-but-to-the-point letter. He folded it, affixed his seal, and handed it to the witch. "Give her this and my love."

"You are her man then?" she asked cautiously.

Brastias laughed. He did like his head securely attached to his shoulders. Becoming Annwyl's man risked that.

"Annwyl has no man because there is no man worthy of her. That includes me. So she has become the sister I lost many years ago in Lorcan's dungeons."

The woman nodded and walked back to the entrance of Brastias's tent. She stopped before leaving. "She asks," the witch spoke softly without turning around, "that you not lose hope."

"As long as she lives, we won't."

Then she was gone. Brastias closed his eyes in relief. Annwyl wasn't dead. His hope returned.

Morfyd landed softly on the glen grounds. Unlike her brother, she'd learned to move silently as dragon.

Once securely on hard earth, she shook her body, releasing the wetness her wings picked up along the flight. She spoke the ancient words of enchantment that allowed her to shift back to human. Moving swiftly, she picked up the clothes she'd hidden away earlier and garbed herself. Her body shook from the chill and she wanted nothing more than to settle in front of a fire to warm her human form.

She'd taken longer than she originally planned to get back. But if Fearghus needed to involve himself in the Sibling War, she wanted to let the queen know now. It would be worse for him if she found out after the fact. Of course the queen didn't seem too interested, but Bercelak was and that could be a problem for them both.

But first she wanted to get the note from the general to Annwyl. She'd learned to like the human girl, with her sudden rages and tendency to end up on the floor. And clearly Annwyl had enthralled her taciturn and cranky older brother.

Fearghus didn't really like anyone. Human or dragon. Among their kind, many considered him rude and inconsiderate. Among humans, they feared the black dragon who smote whole villages. Of course, leave it to humans to exaggerate the truth. He'd only smote one village when their king made killing him into a tournament event.

Morfyd wrapped a cloak around her witch's garb and headed to her brother's den. As always when in human form, she pulled the hood of the cloak over her head to hide her mane of white hair. It was not white from age. Like her mother, she'd been born a white dragon. White dragons were rare and often born with powers far outreaching of other dragons. But she still had a way to go before she could even think to compete against her mother's skill.

She entered her brother's den and moved deep within to reach the girl's chamber. He had practically made that section of the cave into the girl's bedroom.

Very subtle, Fearghus.

As she neared her destination, she heard Annwyl speak and her brother . . . laugh?

Morfyd stopped. Perhaps she heard wrongly. Perhaps she'd finally gone insane. Morfyd inched closer to the chamber and waited.

"Now, I did try to set him on fire once when I was twelve. But, I assure you, I felt awful about it later."

"And how long did that awful feeling last?"

"Until he set the dogs on me."

She heard her brother chuckle and she started at the sound.

"Can I ask you a favor?"

"Another? What do you want now, woman? My gold? My lair?"

"No. No. No. Nothing like that. And this might sound strange . . ."

". . . as opposed to your horse manure story."

"*But* . . ."

"But?"

"Can I touch your horns?"

Morfyd blinked and looked around, half expecting her three other brothers to be standing behind her, proving this was nothing but a joke. Could she have truly heard what she thought she'd just heard?

"I'm sorry. Could you repeat that? Because I think I just got the brain fever."

She heard the girl give a very unladylike snort. "I've never touched a dragon before. Your horns look so beautiful and I would just like to—"

"All right. Stop. Before you say something that will make both of us uncomfortable." She heard her brother move his body. Morfyd realized he was lowering himself so the girl could reach him.

Morfyd couldn't stand not knowing. As silently as she could manage, she peeked around the corner and looked into the girl's chamber. What she saw astounded her, simply because it *was* Fearghus.

The girl stood on tiptoes, Fearghus allowing Annwyl to lean against him as she reached up and ran her strong, battle-scarred hand across his horn, her tanned skin standing out against its shiny blackness. Her other hand moved down his neck and grasped the mane of black hair that flowed across it.

"I didn't know dragons had hair. It's like a horse's mane."

"It is *not* like a horse's mane," Fearghus snapped. To Morfyd's surprise, Annwyl didn't shy away from her brother and scurry across the room. Instead, she laughed, leaning closer against his body.

"No need to get testy. I was merely implying that your kind was really meant to be beasts of burden for us humans. Just like horses. And centaurs."

"Oh, is that all? Well, I apologize, Lady Annwyl. I thought you were saying something insulting."

Morfyd stepped away from Annwyl's chamber. Her brother making jokes? Well, perhaps the time had come for her to completely lose her mind, considering the family she came from. Dragons did do that sort of thing on occasion.

She looked down at the letter she had clutched in her hand. It could wait until tomorrow.

Silently she turned and went to get something soothing to drink. Or, at the very least, some hard ale. She needed something to help her sleep because the last image she'd witnessed before turning away from the chamber would have her awake and obsessing for hours. The image of Annwyl the Bloody, known terror of the Dark Plains, lovingly running her hand down Fearghus's snout . . . and Fearghus the Destroyer letting her.

Fearghus watched Annwyl sleep. They talked long into the night. And she fell asleep lying against his side, a handful of hair wound around her fingers. When she started to slide to the floor, he picked her up, laid her out on the bed, and covered her with one of the furs.

His affection for the human grew steadily by the day. Sometimes by the minute. And it wasn't simply her beauty, but her utter lack of fear of everything and anything except her brother. She didn't fear dying. She didn't fear battle. And, most importantly, she didn't fear Fearghus. She touched him. Ran her hands across his scales and through his mane.

But it was when he covered her up with the fur and she sighed his name in her sleep, that he lost his heart.

Chapter 6

Lorcan threw the table across the room, nearly crushing one of his soldiers. He roared in rage. Seven days and they still hadn't found the bitch girl or any of his men.

He grabbed two heavy wood chairs and flung them as well.

His guards scattered, running for safety. But there was no safety from his rage. A rage rivaled by only one other.

"Find her! Find the bitch!" Several of his men stared blankly at him. "*Now*!" The men ran.

Lorcan leaned his burning forehead against the cool stone of his castle wall.

"My lord?" Lorcan took a deep, soothing breath and looked at his counsel. Hefaidd-Hen still remained the only one brave enough to face him during one of his rages. "Perhaps we are avoiding the obvious."

"Which is?" Lorcan slowly turned, his anger under some control.

"Perhaps your sister has fled to Dark Glen."

"My sister is weak and stupid, but she is not insane. No one goes into Dark Glen. Because no one ever comes back out again. She knows that well enough."

Hefaidd-Hen turned disturbingly milky blue eyes to his master, and Lorcan shuddered inwardly. "She may not have gone there willingly, but it doesn't mean she's not there."

"Then she would already be dead?"

"No. All signs tell me she still lives."

Lorcan snorted. He should have known better than to get his hopes up.

"Then what is your counsel, wizard?"

Hefaidd-Hen smiled, if you could call it that. "Let me take some of your men and go into Dark Glen myself. I will see if I can find her."

"I can't afford to lose you, Hefaidd-Hen. Even if it means destroying her. I need you during these rebel attacks. Every day more troops arrive to fight with her."

"And while she lives they will continue to arrive."

"I said no." Lorcan, his anger spent, sat down heavily in one of the chairs he had not yet thrown. "But send a few of my warriors. Make sure they understand that they go into Dark Glen, or what lies in there will be the least of their worries."

Hefaidd-Hen bowed low. "As you wish, my lord."

Then the wizard took his leave and Lorcan began to breathe again. He thought of his ugly little sister and reveled in the delight he would take in planting her head on a spike outside his castle walls.

"I will have you, bitch," he growled low, hoping his words would find her wherever she was. He wanted her to know that her time would soon end. He wanted her to know he would rule the land in his father's place. He wanted her to know just how much he hated her.

He roared again, his rage returning tenfold. He roared and roared, until he knew she could hear him wherever she was.

Annwyl sprung naked from the bed. Her sword, which she always kept on the floor within arm's reach, firmly grasped in her hand. Her brother's presence surrounded her. She felt him near her. She spun around, expecting to find him standing behind her.

"Are you all right?"

Annwyl barked in surprise at the voice. Without thought, only instinct, she spun around again and threw her sword across the room. The only reason the blade didn't slam into Morfyd's forehead was because the witch moved too fast. She dropped to the floor with a hoarse cry.

"By the gods, Morfyd!" Annwyl, now realizing where she was and that she truly was safe, ran to the woman. "Are you hurt?"

The witch grasped the girl's hand and let Annwyl help her up. "No. No. I'm fine."

"Morfyd, I'm so sorry."

"It's all right." Morfyd sat down heavily in one of the chairs. "I startled you."

Annwyl crouched beside Morfyd. She couldn't bring herself to release the woman's hand. "I thought he was here," she whispered.

Morfyd frowned. "Thought who was here?"

"My brother. I felt him here, Morfyd. As surely as you are standing here now."

"You were just dreaming. He can't hurt you here. Fearghus would never let him."

The witch spoke true, of course. She trusted the dragon with her life, more than any of her own troops. Even more than Brastias.

"Thank you for understanding." Annwyl stood and went back to her bed, wrapping one of the fur covers around her shivering naked body. "And for being able to move so fast. I don't know what I would have done if I . . ."

"But you didn't. So let's not think of it a moment longer. Here." Morfyd handed her a parchment. Annwyl saw the seal of Brastias and grinned.

"You saw him, then?"

"Aye. He seemed heartily relieved that you still live."

Annwyl sat down on her bed. "And my men?"

"They still have hope."

Annwyl nodded. "Thank you for doing this."

Morfyd stood up. "Do not speak of it. I will get you something to eat while you read your letter."

Once the witch left, Annwyl carefully removed the seal and opened the parchment.

Annwyl—
We await your return.
Yours in life, death, and war.
Brastias

Annwyl read the letter again and then held it against her chest. Her army waited. Soon she must return.

* * *

Fearghus watched his sister grab several pieces of fruit. Her human body seemed shakier than usual. "Are you all right?"

"That mad bitch threw a blade at my head."

He studied his sister. "What did you say to her?"

Morfyd swung around to glare at him, fruit flying everywhere. "What did I . . . why do you . . . how dare you . . ." Morfyd stopped and pulled herself together. "*I* did nothing, brother. She was having a nightmare about Lorcan or something. I happened to walk in at the wrong time."

"Or something?"

Morfyd shrugged as she knelt down to pick up the scattered pieces of fruit. "He could very well be contacting her through her dreams."

"I thought you put up protections around the glen?"

"I did," she snapped. "That doesn't mean he hasn't found a wizard to work around them."

Fearghus walked up to his sister. He towered over her in his human form, dressed and ready to start his training with Annwyl. "No one should be able to get past your protections, sister. I don't care if it's the queen herself. I want Annwyl safe. Understand?"

Morfyd's eyes narrowed as she examined her brother. "Why are you dressed like that?" Her frown deepened. "And for that matter, why are you human?"

Damn. "I need to go into town."

"Town for what?"

"Supplies. Now get on with the spellcasting. Please."

He stormed off before she could ask any more questions that would force him to lie to her more.

Annwyl was falling. Then she was landing. Her back hitting the hard ground, then her head. She lay there. Unable to move. Suddenly his face loomed over her.

"Sorry 'bout that."

No he wasn't. He wasn't sorry about anything. She'd gotten in a couple of really good blows and he retaliated, knocking her right on her backside . . . hard.

It took her several moments to get her breath back; by then he reached out to help her stand. She slapped his hands away and dragged herself up so she knelt on the hard ground.

She glared at him.

"What's that look for? It's not my fault you weren't fast enough."

Annwyl punched him in the face. "Was that fast enough?" she snapped.

Now he glared as he clutched his slightly wounded nose.

Annwyl pushed herself to stand up, but the spasm in her neck and shoulder forced her right back down. She moaned in pain and the knight looked at her.

"What is it?"

"Nothing."

"Liar." He moved behind her and placed his hands on her shoulders. His touch sent shocks through her body. Annwyl tried to push his hands off, but he ignored her.

"Stop being difficult."

His strong hands glided across her shoulders and quickly found the spot at the base of her neck where her muscles bunched into tight knots. "Gods, girl. There's a huge knot here." His thumb pushed into the flesh and Annwyl's body jerked.

"Oi! Painful!"

"Sorry."

"No you're not." She stood up while trying to pull away, but he pulled her back.

"Must you be so difficult? If you give me a moment, I can fix this."

Annwyl gritted her teeth.

The knight chuckled, his hands massaging muscles on her shoulder. Annwyl bit her lip and barely stopped herself from moaning. The man had the most unbelievable hands she ever experienced. She closed her eyes and tried to focus on something—*anything!*—that could distract her from the feeling of him touching her.

The muscles loosened under his big fingers and she found herself relaxing . . . grudgingly.

"You know, you still don't know my name."

"And I still don't want to know." When she left the glen with Fearghus she never wanted to see this man again. At least, that's what she kept telling herself.

"Such a difficult girl."

"I'm hardly a girl."

"Oh. Sorry. Do you prefer old maid?"

Annwyl clenched her fingers into tight fists.

"There's that knot again. It just got worse." *What a surprise.*

The knight pulled her arm out, massaging it all the way down. He stopped at her tight fist. "Unclench."

She glared at him but didn't answer. He slapped the back of her hand. "Ow!"

"I said unclench, woman."

She opened her hand and he began to gently massage each finger.

"You don't like me, do you?"

"No. I don't."

"Do you like the dragon?"

"Of course, I like the dragon."

"What do you mean 'of course'? No one likes dragons."

"Then why are you here?" He opened his mouth to answer but abruptly stopped. Annwyl nodded knowingly. "I see."

"You see what?"

"I know what's going on."

"You do?"

"You don't fool me." She pointed at the crest on his surcoat. "That army hasn't been seen in over twenty years."

The knight looked down at his crest as if seeing it for the first time. Annwyl watched as an unruly bit of black hair fell over his eye. She longed to touch that hair. Longed to feel it move across her naked flesh. *I am completely out of control!*

"Really?" He sounded so innocent or at least he tried.

"Yes. Really. Where did you find it anyway? Some castle you robbed? Or the dragon's den? Knight my ass. You're a mercenary. A blade for hire. The lowest of the low."

The knight let out a deep sigh and looked away from her. Ha! She caught him.

He loved the humans' complete inability to see anything even when it stared them right in their faces. He knew what it was, too. Their logic. How could anything the size of a dragon turn into a human? Humans understood nothing of ancient Magick and how powerful it could be.

For a moment, he really thought that Annwyl figured it out. Still, he remained grateful she hadn't. He knew he shouldn't lie to her and, in the beginning, he really hadn't planned to. He trusted her now more than he trusted anyone, but her reaction to him as a human male completely confounded him.

She wanted the knight but hated the knight. Cared for the dragon but, not surprisingly, didn't seem to have any other feelings than general friendliness.

Annwyl continued to be the most complex creature he'd ever met. And, when he wasn't staring at her chest or rear, he found her intelligent, delightful, and extremely funny. Just a joy to be around. But only the dragon seemed lucky enough to see that side of her. When he came to her as the knight, he found her surly, foul-tempered, and downright rude. He still found her a joy to be around, but probably because he liked how she smelled when she became angry. A musk all her own that forced him to fight his erection every time he caught a whiff of it.

Annwyl, the things I could do to you . . .

He needed to focus. Right now. Right this second. Or he would end up doing something very stupid.

He cleared his throat and released her arm. "Feel better?"

"Yes."

"And . . ."

"And what?" He raised an eyebrow and Annwyl scowled. "Thank you."

"Now that wasn't so hard, was it?"

She turned away from him and he caught sight of that lovely rear again. He slapped it with the palm of his hand. Annwyl stopped. Gritted her teeth. But did nothing.

He came up behind her. "Good," he whispered in her ear. "You're getting better. You want to beat me to a bloody pulp but you're able to restrain yourself. Nice." He desperately wanted to touch her, but he fought the desire as best he could. He had no idea his human body could be so hard to control.

"Now," he barked gruffly. "Let's start again."

"So." Morfyd placed a bowl of stew in front of Annwyl. "Tell me about your Brastias."

Annwyl frowned. "He's not *my* Brastias. At the moment, he's no woman's Brastias." Annwyl's frown quickly turned to a grin. "Interested?"

"What?" Morfyd started. "No."

"Oh, then you are just being nosy."

"Oh, forget I asked."

Annwyl dug into the hearty stew. After her long day with the knight, her body demanded sustenance.

"Is it hard to be with all those men? All day? Every day?"

Annwyl drank some of Morfyd's wine. She knew no threat

of infection remained, but the wine still tasted unbelievably delicious.

"Not at all."

"Really?"

"Absolutely. Just let one of the men touch you inappropriately and you take his arm off right at the shoulder joint. Then, as he's bleeding to death, you slam his face into a few things, and you'll find the other men leave you alone."

Morfyd stared at Annwyl with wide eyes. "What?"

Morfyd cleared her throat. "Nothing."

Annwyl could hear Fearghus coming, the cave shaking with each mighty step he took. She didn't look up from her stew until he entered her chamber. "Lord Dragon."

"Lady Annwyl."

"I was wondering when you were going to come and visit me."

The dragon barely glanced at Morfyd. "Don't you have somewhere to be, Morfyd?"

"No."

The dragon bumped her chair with one of his talons. She glared but stood up. "Fine. I'm heading back to the village."

"Good idea. All those sick humans for you to take care of."

Morfyd sneered at the dragon while addressing Annwyl. "See you in the morning, Annwyl."

"Have a good night."

Annwyl finished off her stew, then turned to the dragon, a chalice of wine in her hand.

"So, Lord Dragon, what are your plans for this evening?"

He adjusted his body awkwardly and the end of his deadly tail landed gently in her lap. "Well, I thought we could do that thing again."

"That thing?" Annwyl desperately fought a smile as she ran her hand across the scaled tip. Its very edge shaped like an arrowhead and as sharp. She briefly wondered if the dragon ever needed to sharpen it with a stone. "Do you mean talking?"

"Yes. Yes. Whatever it is called."

"You like talking, don't you? Just admit it."

"I like talking to *you*. And that is all I will admit to."

"Fine. No need to get testy." His snout moved close as well. Without even thinking about it, she rubbed her hand over it. And the dragon let her. "So tell me more about your family."

"Don't you get bored with my family stories?"

"Not at all." She leaned forward and looked at him, her hand once again resting on the tip of his tail. "Waiting."

Fearghus sighed. "Well, one time we shaved our baby brother's head."

Annwyl burst out laughing.

Chapter 7

Annwyl hit the ground. Again. She had to admit it. She grew tired of seeing the world from the flat of her back.

She winced as the pain shocked through her head. The knight had hit her with the back of his hand, the sword he held adding to the power of the move.

"I think you broke my nose."

"Probably." He stood over her, staring into her face. Suddenly she silently cursed herself for removing her shirt while they trained, the rocky dirt digging into her bare back that the bindings did not cover. "No. I just pushed it out of joint a bit."

Annwyl began to stand but he pushed her back down. "Calm yourself." He tossed his blade aside and straddled her hips. She watched him with narrowed eyes as he rested the lower half of his body against hers.

He leaned over and took her nose between both of his big hands. "This may hurt a bit."

He adjusted her nose back into place with a *pop*.

"*Ow*!" She slapped his shoulder.

"Don't be a baby," he admonished with a smile. "So, while I'm down here, any other aches or pains you need me to assist you with?"

Annwyl needed him to get off her because she didn't want him off her. She wanted him to run his hands over her body. She wanted him to kiss her. She wanted this man inside of her. And the thought absolutely terrified her.

"Get off me."

"You know the magic word."

Annwyl rolled her eyes. "Please," she bit out between clenched teeth. The man continued to try what little patience she possessed.

"Now. Now. You can do a little better than that. A little nicer please. Perhaps mean it."

"Oh, come on!"

"Unless . . ."

"Unless?"

"Unless you don't want me to move." He leaned in closer. "Unless you want me to stay right here."

Bastard, it seemed like he could read her thoughts. Just having him on top of her caused her blood to race. And she had the strangest throbbing sensation between her thighs. Not unpleasant, but definitely disconcerting.

"Well," he persisted.

But she couldn't answer him. She couldn't speak. If she did, she truly feared what the hell would come out of her mouth. Instead, she stared into those dark black eyes of his and wondered if his sweat would taste salty on her tongue.

He allowed more of his weight to rest against her hips, and she bit the inside of her mouth to keep from moaning out loud. "Answer me, Annwyl."

She swallowed, hard, and forced herself under some kind of control. Dammit, she was a warrior. The leader of one of the toughest rebellions in known history and still she let some knight completely confuse her.

"Get your ass off me . . . please."

He stared at her stunned, then threw his head back and laughed. He jumped up, grasping her arm and pulling her up with him. "You never fail to amuse me."

"I'm glad I can be so entertaining." She quickly picked up her shirt by the stream and pulled it on over her head. She needed something to hide the hard points of her nipples. The bindings were not helping with that. "I think my nose has gone through quite enough this day. Besides, it grows late. I must go."

He took hold of her wrist. "Are you sure?"

"I said so, didn't I?"

"That's not what I asked you."

"I don't have time for this." She hated how desperate she sounded at the moment, her entire body responding to his touch. Screaming out for him to explore every bit of her flesh.

"Don't leave." His voice low. Enticing.

"One of us needs to go."

He smiled at her. "Why?"

Her eyes traveled the long length of him, taking in the expanse of his wide shoulders, the muscles bulging under his chain mail. "Trust me on this."

He moved in closer to her. He still held onto her arm, but his fingers began to move along the flesh. Traveling up her arm. Her breasts tightened. Her nipples became painfully hard. Her breath quickened. She wanted this man. Gods, did

she want him. More than anything before in her life. And he
knew it. She could tell by the way he looked at her. The way
he moved into her, his body nearly touching hers.

"You *really* need to go."

He lowered his head, his eyes on her lips. "Really? Are you
sure?"

She watched as his mouth lowered to meet hers.

Clearly he'd lost his mind. And he blamed the girl for it. In
the beginning, he had no intention of doing anything more
than training. But with those green eyes of hers staring up at
him and that body calling out to be taken, really, what was a
poor dragon to do?

Kiss her, of course. At least that was the plan as he brought
his head down to taste her, but he felt a sharp slap as a hand
covered his face.

"Hold it." Annwyl reared back from him as she pushed his
face away with her hand.

He pulled back, surprised.

"Exactly what do you think you're doing?" She radiated
anger. Although not her usual rage. It seemed something else
altogether.

"Excuse me?"

"You heard me." She pushed him by his shoulders. "What
do you . . ." Push. "Think you are . . ." Push. "*Doing?*" Shove.

He felt his back slam into a tree and he gritted his teeth.
Was he seriously letting some human push him around his
own glen? As he watched her readjust the bindings under her
shirt to make sure her breasts didn't slip out, he realized that
the answer was yes. Yes, he was letting some human push him
around. But not just any human. Annwyl.

"I'm not some whore you can just grab and take as you
like."

He took a deep breath. "I know."

Annwyl blinked, surprised by his answer. "Um . . . well . . . so long as we understand each other."

He smiled. "We do."

"Well . . . good. Now . . . go away."

"If that is what you wish."

"Yes. Yes. That is what I wish." She waved a dismissive hand as she stepped away from him.

"Of course, a good-bye kiss would prompt me to leave just a little faster," he called after her.

Annwyl stopped and, until the end of time, he would always swear he heard her growl.

Why did he insist on torturing her? What did he want? Why wouldn't the man just leave? Annwyl swung around expecting him to be where she left him, against that tree. But he stood right behind her. The man moved faster than lightning. Startled, she stumbled back from him and almost fell, but he caught her around the waist. She felt searing heat on her flesh where he held her and her breath caught in her throat as he leaned in, keeping her bent over his arm.

"Are you all right?" His low voice slid softly across her flesh. Teasing. Making her body ache with need for him.

"I'll be better when you let me go."

"And I'll be better when you kiss me. Want to make a deal?" She let out another agitated growl and he grinned in response. "I do like that sound."

"Let me go."

"Kiss me."

"How about I just run you through?"

"I believe you need a sword for that task."

She realized she'd left her sword lying on the ground at her feet. *Stupid, Annwyl, stupid!*

His smile softened as he looked down into her face. "Just kiss me." It came out more a plea than a demand. And, as much as her rational mind railed against it, she wanted to kiss him.

She brought her head up slightly as he lowered his. They met somewhere in the middle, and when his lips touched hers, a bolt of heat swept through her. Heat and . . . recognition? Her hands reached up and gripped his shoulders as her mouth opened and his tongue slid in. He swept strong, dry fingers across her bare skin, slipping easily under her bindings to gently graze her breast. Her body jerked in response and Annwyl realized she hovered moments away from letting this man do anything he wanted to her. *Anything.*

She pushed against his shoulders, while pulling her body out of his arms. She forced herself away and the two stood staring at each other, both gasping for breath. Her nipples were painfully hard now as, she guessed, was the erection desperately trying to push its way through the knight's chain-mail leggings.

"Now. As you promised. Go."

"Are you sure?" He took a step toward her and she jumped back.

"You keep asking me that." There was that desperation again.

The knight grinned. "I keep hoping you'll give me a different answer."

"I won't. Now go!"

He nodded and took a deep breath. "As I promised."

He walked off. Once Annwyl knew that he truly was gone, she walked back to the stream and sat in the middle of it, letting the cold water rush past her. After a few minutes, she stuck her head in as well.

Fearghus dived into his lake. Still human, but so was the raging erection he had at the moment. The girl insisted on making him insane. Whether she admitted it or not, her body definitely called to him. Loudly. And what, exactly, did he think he was doing? Why the hell did he kiss her? A human, he reminded himself desperately. Just a human. Just a gorgeous, big-breasted human.

He gritted his teeth. He really didn't know how much more he could stand. But he had to fight it. He had to resist her. Simply for his own state of mind.

When Fearghus pulled himself out of the water he'd returned to his dragon-form once more. He shook the wetness from his body and wings and settled down for a few minutes to get control of his impulse. His impulse to go back outside and find Annwyl. To find her and to fuck her.

"Dragon!" Annwyl's voice rang through his lair, causing his whole body to clench.

"Damn." He covered his eyes with his claw. The woman would be the death of him.

"Dragon!"

Annwyl went deeper into the cavern than she ever had before. She couldn't find Morfyd, and she wanted to see Fearghus. Now. "Dragon!"

"Here." She heard his deep, rich voice and followed. She found him stretched out beside an underground lake, his tail swirling through the water. "What's wrong?"

"Your friend needs to go."

"Not again. What did he do now?"

She climbed up onto a boulder and looked the dragon in the eye. "He's very . . . disconcerting."

"Disconcerting? I didn't know that was a flaw."

"It can be."

"I don't understand why he makes you so nervous and I don't. I can turn you into a fireball."

So can he.

"Well, you're very sweet. And charming."

"They call me Fearghus the Destroyer."

She dismissed that with a wave of her hand. "And they call me Annwyl the Bloody. I'm not impressed."

"You're a very strange girl, Annwyl."

"You get raised by my family and see how you turn out." She clenched her fists in frustration. She'd never been so frustrated before in her life. All over some man.

"I think it would be a mistake to send him away. He's preparing you to fight Lorcan. Eventually you will have to face your brother and kill him." He sounded as if he'd grown weary of reminding her of that fact. But, once again, she blamed the knight. She should tell the dragon to toss a fireball at him.

"I know."

"Unless there is another reason you want me to send him away?"

Annwyl thought carefully on her answer. Tell the dragon that every time she was around the man her body cried out for him? Tell him that every time their swords clashed she became wet with desire? That she continually wondered what he would look like naked and on top of her? Did she admit that to the dragon?

"No." She shook her head. "No other reason." She sighed. "Just . . ."

"Just what?"

Why can't he be more like you? "Nothing."

She looked down at the lake, the water a beautiful clear blue with an active spring constantly replenishing it. She motioned to it. "Do you mind?"

"Uh . . . uh . . . no." He adjusted his large body. "Would you like me to leave?"

"Why?" She slid down the boulder and went to the water's edge. "You've seen me naked before." She dropped her sheathed sword to the ground. "Unless human bodies repulse you?"

"What? No! Just do whatever you must."

She shrugged, quickly undressed, and dived into the water.

He understood now. The gods were testing him. Clearly that must be the only reason this woman now floated naked and faceup in his lake, completely oblivious to his presence. The gods had a cruel sense of humor.

"Dragon?" He realized she'd been speaking to him for quite awhile. But he couldn't stop staring at her breasts. They were amazing.

"What?"

"I said, 'How do you know him?'"

He tore his eyes away from her chest. "Who?"

She frowned. "Am I annoying you, Lord Dragon?"

Annoying wasn't the word he'd use. "No. Why?"

With a shrug, "Just wondering. You seem a little tense."

You have no idea. . . .

She caught the end of his tail with both hands. Her fingers were long and strong, and he could easily imagine those hands stroking him to climax.

No. I shouldn't have gone down that road.

"The tip of your tail is sharp as a blade and the entire length of it muscle. Do you ever use it as a weapon?"

He cleared his throat. Anything to distract himself from her magical hands. "I have."

"Fascinating."

It really didn't help that she insisted on touching him all the time. He never had a human come near him as dragon, much less constantly explore almost every inch of him. He grunted. She *was* trying to kill him.

Why the hell had he involved himself in the Sibling War anyway? He should have just kept sleeping.

"What is it exactly that bothers you about him?"

"Everything." She glanced down at the water. "How deep is this?"

"I can get my entire body into it. And 'everything' seems like a lot."

"He's smug." She gripped his tail between both her arms and held on tight. "Lift me."

"Are you insane? And *I* am smug."

"Yes. But he's irritatingly smug." She still clung to his tail. "Please," she begged with a smile.

With a dramatic sigh, Fearghus lifted his tail, the girl going with it. She squealed and laughed, warming his heart.

"Now what?" he asked her as she hung there, frighteningly far up from the lake.

"Now? I let go." And she did. He watched her crash back into the water, disappearing into the dark blue recesses of the lake. But, within a few seconds, she fought her way back to the surface.

"That," her wet face flush with excitement, "was bloody brilliant!"

Fearghus lowered his head so they met eye to eye. "Have you always been so . . . different?"

She shrugged. "I don't know. Probably." She kissed him sweetly on the snout and swam away.

His claw touched the spot where she'd kissed him. She had such soft lips. He growled low as he watched her naked body swim across the lake and wondered what it would feel like to bury himself inside her, to feel her climax, to feel her soft mouth on his. . . .

"Sorry, Fearghus, am I interrupting anything?"

He gritted his teeth at the sound of his sister's voice and wondered how long she'd been standing there. Knowing his sister, he bet it was quite a while.

Fearghus slammed his tail down and she jumped out of the

way just in time. "No," he innocently replied. "You're not interrupting anything."

His sister glared at him and he feared she might shift right then so she could ensure her blast held enough strength to knock him across the cave floor. He knew he heard "bastard" muttered under her breath.

"I have to go back to the village for a few hours. But tell Annwyl there's food for her." She turned to walk back the way she came.

"As you wish." He lazily swished his tail and heard her curse as he swiped her feet, causing her to trip and stumble out of the cavern. "Sorry," he called after her.

"Was that Morfyd?"

He found Annwyl stepping out of the water. Her brown hair reached down to her knees, covering her long, strong body and, thankfully, those breasts.

"There's food."

"Good. I'm starving." She reached down and grabbed her clothes and sword.

"Annwyl . . ."

"I know. I know. He serves a purpose and I should just give him a chance. Right?"

"Actually, I was going to say you should put your clothes on, there's a chill in here."

"Oh."

"But you should also give him a chance."

She squinted up at him. "Fine, dragon." She grinned. "Anything for you."

And Fearghus's heart missed several beats before it began moving again.

"But he best not piss me off again."

Fearghus cringed. He could practically guarantee he couldn't stop himself from doing that.

Chapter 8

"Here."

Annwyl found the knight holding a sword out to her. "What's wrong with my blade?"

"Nothing. I want you to start using both."

Annwyl took the sword from his hand. It bore beautiful workmanship. A noble's blade. A little heavy for her, but a weight she would be able to get used to. And she bet it could cut through anything. She wondered where he got it from. What noble died at his hand? She shrugged. She never liked nobles much, so she really didn't care.

"How does it feel?"

"Good."

"Want some time to get used to it?"

She didn't answer. Instead she swung at his head with her new blade. He ducked and she blocked his retaliatory blow with her other sword. He smiled at her sudden attack and she felt pride. It took much to impress this man.

As the morning progressed into afternoon, the contact of their blades and the grunts of exertion the only sound in the glen.

Morfyd pulled away from the flames and growled. No matter how hard she tried, she just couldn't see Lorcan. She couldn't see into his world. She recently heard he had joined forces with a powerful wizard whose name no one ever seemed to remember.

Powerful indeed. There were very few humans who could
block her. She'd have to warn Fearghus. Let him know that the
girl may have more to worry about than that demon brother
of hers.

Fearghus. What exactly was going on with him and that
girl? Morfyd wasn't blind. She watched him watch her.
Clearly he'd become enamored of the female. But she sensed
something else going on. As Annwyl became stronger,
Morfyd began to spend most of her time in the local village.
A recent bout of fever required her skills. But she sensed that
neither Annwyl nor Fearghus spent their days in the lair. And
if they weren't in the lair, where the hell were they?

Morfyd knew her curiosity would soon get the better of
her. But something was going on, and she planned to find out
exactly what.

Annwyl watched the shadows move through the glen. She
knew the hour grew late. And her body tensed in anticipation.
She saw it now as a kind of ritual. They would meet and train
for hours. Break to eat in silence. Train for several more hours.
And at the end of it, something would happen. Something that
usually caused increased wetness between her thighs.

Their blades clashed one more time.

"Hold," he barked. She smiled. The stronger she grew, the
more she seemed to be wearing him out. She had no doubt he
could continue for a few more hours, but she liked that her
skills had improved since they'd first started.

He sheathed his sword and turned from her. She crouched
down and picked up her shirt, pulling the soft, plain cotton
material over her head. She sheathed both her weapons and
looked up to find boots standing in front of her. She fought to
control her breathing as she slowly looked up at him.

He stared down at her, his face inscrutable and half
covered by his black hair. He almost looked angry at her, his

silence driving her to distraction. "Is there a problem?" she snapped.

A low growl erupted from the back of his throat as he reached down and took hold of her shirt, pulling her to her feet. Then his mouth latched onto hers. Annwyl didn't fight him. She had no desire to. Instead she wrapped one arm around his neck, the other around his waist. He had her by the nape of her neck, his other hand slipping under her shirt. His rough fingers moved across the sweat-covered flesh of her back while his mouth claimed hers in a kiss that was so desperate, so passionate, she thought for sure he would take her right at that moment.

Instead, he let her go as abruptly as he'd grabbed her. And she couldn't stop the whimper that escaped her throat when he broke off contact. He stared at her for a moment longer, then he stormed off. Just like that. Leaving nothing but the dull ache between her legs to keep her company.

Morfyd placed food in front of Annwyl and watched the girl ignore it. In fact, she hadn't spoken since her return. Morfyd glanced over the girl's body. She wore only her bindings and leggings, and for the first time Morfyd noticed the bruises, bloody nicks, and deep cuts that covered Annwyl's body.

"Annwyl." The girl's green eyes flickered toward Morfyd. "Where did those bruises come from?"

"My training." She made the statement as if Morfyd were supposed to know what the hell she spoke of.

"Your training?"

"Aye. With the knight."

Morfyd's eyes narrowed. "What knight?"

"The one who was here when I was healing. The dragon's friend."

Morfyd couldn't hide her surprise as she took a sudden

step back. Her brother with a knight friend? Not in this lifetime. Or any lifetime for that matter. And suddenly his recent
desire to traipse into the village as human made sense.

"Ah, yes. His *knight* friend. And he's done this to you?"

"You could say that."

Morfyd nodded. She needed to find out what was going
on. Now. The curiosity was killing her!

"Is the dragon here?" Annwyl asked hopefully.

"As a matter of fact, no. He's not." The girl went back to
staring at the wall. "Eat, Annwyl. I need you to keep your
strength up. Understand?"

The girl nodded but made no move to eat and continued to
stare at her fascinating wall.

He looped around the glen, moving past a large boulder,
heading for the back way into his den. He'd gone into town,
running all the way, to order a few things and hopefully work
the girl out of his system. It didn't work. If he stumbled across
her now, he'd have a hard time not taking her up against a tree.
So, again, it looked as if his cold lake would be his only
respite.

But as he came around the boulder he stopped. Morfyd
stood waiting for him. Her eyes narrowed in anger, her arms
crossed in front of her chest, one foot tapping sharply against
the grass.

She glared at her brother for several moments. "I'm
telling!" she barked. Then she was off.

"Morfyd!" He charged after her, snatching her around the
waist before she could get away from him. She slapped at his
hands. But when that didn't work she slammed her elbow into
his face. He released her and she spun around to face him.

The two siblings stared at each other. "Keep your mouth
shut, sister."

Morfyd hissed just before she latched onto a handful of Fearghus's hair and pulled.

"You little . . ." He winced in pain and wrapped his arm under his sister's leg, tossing her on her back. She didn't let her grip on his hair go though, and instead reached up and punched him in the head. "*Ow!*" He slapped her hands away. Could this be more ridiculous? They were dragons. The mightiest killers in the known world. What the hell were they doing?

"Hold it! Just hold it!"

Morfyd stopped. "How could you lie to her like that?"

"I'm not lying."

"Did you go up to her and say 'It's me. Fearghus.'"

"Well, not exactly . . ."

"Liar!" She dragged herself off the ground by using her brother's hair to pull herself to her feet.

"Stop yelling!"

She finally released her hold on Fearghus's hair. "What are you up to, brother?"

"Getting her ready."

She raised an eyebrow. "For what exactly?"

Dirty little . . . "That's not what I meant. Soon she will face her brother, and I'm making sure she's ready to do that. I won't watch her die."

"That's admirable, brother. But I still don't know why you haven't told her the truth. Told her who you are."

"Our power to shift is one of our most sacred secrets. Do you think I'm going to reveal it to some little girl?" He motioned to his sister's scarred face. "You even kept our secret while they cut your face." For a moment, even Fearghus believed that excuse. Morfyd however . . .

"Ha! That's a weak excuse, brother. If they'd known what I was they would have killed me or at least tried to. And I'd rather not be like old Terlack with only one wing. And I'm sure she wouldn't harm a hair on that big, thick head of yours. So why don't you simply admit the truth?"

"And what truth is that?"

"That you're afraid. Afraid that once she knows who and what you are you don't stand a chance with her."

"What are you talking about?"

"I've seen how you look at her, brother. I'm not blind."

"No, but you are insane. I have no interest in some human girl." If he wasn't careful, his lies would choke him. He wanted that girl more than life itself. He'd tried to walk away earlier, but he couldn't. He just had to taste her again. And it took all his strength to stop himself from going further. From ripping off her clothes and burying himself inside of her until morning.

"You're afraid that if she finds out her knight is really you . . . really a dragon, she won't give you another look." His sister stood in front of him now. Her blue eyes boring into his head. "You desire her, brother. And you don't want anything to jeopardize that."

Fearghus looked down at his sister. "Are you done?"

"Aye."

"Then hear me well, sister. I don't have to explain myself to you." He leaned into her. "You just keep your mouth shut. I'll tell her when I'm ready."

"Fine. But you best hope it's not too late, brother." She punched him in the chest—hard—and walked away from him.

Fearghus sighed—he had too many damn females in his life.

Annwyl just started eating when Morfyd stormed back in. She stopped and looked at the witch. Watched her pace in front of her. "Is everything all right, Morfyd?"

Morfyd looked at her and Annwyl put her spoonful of food down. Based on the expression Morfyd wore on that scarred face of hers, Annwyl wanted to make sure she could sprint to the door if necessary.

"What's going on with you and that knight?"

"What? Uh . . . nothing?"

Morfyd pulled a chair over, sat in it, and stared at Annwyl. She'd always heard it was a bad idea to lie to a witch. "Well, he's kissed me a few times."

"And?"

"And nothing."

"Nothing else has happened between the two of you?"

"No."

"But you want more, don't you?"

Annwyl's face got hot. A blast of the dragon's flame couldn't make it any hotter than it was at this very moment. "I . . . uh . . ."

"Annwyl."

"Yes. All right. I do want more."

"So why has nothing more happened?"

Annwyl shrugged.

"Are you afraid? I know he'd be your first."

"No. I'm not afraid."

"Is it because you might become with child? Because as long as you keep drinking the wine—"

"No. No. That's not it." Morfyd waited for her to continue, but she didn't think she could speak the full truth. Not out loud. "You'll never understand."

"Annwyl, I'm a witch. I understand much more than you could ever conceive. Just tell me before you shred my nerves."

Annwyl looked into those clear blue eyes as she found herself wringing her hands. "I . . ." she swallowed, "I feel guilty."

Morfyd tilted her head. Her brows pulled together in confusion. "Feel guilty about what?"

Annwyl closed her eyes and rushed forward before she lost all nerve. "I can't help but feel I'm betraying the dragon."

Silence followed her admission. She slowly opened her eyes to find Morfyd still staring at her. But her expression of anger and confusion were gone. Instead, she smiled. A smile of such kindness that Annwyl felt her heart warm for the scarred witch.

"I want you to do me a favor, Annwyl."

"Anything." And she meant it.

"If you want the knight, take him."

Annwyl blinked. That wasn't the response she'd expected. *Ever.* "What?"

"I'm sorry. Was I not clear? I said if you want him. Take him."

"But . . ."

"Do not worry about the dragon. Just promise me. If this is what you want, you'll take him." She reached out her hand and ran it along Annwyl's cheek. "Trust me, my friend."

Annwyl watched Morfyd leave. Her confusion continued to grow by the day. The minute. The second.

She pushed her chair away from the table, slowly standing on wobbly legs. She needed to see the dragon. The one calming thing in her life. He was what he was and she loved him for that.

Fearghus, his head resting in the palm of his claw, sighed. Again.

"How many times must we do this?"

"Until I get it right."

"Aren't you tired? You had your training today, didn't you?"

"Yes. But all we do is sword train. This hones my reflexes. Now do it again."

Fearghus again sighed and swung his tail. Then he swung it back. He heard her squeal, but unlike before he didn't hear her lovely bottom hit the ground. "Annwyl?" He turned around but she'd disappeared. His confusion lasted only a moment. He felt the weight on his tail. Slowly, doing his best not to laugh, he brought his tail around. The tip of it caught under her shirt and there she hung. "Are we done now?"

Her face took on a charming beet-red color. "Yes. We're done now."

"You sure? I mean, we can keep going if you like."

She growled at him. "Enjoying this, are you, dragon?"

"As a matter of fact, yes I am."

"Down." He carefully lowered her to the ground and watched her struggle to get untangled from his tail. She finally had to yank off her shirt and Fearghus took in a shaky breath. She wore no bindings.

She really needed to stop getting naked around him.

"I should be faster than that."

"Annwyl, you're tired. You had a long day. As did I."

Annwyl raised an eyebrow as she pulled the shirt back on. "And what did you do all day?"

"Many things. Dragons are very busy higher beings."

Annwyl smirked at him, her arms crossing in front of her voluptuous chest. "Higher beings, eh? It must be nice."

"You need not feel jealous. You are much better than most humans."

Annwyl laughed outright. And Fearghus realized how much he loved to see her smile. "Why thank you, oh mighty dragon." She curtsied low.

"Now. Now, Annwyl. No need to curtsy. A simple nod of your head and absolute worship will be more than enough."

Annwyl liked Fearghus more and more every day. At some point she began to think of him as *her* dragon. As if the great beast belonged to her and her alone. Ridiculous, of course. The dragon belonged to no one, but she found the feeling comforting.

She laughed now when she thought of how afraid she had been of him. Afraid of him and all his kind. That feeling seemed like ages ago. Now she found herself almost dreading the day she would have to leave. She and the dragon never spoke of it. They spoke of everything except her leaving.

And Annwyl did love talking to her dragon. She loved to hear the history of his kind. The stories of his family. She loved to hear him. Just the deep, rumbling sound of his dragon voice calmed her. Eased the rage that always pulsated just beneath the surface.

"Absolute worship? That's a very tall order."

"You are a very tall girl."

Annwyl chuckled as she knelt before the dragon and held her hand out to him.

"I thought you knelt before no man."

"You are a dragon. And don't get your hopes up. I only want to see your talon."

"I'm under such scrutiny," he grumbled in annoyance, but laid one of his talons into her palm nonetheless. Coal black and smooth, its tip sharp and quite deadly. She closed her hand over it, marveling at the fact that her long fingers could barely reach around.

"What's it like?"

"What? Being a dragon?"

"No." She smiled as she released the talon. "Flying?"

He laughed. "Fine."

"Fine? Just fine? That's the best you can do?"

"Well, I've been flying most of my life so it's not as interesting to me as it seems to be to you."

"You take your gifts for granted, dragon."

"As do you."

"And what gifts do I have exactly? The ability to have my own brother trying to kill me?"

"The ability to inspire hardened warriors to follow you into battle. I know few who have such a gift as that."

Annwyl shrugged. "They were desperate. No one else knows much about my brother."

"If they were desperate, they would have sent you back to him with a ribbon around your head."

Annwyl smiled at the dragon. He possessed the uncanny ability to make her feel as if she could challenge the entire world and win. And after a long day of being thrown on her back and told her rage would only get her killed, it was nice to come back to the lair and have the dragon make her feel like she was worth something.

She sat down on his front claw, leaning back against his forearm. She let out a deep, contented breath and felt her sore body begin to relax. She put her hands behind her head and looked off into the dark cavern, amazed at the size of the dragon's home.

With mild sarcasm, "Comfortable?"

She wiggled her rear against his scales. "Yes. As a matter of fact, I'm quite comfortable, thank you." She let his chuckle wash over her and her body relaxed even more.

"Annwyl?"

"Aye?"

"Did you get those marks on your back from your brother?"

Annwyl didn't even have to look to know which marks he spoke of. There were scars from battle all over her body. But the ones her dragon spoke of were brutal whip marks that covered her back. Those scars had belonged to her for more years than she could remember.

"No." Annwyl cleared her throat, and she admitted something to the dragon that she never admitted to anyone ever before. "I got these from my father." She still hated the man. Even though he had been dead for so many years, she still hated him. She lowered her arms and laid her hands in her lap. "My brother has the same marks. One of the few things we have in common."

Annwyl didn't even realize at first that she clasped her
hands together. Clasping them so tightly that the knuckles had
gone white. Then the dragon placed two of his talons against
them, and she realized that only her father ever caused her to
feel this way. She closed her eyes and willed herself not to
cry. She'd shed enough tears over that bastard. She would
shed no more.

She opened her eyes when the dragon stretched himself out
and crossed his forearms over each other. He adjusted her so
she rested in the crook of his forearm, his claws ensconcing
her safely. He lowered his head until it rested over her outstretched legs. She stared at him for several long moments.
His eyes closed; he didn't make any further moves. She realized he wanted her to feel safe. And she did. He was giving
her his strength, his power, his protection. She didn't fear the
razor-sharp talons that laid so close to her body or the mighty
head with all its dangerous fangs. She didn't fear Fearghus the
Destroyer at all. She marveled at the feeling. The feeling of
being safe. It seemed strange to feel neither fear nor rage. As
new a feeling to her as her desires for the knight. And, she had
to admit, she liked both. That two different beings could introduce her to such opposite emotions shocked her to her very
core. No matter what happened, both dragon and man would
forever share a place in her heart.

Annwyl reached out her hand and brushed her fingertips
lightly over the scales on his snout. She let her hand rest there
as she closed her eyes and leaned back.

She had no idea how long they stayed like that, but when
she finally couldn't stifle a yawn any longer, Fearghus spoke
up. "You'd best get to bed, Lady Annwyl."

"Aye." Annwyl pulled her legs out from under the dragon
and stood up, shaking off the pins and needles that ran
through them. "That demon knight you've trapped me with is
quite the task master." His head still remained close, so she

bent down and kissed the dragon on his black snout. "Good night, Lord Dragon. And thank you."

"For what?"

She smiled. "For nothing at all. Which is exactly what I needed."

Annwyl walked past him to get back to her chamber. As she left she couldn't help but slide her hand across his leathery wings and the scales of his body.

Fearghus closed his eyes as her hand swept across his body. Something she did almost every night now before going to bed. Although he didn't expect her to kiss him. It took all his strength to not shift right then and there. To kiss her back as he wanted to. To do what he could to take away her pain over a cruel father and a sadistic brother.

His sister was right, of course. *Unforgivable brat.* He did long for the girl. Longed to make her his own. But the reason she felt so comfortable with him was because he was not a man. From men she'd only known pain and abuse. Yet a dragon protected her. Cared for her. Saved her life.

He thought of her touching his human flesh the way she touched his scales. Running her hands along his body, the skin sensitive to the touch because of the shifting.

His entire body shuddered at the thought, and he headed toward his lake. The water, cold and bracing, was just what he needed right now.

Hefaidd-Hen glared at the flames and wondered what the hell was going on. He'd never really focused much energy on seeing into Dark Glen before. He never cared. But his instincts, which were never wrong, told him he could find the girl there. And he needed to find the girl.

Not for Lorcan. He could care less whether the fool ever

got his precious revenge. It seemed that the girl had more reason to want her brother dead. But Hefaidd-Hen needed the girl for other reasons. He had to stop the rebellion and she was the key.

For he had plans. Important plans he needed Lorcan for. The girl, however, would never be stupid enough to trust him. He could never have made her an ally. But Lorcan, so lost in his rage, didn't even realize that someone like Hefaidd-Hen would never waste his time on such petty battles. Unless he wanted something in return.

So he needed the girl out of the way. Every day she pulled more and more loyalty from the other kingdoms to her side. What had started out as a poor and rather ineffectual rebellion had become something much more deadly and decisive in the girl's capable hands.

Lorcan insisted he wanted her alive, so he could have the pleasure of taking her head. And Hefaidd-Hen would do what he could to keep the fool happy. At least for the time being. But if the girl had to die first, she had to die.

Hefaidd-Hen looked back into the flames and frowned. He still couldn't see anything. What could possibly be strong enough to block him? It must be powerful Magick because there were few who could match him.

Whoever or whatever protected the little whelp needed to die as well.

All these little distractions took him away from his plans. And soon his patience would run out. Especially with Lorcan. He didn't realize someone could be so dislikable. But the man was. Never happy. Never satisfied. Any failure met with brutal and uncontrollable rage.

Hefaidd-Hen wondered how long before he lost his patience with the puny man. He had a feeling he'd know soon enough.

Chapter 9

"If you want him, take him." It sounded more like an order than anything else. And Annwyl felt compelled to obey. She smiled at her own centaur shit. She wanted the man. Nothing the witch could say either way would ever change that.

Annwyl reached the stream where she and the knight always met to practice. She stopped short, taking in those broad shoulders and back that tapered into the narrow waist. He crouched by the stream, his body taut and ready under his chain mail. Even before he turned around she knew he was beautiful.

He glanced over his shoulder, sensing her presence. "Well, hello, pretty lady." He pushed thick golden blond hair out of his eyes and leered at her. Openly. Didn't even try to hide his lust.

"Who the hell are you?" Considering almost all feared Dark Glen, there seemed to be many visitors here of late, her included.

"Gwenvael is my name. And you are?"

"Your worst enemy, unless you tell me your business here, knight."

She glanced down at his surcoat and noticed it bore the same color and crest as the one worn by her knight. Another mercenary it seemed.

Gwenvael stood up to his full height and Annwyl tightened her grip on her sword, ready to unsheathe it if need be. He was enormous. And she had no doubt her knight and this man were brothers.

"I'm here to see the dragon."

Her eyes narrowed. "Why?"

"My, we are protective."

"Yes. *We* are. Now answer my question."

"I have a message for him. From family."

"Really? Well, give it to me. I'll make sure he gets it." She held out her hand.

The knight smiled. "Actually, the message is in my head, sweet one." He took her hand, and brought it up to his lips. Annwyl watched as he kissed the tips gently, all the while staring into her eyes. She let him finish, then pinched his nose between her thumb and forefinger. She twisted until she got a cry of pain from him.

"Don't touch. I don't like to be touched."

"I see that."

"Say you're sorry or I'll take it off."

"Sorry. Sorry!"

She released him. He rubbed his nose and pouted. She couldn't help but smile. So very cute. And so very charming. Of course she still wouldn't trust him with her dead horse.

His sister was up to something. He could tell. He'd known her for over two hundred years and she'd been annoying him senseless that entire time. But she would tell him nothing now. She was still too angry at discovering his double life.

But she would never be as angry with him as he was with himself. Yesterday had been the final straw. He had no intention of touching Annwyl, much less kissing her. He, in fact, had started to walk away. But, once again, he couldn't help himself. And when she kissed him back. . . .

Yet today would be different. Today he would get control of this human body of his. Today he would not touch her. He wouldn't even look at her. Today he would face the fact she was human and he a dragon.

Fearghus sighed. When had everything become so difficult? *When you just had to rescue her, you idiot.* He now realized he should never have gone out to help. He should have let the humans fight their war as they'd been doing for centuries. As soon as he became involved, everything became difficult. Complicated. Now he had his sister and some human girl living with him. Who else exactly would appear to drive him insane?

He realized too late he should never have entertained that thought as he came upon them. They sat by the stream. His unmistakable charm oozing from every pore while she laughed loudly at whatever he'd just said. She almost looked as if she were flirting.

Brutal jealousy came up and choked him. He would throttle the little bastard. Send him back to their mother without the rest of his tail.

He walked out of the trees and Gwenvael looked at him. "Oh. Greetings, big brother."

He gritted his teeth. Had the little bastard told her anything? Gwenvael, unlike the rest of their kin, did not believe in discretion. It didn't take long to realize that if one asked Gwenvael a direct question about dragons or anything for that matter, he would give a direct answer.

"I'm here to see the dragon." He winked at Fearghus. And Fearghus barely contained the near overwhelming desire to take the boy's head completely off his shoulders and kick it right out of his glen.

"Is that a fact?" Fearghus spit out between clenched teeth.

"Oh, yes. Important family business has sent me this way."

"Well, why don't you find Morfyd? I'm sure she's in the cave. She can help you."

"Really? Do you think so?" Gwenvael's glee almost caused the little bastard to froth at the mouth. He had Fearghus right where he wanted him and they both knew it.

"I'm sure of it."

"Well, then. I guess I better go find this elusive Morfyd."
Gwenvael's grin practically blinded him. But when the bastard caught Annwyl's hand in his, and kissed it, Fearghus
realized he would definitely have to kill the little toe-rag.

"I thought we discussed this, knight," she chastised with a
smile.

"We did. But I just couldn't help myself, lady."

Gwenvael stood up and walked toward Fearghus. "I'll see
you soon, brother."

The two brothers stared at each other until Gwenvael disappeared out of sight.

Fearghus turned back to find Annwyl standing, brushing
dirt off her backside. "You never mentioned a brother before.
You two look very much alike."

"What were you doing with him?"

She looked up startled and caught on to his implications
almost immediately. "Anything I like."

He snarled. She snarled back. He moved on her, his hands
slipping under her arms, lifting her off the ground and pushing her back against a tree. He could smell the lingering scent
of his brother surrounding her and he wanted that smell gone.
If she smelled of a male, it would be of him and no other.

"You need to stay away from him."

"Don't try and tell me what to do. I answer to no man."

He lifted her up higher so they were eye to eye. "You'll do
as I say."

The look on her face. The smell of desire battering his
senses. The fullness of her lips. None of that moved him. It
was what she said next that did the most damage.

"Make me."

This couldn't have been what Morfyd meant. She must
have meant something else. Something less . . . dangerous.
Or, at the very least, less stupid.

But Annwyl challenged him. Not with a sword or a mace. Those she could handle. She challenged *him*. Had she lost her mind? Had she finally become as mad as her brother?

She stared into those beautiful dark eyes, one of them almost blocked by the hair that continually fell across it, and realized that for once she might be in over her head. Her feet weren't even on solid ground. He lifted her as if she weighed no more than a babe. And, even worse, she *still* didn't know the man's name.

By the gods, woman. What have you done?

But she wouldn't back down now. She had her pride to think about. At least that's what she kept telling herself.

He leaned in close to her. His mouth brushing against her cheek. His hot breath tickling the inside of her ear.

"A challenge? Woman, are you trying to kill me?"

Annwyl frowned in confusion. What was he talking about? "Do you speak of the dragon? He would not harm you."

He ran his tongue along her jaw. "You think you control the dragon, do you?"

Annwyl had to force herself to focus. His tongue against her skin made her crave more. More of his touch. More of him. "He's not mine to control." Annwyl bit back a moan when he pinned her against the tree. His body, hard and tight against hers, the only thing holding her up.

"Then what makes you think . . ." He kissed her collarbone. "You can stop him . . ." He kissed her neck. "From harming me?" He nipped her earlobe.

"A creature he may be, knight, but an honorable one. I'd trust my life with him before any human."

His hands stopped moving. His body became still. His lips rested gently against her ear. Had she insulted him? She didn't want him to stop, but she would never beg him either. So she waited.

"You care for a dragon?"

"I care for this dragon, knight. He is my friend."

"And I?"

"You? I have no idea. But I wouldn't exactly call us friends."

He released her, letting her drop to the ground like a sack of potatoes. "Then why are you here with me now, Annwyl?"

"I didn't say I didn't want you. I just said I wasn't sure if I care for you."

He stepped back and stared at her long and hard. "Honest girl," he finally managed.

"My family can be called a lot of things, Lord Knight, but liars aren't one of them."

"Fair enough."

Annwyl fought to understand the confusing man. She sensed he wanted something from her, but she had no idea what. And her frustration was too great to try and figure it out. With an aggravated sigh, she pushed past him.

"We're not done."

She stopped in midstride, annoyed by his tone. Annoyed by him. "We're not?" She faced him, arms crossed in front of her chest.

"No. I'm still waiting." He walked toward her, and she felt like a hunted doe in the woods.

"Waiting? For what?"

"For your promise to me." He stepped in front of her and what little light the two suns poured into the dragon's heavily wooded glen was completely blocked out by the man's huge body. She now stood in shadow.

"Promise?"

"Your promise to stay away from Gwenvael."

Now she really was annoyed. She could care less about Gwenvael. A mischievous little troublemaker that one. But she also understood how brothers could make each other insane. "I do not intend to make such a promise." She could see his jaw tighten and she had the sudden desire to be wicked. *Very* wicked. "Truth be told, I just can't stop thinking about the man. Tell me." She cocked her head to the side as she looked up at the knight's dark handsome face. "Does he already have a woman?"

"You test me, wench."

"And you push me. I strongly suggest you not."

"Or you'll what?"

She gave him the same smile she gave an enemy soldier in battle. She didn't practice it, but she knew it when she gave it. Men blanched at this expression. Most ran. All died. Her knight didn't even flinch.

"Or I'll make your brother a very happy man. He seems more than willing."

With a feral growl, he grabbed her arms and pinned them behind her back. He pulled her close and she felt the intense heat from his body. The anger. And the lust. "You play where you should not, Lady Annwyl."

She could have backed off. She probably should have. But Annwyl had always been reckless. Foolish. And this man . . . this man brought out something base and primal in her. Something that she couldn't control.

"Only one man ruled me. Now his bones lay rotting in the ground. And since his death I answer to no man. And especially not to you."

The knight gave a painful groan, just before his lips slammed against hers. And for Annwyl there would be no going back.

Fearghus wanted to be stronger than this. He wanted to hand her sword to her and begin their daily training session. Instead he ripped her swords from her back and threw them across the glen floor.

Annwyl the Bloody was more dangerous than anyone realized. She took no prisoners whether in love or war. Her response to his kiss was as desperate and demanding as he felt. But he had to remind himself that she was still a virgin. As much as he wanted to find a boulder and bend her over it, he couldn't. He didn't want her first experience to be a painful memory that made her wince.

He fought for control, pulled away from her, leaving her gasping, and annoyed.

"Take your clothes off," he ordered as he stepped away from her. She frowned in confusion. "I'll rip them off your back if I do it myself. Take them off."

Annwyl stared at him, her entire body tense. For a moment, he thought she might have changed her mind. Her eyes flickered to the path that led back to the cave. But then she pulled the shirt over her head. Followed by the bindings. She slid the breeches off past her hips and long legs, dropping them in a puddle at her feet. She kicked them as well as her boots aside. She stood before him completely naked. He studied every inch of her. Every scar. Every freckle. She was so beautiful. And his.

"You stare, knight."

"Yes. I do. You're beautiful."

Suddenly she appeared awkward and shy. Her gaze shifted to the ground and it seemed as if she might bolt.

"Has no one told you that before?"

"They have. Usually when they wanted something from my brother or myself. They've never meant it."

And suddenly he saw the woman behind the warrior. A woman who grew up among evil men but still somehow managed to keep her soul. A woman who fought for the freedom of people she didn't know and who risked her life every day to defend them against her own kin. A woman who easily called a dragon her friend. And whether she knew it or not she belonged to him. His woman. His warrior. His life. He'd do anything to protect her. Anything to keep her.

He reached out and pushed her long hair off her shoulder.

Gently he ran his finger down her chest, across her breast, circling the nipple. He watched it harden at his touch. Watched her breath come hard and fast. She smelled of desire and the forest. And soon she would smell of him.

His arm slipped around her waist and he roughly pulled her flat against his body. His mouth captured hers as his hands trailed down her back and bottom. Her strong hands gripped fistfuls of his hair. Her tongue tasted his.

He moved away from her long enough to snatch off his own clothes and weapons, then he had her in his arms again. Fearghus nipped the soft flesh at her neck and heard her give a growl. The sound played across his every nerve, testing the very control of his human body. He lowered her to the soft grass of the glen, settling down beside her.

Annwyl loved the feel of his body. His hips fit snugly against hers. His hands were rough and large, capable of holding her sizable breasts. His skin hard and smooth. Her fingers reveled in flowing across his body, through his long thick hair.

As he slowly trailed his tongue down her chest, she feared she might come out of her skin. But his hands held on to her, grounding her, as they trailed down her back until they cupped her rear. His tongue slid between her thighs, causing her back to arch. But when his teeth rasped over her clit a feral moan tore from her throat.

Annwyl always believed herself beyond this. That desire would never trap her like the few women she'd known over the years. But now she realized that her body had become a treacherous thing. In battle it responded to her every command. Did things she never believed that it could. Had strength she never knew it possessed.

But now her body completely ignored her. It responded to something else altogether. And until it got what it needed, it would no longer respond to anything she thought or rationalized. It would only respond to her desires. To her needs. And at the moment, that meant her body would only respond to him.

He loved the taste of her. The scent of her. Everything about her brought him to life. Making him more human than he'd ever been before. She panted, her body tight and coiled, afraid of this new feeling. This new sensation she'd never had. But when she tightened her hand in his hair, winding the strands around her fingers, he realized how much he needed her. How much he would risk so that he could have this time with her.

He swirled his tongue slowly around her clit as he slipped a finger inside of her. Her whole body jerked, and he smiled as he licked her over and over while slowly fucking her with his hand. She moaned aloud and he wondered how much more of this he could stand before he could be inside of her. But her body jerked again and the muscles of her sex tightened around his finger. She gasped loudly and gripped his hair tighter as she came, her juices sliding down her thighs.

He licked her clean as the spasms passed and moved slowly up her body, kissing and licking every scar as he went.

His lips reached her mouth and he groaned in surprise to find out how hungry she was for him. Fearghus hadn't satiated her as much as he made her want more. Her passion increased his.

He settled his hips between her thighs, his erection pushing against her. She panted in his ear, her body shifting beneath his, preparing herself for his shaft, her legs opening wider. Fearghus kissed her along her neck, moving up to her earlobe. He licked the sensitive bit of flesh, and then bit down on it.

She gave out a sharp cry of surprise and that's when he

slammed home, breaching her maidenhead, and filling her completely, his cock buried deep inside her.

She wrapped her arms around him and Fearghus waited until she became used to the size of him, until she became comfortable having him inside her. In moments, she began to kiss his neck and along his jaw. He kissed her again. And while he slowly explored her mouth, he began to thrust into her. He enjoyed the feel of her, the way her body moved beneath his. He didn't want to do anything to hurt her, so he took his time, keeping his own pleasure at bay until she could have hers.

Then he heard her mutter something against his throat. "What?" he asked softly, and he started at her answer.

"Harder."

She couldn't believe she said the word once, much less twice. But she had always been a woman who knew what she wanted. And she needed him to move inside of her harder. She appreciated the time he took, the gentleness of it all, but she was over the hardest part. He had breached her maidenhead in expert fashion and now she wanted to move past that.

He paused. "Did you just say 'harder?'"

"Yes." She cringed. "Guess that was rude." An accusation flung at her more than once.

He licked the hollow of her neck. "Not at all."

He slammed into her and Annwyl felt every nerve in her body come alive. He pulled out and slammed into her again. She closed her eyes and let the pleasure wash over her.

As he moved inside of her, she ran her hands down his back. When heat spread from her loins and up her spine, she dug her nails into his back as her whole body began to tighten and she lost her breath. When the first spasm tore through her, her nails ripped across his flesh and she screamed out, her body arching against his.

He slammed into her again, his whole body shaking as he released inside of her.

Annwyl leaned her forehead against his neck. She closed her eyes and listened to his breathing. His heart beat against her chest as his warm body held her close. Before she knew it, Annwyl was asleep.

He could feel Annwyl's even breathing against his hot flesh as she fell asleep against him. He smiled as he relaxed them both against the grass. He smoothed her long hair away from her face and stared down at her. No frowns. No worries. It looked as if she were having a dreamless sleep.

He cradled her in his arms and kissed her sweat-covered forehead. He closed his eyes. When they awoke he'd tell her the truth. All of it.

Whether his mad little warlord wanted to hear it or not.

Chapter 10

Annwyl awoke to find the shadows deepened and herself naked in the knight's arms. She turned her head, and their eyes locked. He watched her silently. And she guessed he had been for quite a while.

He started to speak and Annwyl stopped him. "Don't." She pulled away from him, picked up her clothes, and walked off. "See you tomorrow."

* * *

See you tomorrow? Fearghus sat up and watched her walk off. She didn't even look back at him as she walked and put her clothes on at the same time. She barely acknowledged his existence. She wouldn't even let him speak.

Fearghus clenched his fists, his rage swarming around him. He needed to hurt something. To destroy something.

Fearghus's eyes narrowed. *Gwenvael.*

He stood up with a growl. He needed to find his brother. He needed to kick the shit out of something and Gwenvael would do quite nicely.

Gwenvael sat in one of the chairs in Annwyl's room, his feet up on the table. He'd done his task. He'd given Morfyd the message. And she would make sure that Fearghus got it. Now he could play. And he'd bet all his gold that Annwyl could be quite the entertainment. Sweet. Innocent. And his brother was crazy about her.

He didn't blame him. She was a beautiful girl. Tall. Scarred. A little mean. And he'd always liked that in a female. He loved it when they were mean. But that wasn't what really interested him. It was the fact that "Don't bother me" Fearghus had finally fallen. And fallen hard by the looks of it. He thought his brother would rip his guts out when he saw him talking to Annwyl.

Absolutely nothing made his day more fun than when he could drive Fearghus insane. True, Fearghus might be first-born, but Gwenvael always felt his particular birthright was to torture his siblings. And Fearghus had always been his greatest challenge, therefore his favorite. Mainly because Fearghus was the quintessential dragon. He never moved faster than he had to. He never got upset or seriously angry.

He never worried. And he never seemed to care about anything except his privacy and his quiet.

Then the human came along. When he heard that Fearghus rescued a human, Gwenvael had been shocked. When he found out it had been Annwyl the Bloody, notorious sister of the Butcher of Garbhán Isle, he became intrigued. And now that he'd seen his brother desperate with lust . . . well, things just became much more interesting.

Besides, he thought with a growl, *I still owe him for my tail*.

He heard her coming a league away. The woman stomped like an elephant.

Annwyl stormed into the chamber and stopped as soon as she saw him.

"I was wondering where you'd gone."

"What do you want, Gwenvael?" She wasn't in the same mood she'd had been in a few hours before. He fought back the smile. He could smell his brother all over her. It seemed that Fearghus had finally stopped being a prat.

"I just stopped by to see you. Is there anything wrong with that?"

She sighed, heavily, and stomped across the room. She stopped in front of a large wood chest. "Where did this come from?" At his shrug, she smiled. "Fearghus." She said it so softly, he almost didn't hear her. Annwyl knelt down and opened it. There were clothes inside, but she ignored them for the dagger that lay on top.

He wondered what dead nobleman's hand his brother pried that little item from. Gwenvael watched her examine the blade and became bored. Time now to have a little fun.

"So, where's my brother?"

"I have no idea." She tested the weight of the blade.

"I hope you're not . . . well, getting any feelings for him. That would be a mistake."

"Really? And why is that?" She gripped the handle of the

dagger with one hand, while checking the sharpness of its blade with the other.

"I just don't think he could appreciate a woman like you."

"And you?"

Gwenvael gave that smile that had gotten him more pleasure than he cared to admit. "I am not my brother, lady."

That's when she moved.

She was up and across the room, snatching him out of his chair in mere seconds. Annwyl slammed him face down on the table, her knee against his back to hold him in place. The point of her blade burrowed into the skin of his neck. As human, that blade could easily kill him.

She leaned in and spoke quietly. "I don't know what's going on between you and your brother. And I don't want to know. But I'll not be the bone between you two dogs. So take yourself from my sight. I am in no mood."

With that she lifted him off the table and shoved him from the chamber.

The crazed bitch had more strength than he had known, he realized as she sent him tumbling from her presence. He fell and slid across the cave floor, coming to an abrupt stop when a large boot slammed into his head.

He looked up and braved a smile. "Oh. Hello, brother."

With a growl, Fearghus lifted him off the ground by the back of his neck.

Morfyd reached down and pulled an Aouregan root. The materials she collected were for a spell that might help her destroy the protective barriers surrounding Lorcan. But she found the yelling simply too distracting. And when her baby brother literally flew over her head and landed in a heap not a quarter league from her, she decided it was time to say something.

"Fearghus!" She stepped in front of her advancing brother and put her hand on his chest. "Leave him alone."

"Just let me kill him. Please."

Morfyd bit the inside of her cheek to stop herself from laughing. After all these years her brothers still couldn't get along.

"No. She'll never forgive you if you kill him. She still resents you for his tail." To this day she remembered her three other brothers playing catch with the tip of Gwenvael's tail and her mother raging like never before. It was funny then and it was still funny now.

"I hate him, Morfyd. I hate him."

"I know." She patted her brother's shoulder. "But he is all our burden to bear. Our pain."

"You know what?" Gwenvael jumped up, his rage pouring off him in waves. "You're all bastards. And I hope the lot of you rot in hell."

"You just stay away from her, you little toe-rag!"

"What's wrong, big brother? Can't handle your woman?"

Morfyd barely dodged in time to avoid the fireball Fearghus let loose. But it hit Gwenvael full in the chest, sending him flying back into the trees.

"Keep him out of my sight, sister."

"Fearghus . . ."

"*No!*"

She'd never seen her brother so angry. And she had the distinct feeling it had very little to do with Gwenvael's presence—for once.

"Wait." She caught up to Fearghus and grasped his arm. "Gwenvael brought a message."

Fearghus stopped walking. "From who?"

She smirked. "Who do you think? And he's not happy. He doesn't want us involved in this Sibling War."

Fearghus looked at his sister. "And this means what to me?"

She sighed. "We can't just ignore him."

"I can and I will. You do whatever it is you need to do, sister."

He snatched his arm away and walked back into his cave. She wouldn't bother going after him. There would be no point. She knew as soon as she got the message from Gwenvael that this would only set Fearghus's resolve. He never liked anyone telling him what to do . . . anyone.

She heard Gwenvael moaning and headed toward the sound. Then Morfyd stopped. She sniffed the air and looked around her. She felt a presence. Something deadly and evil.

She had to move quickly. She began a chant in her ancient tongue, and soon flames covered her body. Flames that didn't burn. She wrote sigils in the air and, with a roar that shook the glen, she sent the flames off.

Once the flames disappeared from her sight, she again headed off toward Gwenvael. She would tend her little brother's wounds and hope that Fearghus didn't merely open them up again tomorrow.

Hefaidd-Hen flew back out of his chair and across the room, slamming into the far wall. He collapsed to the floor and stayed there. His head feeling as if it might split open, his body racked with lightning strikes of pain. He should be dead. And, if he were any other wizard, he would be.

Two of his three acolytes were immediately by his side. "Master?" He slapped their hands away and continued to sit on the floor. He gasped for air, stunned.

So, it had been Morfyd. The Dragon Witch. That explained so much.

He smiled, even through the pain, and watched as his apprentices fearfully backed away from him.

* * *

Fearghus shifted back to dragon before returning to his lake. He was glad he had, too, because Annwyl waited for him. She sat on one of the large boulders that, because of its height, would bring them eye to eye. Her wet hair told him she'd bathed. Probably trying to wash him off, attempting to remove his scent from her body. That tore his heart more than he could admit.

But when she saw him and smiled, he became completely confused. It was the warmest smile he'd ever seen and she seemed absolutely relieved by his presence.

As long as he existed, he would never understand the girl.

"Fearghus. I wondered where you'd gotten to."

"Is everything all right?"

She sighed. "I guess."

The woman was killing him. Slowly. Bit by bit.

He settled down next to her and she immediately grasped a handful of his hair. "All right, Annwyl. What is it?"

"The knight."

Fearghus tensed. "Yes?"

"I lost my virginity to him today."

Fearghus's head snapped around so fast he dragged the girl off the rock, her hand still gripping his hair. "Oi!"

"Oh. Sorry." He never expected her to tell him. Never expected her to tell anyone. The way she walked away a mere hour before led him to believe she'd go to the grave with that secret. "Are you all right?"

"My butt hurts."

"*What*?"

"From dragging on the rock. And do get your mind out of the gutter, dragon."

Fearghus chuckled at that. "Sorry."

She lowered herself to the ground but still had a firm grip on his hair. She leaned into him and Fearghus couldn't believe how warm her body felt against his.

"What do I need to do to mount you?"

"*What?*"

"For battle! Honestly, Fearghus."

"Oh. That. Just catch hold of my hair and climb."

"Won't that hurt you?"

"No."

She seized two handfuls of his hair and pulled herself up until she placed herself on his back. She sat low on his shoulders, her legs straddling him at his neck.

"No saddle?"

"I'm not a horse."

"No need to get testy. Just asking."

She squeezed her thighs tight around his neck and he wondered how much more the gods would make him endure before he lost all reason.

"Did he . . . hurt you?" Fearghus had to know. Had to know what she was feeling, thinking. And she wouldn't tell the knight. So maybe she would tell the dragon.

"No."

"I can't help you if you don't talk to me, Annwyl." Yes. He would go to hell and this girl would be the one to send him there. A special hell for evil dragons that lied to beautiful women.

She gave a great sigh as she combed her strong fingers through his mane. He fought the desire to purr like a cat. "I don't know what I want."

"Do you want him?"

"Oh, yes. I want him. I *really* want him. But . . ."

"But . . . ?"

Annwyl could easily spend the rest of her life right here. Right on top of this enormous beast. Her legs straddling his neck. Her hands buried in his mane of black hair. She wondered what it would be like to ride with him into battle. To feel his strong body soar through the deep blue skies of Dark Plains.

But would she be happy? Could she give up her life as a leader and a woman to spend the remainder of her days in this cave with this dragon? Her dragon?

The knight had opened a new door for her. She never trusted anyone enough to let them get that close to her. He hadn't made love to her, as she'd heard the kitchen maids call it. What they had was much more primal. Much deeper.

Could she give that up to stay with her dragon and be no more than a friend? That's all the dragon could really offer her and there would be no guarantee he wanted to give her even that much.

And although the knight gave her insurmountable pleasure, it was the dragon that she wanted to talk to when she awoke in the knight's arms.

Perhaps her father had been right. Maybe she did go out of her way to make things difficult.

"Annwyl?"

She realized that the dragon waited for her answer, but she really had none to give.

Annwyl stood on the dragon's back and stretched. "I don't want to talk about this anymore."

"Then what do you want to talk about?"

Annwyl, on a whim, did a handstand.

"What are you doing back there?"

"Nothing to worry yourself about, dragon." She balanced her body and proceeded to move across the dragon's back, inch by inch using only her hands. "Tell me more about your family."

Fearghus stretched out and Annwyl let out a squeal of surprise as she lost her balance and landed heavily against his back. Ignoring her, the dragon rested his enormous head on his arms. "I cut the tip of my brother's tail off once."

Annwyl sat up with a laugh and wondered what the hell she was going to do.

Chapter 11

Hysterical laughter. Why did he keep hearing hysterical laughter? Fearghus opened one eye to stare at his two siblings. They were practically falling over each other they were laughing so hard. They woke him up from a sound sleep for this?

"What?" His current mood wouldn't allow for this. And definitely wouldn't allow for *him*.

Gwenvael choked out an answer. "She braided your hair, brother."

"Like a horse's mane," his sister added.

He growled and watched Gwenvael snatch their sister out of the way before the stream of white flame hit them both.

Of course, that didn't stop the laughter.

"If that's how you feel, you should tell him." Morfyd tossed two apples to Annwyl. "But you can't hide in here all day."

"I know." Annwyl looked at her friend. "I'm just not sure what I should say."

"Whatever feels right."

Annwyl nodded and left the chamber. She passed Gwenvael as she walked out of the dragon's lair. "How's your neck, Gwenvael?"

He glared but said nothing. Although she noticed he moved as far away from her as possible.

She bit back a smile and headed out in search of her knight.

She was so confused. And she wasn't used to that feeling.

She made life and death decisions every day. Even before she took over the rebellion, she risked her life and her brother's wrath to help innocent people trapped in the Garbhán Isle dungeons. But her feelings over two males were making her completely useless.

But she would talk to the knight. Tell him how she felt. And most likely end it. Her heart didn't belong to him, even if her treacherous body did.

She found him crouching by the stream, much as Gwenvael had done the day before. Unlike Gwenvael, however, the sight of his body sent a thrill through her that knocked the air from her lungs.

She forced herself to walk up to him. To face the man and tell him exactly what she thought. She knew he sensed her presence, his whole body tensed at her approach. Waiting. Waiting for her. She stood behind him for several long moments. Neither speaking. Annwyl crouched low, her body close to his.

Before she realized what she was doing, she slipped her arm around his shoulders and kissed the side of his thick neck. His whole body suddenly loosened up at her touch and he turned his head to look at her. He gave her the perfect opportunity to say something. To tell him the truth. But she couldn't stop staring at his full lips or wondering what it would be like to have him inside her again.

She kissed him and his moaning growl set her body on fire. Wanting someone was one thing. Knowing he wanted you just as much was something else entirely.

Tomorrow, she thought as he ripped the shirt from her back. *I'll tell him everything tomorrow.*

Tomorrow. I'll tell her everything tomorrow. Only a twinge of guilt needled his heart as Annwyl eagerly pulled his chain-mail shirt over his head. Morfyd convinced him that morning that he should finally tell Annwyl the truth. Tell her that her dragon and her knight were one.

He promised himself he'd do it, too. He could feel her standing behind him and he had his speech all prepared. Then suddenly her arms were around him and her lips were on his neck. With those simple gestures all logic disappeared and all he could think about was burying his head between her thighs.

It seemed like they were both naked in a matter of seconds. Fearghus licked his way down her body, loving the feel of her hands on his skin, and in his hair. He settled between her thighs, her legs on his shoulders, and ran his tongue between the lips of her sex. He marveled at how wet she already was, how clearly she wanted him. He dipped his tongue inside of her and her body arched off the ground. She tasted so good, felt so good. He realized, as he slowly dragged his tongue across her clit, that she was everything he wanted and more.

He couldn't give her up. He wouldn't let her go. There had to be some way to keep her. To prove to her that they were meant for each other. And he would risk absolutely everything to make that happen.

Lorcan stared at his advisor. "I'm sorry. Could you repeat that?"

Hefaidd-Hen spoke with his usual measured slowness. "Your sister is being protected by a dragon, milord. Perhaps two. The vision was not clear."

"I don't understand. How is she *protected* by dragons? People like her are *eaten* by dragons. *I'm confused!*" he bellowed.

"I can't explain the relationship, Lord Lorcan. I can only tell you my vision."

Lorcan rubbed his head. "Am I asking too much to want the little bitch dead? *Am I?*" It seemed Hefaidd-Hen learned long ago not to answer certain questions. "All I want is for her to suffer a painful, horrifying death. And for her head to be on a spike in front of my castle. That's all I want."

"We can still achieve that."

"Go up against a dragon . . . or two? I think not, Hefaidd-Hen. I'd rather my last memory not be of flames."

"Trust me, lord. I can find a way to get your sister and all that you desire."

"How?"

"By doing what I do best."

Lorcan looked at his advisor, a brutal chill running down his spine. Those cold blue eyes stared back, telling him nothing about the man behind them. But Hefaidd-Hen had proven himself time and time again in the past. As much as his very presence disturbed Lorcan, he could not deny that the man was a powerful ally.

"You have three days. After that, Hefaidd-Hen, I start to get angry."

"I understand." Hefaidd-Hen gave Lorcan the oddest smile before he bowed low and quietly left.

Morfyd needed to go to the village. A woman in her care would give birth in the next few days and all the signs told her it would not be an easy delivery. She'd already warned Fearghus she might be gone off and on for a bit, but Annwyl's body healed well. She no longer needed Morfyd's care.

As she walked out of the cave she passed Annwyl walking in. The girl had her swords in one hand. The other hand held her ripped shirt and bindings over her ample breasts. Her brows angled down into a dark frown and she wouldn't even look at Morfyd as she passed.

"How did that talk go then?" Morfyd called over her shoulder.

"Shut. Up."

Morfyd laughed as she advanced into the glen toward the clearing where she could take off. She rounded a corner and came upon her brother, his chain-mail shirt and sword in his big hand, heading toward the hidden entrance of his cave. She watched him as he passed and she noticed the long scratches across his back.

"How did that talk go then?" Morfyd called over her shoulder.

"Shut. Up."

Morfyd shook her head. If love always made you this pathetic, she wanted nothing to do with it.

Brastias tugged the hood of his cloak over his face. Again he wondered how much longer they had before Lorcan made his move. He could feel it. Feel it coming. Even before his spies told him to start getting his men ready, he knew that something had changed. Lorcan's troops were readying for battle at Garbhán Isle. And he sensed that a strike would be coming from Lorcan himself, but he wasn't sure when or how.

He wished he could see Annwyl. Discuss it with her. She knew her brother better than anyone else. She'd know exactly how and when Lorcan's forces would strike. Instead, all he could do now was wait for more information to come their way and hope they'd have time to react.

The door to the busy pub smashed open and again he turned to see who entered. Already he'd lost three hours waiting. Waiting to see her.

Danelin brought him over another ale and sat across from him. "How much longer?"

"Until she gets here."

Brastias didn't mean to be so abrupt but he didn't like being out in the open any more than Danelin. He'd rather be back at the camp, safe, with a lot of troops surrounding him. But he had to know how Annwyl fared. It had been days since the witch called Morfyd came to see him that first and only time. He hoped she would bring more messages from Annwyl. But she never returned. So, when he heard she was in the village visiting one of the women about to have a baby, he decided to go to her himself. He heard she always stopped at the pub for food or drink later in the evenings. So he waited and worried. Not about her or even about Annwyl. But about the rebellion.

He could tell the rebellion would soon come to an end. Tension grew daily. Many of the local villages emptied out. All except this one. Many of the rebellion's families lived here. Their wives and children. He debated whether to give the order to move them all into the Citadel of Ó Donnchadha where they would hopefully be safest. He knew the women would never willingly leave their mates.

As he wondered about the logic of this move, he saw her. How could he miss her? She stood taller than Annwyl and almost the same height as him. A grey cloak covered her witch's robes. She found a table in the back and ordered food. After the bar wench left, Brastias walked over to her table.

"Remember me?"

Glittering blue eyes turned to look at him. Her eyes were almond shaped, almost like a cat's. "How could I forget? You're so compelling."

Brastias smiled as he sat down opposite her. "How is she doing?"

"Better. Stronger every day."

"How much longer before she returns to us?"

The witch blinked. "Not sure really."

"What do you mean you're not sure?"

"What exactly do you think I mean?"

The witch's vagueness caused the hairs on his neck to rise. He didn't like this one bit. "Is she safe?"

The witch hissed at the insult. "Of course she is. Safer than if she were with you."

Brastias glared at the witch. "Really? And how is that possible when you are here and she is wherever you left her? Alone."

Perhaps it was the look in the witch's blue eyes or the way she didn't answer him, but it suddenly became clear. "She's not alone, is she?" When the witch didn't answer, he grabbed her hand. She snatched it away as if he were on fire.

She stood quickly. "Be well assured that she is safe. And soon she will return to you. You'll be able to find me at the village from time to time should you need to get an *actual* message to her." She tossed a few copper coins on the table and stormed out.

"What the hell happened?"

Brastias looked up at Danelin. He shook his head. "I don't know. But something's going on."

Danelin sat down as the barmaid left the witch's food on the table and scooped up the coins she left. "What?"

"I don't think the witch is taking care of her. It's somebody else."

"Who?"

"I don't know."

"Do you think she's safe?"

Brastias thought about it a minute, listened to his gut. "Yes. I think she is."

Danelin seemed surprised by that. "Then why do you have that look on your face?"

"Did you see the way she ran out of here? Like I had the plague or something."

"Who? The witch?"

"Aye."

"And this bothers you because . . ."

"Well . . . it's rude."

"Uh-huh."

Brastias growled at his second in command. "Shut up."

Fearghus turned the page of his book with one of his talons. He never bothered to read the story about his grandfather, Ailean, before. But Ailean spent most of his life as human. And lately, Fearghus began to wonder what that was like.

Completely engrossed in the chapter about Ailean and three bar wenches, he didn't know Annwyl sat down beside him until she pushed herself up against his side, near his wing. She brought wine, cheese, bread, and a book. She didn't say a word, just began reading and occasionally drinking or eating.

Fearghus watched her. "What are you doing?"

"What does it look like?"

"No talking tonight?"

She smiled softly. "No. Not tonight."

"Good."

Tonight he didn't want to talk. He just wanted to read his book and enjoy Annwyl being beside him.

He didn't know when he fell in love with her. It might have been when he first saw her outside his cave, fighting for her life. Or when she yanked his tail. Or possibly when she swam naked in his lake. In the end it didn't matter. It didn't matter when he fell in love with her. All he knew was that he loved her now. And would love her until his ancestors called him home.

He thought of the too-short life span of the humans. Or, at least of his Annwyl. Even if she survived the Sibling War she still wouldn't survive as long as Fearghus. The thought of living without her cut him like a lance through his heart. A very selfish part of him wished he could walk away from her. Leave her to live her human life with some human male. But when he looked at her, he realized that wasn't possible. She dipped her forefinger in the chalice of wine, leaned her head back, and let the wine drip into her open mouth. He shook his head at the woman's overt silliness. Still, he couldn't help but think about that mouth of hers exploring his entire body. That finger running over his shaft and wiping the fluid off its head.

Annwyl put her finger in her mouth and sucked it clean. Without meaning to, he gave a little moan and she turned to look at him. Oblivious, she winked at him and went back to her book.

There was one thing he could do, but it risked too much and could lose him everything. He shook his head again. No. The queen would be his last resort. She was *always* his last resort.

The air shifted in front of her as the blade slashed by her throat. With a laugh, she danced back several steps and brandished her two swords. He attacked and she blocked the move while she swung out her leg, aiming for his groin. He stopped her, catching hold of her ankle, then flipping her up and over. She landed facedown but forced her body up and moving before he could get his hands on her.

Annwyl really did have herself to blame for this. Throwing out "If you can take me, you can have me" before their swords clashed was, in retrospect, probably a bad idea. She really should stop challenging the man but she had to admit that she did enjoy a good fight.

Her father always accused her of making everything difficult. Perhaps he was right. If she wanted the knight, she could have easily taken him. From the time she walked up to him that morning, he had been more than ready. She knew it and he never said a word to her. But she realized now that she liked the challenge. She liked making him work for it. And work he did.

He knocked one of her swords out of her hand, so she backhanded him, causing the big ox to stagger away from her. She tried to charge past him, but he reached out that long arm and grabbed her. She struggled to get away from him, but his ironlike grip held fast. He pulled her struggling body into his chest with one arm. With the other he twisted her wrist until she dropped her sword.

"Seems, my lady, that I've got you."

"Bastard!"

"Now I guess I can have you."

"Let me go!"

"You made a bargain, my lady."

Annwyl growled in frustration, loving the feel of his arm around her, his hard body pushing into her back.

He forced her up against a tree, her back still to him. He leaned in close and whispered in her ear, "I'd hate to think the future ruler of Dark Plains would not keep her promises."

Then he ripped her leggings off.

Hours he spent creating the spell that would drag Annwyl from her protective cocoon with the dragons right to *his* lair. Days he spent gathering all the necessary ingredients. He even had to sacrifice one of his favorite acolytes who, tragically for him, was a virgin.

But the virgin blood opened the doorway between space and time. And that's when he saw her. Stark naked and astride some male. She rode him as if he were a favored stallion, her hips grinding against the man's body. Hefaidd-Hen's view took in her back and he could see her muscles flexing as she came closer and closer to release. He could see the sheen of sweat on her tanned skin, the sweat-drenched hair draping across her rippling muscles. He could hear her moans and cries of pleasure. Hefaidd-Hen's fingers neared her, about to touch her flesh. She was nearly his. But Lorcan burst in. Stormed in, actually. Pushing about his acolytes, demanding Hefaidd-Hen's immediate response to his presence.

With his concentration broken, the doorway slammed shut and the girl slipped his grasp. He roared in anger.

And Hefaidd-Hen turned all his fury toward the Butcher of Garbhán Isle.

Fearghus snatched Annwyl's naked, sweaty body protectively to him and sat up.

"Wait. Don't stop." He'd never gotten the stubborn, demanding, insatiable wench that close to begging before, but he had to ignore her. Something wasn't right.

The energy surrounded him. A presence. Not quite human. He looked around him and sniffed the air.

"What? What is it?" She reached for her sword, but he stopped her.

They were alone in his glen again. But a dark sense of foreboding invaded his very soul at that moment. Things were about to change. Forever.

He looked at Annwyl. She stared at him, a small smile on her lips. "Everything all right, knight?"

He didn't answer her. Instead he kissed her collarbone and stretched back out, his hard, demanding cock still inside her. "Finish what you started, woman."

Her smile grew wide. "My pleasure, knight."

Lorcan slowly opened his eyes. The brutal pain in his head made him wish for death. Just the dim light from a close-by pit fire caused a moan to escape. He couldn't remember what happened. Not clearly. But he knew from the sound of loud breathing in the room that something was terribly, terribly wrong.

"Ah, my lord. I am so glad to see that you are finally coming around." The voice sounded familiar, but he couldn't quite place it. He tried to push himself up with his arms, but something powerful and large slapped flat across his back, forcing him back to the ground.

"No. No. Stay down. I want you to rest before you try getting up." The voice sighed heavily. "I am so sorry, my lord, that it was necessary to be so harsh with you. But I think that it is time we made some things clear, mhmm?"

Lorcan didn't try to rise again. Whatever pushed him down still rested against his back, holding him in place. But he slowly swiveled his head around to see what spoke to him.

On sight of it he immediately tried to pull away, but it wouldn't let him go. "Now. Now. There is no reason to fear me. I am your ally. Just like I have always been." Lorcan retched and his meal from several hours ago burst across the floor.

"Well, that is lovely. You humans. So quick to panic. It amazes me that any of you still live."

Lorcan closed his eyes tight and refused to look at it anymore. He couldn't. Not if he hoped to keep his sanity.

"This can be a very profitable relationship for us both, Lorcan. As long as you understand that *you* belong to *me*. Body. Soul. And what little bit there is of a mind. I will give you your sister, but, in return, you will give me what I want as well. As long as you agree to that, you will live a very long time. But if you do not . . ." It pushed against his back and he knew that at any moment his ribs would break. But it stopped itself before going that far. "Do you understand, Lorcan?"

For the first time since his father died, Lorcan shook in fear. "Yes. Yes. I understand." Tears slid down his face and he realized he hadn't done that either since the death of his father.

"Good. Good. I do like when things are clear and concise. It's just in my nature." It patted his back almost lovingly. "We have so many plans to make. There will be much bloodshed soon. But you just rest now, my pet. You will have your sister soon enough."

Lorcan cried silently and prayed for oblivion.

Annwyl stared up at the cave ceiling, her hands behind her head. The dragon's even breathing causing his scales to move gently beneath her. He'd let her climb up his back and lie there. He didn't complain and she let herself enjoy the moment. His mane of hair spread across his scales and felt silky next to her bare skin. She wore nothing but her recently mended leather leggings and her bindings. She'd spent another day entangled with her knight. They had barely trained in days. Instead choosing to rut around the glen like two dogs in heat. But she couldn't help herself. The man did things to her body; made her feel things; took her to heights she never thought possible. And every evening, as the shadows darkened, she'd leave him and return to her dragon. Shame she couldn't live her life in this manner for the next thousand years or so.

"How was your training today?" His low voice rumbled through his body, vibrating against her flesh.

"Fine," she lied. She hadn't touched a sword—at least one made of metal—in two days.

"Good."

"Dragon?"

"Yes?"

"Have you ever had a woman?"

"What?"

"I mean a female. Mate. Whatever your kind calls them?"

"Oh." His body moved a little beneath her. "No, I've had no mate. Why?"

"Just wondering."

"What is it, Annwyl? What's bothering you?"

Nothing now. In fact, she felt relieved.

"Annwyl?"

She turned over, her head resting on her arms. "I'm fine, Dragon. Just curious." She closed her eyes. She'd never felt so safe before in her life. So at peace. She realized now there was no man alive who could ever make her feel this way.

She smiled. *Only I would fall in love with a dragon.*

Fearghus loved the feel of her body against his. Loved the fact she felt safe enough with him to fall asleep while stretched out across his back. He didn't realize how much that feeling would mean to him. How much this girl would mean to him.

He never realized that his feelings for Annwyl could get any stronger than they already were, but he was wrong. They were stronger and becoming stronger every day.

By day he lay with her as human, and every night she found him by the lake and they talked for hours. She still confused him, but he wouldn't give up their time together for all the gold in the world.

But he still feared the day he would have to tell her the truth. Tell her that he'd been lying to her. Would she hate him? Would she ever forgive him? He didn't know. And he didn't want to think about it too much. Because his gut would twist up and a sudden sense of panic would set in. He thought only humans could experience panic. It annoyed him to discover he was wrong about that, too.

No, he thought as Annwyl tightened her grip in his mane of hair and sighed softly in her sleep, *I'll not give her up without a fight. Never.*

Chapter 12

It had been a hard birth, but both baby and mother survived. Besides, Morfyd had needed to be away. Give her brother and his human some time alone. Of course, Gwenvael refused to leave until he got an answer from Fearghus, but she was able to bribe him to stay out of the lovers' way. She would have thought her baby brother would be too embarrassed to take money from his sister. She quickly discovered how wrong she was on that point.

Dark Glen lay only a few leagues away, but she wasn't ready to go back yet. She never knew where or when she might stumble across Fearghus and Annwyl "going at it," as Gwenvael so eloquently put it. The late hour and a brief check around assured her that she was alone.

Morfyd quickly stripped off her robes and dove naked into the lake. She enjoyed the rush of cold water over her human form. She didn't know why but her kind did love water. She'd envied Fearghus a bit when he found his lair. A cave with its own freshwater lake. Now that was heaven.

"She couldn't have gotten far. Go that way. I'll check the lake." Morfyd froze. She heard male voices and knew they were looking for her. She swam to the edge of the lake and had just pulled herself out when a man stumbled from the bushes. She stood tall, ready to burn him to embers when he straightened up, turning to face her.

"Brastias?"

"Morfyd. Good. We were . . ." Brastias stopped. Apparently he just realized she was naked and he became transfixed.

She waited, but he kept staring. His light eyes seemingly unable to look away. With a growling groan, "Damn, woman."

"Brastias?" She snapped her fingers. "Brastias!"

"Uh . . ." He yanked himself out of his trance and turned away from her. "Sorry. Sorry. I just didn't . . . I . . . uh . . ."

Morfyd grabbed her robes from off the ground. "What is it? What do you want?"

"I need you to get word to . . . um . . . um . . . uh . . ."

"Annwyl?"

"Yes, that's it."

Morfyd wanted to laugh but her sudden awareness of her own naked body trapped the sound in her throat. She pulled on her clothes. "You can," she cleared her throat, "turn around now."

Brastias looked over his shoulder at her. "I'm very sorry. I heard you'd just left the village. I didn't know you'd be here . . . uh . . . bathing."

Morfyd pushed her wet hair off her face. "No bother. Really. We'll simply never speak of it again. *Ever*. Now you said you had a message for Annwyl."

"Yes." He slowly turned his body to face her. "We've received word that Lorcan will be attacking this village in three days' time. We're going to move the women and children to the Citadel of Ó Donnchadha. We think they'll be safe there. . . . I never knew your hair was white."

Morfyd's head snapped up, her eyes locking with Brastias's.

"Uh . . . I mean," he continued in a rush, "we believe Lorcan himself will be attacking. I haven't seen him in battle for quite some time, but I know Annwyl's been waiting for this chance. I need you to let her know."

"I will."

"No matter what, we will fight to protect this village, so if she's not ready . . ."

"She's ready."

"Tell her we'll carry on until we hear from her."

Morfyd nodded. "I'll let her know."

"Thank you." Brastias stared at her for a moment longer, then quickly turned away, slamming into Danelin who had just emerged from the trees. He spun Danelin around and, before the man could say a word, pushed him back into the trees and away from the lake.

Morfyd covered her face with her hands. "Just bloody wonderful."

Fearghus walked past his treasure room toward his lake. He stopped, taking several steps back. Gwenvael sat on his pile of riches like he owned it.

"What are you doing?"

"Waiting for you. You've been avoiding me."

"As if you are worth avoiding."

"Well, it was either sit here or go sit on Annwyl. But she'd hurt me. Of course, I'm not sure I'd mind."

Still drenched in sweat from his last encounter with Annwyl, he could still smell her all over his body, still taste her on his lips. So, he wasn't about to let his idiot brother upset him. "What do you want?"

"I'm waiting for you to give me a message to take back."

"There is no message. It's none of their business."

"Do you really think it's that easy? Do you really think you don't have to live by the same laws the rest of us do?"

Fearghus snorted. "What laws do you live by, little brother?"

Gwenvael grinned. "The ones that keep me alive and healthy."

"Go back to them. Tell them anything you want. But when Annwyl leaves to fight her brother, I will be by her side."

Gwenvael sighed. "She could never love you, brother. She's human. I'd hate to see you give up your family for a girl that as soon as she finds out the truth, will run fast and far from you."

Fearghus gritted his teeth and tamped down his desire to blast Gwenvael where he sat. He didn't dare go near him. He might shift and rip the little bastard's guts out. "Get from my sight, boy. Before I send your head back to them as a gift." Fearghus headed toward his lake.

"Don't say I didn't warn you." Gwenvael yelled after him.

Annwyl leaned her forehead against the dragon's snout. "You've been very quiet this evening. What's wrong?"

"Nothing."

She knew he was lying. He'd barely spoken two words in the past hour. "Did I do something?"

"No. Of course not. It's just family problems. Nothing to concern yourself with."

"That message Gwenvael brought with him. They don't want you involved with my war, do they?"

The dragon sighed, heavily. "What they want doesn't concern me."

"I won't come between you and your kin. You saved my life, you owe me nothing more."

He pulled his majestic head away from her. "This isn't about owing you anything, Annwyl. I fight by your side because that is what I choose to do."

He moved away from her. Restless, he didn't stand still for long this night. She also sensed his anxiety and annoyance. And she knew that somehow she stood at the heart of it, but she didn't know what she'd done. Unless, of course . . . "Is this about the knight?"

The dragon stopped moving, but he didn't turn to face her. "If I asked you to stop seeing him, would you?"

Annwyl closed her eyes. Finally, the question she dreaded

since this all began. But she only had one answer for the dragon. Only one answer that would not be a lie.

"Yes."

"Why?"

"Because you asked me to. And I am loyal to you and you alone. I'll always be loyal to you, Fearghus."

"Because I saved your life?"

"No. I owe you my life for that. If you hit me with a ball of flame I wouldn't try and stop you. My life is yours to take. But my loyalty is not. That has to be earned. And you have."

"How?"

"You've made me feel safe. When no other has."

Annwyl drifted slowly to him. Once in front of him, she rested her hand on his snout. He closed his eyes at her touch. "For that you'll always have my loyalty."

She walked around the dragon and wrapped her arms as far around his neck as she could. She hugged him and, as always, he let her. "Good night, my friend."

"Good night, Annwyl."

She headed back to her chamber, but couldn't help but slide her hand across his leathery wings and the scales of his body. Like she did every night.

Fearghus didn't watch her leave, as he often did. His emotions a jumble in his head. The man that he played by day railed against the fact she could so easily give him up. The dragon agonized in confusion because she was willing to give up for him something that she clearly desired. But not once had she mentioned love. Only loyalty. Of course, he had not mentioned love either.

The little human managed to completely confound him and he wasn't sure he would ever be able to forgive her for it.

* * *

She watched the soldiers quietly flow into the glen. She could smell their fear. They didn't want to be in Dark Glen, no sane person would. So their other option must have been much worse. And once she recognized their armor, she realized it was. They were Lorcan's men. He sent them to her brother's glen. Sent them to find Annwyl.

She let them get farther in, away from any troops that might be waiting in safety outside the glen. She waited and she watched. When the time was right, she moved behind them, clearing her throat. The men stopped. At first, they wouldn't turn around. Afraid of what they might find. But she waited, knowing their human curiosity would get the best of them. It did. When she saw their eyes, Morfyd let go a stream of fire that scorched them to cinders before they could scream.

Gwenvael appeared beside her, his golden scales glinting brightly in the moonlight. He sniffed the air and looked at the still-smoldering remains of the soldiers.

He smiled at his sister. "Dinner."

It had gone on for days. The two of them constantly "at it." Like two mating beasts. Gwenvael shook his head in disgust. He understood lust. Actually, he appreciated lust greatly. But love? A strictly human emotion. And although he enjoyed gallivanting around town as human, he had no intention of making a muddle of his life as they all seemed to.

Of course, he would never have thought Fearghus the Destroyer would either. If there was one thing he could always count on from his large, less-than-social brother, it was his seemingly innate ability to feel nothing for anyone. So, to now watch him moon over some slip of a girl made Gwenvael question all his beliefs.

His head snapped up and he studied the sky. For a moment he thought he'd heard the flap of large leather wings. But as he searched the sky he saw nothing. He dismissed it and went in search of his sister. The soldiers from the previous night were not sitting well in his stomach and he needed one of her soothing concoctions.

She always did have a tendency to overcook their food.

Annwyl followed the sounds of retching. She found Morfyd by the stream. Her arms around Gwenvael's shoulders as he vomited into the water.

"He all right?"

Morfyd shrugged. "He ate too much. But he'll be fine. And I have a message for you from"—she cleared her throat—"Brastias."

Annwyl frowned. Did Morfyd just blush? "What message?"

"Your brother plans to attack the closest village in three days' time. Maybe less. I tried to tell you last night but you were sound asleep."

Annwyl shrugged. "All right. Thank you." She'd already planned to return to her troops in the next day or two.

"Is that all your brother warrants? A shrug and a thank you?"

"As a matter of fact, yes," Annwyl snapped, unable to help herself. "I have other things on my mind besides him. Oh . . ." she waved her hand. "I'll come back later." Annwyl made to go, but Morfyd stopped her.

"Wait. Annwyl. What is it?"

"I can't go on like this."

Morfyd dropped Gwenvael, his head slamming into the stream. Annwyl grinned as Gwenvael cursed the woman.

Morfyd moved over to Annwyl and looked at her. "You can't go on like what?"

"My days with the knight. My nights with the dragon. It's becoming impossible."

"Annwyl, talk to him."

"I tried that. I can't think when I'm around him. He does this thing with his tongue. . . ."

"Annwyl! I mean the dragon. Talk to the dragon."

"I tried last night, but . . . I think he grows tired of me. And what if he laughs?"

"He hasn't. And he won't." Morfyd smiled. "Trust me."

"But . . ."

"No. I don't want to hear it. Just tell the big bastard how you feel. How you feel about *him*. He needs to hear it. And you need to say it."

"But the knight . . ."

"Don't worry about him. Talk to the dragon. The knight can wait."

Annwyl took a deep breath. She had to do something. Soon she would face her brother and most likely death. She didn't want to go to her grave knowing that her weakness held her back from the one thing that truly mattered to her.

She nodded and headed back to the cave. Back to her dragon.

Fearghus followed the sound of retching. He found his brother doubled over and Morfyd patting him on the back.

"What's wrong with him?"

"He ate too many soldiers last night."

"Soldiers? Here?"

Morfyd nodded. "Lorcan's men. Don't worry. I took care of them."

"But this means they know Annwyl is here."

Morfyd shook her head as she rubbed Gwenvael's sweaty brow. "Not necessarily. It looked more like they were just checking the area. You know, a scouting party." Morfyd looked up at her brother and frowned. "Why are you here?"

"What do you mean why am I here?"

"I just sent Annwyl to find you. She wants to talk to you."

"Talk to me?" He pointed to himself. "Or to me?" He pointed toward his cave.

Morfyd laughed and seemed about to answer when she stopped and stared off behind him.

Fearghus turned around. "What are *you* doing here?"

Briec, next in line behind Fearghus, leaned against a tree and watched his siblings quietly. Naked, fresh from shifting, his long silver mane of hair stretched down his back and fell across his face and shoulder.

"When there was no answer from you or Morfyd and baby brother didn't return . . ."

Fearghus shook his head. "Not this again." He didn't want to hear it. He wanted to find Annwyl. Hear what she had to say. And no matter what she said, he would tell her the truth. Tell her everything. He couldn't go on like this anymore.

"I told you not to ignore him." Morfyd chastised as she helped a very green Gwenvael to his feet.

"Go back to the old bastard and tell him to stay out of my life."

Briec shook his head. "I can't."

Fearghus frowned. "What do you mean you can't?"

"I mean I can't . . . because he's already here. He awaits you in your den."

Before Fearghus could react, Morfyd's hand suddenly gripped his arm, nearly tearing the skin off. "Gods, Fearghus. Annwyl."

"Dragon!" Annwyl called out before she even entered his part of the lair. "Dragon! Are you here?"

She marched into the dragon's main chamber, the words she needed to tell him on her lips. "Fearghus, I . . ." She stopped.

Although the dragon she now saw before her bore the same

size and color as Fearghus, this one's black mane had silver and white hair streaked through it, and his scales were not as bright. Clearly an older dragon.

And he definitely wasn't Fearghus.

She stopped and stared at him. The old dragon looked at her.

"You."

The look of welcome she always saw in Fearghus's eyes did not spark in this dragon's. And she knew in that split second he wanted her dead.

She burst into a run, the dragon's flames just missing her. The dragon took in another deep breath so Annwyl dived behind a large boulder. Flames erupted all around her as she crouched down low. The flames went around the boulder but its heat scared her beyond anything she'd known. He could kill her with one blast. She ignored the panic that began to rise and unsheathed her sword.

After several moments, the flames stopped and she could hear the dragon stomping toward the boulder. She held her breath and waited. He stopped and she glanced over just as his snout came around the boulder, latching on to her scent.

She waited until the beast's head was close enough, then she slashed him across the snout. Dragon blood spurted across her arm and the dragon roared in pain and anger as she sprinted out, heading away from the beast. He charged after her. Annwyl knew that in order to survive she needed to let her instincts take over. She weaved between other boulders, using the beast's size and weight against him. When he stopped to strike her with flame, she would again hide behind a boulder or a stone wall. But she couldn't keep it up much longer. She needed to kill the dragon before it killed her. She stayed behind a boulder longer than normal and this time, just as she somehow knew he would, the dragon came from overhead.

As his head silently lowered to get close to her she jumped up on the boulder and onto the beast's snout. Startled, he gave her the time she needed to run up and over his head, down his neck, across his back, until she reached his tail. She knew he could use it as a weapon, so she moved quickly. She held the tip down with her foot and slammed her sword between it and where the scales were at their smallest and weakest. Where Fearghus once cut his brother's tail off.

She impaled the tail, burying the blade into the ground. The roar he sent out shook the cave and Annwyl knew she only had seconds before he got himself loose. So she unsheathed her second sword and ran under the dragon.

She could only pray that a dragon's weakness was the same as a human's. The groin. She lay flat on her back and, using her legs, slid completely under him. She had to move quickly. Once he realized she was there, all he had to do was lie down.

As she hoped, the hard scales that covered the rest of his body did not cover his groin. His shaft protectively tucked up inside the flesh, thankfully out of sight and away from her face. She'd already seen more of this dragon than she'd ever wanted to. She raised her sword and dug it into the beast's fleshy underbelly, readying herself to push the blade through. She hoped the move would allow her time to get out of the cave and out of the glen if she had to.

"*Annwyl! No!*"

Annwyl froze. Blood began to seep where the tip of her blade rested, but she pushed no further. The dragon above her stopped breathing. He couldn't sit now. True, he'd crush her, but he'd impale himself in the process.

"Annwyl, love. Give me your hand."

Annwyl glanced over and saw the shiny black talons of her dragon. Breathing hard, a war raged in her soul between the warrior ready to strike the killing blow and Annwyl the woman who knew this dragon was Fearghus's father.

"Fearghus?"

"Annwyl. Trust me."

Annwyl looked back at the bleeding beast above her. If the old dragon killed her now, she knew as sure as she knew her own name that Fearghus would kill him. The old beast wouldn't risk that. She decided to trust the one being she'd trusted all along.

She grabbed onto his talon and allowed him to snatch her out from under the great dragon. He pushed her back into Morfyd and Gwenvael and turned to face his father, protecting them all with his own body.

Chapter 13

Never before had anyone gotten so close to killing Bercelak. And if he hadn't stopped her, Annwyl would have killed him. She found the one weak spot on a dragon. The one place with no protective scales.

When the four of them charged in, Annwyl had just slid her long body under the dragon's. Fearghus called her name but the bloodlust had her, and she couldn't hear him. So he shifted, his voice shifting with him, almost bringing the walls down with his call to her.

Part of him didn't want to stop her, he was so angry at his father. But he knew that if Annwyl killed him, there would be no going back for the queen. She would move heaven and earth to destroy Annwyl and he would do the same to protect her. But at the sound of his voice, she stopped. Cold. He wasn't sure she had that kind of self-control. But, as always, Annwyl continued to amaze him.

"You son of a bitch!" Fearghus's rage shook the walls of his lair, and he itched to beat the old bastard to death.

His father had his claw over his slashed snout while desperately trying to get his tail released from the blade that held it. "Did you see what that mad bitch did to me?"

"I should have let her kill you."

"I gave you strict orders. . . ."

"I don't answer to you! Get out. *Now!*"

"What is your attachment to this human?" His father's shrewd eyes stared closely at his son, his nostrils twitched. "I smell her all over you."

"I said go!"

His father looked around him to see Annwyl. "What did he tell you, little human, to get you to spread your legs?"

Fearghus released a fireball that sent his father flying across the cave, part of his tail torn off where the blade impaled it.

"Fearghus, no!" Morfyd shouted behind him. But he only glanced at his sister. His anger had a stranglehold on him now. Too blind with rage to acknowledge anything. Until he heard Annwyl.

"Fearghus?" She didn't shout. She didn't scream. She said it so quietly the rest of his family probably never heard her. But he did.

Annwyl sheathed her sword and listened to the fight between father and son. It almost reminded her of Lorcan and their father, but she doubted the fight would end with Fearghus crying and cowering in a corner.

The old dragon's cold eyes turned to her. She pulled away from Morfyd, ready to face the old bastard when something caught her eye. The bright red of a surcoat. Shredded and sitting at the entrance to the chamber. She walked over to it as the family squabble continued. She crouched down beside the garment and also found chain-mail leggings, chain-mail shirt, and leather boots. All shredded and ripped apart. For a moment she worried that maybe her knight had become food for the old dragon, but she could find no blood and the garments seemed split apart.

She looked up at Fearghus who had just blasted his father across the room. What did the old bastard say to her? *What did he tell you, little human, to get you to spread your legs?* At that moment, Morfyd called out to Fearghus, and in anger the dragon's head snapped around to briefly look at her. The action caused his mane to flip to the opposite side and an unruly bit of black hair fell over his eye. Annwyl stared. How had she never noticed it before? That black hair that she loved so much on both her knight and her dragon. The hair she insisted on running her hands through when she talked with her dragon or gripping in passion when she rode her knight.

"Fearghus?"

He moved to descend on his fallen father, but her voice stopped him. He looked at her. Their eyes locked. And Annwyl felt a wave of cold spike down her spine. Her gaze shifted to Morfyd, but the woman looked away from her. Gwenvael, although still a little green, turned his entire body away. His eyes downcast. Then she realized that there was another. She looked up to find a silver-haired naked man staring at her. He grinned in greeting. Then he winked.

Annwyl stood and walked to Fearghus. She stood in front of him. "Fearghus?"

"I can explain everything. . . ."

"Can you, boy?" Fearghus closed his eyes at the sound of

his father's voice. The old dragon had hauled his enormous bulk up and stood behind his son.

Annwyl felt it at that moment. She had kept it at bay so long she forgot how good it felt to wrap it around herself like a warm cloak in the middle of winter. She unsheathed her sword as her rage spread through her limbs.

Fearghus's eyes snapped open in surprise at the sound. "Annwyl." She moved around him, her eyes locked with his. He turned his body as she walked. He waited for it. Waited for the blow. And he'd take it too. She was sure of that.

"Are you going to let some human do this to you, Fearghus?" His father barked in disgust. Annwyl now stood between the two dragons. Her eyes still locked with Fearghus's, her blade pointing tip down, the handle gripped by both her hands. She held the weapon so tightly that her tan knuckles now white with the effort.

"You lied to me."

"Yes."

"Why?"

"I didn't think you'd understand."

"Just kill her, Fearghus. Kill her and be done with it," his father sighed heavily.

"Tell me, Fearghus." She raised the sword high, her rage singing through her veins. "Do you understand this?"

She spun on her heel away from Fearghus and, using all the rage she contained, slammed the blade into the old dragon's claw between his talons where the scales were at their thinnest, nailing it—and him—to the hard ground.

The dragon's head fell back and the roar he let out most likely rang out hundreds of leagues away.

Annwyl turned to her lover. "Burn in hell, Fearghus."

She walked away, leaving the dragons to tend their wounded father.

Chapter 14

His siblings stood there silent, stunned by their father's scream of pain. But Fearghus watched Annwyl. He watched her walk toward the exit. Watched her notice Briec staring at her. She stopped and stared back at his silver-haired brother. When he smiled at her, she backhanded him across the head, knocking the dragon's human form into Gwenvael.

He glanced at his younger brother. "Go with her."

"*Have you lost your mind?*" Gwenvael demanded as he helped Briec to his feet. "She's insane! I'm not going anywhere!"

Fearghus growled low, making sure his fangs showed. Gwenvael winced back and grudgingly followed.

"Keep her safe," he called after his brother. He looked at Morfyd who finally snapped out of her surprise and now tended their father.

"How bad is it?"

Morfyd looked at her brother with wide eyes. "She went straight through to the cave floor. I think it's stone." She didn't bother hiding the awe in her voice.

"No. There's some dirt there."

"Well, it's going to have to be pried out. It's imbedded."

He sneered at his father. "He'll live. I'm going after her."

"What?" His sister stood up in front of her brother. "Fearghus, don't. She's angry. *Very* angry. She impaled your father . . . twice. Give her some time to calm down."

"I lied to her, Morfyd. She has every right to be angry. Besides, it wasn't me she hurt."

"No. You're not going anywhere until you help me with him." She went back to Bercelak. "I can't do this alone."

Fearghus shook his head. His sister didn't need his help. But she wanted to give Annwyl at least a few minutes to calm her rage. Perhaps not a bad idea, when he thought about it a moment.

He watched his father struggling to pull his claw from the cave floor, but he couldn't do it without tearing open the wound. The bastard was effectively stuck until he and Morfyd helped him. Fearghus smiled a little at his father's suffering and the female who caused it.

I do love that woman.

"Stay away from me, Gwenvael."

"I don't want to be here, but my brother gave me no choice." Gwenvael struggled to keep up with her. His stomach still threatened to remove the rest of the soldiers he'd eaten the previous night and she had very long legs. She didn't run but rather stalked. And he knew if he got too close he could end up like Briec. Or worse . . . like his father.

He finally understood what his brother saw in this woman. Dragon females were dangerous, but very calculating. And sometimes very cold. For them it was all about the politics. Not for Annwyl, though. She cared nothing for politics. She ran on instinct and emotion. Her instincts kept her alive. Her emotions made her a lethal weapon. How could Fearghus not fall in love with her? If Gwenvael thought about it himself, he might have to admit he'd fallen a little in love with her himself.

It didn't take long for her to reach the edge of Fearghus's glen. He followed her out but found himself slamming into the back of her. He thought once she hit open ground she'd run for it, back to her troops. But when he looked up he saw what stopped her.

Two battalions of soldiers waited for her. They wore Lorcan's colors and they clearly had every intention of taking her back alive for their leader to have his revenge. At least ten men had nets to snag the female.

"I have no weapons," she muttered under her breath as she took a step back toward Gwenvael.

"Yes you do." He tossed his sword to her. Annwyl stared at the weapon. And Gwenvael quickly realized the girl had lived in safety with Fearghus too long. Well, no matter. He knew exactly how to get Annwyl the Bloody back. "And don't forget, Annwyl. My brother lied to you. Made a fool of you. And he's probably having a good laugh with the old dragon as we speak. Now"—he shoved her toward several advancing men—"go get 'em." He watched as the girl gave a bellow of rage and took off the head of the first man who came near her. Then she turned and swiped off another. Gwenvael shivered. Her name fit her well.

Gwenvael saw soldiers moving toward him. He shifted, forcing the girl to dash off to the side to avoid the crush of his dragon body.

"Dragon!" He expected them to run. They always ran before. But these troops didn't.

And he suddenly realized that Annwyl hadn't been the only one expected. So had a dragon.

Annwyl slammed her blade into another soldier's belly and sliced him open. She snatched the man's sword from the sheath at his side, ignoring the bowels that fell to the ground in front of her, and turned to face the next attacker. They wanted to get her in those nets, but she knew what that meant. Going back to her brother and any tortures he had planned for her. The thought chilled her to the bone and spurred her speed and malice.

She began first by hacking off arms. Any arms holding

nets. She realized quickly how her training with Fearghus benefited her as she lobbed off another arm and removed the man's head. She moved faster now. Her attacks more pointed, more deadly. For a moment she forgot how angry she was with him. But then she remembered and practically cut a man in two with her rage.

She heard Gwenvael's roar of anger and turned to find that a separate group of men were trying to take the dragon down. They had ropes wrapped around his neck and at least thirty men were trying to pull the beast to the ground. He blasted a few with a breath of fire, but she recalled that in his human form Gwenvael had been quite ill. She now realized that same illness affected the dragon as well. A few more moments, and he would be down and the soldiers would take him.

She ran toward him, taking another soldier's head as she passed by. She slid to a stop under the dragon's neck and slashed at the ropes holding him, slicing as many as she could into two. Gwenvael pulled up as some of the pressure lessened, dragging the men holding the last few intact ropes with him. As they came close, Annwyl gutted several of them, and took a few heads.

"Fire!"

Annwyl crossed her blades in front of her as archers released a volley of arrows. But they never reached her as white flame destroyed them in mid-flight. A silver dragon appeared over the battle, his flame taking out almost an entire battalion. A white dragon swooped down and snapped up a carriage of soldiers, tossing them like toys. Then Annwyl saw him.

He landed beside his golden brother, blasting the last of the men still holding ropes.

"Take her!" he barked at the now-free Gwenvael.

"What about you?"

"We're fine. Take her!"

Another group of men charged Annwyl. She readied her blades but suddenly found herself gripped firmly about the waist and airborne. She watched the land recede from her sight.

"*You bastard! Let me down!*"

"Not on your life, beauty." The golden claw gripped her tighter. "You get hurt, he'll kill me. Now quiet. I'm trying not to vomit."

Fearghus watched Briec and Morfyd unleash lines of flame, destroying anything in their wake. A small group of men, about twenty, ran toward him, their blades drawn. In disgust, Fearghus spit out a fireball and watched with little satisfaction as the men writhed and screamed.

He saw another group trying to escape. "Briec! Kill them! Leave none alive!"

Briec followed and Fearghus walked out among the remains, stepping on any men he thought still lived. Morfyd landed in front of him.

He nodded toward the empty spot where Gwenvael first stood and the ropes that lay there. "Seems I was expected as well."

His sister nodded. "Seems so."

Fearghus growled. "I am not happy, sister."

"I can tell."

"And you still have no idea who's helping Lorcan?"

"It's Hefaidd-Hen." Fearghus watched as a wounded Bercelak landed gingerly in front of him, making sure not to further damage his wounded claw.

"Hefaidd-Hen? *The* Hefaidd-Hen?"

"Well, that's just bloody wonderful," Morfyd spat out as Briec continued to fly overhead blasting flames.

"And when were you planning to tell us?"

"Never. The girl shouldn't have even been here. And you shouldn't have been helping her."

"Why would Hefaidd-Hen help Lorcan?" Morfyd cut in before Fearghus could go for their father's throat.

"How should I know? And why should I care? These are human concerns, not ours."

"You should care because Hefaidd-Hen's a dragon," Morfyd snapped angrily.

"If he gets Lorcan's loyalty, then he gets his troops, which no doubt would triple once he's secured the loyalty of the other regions."

"And once he gets his troops, he moves on the queen," Morfyd summed up quickly.

Fearghus saw his father suddenly realize the implication to them all of Hefaidd-Hen's involvement.

"He wouldn't dare." If there was one thing Fearghus had always been sure of it was his father's feelings for the queen. He had no doubt this little revelation would change everything.

"That dragon craves power more than anything," he reminded Bercelak. "And all he's ever wanted is the queen's throne."

"There's much power in her blood," Morfyd added. "If he takes it . . ."

"That won't happen."

"Then you best hope Annwyl defeats Lorcan, Father. If she doesn't, however, then we'd best prepare for war. Because no dragon will be safe."

Fearghus watched Bercelak struggle with all this. The old dragon hated being wrong. Especially when his own children pointed it out to him. But Bercelak knew, in his heart, how right they were. And Fearghus knew that he would do what was best for the queen, as Bercelak always had.

His father's head snapped up. "Briec and I will return to the queen. And you two make sure the girl wins, I don't care what you have to do."

"If she lets us near her, Father," Morfyd bravely chastised. "Her last memory is of you trying to kill her and telling her about Fearghus before he could."

Briec finally landed behind his father. He tossed his silver mane. "She still saved Gwenvael. I saw her. She's a brave girl . . . for a human."

"I know that," Fearghus snapped. He looked at his father. "I'm just not sure how I'm going to fix this."

"Well you better find a way, *boy*. Use whatever charm she seems to think you possess. You got her on her back at least once before."

Morfyd slid between Fearghus and their father before he could kill the old bastard. "Fearghus!"

"Just let me kill him. I'm begging you!"

"Father, go!"

The dragon didn't waste time; he took to the skies. Briec nodded at his siblings once and followed.

"Really, Fearghus. You need to stop asking me to let you kill our family."

Fearghus shook his head. "They just keep irritating me."

Morfyd gave a smile he knew would frighten any human. "I know. But that's what most families do. Irritate." She stepped back. "I need to do something, Fearghus. And you need to go to Annwyl."

Fearghus looked down at his large claws and sighed. "She hates me."

"Yes. I believe she does."

"*How is that supportive?*" he bellowed.

"I'm not going to lie to you, brother. But I also know she loves you. She must. She risked her life to save Gwenvael."

"Yes. She did."

"And now she's alone with him." Fearghus looked at his sister. "She's alone with big, golden, charming Gwenvael. And he's probably feeling so indebted to her right now for saving his life."

Fearghus knew what his sister was doing. Knew how she was trying to manipulate him. That didn't change the fact that it worked.

He took to the skies, only briefly wondering what "something" his sister must do at that very moment. But he thought of Gwenvael alone with Annwyl and he forgot all about his sister.

Annwyl's rear hit the ground hard. The shock traveled all the way from her spine to her teeth. But she knew that in the dragon's mind he'd dropped her gently to the ground.

She heard him land behind her and felt human hands grip her under her arms and lift her to her feet. "That wasn't too hard, was it?"

"No. Like landing on pillows." She pulled away from him.

"I could have taken you directly to your camp."

"True, but then I'd have a camp full of screaming men wetting themselves over the dragon."

"Oh. Good point."

She didn't know what to do with this Gwenvael. And not just because he was naked and very much like his brother. But because up until now he'd never stopped flirting with her, although he'd always kept a healthy distance from her and Fearghus. But this Gwenvael seemed almost sweet, the smug bravado gone.

"Well, you can go." She waved him away, hoping he'd leave. She wanted to be alone. She wanted to be angry. *Really* angry.

"Yes. I just wanted to say . . . well, thank you for saving me."

She had, hadn't she? Why? At the moment, she hated all dragons. Especially large black ones. Must have been instinct. Anything that fought against Lorcan or his men, she needed to protect.

"You're welcome." She realized he was leaning into her. His eyes focused on her mouth, his lips slightly open. She

slapped her hand over his face, just as she had his brother.
"What are you doing?"

"I was going to give you a kiss. . . ."

"Don't even think about it, Gwenvael. I am in no mood."

The dragon nodded sagely. "You still love him."

"No, Gwenvael. I don't love anything. And I don't think I'll
love anything *ever again!*" He stepped back at her sudden
spurt of rage. "*Now get out of my sight!*"

She stomped off toward camp, her rage walking beside her
like a pet panther.

Chapter 15

Brastias dismissed the other lieutenants. Once alone with
Danelin, he asked him the question that had plagued him all
day. "Anything more on Lorcan?"

Danelin shook his head. "No. And I'm worried."

"That bastard's going to move soon. I can feel it."

"Have you seen the witch again? Do you know if Annwyl
is still returning?" At the mere mention of Morfyd, Brastias
felt his whole body tighten. "I don't know," he barked gruffly.

"What if she's still healing? She'll be no use to us if she
can't fight."

Brastias walked out of the tent, Danelin beside him. "I
want the men prepared and ready. When Lorcan moves, I
don't want us surprised. By anything."

"I understand."

The two men stepped aside as a woman pushed past them heading to Annwyl's tent.

Brastias stopped. "Was that . . . ?"

"I . . . think so."

Brastias and Danelin followed. They found Annwyl just as she threw a chair across the room.

"*Lying, conniving, toe-rag!*"

Danelin gave Brastias a look, turned, and ran.

"Annwyl?"

Angry green eyes locked on to him, and he'd wished he'd run like Danelin. When he still had the chance. "Brastias. My friend." *Uh-oh, this couldn't be good.* "Do you lie to me?"

"Uh . . . no."

"See? *That's a lie!*"

"Annwyl, calm down. Tell me what happened."

"Happened? Nothing. Nothing happened. Everything is just fine. Perfect. Better than perfect."

Brastias wanted to pursue this further, and probably take his life in his hands, when he heard the screams of the men from outside the tent.

"Lorcan." He ran out of the tent and slammed into Danelin, who couldn't move. He stood trapped. In fear. Fear of the mammoth black dragon that landed in the middle of their camp.

"By the gods."

The dragon looked around at the surrounding troops, but still hadn't sent anyone to hell.

"*Annwyl!*"

"Oh, gods. It's . . . talking." Danelin looked like he would piss himself any moment.

But fear for Annwyl kept Brastias moving. He drew his sword, intent on challenging the creature when she stormed out of the tent. He seized her arm in what he thought a powerful grip to stop her, but with her formidable anger she easily pulled away, stomping off to face the dragon.

The men watched as Annwyl the Bloody took a stand against something from their darkest nightmares. Too afraid to fight, but too terrified for their leader to run away.

And then Brastias saw the girl do something he would never forget.

She kicked the beast. Right in the knee.

Brastias and Danelin exchanged glances.

"Well, you always thought she was insane," Brastias offered.

"I didn't think I was right."

"You lying toe-rag!" she yelled up at him.

"Let me explain."

"*Go to hell!*"

"Annwyl."

"*No!*" She headed back to her tent. "Leave me, Dragon. I never want to see you, or your family, again. *Ever!*"

Danelin glanced at Brastias. "Family?"

"Don't ask."

The dragon silently watched Annwyl's retreating form. He began chanting and flame surrounded him. That's when Brastias wondered if he would die this day. The flames grew, enveloping the beast, but eventually the flames died away, leaving a very large, very naked man.

With a growl, he followed after Annwyl, disappearing into the tent after her.

"So they can shape-shift then?" Danelin asked quietly.

"Seems so."

"Should we go after him?"

Brastias looked at Danelin. It took him awhile, but he'd finally figured out what he'd just witnessed. A lover's quarrel. Leave it to Annwyl.

"Uh . . . I think not. We need to ready the troops. And let's ready them somewhere away from camp, I think."

He glanced at the tent, shook his head, and walked off. A quaking Danelin followed quietly behind.

* * *

"Why won't you talk to me?"

"You want me to talk? Fine. How's your father?"

"How do you think he is? You stabbed him in the foot."

"I would have aimed for his heart, but I wasn't sure he actually had one. Do any of you have one?"

"Annwyl, I couldn't tell you the truth."

"Why?"

"I . . . uh . . ." He didn't know this would be so hard. Was he joking? Of course, he knew it would be this hard!

"Still waiting." He got the feeling he could claim being one of the few who actually got her this angry. Funny, that didn't seem like such a good thing to him at the moment.

"I was going to tell you. I swear."

"Really? You were *going* to tell me?" Her sarcasm thick, her bitterness filled the tent. He couldn't blame her. He'd asked for this.

"Yes, Annwyl, I was. Today. My father just beat me to it."

"And why didn't you tell me before?"

He moved into the room toward her. She took a step back, drawing her sword. "Everything changed."

He stood before her now, her blade at his throat. "I couldn't stop thinking about you, Annwyl. I wanted you, more than anything. And I didn't know how to tell you the truth without losing you. You trusted the dragon, but you absolutely hated the man. I needed you to accept all of me. Today I thought maybe you could."

He took a step forward and felt the tip of the blade just pierce his flesh. A trickle of blood eased down his neck to his chest. Annwyl's breath came out in short gasps as she stared into his eyes. "You could kill me now. Easily. If that's what you want." He moved in a bit more. Any more and the blade would tear through his throat and kill him. "Is that what you want, Annwyl?"

She stared at him for several long moments. "Yes, Fearghus," she growled out. "It is."

Not the answer he'd hoped for, but he was quickly distracted by the pain in his knee where she kicked him.

He barked in agony as she pushed him out of her way and moved a safe distance from him, against the far tent wall beside her bed. "Luckily for you, I owe you my life. Bastard."

Annwyl knew her rage could snap loose at any moment. She wanted to run the lying bastard through. Wanted him to know the pain she'd suffered when she'd realized the truth. Fearghus knew she had little knowledge of dragons except they were something to fear. She had no idea they could turn human. Live as human. And, based on what they'd been doing all over his glen recently, mate as human.

She felt like a fool. A whore and a fool. And she hated him for making her feel that way. So, yes. She did want to see him dead. His blood on her sword. And although he gave her the perfect opportunity, she couldn't bring herself to do it. At the moment, she hated herself for that weakness.

He rubbed his knee and looked at her. "I need you to calm down so we can talk about this."

"I hate you."

He stood to his full height, already recovered from the blow. Clearly he wasn't that easy to kill as human. Any other man would be nursing a shattered knee from that practiced kick.

"Can't you give me a chance?"

"No." He seemed startled by that.

"Can't you even try?"

"No."

"Can you tell me you feel nothing for me?"

"I felt for the dragon who rescued me. Took care of me."

"And the man?"

She shook her head. "I don't know what I felt for him . . . you . . . whatever."

For the first time, she was lying. She knew exactly what her feelings for the man were. Lust. Pure, simple, and quite exquisite. But she couldn't tell him that. She could never admit that to him now. Even as she had to cross her arms in front of her chest to hide her hardening nipples or that damn distracting pulse coming from between her thighs. No, she could never admit any of that to him.

But when she glanced up at him, she realized he already knew. Just by the expression on his handsome face.

Fearghus moved to her again so that he stood in front of her. *Brave man*, she thought with intense bitterness. He looked down at her, then lowered his head until his forehead rested against hers. He didn't try to kiss or grab her. He simply rested against her. And it felt wonderful.

She stood stock-still, wondering exactly what he was up to until she heard him whisper, "I'm so sorry, Annwyl. Please. Please forgive me."

No. He wouldn't get out of this with a simple apology. Not in a million years. Even with an apology as sweet and heart-felt as that.

"There is nothing you can ever say or do that will make me forgive you," she whispered back.

He pulled away from her and stared. She wondered what he was thinking, but she wasn't expecting the grin that spread across his face.

"Was that a challenge, Lady Annwyl?"

Her face grew hot as she pushed away from him. "It was most certainly not!" She scrambled away from him, scooting around the table. He stood on the other side, his hands resting against the hard wood.

"It sounded like a challenge."

"It was *not* a challenge, but a statement of fact. I will never forgive you."

"Challenge."

"Stop saying that!" She tried to look away from him, but she kept seeing his gloriously naked body. But when she looked up into his eyes, she kept seeing him. His soul. Staring at her.

She moved around the table again and he slowly followed, every muscle moving, anticipating the chase.

He looked at her and she found herself marveling at how long those black lashes of his were.

"I bet I can *make you* forgive me."

Damn him to hell. She hated him. She hated him with every fiber of her being. But her damn treacherous body responded like never before. She kept forcing herself to move away from him, but it became harder and harder. Especially when all her body wanted to do was climb onto the wood table that separated them and let him climb onto her.

"I'm not going to do this." She cringed. That probably would have sounded a lot more convincing if she weren't panting when she said it.

"Do what?"

"Stop it!"

"Stop what?"

"You know most men try not to get me this angry."

He stopped, his dark eyes burning into her very soul. "I'm not most men. I'm not a man at all."

And that's when Annwyl charged for the tent opening, but he caught hold of her before she could even get within arm's length of it.

He pulled her to him, her back against his chest. He snatched the sword from her hand and tossed it across the tent. He leaned in close to her ear, while the hand on her waist skimmed under her shirt. "Forgive me, Annwyl."

"No."

His free hand pulled her long hair out of the way. His fingers brushing against the skin of her throat, causing her entire body to shudder. Her damn treacherous body. Then his hot mouth was on her neck, his tongue running along the side. The hand under her shirt went right for her bindings, gliding under them, pushing them out of the way.

It felt like her head and her body were completely separate. Her head kept screaming at her to pull away. Telling her to make him stop. While her body ignored her head. Instead, her body did things like reach her arms back so she could dig her fingers into his hair, while also stretching the entire length of her taut so his fingers against her swollen breasts would feel that much more wonderful. She hated her body. Hated its weakness. Clearly her body only thought about her immediate pleasure and not what this would all mean later. No, only her poor head thought about that.

He gripped her nipples with both of his large hands as he gently bit the flesh at her throat. He let the bite get a little harder, and Annwyl realized with horror that she rewarded his actions with a moan.

"Forgive me, Annwyl," he said again, his voice a dark, husky whisper in her ear.

She knew she should just say it and get it over with. But she wanted him to make her say it, and he had a way to go before that happened.

"Never."

No female had ever made him feel this way. Dragon or human. But Annwyl stood apart from the others. She wasn't dragon. She wasn't human. She was something more. She was his.

He pulled the shirt off her body and tore the bindings from her back. He turned her around, his gaze immediately falling on those breasts that he so loved. He gripped her close, leaning his head down, sucking a nipple into his mouth.

She moaned and leaned back, both her hands in his hair.

He ran his tongue over the already hard nipple again and again, teasing it. Teasing her. Her grip on his hair tightened.

"Say it, Annwyl," he demanded against her hot flesh. "Say you forgive me."

"No."

He slammed her against the wood table and ripped the breeches from her body. She let out a startled, hungry gasp and he leaned into her, running his tongue up her neck until he reached her mouth. He swiped his tongue along her full bottom lip. She leaned up, capturing his mouth in a searing kiss. Her tongue sliding along his teeth, gliding along the inside of his mouth.

He ran his hand down her body and between her legs. Her head fell back as he slipped his finger inside of her, slowly moving in and out.

"Tell me, woman."

"Go to hell."

He jerked back startled. She stared up at him, her eyes full of lust and challenge.

"Want it that way, do you?"

He pinned her to the table with his body while his eyes wandered around the room. As the leader of the rebellion she received the best of what they could manage. That meant she had an actual bed. Made of a solid wood frame, it wasn't very large, but long enough to suit her height. It would do quite nicely.

In seconds, he caught sight of what he needed lying on the floor, conveniently beside the bed.

"Come on then."

He gripped her wrists in one hand, stepped back, and pulled her up.

She watched him with wary eyes as he dragged her to the bed. But when he reached down and snatched up a good length of rope that someone had been practicing knots on, she burst into laughter and began to fight at the same time.

"Not on your life, Dragon!"

"You started this."

"No I did not!"

He leered at her as he held her tight. Ignoring her struggles, he hauled her to the bed and threw her facedown on the fur coverings. His knee, well placed, held her down.

"You bastard! Let me go!"

"No." He mimicked her recent simple delivery as he took her wrists, bound them securely with the rope, and tied the end of the rope to the wood frame.

"Fearghus, let me go! Now!"

He ignored her, instead crouching by the bed and running his hand along the entire length of her body. She closed her eyes and gave a shuddering moan.

"Tell me what I want to hear, Annwyl. Tell me, and I'll let you go."

"No!"

In response, he slapped her rear.

Annwyl froze. Her eyes wide in shock. Did he just slap her ass? As if in answer, he slapped the other cheek.

She glared at him. "Have. You. Gone. Mad?"

He smiled at her and she couldn't believe how beautiful he was. "Just forgive me. Unless, of course, you want me to . . ." He raised his hand above her rear. Annwyl snarled. How could she hate him and want him at the same time? How could she feel completely betrayed and still be having the time of her life?

Fearghus kissed her, taking her breath away as he smoothed his hand across her rear. He slid two of his fingers inside her. Already so wet and ready for him, her body offered absolutely no resistance.

He began again to slowly move his fingers in and out of her, making her writhe on the bed. She closed her eyes and moaned. The man must have some kind of spell he used on her. Nothing, absolutely nothing, could feel this good on its own. Her body tightened as heat spread across her groin and up her spine.

Then he stopped.

Annwyl's eyes flew open and she groaned in frustration. "Don't you dare stop!"

He stared at her mouth. "Then say it. Say you forgive me."

She wanted him to finish. Wanted him to bring her the pleasure only he could. But she would never give in that easy. Unable to speak for fear she'd start begging, she shook her head.

He gently pushed her tangle of hair out of her face and stared at her. Her eyes boldly swept across his body, lingering on his erection. He growled in response, standing up. His body towering over her, Fearghus placed his knee on the bed and leaned in, his engorged cock right by her mouth. Without a second's thought, she pushed her mouth onto it, taking in as much of it as she could until the head tickled the back of her throat. She began to deeply suck his shaft, while her tongue ran along the underside.

His eyes closed and he growled her name.

Clearly her mouth was a gift from the gods. There could be no other explanation for something that felt so wonderful. He let himself get lost there for several minutes, as she sucked and licked him. He pulled away before he came in her mouth, although the little moan of disappointment she gave when he did almost made him reconsider. But he wanted to release while buried deep inside her.

Panting, he stood back and almost came just looking at her. Laid out on the bed, bound at the wrists, her body vibrated with her need for him. He couldn't wait any longer, whether she gave in or not. He had to have her.

He knelt between her legs, pushing them up and under her so that he had a delicious view of her rear.

He entered her from behind, gritting his teeth as her head dropped forward, and she gave a guttural gasp. He moved in slowly, taking his time, ignoring her pleas and rude demands. He waited until he imbedded his cock deep inside her, then he leaned forward.

"Tell me, Annwyl," he panted desperately in her ear. "Tell me you forgive me."

"No."

He sank his teeth into the flesh of her back and she bucked under him. He ran his hand down her body until he had his hand at her bottom, then he slapped her rear again.

"*Why do you keep doing that*?"

"Because now it's getting fun. Besides, you wench, you're enjoying it."

"No, I am not!"

"Liar." His hand slapped the firm flesh of her rear and she growled. "Now tell me you forgive me."

She took a moment to get her breath. "Why? Why do you care?"

Fearghus blinked. *By the gods, she doesn't know.*

He smoothed his hand across her back as he nuzzled the back of her neck. "Because I love you."

Annwyl's entire body started at the whispered pronouncement. Her dragon loved her. That's all she wanted to know. All she ever needed to know.

She tossed her head back and looked at him. Saw the truth in his eyes. "Untie me, Fearghus." He leaned forward and released her bonds. Once free, she pulled away from him. A moan escaped his lips as he slid out of her. She turned her body so that they faced each other.

Annwyl stared at Fearghus, her hand brushing against his cheek and skimming along his chiseled jaw. Then she growled and punched him in the chest. "You idiot!"

"Ow!"

"Why didn't you tell me that before? *You're making me crazy!*" She punched him in the shoulder.

"Stop hitting me!"

She stood up and stormed away from him to the middle of the tent, her arms crossed in front of her chest. "I thought I was finally going insane. Because of you!"

"Are you done?"

Annwyl stopped pacing, slowly turning to face Fearghus. He leaned back against the bed, his long legs on the floor, his long erection at the ready. "Excuse me?"

He smiled as his smoldering gaze swept over her. "I asked if you were done. I mean you can go on all day about how I wronged you, if you like. Or you can come over here and let me make it up to you."

Annwyl bit the inside of her mouth to stop herself from smiling. *Cheeky bastard.* "I'm very wounded, you know. Devastated. May never recover from this."

"Come to me, Annwyl." He held his hand out to her, a beautiful smile spreading across that gorgeous face. "Bring that pretty ass to me."

Annwyl rolled her eyes, but went to him nonetheless. She took his offered hand. Fearghus squeezed it as he gently turned her away from him. He grasped her hips and pulled her back to him, lowering her body until his hot shaft slowly entered her from behind. She gasped as he placed her on his erection, taking his time. Moving slowly.

Once she fully enveloped him, he slid his hands to her breasts. He gripped the nipples tight between his calloused fingers, while he rubbed his forehead against her back and nuzzled her neck. Annwyl groaned and she wondered how she ever thought she could give this up. Give *him* up. She realized she no longer had to worry about it. She had them both. Dragon and knight were one and the same. And he loved her.

He nipped the nape of her neck and gripped her hips. He slowly moved her up and down his shaft. Over and over, until Annwyl felt sure she'd go insane. His tongue glided up and down the back of her neck, his hair cascaded over her shoulders and rubbed against her sensitive breasts.

Annwyl placed her hands over his. She gripped them tight, digging her nails into his flesh. "Gods, Fearghus. You're driving me mad."

He chuckled against her neck. "Too slow?" She could only manage to nod. "Then tell me what I want to hear."

She gasped as his hands tightened on her. She shook her head. She had no idea what he was talking about. "Tell me you forgive me, Annwyl. Forgive me and I'll fuck you until you scream."

Hell, she'd forgiven him a hundred times over. At least she had in her head. But to verbalize it, right at this moment, when she couldn't even see straight. That was the real challenge.

"Uh . . . yes."

"Yes what?"

She moaned. She was so close. So close. "Forgive."

"Forgive what?"

What an utter bastard! "You."

"Say it, Annwyl. Say it, because I can keep this up for hours."

Hours? She couldn't handle five more seconds of this, much less hours. She forced herself to concentrate, using the same skills she used in battle.

"I forgive you, Fearghus. I forgive you."

Suddenly he lifted her off his cock and threw her back on the bed. He pushed her ankles up around her ears, slamming his cock into her. She gripped the headboard with both hands and growled Fearghus's name. Already so close, it didn't take much more to push her right over the edge and the growl became a scream as she exploded around him. Wood splintered in her hands, the headboard an unlikely casualty of their mating.

His climax followed close behind, a savage groan torn from him as her muscles gripped him, attempting to wring every last drop from his body.

They stayed locked together. Neither moving nor speaking. Eventually he pulled out of her, gently lowering her legs. He stretched out beside her on the bed so she could nuzzle against him.

Annwyl smiled as he kissed her forehead.

"Now what, Dragon?"

He ran his hand across her cheek. How close he'd come to losing her. The only thing he ever wanted. "I think we have a war to win."

Annwyl shook her head. "No. I don't . . . I didn't . . ."

He kissed her mouth and she stopped babbling. "I know. I want to. Actually, I've been ordered to." He grinned. "Besides I really want to see you go up against that brother of yours."

"Are you sure?"

"I'm sure." He reached down and pulled fur coverings from the floor over their entwined bodies. She settled in close to him, nuzzling his neck while he ran his hands along her back.

He would help her win this war. Not for his father or the queen. But for her. For his Annwyl. For the love of his life.

Chapter 16

Annwyl's eyes flew open as the hand closed over her mouth. But once she saw Morfyd's blue eyes, she relaxed. Morfyd took several steps back and motioned for Annwyl to follow, then she quietly slipped out of the tent.

Annwyl tried to move out from under the large possessive arm slung over her waist. But it tightened, and Fearghus snuggled into her back. "Where do you think you're going?"

Smiling, she rubbed the hand at her waist. Just his low, rumbling voice gliding across her back had her wet and ready for him. "Can't a girl have some time to herself? I'll be back in a bit."

His teeth nipped her shoulder. "Better be."

She tumbled out of bed, grabbed a fur covering, and stepped out of the tent. She walked around the corner and found Morfyd impatiently waiting for her.

"What is it?" She liked Morfyd, but she really wanted to be back in bed, Fearghus's arms wrapped tight around her. His cock inside her, hard and ready.

"I need you to come with me."

"What? Where?"

"I can't explain now. Here." She handed Annwyl her clothes. She had no idea when Morfyd took these. Nor could she understand the secrecy.

"Morfyd, what is going on?"

"I need you to trust me, but we need to get moving before Fearghus comes looking for you."

Annwyl put her clothes on while she watched Morfyd. "You too, huh?"

"Me too, what?"

"You and Fearghus. I never noticed before but you look a bit alike."

"He's my brother."

"Big family." Annwyl tugged on her boots, pulled her surcoat over her head, and wrapped a leather belt around her waist. Once dressed, she put her hands on her hips and raised an eyebrow. "What now, Lady Dragon?"

Morfyd watched Annwyl address her lieutenants. True, she'd seen a side of Annwyl that these men never had. The wounded warrior struggling to live. The woman who loved her brother. And the warrior woman she'd taken as a friend.

But she now saw why these men followed her. Annwyl radiated strength and determination. She was more than the leader of the rebellion. She was the heart of it.

"Move out tonight. We've gotten word that when the two suns rise tomorrow, Lorcan will attack the village. We can't let him get through, or he'll make for the Citadel of Ó Donnchadha and our women and children are there. Kill anyone that wears Lorcan's colors. No survivors. No prisoners."

"And you?" Brastias asked.

"I leave with Morfyd. Now. But I'll be back by morning. Tomorrow I will face my brother."

"And what of . . ." The men shifted uncomfortably, unwilling to meet Annwyl's eyes.

She smirked. "And what of my dragon?" Morfyd blinked in surprise. Annwyl wasn't even trying to hide her relationship with Fearghus.

Brastias cleared his throat. "Yes, Annwyl. What of your dragon?"

"Let him sleep. When he awakes tell him that I will return by sunup. Not too hard, is it?"

"And are we safe around him?"

Annwyl sighed in annoyance at the question, but Morfyd answered for her. "Yes. You are safe around him. But when you tell him about Annwyl, I wouldn't stand around. I strongly suggest moving away quickly. Very quickly."

Annwyl and her men stared at Morfyd. She shrugged at Annwyl's raised eyebrow. "He is my brother. I know him well."

The men, en masse, stepped away from her. All except Brastias, who stared at her. She realized that they were completely unaware that she, too, was a dragon. "Don't worry. You're safe around me as well." She smiled but only Brastias and Annwyl smiled back.

"All right, then. We're off." Annwyl stepped away from the large table strewn with maps that she'd been leaning against. "I'll see you all at dawn."

Morfyd walked out of the tent, Annwyl behind her. Brastias's voice stopped them.

"Annwyl." The two females looked at him. He braved another smile at Morfyd before speaking to Annwyl. "Your weapons?"

"No." Morfyd shook her head. "No weapons, Annwyl."

Annwyl looked at Brastias and shrugged. "No weapons."

"Then please be careful."

Annwyl nodded and followed as Morfyd led her away from the camp to the clearing where she'd landed earlier.

The girl stepped back as Morfyd shifted, shaking out her wings and mane of hair. "You ready, Lady Annwyl?"

Annwyl grabbed on to the white mane of hair and expertly hauled herself up onto Morfyd's back. "Aye, Lady Dragon. I'm ready."

* * *

"I just don't understand our brother. A human." Briec gave a great sigh, causing Gwenvael to roll his eyes in annoyance.

"You don't know anything, Briec. She's different."

"Don't you really mean crazed, baby brother?"

Gwenvael saw Morfyd's white scales swooping toward them. He stood up. Both he and Briec were already in human form and dressed.

"You're just mad she slapped you around." Gwenvael looked at his brother. "Like a bitch."

Briec stood up. Slightly taller than Gwenvael, but still shorter than Fearghus, he tended to be just as much fun to torture as their older sibling. "I let her hit me."

"You had to. Otherwise she would have killed you where you stood."

Morfyd made one of her soundless landings and patiently waited while Annwyl dismounted. She shifted to human and Annwyl wrapped a fur covering around her shoulders.

He rushed down the stairs to meet them. "Lady Annwyl."

"Gwenvael."

"Feeling better?"

She couldn't hide her smile or the blush to her cheeks. Now he knew what he'd always suspected—his brother was a brave, brave dragon. "Much, thank you."

"Good."

Briec now stood beside him. His arms crossed in front of his chest. "Lady." He nodded coldly to her, and Annwyl glanced between Gwenvael and Morfyd.

"I'm sorry, do I know you?"

Briec blinked in surprise. "I am Briec the Mighty."

Annwyl examined Gwenvael's brother over from head to toe. "Really?" she remarked at last. "Did you give yourself that name?"

Gwenvael and Morfyd choked back a laugh before Morfyd pulled the girl away and up the stairs. "Come, Annwyl. We don't have much time."

Briec sneered after their retreating forms. "I hope the queen eats her marrow like pudding."

Gwenvael scowled. If those two became enemies—Annwyl and the queen—who knew who would come out the winner. They were equally frightening females.

Gwenvael jogged up the stairs, Briec closely behind him. "Just remember, Briec. She almost took down Father. So we best hope they get along."

Annwyl thought they would travel for long distances across land. She guessed wrongly. Morfyd instead went straight up. Higher and higher until they reached the crest of Devenallt Mountain just above the clouds. It contained the court of the infamous Dragon Queen. Believed to be a myth, she, like Fearghus, turned out to be all too real. And little did Annwyl know a whole community of dragons were always so close. They truly did keep their lives secret from humans. And now, here Annwyl was. A common bastard girl, walking into the majestic halls of the queen's court.

As she entered the main hall with Morfyd, all conversation stopped. The dragons all turned to her. They watched her. Closely. Annwyl felt naked and alone. She wished that Fearghus accompanied her, but she knew he'd never let her come. He wouldn't risk it. He wouldn't risk her. The thought brought a smile to her face and she didn't notice Fearghus's father until she practically climbed on top of the old bastard. Still in dragon-form, his claw and tail freshly bandaged. His damaged snout smeared with some kind of ointment, probably to stop the bleeding.

He glared down at her with those cold eyes and Annwyl felt that desire to run again. But she wouldn't give the old bastard the satisfaction.

"How's the claw?" she called up to him. Morfyd gasped

and seized her arm, dragging her up another set of steps and into another hall.

"Please try not to get yourself killed, Annwyl. Fearghus would never forgive me."

"I'll keep it in mind." As they entered the next hall, she again halted all dragon conversation. Instead they watched her walk by.

"They all stare."

"Yes. It's been hundreds of years since a human has been here."

"You mean a human who wasn't brought here as a meal?" Morfyd shrugged but would say nothing else.

"I see."

A dragon walked toward Annwyl and Morfyd hissed at him. "Keep back, Kesslene."

"I just wanted to see the pretty thing," the dragon announced to the room.

"Oi!" Annwyl snapped. The last one who referred to her as a "thing"—Lorcan—she had every intention of killing soon.

Morfyd kept Annwyl moving, although the large dragon kept pace with them. "Don't be cute, Kesslene. Besides, she's with Fearghus. And you remember what he did to you the last time you caused his displeasure." Morfyd went down another flight of stairs this time and the dragon Kesslene stopped following, but he wasn't done.

"With Fearghus? Really? Then why has he not 'Claimed' her?"

"Claimed me?"

"Worry about that later, Annwyl." After several minutes, they stopped in front of another set of stairs.

"You dragons really like stairs."

"Up these stairs and inside. You know what to do."

Annwyl nodded once, took a deep breath, and walked up the steps and into the queen's chamber.

* * *

The great queen tossed her mane of white hair out of her eyes, and turned the page of the book she read. As she did, the chain linked to the collar around her throat rattled lightly and she smiled. Then a familiar scent hit her nostrils. She sniffed the air.

"Fearghus?" She closed the book in her hand and turned, her chain rattling more. But it wasn't Fearghus standing in front of her, but a tiny human. *How cute.* Bercelak sent her a little something to munch on.

"And who are you?" She always liked to chat with her meals before disemboweling. You never knew what you might learn.

The human female did not answer. She just stared at her. A typical response when humans saw her. She stood much larger than most dragons.

She snapped two talons together. "Hello?"

It came alive, clearing its throat. "Um . . . I am Annwyl."

"Annwyl. Annwyl. I do not know an Annwyl. So, are you my dinner?"

"No." It took a step back. "No. I'm not dinner. Let's never say that again. I am Annwyl of the Dark Plains." The queen stared at it.

"Annwyl of Garbhán Isle?" Still nothing. It sighed.

"Annwyl the Bloody."

"*You* are Annwyl the Bloody?"

It looked slightly defeated. "Yes."

"You are awfully tiny to be Annwyl the Bloody."

"I'm taller than most men."

"That simply does not impress me."

Morfyd should have warned her. She should have let her know that she would be facing a being this large and imposing. How could the dragon before her be anything *but* a queen?

She reminded Annwyl of Morfyd. Her scales a glossy white. Her mane the color of fresh snow. But she stood as tall and wide as Fearghus, if not a little bigger than that.

"Is Fearghus here? I smell him."

Annwyl now wished she had bathed before leaving the campsite, but there hadn't been time.

"Uh . . . no, he's not here." She cleared her throat. "That's me . . . you . . . uh . . . smell."

Intense blue eyes shifted and the queen leaned in closer as if to get a good look at her.

"You? He's been with you? A human? Whatever for?"

This was one of those times where Annwyl had a really crude remark at the ready. Something that would include the word "suck." But she kept her tongue in check. Controlled her impulses. It wasn't easy.

"He loves me."

"Does he now?" The queen sat up and for the first time Annwyl noticed she wore a collar around her throat with a chain connected to it. The chain led to a stone wall, securely attached to a thick metal circle. She frowned but didn't have much time to think about it as the queen moved closer to her.

"Whether he does or doesn't, concerns me not. Why are *you* here?"

"I must fight Lorcan of Garbhán Isle in a few hours. . . ."

"I do not concern myself with the problems of humans."

"But my problem isn't human, lady. It is Hefaidd-Hen."

"Ah, yes. Bercelak told me of his involvement with your brother."

"Morfyd said you could give me some kind of protection. He will surely use Hefaidd-Hen against me."

"Are you afraid you'll die, human?"

Annwyl shook her head. "No, lady. That has never been my worry. I worry that I will not be able to kill my brother *before* I die. That has always been my greatest fear. I know what he can do. He'll destroy all that oppose him and Hefaidd-Hen will help him do it. I only need protection from Hefaidd-Hen long enough to kill my brother. After that I don't care what happens to me."

"And what of Fearghus?"

"Fearghus said he will fight with me."

"So you risk his life as well as your own?"

"My life is forfeit, lady. All I care about now is killing my brother. He must die this day so that my people can be free. And I truly believe I'm the only one who can do it. Fearghus can take care of himself."

"But if you die, what of Fearghus?"

Annwyl shrugged, uncomfortable with these questions. "He will find another, I guess. I don't know."

The queen snorted. "You don't know dragons at all, do you?"

"I never said I did."

"And if Fearghus dies, but you live. Then what?"

Annwyl's face tightened. The thought of something—anything—happening to Fearghus caused her anger to vibrate right below her flesh. Her voice low, her rage barely contained, "You best pray that never happens, lady. For if he dies and I live, then I will tear this world apart with my rage. And no one will be safe. I promise you that."

The queen watched Annwyl for several long moments. "You are an interesting . . . thing. I think I understand what my son sees in you."

Annwyl swallowed. "Son?"

"You didn't know?" Annwyl slowly shook her head. "Yes. I think all my children are quite unimpressed with their rank among dragons."

"Yes. Apparently they are."

The queen smiled at that, and Annwyl had to stop herself from running from the chamber. Her smile revealed a frightening display of what seemed to be hundreds of teeth. Mostly fangs. The dragon moved to the other side of the cave, reaching into a tiny cavern. She dug inside, then came out with a small but shiny object. She walked over to Annwyl and held the item out to her.

Annwyl took it from the queen's white claw. She examined it carefully. A necklace. Made of a strong, but extremely thin, silver-colored metal, twisted into an intricate design, the thin lines swirling around and through each other.

"Remove your shirt and put it on. It needs to be right next to the flesh."

Annwyl followed the queen's direction, quickly pulling off her surcoat and shirt, and placing the necklace right at the base of her throat. It lay flat against her collarbone and the top part of her chest, while two thin bits laced around her neck and clasped at the back. She redressed quickly, eager to be away as dawn and the fight for her people drew near. She prayed there would be no more questions.

"How does that fit then?"

Annwyl nodded. "Fine. And this will protect me from Hefaidd-Hen?"

"No. That will not help you." Annwyl sighed in exasperation. Then why waste her time putting on bits of jewelry? But before she could ask the question, the queen cocked her head to one side. "That will not help you with Hefaidd-Hen, but this will."

Annwyl looked up just as the queen let loose a ball of flame that threw her from the chamber.

Morfyd and her three siblings waited outside the queen's chamber. Éibhear, the youngest brother, anxiously jumped around them. "When are we going? When? When?"

Briec calmly looked at him. "You ask that question one more time, and we're going to shave your head . . . again."

Éibhear sunk into a moody silence as Morfyd wondered what kept the girl so long. She risked Fearghus's wrath by bringing Annwyl here and taking her to the queen. There was every chance the girl would not survive. But she had to risk it and Annwyl agreed. In her more than two hundred years alive, she never knew a braver human. One willing to face the Queen of Dragons. And Morfyd had warned her. Warned her that the queen had no sympathy for humans. Annwyl had laughed. Not dismissively, but after fighting off Bercelak a lack of sympathy just didn't sound that scary to her. So she walked in alone to face the one being who could protect her or turn her to ash where she stood.

Morfyd still had no idea which the queen would choose. She gave up long ago trying to guess her moods and whims. All she could hope for now was that her fondness for Fearghus kept the girl alive.

The siblings stopped talking. They all heard it. The unmistakable sound of air sucked into lungs. They all turned to each other, just as a ball of flame flew out of the chamber. It hit the wall and crashed against the floor.

"Oh, gods! Annwyl!" Morfyd and Gwenvael rushed over as Annwyl rolled herself on the floor to put the flame out. But by the time they reached her the flame disappeared.

No. That wasn't right. It didn't disappear. It went *in* to her. Her skin soaked up the flame. Annwyl, however, still screamed and rolled around, completely unaware that the fire was gone.

Morfyd caught hold of her. "Annwyl! Annwyl! It's all right!"

After a few moments, Annwyl stopped. She rolled into a ball and breathed in gulps of air, her entire body shaking. They all waited. Silently. Expecting her to snap out of it. But the queen's voice called from inside her chamber, "It's not over yet, my loves."

That's when Annwyl started screaming again. Not in fear

and panic. But in pure, unbridled pain. "Get it off me! *Get it off me!*" She ripped off her surcoat and her chain-mail shirt and dug at the flesh on her throat and neck. "*Get it off me!*"

Morfyd hit the girl with a spell that knocked her out instantly. Annwyl fell back and Morfyd looked closely at her.

"What are those markings?" Gwenvael asked, next to her.

"I don't know." Morfyd ran her hand along the flesh and felt something right under the skin. Something imbedded in the girl's flesh. Something that she knew hadn't been there a few hours before. Within seconds the markings turned a deep rich brown and Morfyd gasped. "The Chain of Beathag!"

Gwenvael stared in awe. "She gave her *that*?"

Briec snorted in disgust. "The only reason she gave that to this human was because of Fearghus."

"Well, she never liked you," Gwenvael muttered.

"Amazing breasts," Éibhear noted casually.

"Would you control yourself," Morfyd snapped at her oversized baby brother. She lifted the girl up. "Help me get her clothes back on. We need to get her out of here quickly and don't let the others see." The dragon court would find out about the queen's gift soon enough.

Her chain mail was scorched. Her hair was darker, the gold streaks that ran through it brighter. And her skin looked like she'd spent several days under the hot desert suns of Alsandair. But other than that, Annwyl lived.

They dressed her quickly and stood her up; Gwenvael took one arm, Briec the other. Morfyd muttered a counterspell and Annwyl awoke, still screaming.

"Annwyl!" She'd made sure to put a healing spell on her chest to stop the pain. She grabbed the girl by the face and yelled her name again.

Annwyl finally stopped screaming. She looked around.

"Better?"

Annwyl's eyes latched on to her, and that infamous rage exploded around her. *"What did that bitch do to me?"*

"I heard that!" The siblings all cringed and began dragging Annwyl down the stairs, ignoring the girl's angry protests. But when she shuddered and began to shake uncontrollably, they stopped.

Morfyd pushed the girl's hair from her face. "You all right, Annwyl?"

After a few moments, Annwyl nodded. Gods, the girl carried some strength within her. More strength than even some dragons possessed.

"I'll be fine. Just give me a bit . . ." Annwyl's eyes focused on Éibhear. "Your hair is blue."

"I'm a blue dragon," he announced with his usual pride. Morfyd rolled her eyes. Éibhear did love his blue hair.

Annwyl glanced at Morfyd. "Another brother?"

Morfyd shrugged as they went up another flight of stairs, meeting Bercelak at the top.

He looked down at Annwyl. "So she survived?"

"Looks that way, Father." Morfyd answered, a little smugly.

Annwyl, still supported by Gwenvael and Briec, raised her head and looked at Bercelak with narrowed accusing eyes. "Why is the queen chained inside her chamber?"

Morfyd closed her eyes in utter embarrassment. *For the love of . . .*

Bercelak's relationship with their mother never failed to either embarrass or annoy all their children. If she didn't know for a fact that they loved each other more than anything, Morfyd would have divorced herself from the clan long ago out of sheer disgust.

Her father grinned. "Did she complain?" Morfyd and Briec exchanged mortified glances while Gwenvael and Éibhear bit back their laughter.

Annwyl shook her head. "No."

"Then what do you care what goes on between me and my mate?"

Annwyl stared thoughtfully at him, then recognition dawned. "Oh, by the gods!"

"Time to go!" Morfyd started moving again. "The suns will rise soon."

"Yes. All of you must be off."

Morfyd stopped and looked at her father. "All of us?" She'd already talked her brothers into helping Fearghus, but they were planning to do it without Bercelak's knowledge. Now it seemed their father finally realized the danger of Lorcan and Hefaidd-Hen winning this battle and perhaps the Sibling War.

"Aye. You can't let your brother fight alone with some humans. You all must go with him. I will stay here with the queen."

"I bet you will," Annwyl muttered under her breath.

The siblings exchanged glances as Bercelak began pushing them toward the exit. "Go. Now. You haven't much time."

"Wait!" Morfyd watched as her younger sister, Keita, in human form ran toward them. She wore a beautiful gown, probably given to her by some noble who thought her a sweet maid before he took her to bed and found out otherwise. Well, perhaps a noble, his brother, and his cousin took her to bed. All at the same time. *Slut.* "Sorry I'm late!"

"What are *you* doing here?"

"Daddy asked me to come." She gave a toss of her long red hair before smiling up at Bercelak who smiled back and patted her shoulder.

"'Daddy asked me to come,'" Morfyd mimicked brutally. Her sister sneered at her and she wanted to kick Daddy's little princess in the face, but Annwyl's voice stopped her.

"Exactly how many are in your family?"

"Too many," all the siblings answered at once.

Chapter 17

Danelin lived the first nine years of his life in Garbhán Isle's dungeons. He'd been battling the troops of the Isle since he turned twelve. And learned to fear nothing besides the Siblings' wrath, which all men of any intelligence feared.

Until the day the black dragon landed in the middle of their camp. For the first time he learned the meaning of true fear. Seeing the black talons of the beast touch down. Watching the mighty horned head turn slowly as it watched the troops surrounding it. Hearing it roar Annwyl's name. He thought he would never experience fear quite like that again.

He turned out to be very wrong.

Standing across from a dragon who had shape-shifted into a man and explaining to him how his lady love left, but "Don't worry, she'll be back soon enough," introduced him to a whole new world of fear. Especially when the dragon stood naked across from him and Brastias, big arms crossed in front of a big chest, big legs braced firmly apart and, most disturbingly, black smoke curling from his nostrils.

Luckily they had already sent the troops ahead. But the two suns were rising and he needed to get Brastias to the village. Someone needed to lead since they really had no idea when Annwyl would return. Although he and Brastias had no intention of telling the dragon that. Of course now they realized they should never have told the dragon about Annwyl while his big body blocked the exit. Now he stood between them and the way out of the tent.

And the dragon wasn't moving.

"So you just let her leave?"

Danelin exchanged glances with Brastias.

Brastias raised an eyebrow. "Perhaps you haven't actually *met* Annwyl the Bloody, but you don't let her or not let her go anywhere. You just stay out of her way."

Danelin forced himself not to cower as the dragon growled in displeasure.

He watched the two humans stare at him. Brastias looked annoyed. The boy looked like he might start screaming at any second. He knew he shouldn't take his anger at Annwyl out on these two men, but they were here and she was not.

The last thing he remembered was her slipping that lovely body out of bed with whispered promises to return quickly. He awoke several hours later to the sounds of Annwyl's troops moving out. He also discovered his bed cold and no sign of his woman. A feeling, he found, he did not relish.

By the time he dragged his human body out of bed, most of the troops were gone, leaving Brastias and the boy. He cornered them in one of the supply tents and refused to let them go. Their cavalier attitude about Annwyl's disappearance with his sister did nothing but raise his anger. Where Morfyd may have taken her, he could only guess. But if he guessed right, his sister would pay.

"She's not our responsibility, Dragon. Nor is she yours."

He had to admit, Brastias turned out to be a lot braver than he thought. The boy, though, didn't look like he could handle much more. But he wasn't done with them. Soon he would start threatening body parts, but a hand on his bare shoulder stopped him.

"There you all are." Annwyl smiled. "Everything all right?"

Fearghus scowled. "No. Everything's not all right. Where the hell have you been?"

"Discuss later. Fight war now." Obeying a motion of her

head, Brastias and the boy quickly left. "You better not have been terrorizing them."

"Annwyl." He caught her arm. "What's going on?" He looked at her face and wondered what was different. The two suns had just begun to rise, darkness still filled the tent, so he couldn't see all that clearly, but he knew something had changed.

"Later. Right now my people need me, Fearghus." She reached up and kissed him lightly. "Trust me."

He brushed his head against her cheek and breathed in her scent. "Try not to get yourself killed, Annwyl."

She laughed. "Why do all of you keep telling me that?"

He kissed her, long and deep until she pulled away. He enjoyed the fact that it seemed to be a struggle for her.

"We . . . uh . . . better go." She stared at his lips for a moment longer, then, with a deep sigh of regret, stepped away from him and through the tent opening.

He followed, but stumbled upon finding his siblings waiting for him. *All* his siblings.

"Took you two long enough," Briec snapped.

"What exactly were you two doing in there?" Gwenvael smirked.

"Big brother!" Keita spread her wings wide, completely blocking out Morfyd.

Morfyd slammed her claw down, causing the ground to shake. "You do that one more time, Keita, and I'll start taking pieces of you right here!"

"Let's go! Let's go! Let's go!" Éibhear took off and continued to swoop around the group, "Come on! We'll miss all the best kills!"

Fearghus glared at Annwyl. She backed away from him with a shrug. "They wanted to help."

"When we're done with your brother, woman, we *will* discuss this."

"Promises. Promises." Annwyl leered as she quickly

strapped her swords to her back, leather gauntlets on her wrists, and tied her hair back with a long leather strap.

Fearghus walked out into the middle of the campsite and shifted, doing his best to ignore his squabbling kin. He shook out his mane and turned to Annwyl as she secured her swords to her back.

"Lady Annwyl?"

Annwyl finished adjusting her weapons. "Lord Dragon?"

"I think it is time we make you queen."

Annwyl nodded once . . . and smiled.

Brastias rolled on his side, avoiding the war hammer aimed at his head. He stood and brought his ax up, splitting the man from groin to neck.

"Behind you!" Brastias didn't turn but swung his ax back and up. He took off a soldier's sword arm, then turned to finish the man off. Prying his ax from the man's corpse, he glanced at Danelin who called the warning.

"Where is she, Brastias?" the warrior yelled over the din of battle.

"She'll be here."

"Well, she and those dragons better be here soon."

"Why?"

Danelin pointed to the sky and Brastias turned to see why the color drained from his lieutenant's face. It wasn't just that it was a dragon. Or that Lorcan rode him. But the fact that they were not alone. Eight other dragons flew with them, geared for battle.

Brastias cringed. Things just became more difficult.

As they flew toward battle, Fearghus gave explicit instructions, while Annwyl clung to his back. "Lorcan belongs to

Annwyl. Hefaidd-Hen is mine. Kill every one else who wears Lorcan's colors. Understand?"

"Wait. Is that it? Has our brother no words of wisdom before we go into battle?" Gwenvael demanded with sarcasm.

"As a matter of fact, I do. Don't get killed." Morfyd and Keita laughed as they moved out. His three brothers following.

"And Annwyl. Remember what I told you."

"Protect my right side?"

"No."

"Feint with my left?"

"No."

"Nice ass."

"No!" His growl of annoyance only elicited a sweet chuckle from his woman.

"Watch my rage, heart of my heart?"

"Condescending cow."

Chapter 18

The ball of flame narrowly missed her and she desperately clung to Fearghus's neck and hair as he spun and dove down toward the middle of the battle. For several agonizing moments her world turned upside down and she felt certain she would retch at any second, when the dragon thankfully righted himself. She didn't care what he said, she was getting him a saddle.

As they neared the ground she caught sight of Brastias. "There! Land me there!"

Fearghus dropped lower, plowed through a contingent of horse-mounted soldiers, and slid to a halt in front of a startled Brastias.

Annwyl slipped off the dragon's back. She unsheathed both her swords and turned to her dragon-lover.

The two stared at each other.

"Stay well, Lady Annwyl."

"Stay alive, Lord Dragon."

Fearghus unfurled his mighty wings and lifted off into the air to join the battle already raging with the other dragons and his siblings.

"We're glad you're here." Brastias stood beside her now, covered in blood, the majority of which she doubted belonged to him.

"Sorry I took so long, my friend." She tested the weight of her blades. As always they felt good in her hands. She was ready.

"Where is he, Brastias?"

"Up there." He pointed to a ridge where she could hear the war cries of men. But between her and her brother lay a battery of troops screaming for her blood.

One soldier ran for her, the bloodlust having grabbed hold of his mind. She brought her two swords together, stepping aside as the man's head snapped off his body.

Annwyl smiled at Brastias. "Perhaps you should let me take this from here."

She wondered what he saw on her face when she looked at him, because he visibly blanched and backed away from her. "As always, Annwyl. They're all yours."

Annwyl smiled and charged in, killing all that stood in her way and did not wear the colors of her army.

* * *

A bolt of lightning hit Fearghus dead in the chest. He flew back with a roar. Leave it to Hefaidd-Hen to find lightning dragons. Purple beasts from the Northlands with awesome powers, but he already tired of the stinging pain their lightning caused. Plus, he knew they were singeing his hair.

He could see Gwenvael coming up behind the dragon. He moved in again to distract him and barely missed the bolt the beast sent out. As the dragon reared back to send out another, Gwenvael wrapped his maw around his neck and held it. Fearghus dived in and slammed his talons into the beast's groin and belly, ripping up. The dragon roared in pain as he lost his bowels over the battlefield. And when they released him he dropped to the ground, taking out some of Lorcan's men in the process.

The two brothers stared at each other. They got along at no other time as when they were in battle together. And Fearghus finally admitted to himself it brought him joy that his family fought with him this day.

The two brothers separated and Fearghus went over to help Morfyd. But as she dispensed with two dragons, one with flame the other with a spell, he wasn't quite sure why he'd bothered.

Then he saw Éibhear tumble past him. He caught his brother's arm before he could fall to the ground while he hit the enemy dragon with flame, knocking the beast back.

"Éibhear! Are you all right?" he demanded in the ancient language of dragons.

"Aye, brother. That bitch caught me by surprise, is all."

"Well, watch your back, pup. I'll never hear the end of it if anything happens to you. You she likes."

Éibhear took to the air once again, going after the bitch dragon who had just tried to kill him.

"Morfyd!" Fearghus flew to his sister. "Hefaidd-Hen. Where is he?"

His sister closed her eyes and tried to reach out with her

Magick to find the dragon. Suddenly her eyes snapped open and she looked at her brother.

"What is it?"

"Annwyl."

Annwyl tore through her brother's troops. Most of them she beheaded as was her way. She only wasted time with arms and legs when the head wasn't readily available. And she only took those limbs to slow the enemy down long enough so she could take the head.

A soldier dived for her. She blocked his blow and brought her other sword down cleaving off half his skull and silencing the man's screams. She turned as another soldier hoped to sneak up on her from behind. She gutted him, which she also liked to do. Especially when her blade released the entrails.

She realized with a smile that she truly did earn her name. She really *was* Annwyl the Bloody. And proud of it. But she tired of wasting herself on these men. She wanted her brother. She wanted *his* head. And by the gods, she would have it.

She killed off two more soldiers stupid enough to get in her way, and then charged up the ridge, screaming for Lorcan. As she made it to the top, she slid to a halt in the wet grass. Lorcan waited for her. Waited for her with his dragon.

She glanced behind her and realized that more of his troops blocked her escape.

Annwyl glared at her brother. "Afraid to face me yourself, Lorcan?" He wouldn't even meet her eyes. "Can't you answer me, brother?"

"You can direct your questions to me, Lady Annwyl."

She looked at what could only be Hefaidd-Hen. Unlike Fearghus and his kin, she saw no beauty in this beast. No sense of grace or elegance. Just a cold-blooded killer. His dragon body appeared almost skeletal. His color a sickening maggot white. His dragon eyes a pale, watery blue. Just looking at him made her skin crawl.

"Are you ruler of Dark Plains now, Hefaidd-Hen?"

"I am merely counsel to Lorcan."

"And what has been your counsel to my brother?"

"That he should not waste his time killing you. He should leave that to me."

Annwyl stilled her panic. The queen supposedly gave her a gift that would help her fight Hefaidd-Hen. She had no idea what her flames would do, but she prayed that the queen really did help her. She prayed hard. For although she could hear Brastias calling to his men, hear them battling to get through the line of troops separating her from them, she still knew. She knew, as Hefaidd-Hen reared back to take in a lungful of air, that they would never get to her in time.

She looked at her brother. "No matter what happens, this isn't over, brother."

Fearghus flew as fast as he could, Morfyd doing her best to keep up with him, calling his name. He ignored her. Morfyd saw the ambush. An ambush for Annwyl only. As strong as she was now, she would never be able to face Hefaidd-Hen down. Never be able to win against him. He wasn't just a dragon, but a wizard as well. His flame, like Morfyd's on occasion, would be rife with Magick.

But as he closed in on the ridge his woman now stood on, he could see he wouldn't be in time. No matter how fast he flew. No matter what he did. He would lose her.

Brastias couldn't clear the enemy troops and make it up the ridge before the foul beast sent a blast that completely covered his leader in a white-hot flame. And no ordinary flame, like the one he saw her dragon-lover spew. But something different. And seemingly a waste of Magick, considering she was just a girl.

But when the flame and smoke cleared, there she still stood. Her eyes shut tight, her face turned away. Everything as it should be. Even her chain mail and surcoat.

Brastias stopped. That wasn't possible. There should be nothing of her left. Not even ash.

He saw the dragon rear back in confusion as Annwyl slowly opened her eyes and looked around. She most likely expected to see those of her ancestors welcoming her to the next world. Instead her eyes focused on a startled and a little bit disturbed Brastias.

She grinned and wiggled her eyebrows at him. "She's bloody mad," he whispered as she swung around and looked at the dragon.

"Did you miss?" she asked sweetly.

The dragon looked as if he were about to answer, but he never got the chance. Fearghus swooped down and snatched him up. The beautiful Morfyd right behind him.

Brastias threw himself back into the fray, but not before he heard Annwyl address Lorcan. "I guess it's just us then. Eh, brother?"

Lorcan smiled. Things had turned in his favor. He knew he couldn't battle Hefaidd-Hen on his own. He'd killed dragons before. But Hefaidd-Hen wasn't just a dragon. He was something completely different. Unnatural. Unholy. Evil. But with Hefaidd-Hen off battling his own kind, Lorcan could finally do what he'd wanted to do since the day the little bitch became part of his life.

He would kill his only sister.

Lorcan brought his blade up and charged.

Annwyl dodged the blade, slicing her brother's back as he

passed her. But the blade barely touched him. He swung around to face her again.

"You've become fast, little sister." He openly leered. "Did the dragon teach you that before he pushed you to your knees?"

The siblings shadowed each other. Moving slowly, purposely. Waiting for the other to make the next move.

Annwyl knew exactly what her brother was doing. He was baiting her. And it would have worked . . . a few weeks ago.

"He taught me many things, brother. Although I think it is you that has become the bitch of a dragon. Did Hefaidd-Hen make you moan as he took you?"

Lorcan began to growl, but quickly it became a full-blown roar. He attacked. A straight thrust to her belly. Annwyl parried with one blade and slashed his midsection with the other. She danced back away from him.

Her brother looked down at the blood seeping from under his garments. Annwyl knew the damage was slight. But Lorcan's shock went to the fact that few ever came that close to striking him before. And that's when she knew she had him.

His rage exploded out, surrounding her. She knew she should be scared. Or angry. She felt neither. His anger calmed her. Soothed her. She knew the control belonged to her, while he drowned in his own rage.

She stayed on the defensive, letting him come to her. He attacked again, this time swinging at her neck. She blocked the blade and slammed her body into him. Lorcan stumbled back. He righted himself quick enough, though, and brutally backhanded Annwyl. Her body flew several feet before landing. Yet her dragon had hit her like that before while training, so she barely felt Lorcan's fist. She scrambled to her feet before he ever reached her.

After fighting Fearghus, Lorcan's moves seemed slow and blocky. Not the fluid movements of her dragon. Suddenly she couldn't understand what she'd so greatly feared all these years. Hell, she'd faced Bercelak the Great and almost destroyed him. Was her brother really that much of a challenge?

She found herself getting calmer. Seeing his moves long before he ever made them. She could also see his rage burning through his body. He wanted her dead so badly his attacks became sloppier. Soon blood covered him. And none of it belonged to her.

Fearghus took Hefaidd-Hen up toward the suns, his talons digging into the soft white underbelly. He no longer had the protective scales of their breed.

What did this dragon do to himself?

Hefaidd-Hen spat out a spell and an almost unbearable pain racked Fearghus's body. A pain that came from within. Now he saw that the beast gave parts of himself for the Magick that coursed through his veins. The Magick that Hefaidd-Hen now used on him. But Fearghus wouldn't let the bastard go. He'd only go after Annwyl again. He couldn't risk that. So he kept his claws dug deep into Hefaidd-Hen's flesh and held on.

Another wave of pain tore through Fearghus's body. He roared. But his roar could never match Hefaidd-Hen's brutal scream. He opened his eyes to see that Morfyd had attached herself to Hefaidd-Hen's back. Her claws dug in deep to the white flesh as she spoke a spell that set the beast on fire. And without scales, he had no protection from the unholy flames Morfyd unleashed.

"Now, Fearghus! Now!"

Fearghus dug his claws deeper into Hefaidd-Hen's lower body and opened him up from bowel to throat.

Hefaidd-Hen screamed. A scream of surprise and utter pain. Fearghus and Morfyd released his body. The unnatural beast plummeted to the ground, vainly attempting to keep his entrails in and put out the fire that covered him. Morfyd spewed another spell at the retreating form and Hefaidd-Hen burst into pieces.

Fearghus glanced at his sister. "That was a bit much, don't you think?"

She gave an innocent shrug. "I like to be certain."

Annwyl saw an opening and took it. She lunged and thrust her blade into his thigh. Lorcan roared in pain and slapped her across the face, his gauntleted hand opening a slash across her cheek. She went down on her belly and he straddled her from behind, his two hands on her throat. His rage had him out of control, but she never thought he'd use his bare hands to kill her. She only had seconds before she blacked out. She pulled her dagger from her side and slashed backward. Screaming, he stumbled off her.

Jumping up before Lorcan could recover, Annwyl turned and saw her brother's hand over his face, blood pouring from between his fingers. She'd slashed him across his eye. Quickly, not wanting to give him any time to attack again, she moved behind him while he kneeled on the ground, cradling his bleeding eye. Her father always taught her that if one destroys a man's legs, you've destroyed the man. Remembering that, she slashed the tendons on the back of Lorcan's ankles. She ignored his screaming as it intensified tenfold. Knowing that he couldn't walk or run, she kicked him in the back, knocking him to the ground.

Annwyl straddled him, just as he'd done to her. Snatching off the strip of leather she used to bind her hair back, she pushed her brother's hands out of her way and wrapped it around his throat. She pulled the ends tight and ignored his flailing arms, keeping the pressure up.

There would be no noble death for him. She would not take his head while he still breathed as she would have any other warrior. He deserved no such courtesy. Instead, she gritted her teeth and kept up the pressure.

Soon his movements slowed and desperate needy sounds came from the back of his throat. She waited until he dropped off unconscious and with one strong pull, she snapped his neck.

She released him, and his lifeless body dropped to the ground. She realized that it took less time than she thought it would. The task of actually killing her own brother.

"Annwyl."

Annwyl tore her eyes away from her brother's body and looked up at the looming form of her dragon-lover.

"You need to turn the tide of this battle."

She glanced over the battlefield and saw that her men and Lorcan's were at a standstill. Both sides fighting equally well. Neither side giving up any ground.

She nodded as she retrieved her sword. "You are right."

Brastias raised his ax to cleave another man in two when he heard her voice. Clear and strong, booming over the battlefield and the land.

"Hear me!"

On her command, they all stopped fighting and focused their attention on her. Even the enemy paused. She stood upon the black dragon's back as if she were born to be there.

"I lead Dark Plains! I lead these troops! And now Garbhán Isle belongs *to me*!" With that final screech, she raised her brother's head high in the air.

Her men screamed her name as Brastias turned to the soldier before him. "Now where were we?" he asked, just before cleaving the man in two.

Chapter 19

Fearghus sank deep into the metal tub someone placed into Annwyl's tent. He let the hot water wrap around his human body, soaking the aching muscles. He would rather be back at his lake, but this would do for now. Besides, he would be home soon enough.

"Annwyl?" Morfyd entered the tent, but stopped short on sight of her brother. "Oh. You."

"Yes. Me."

"Where's Annwyl?"

"Still celebrating with her men, I presume." He closed his eyes and leaned back against the tub. "Did the family leave?"

"All except Gwenvael. He's enjoying the camp girls, I think."

"That better be all he's enjoying," Fearghus growled out.

Morfyd chuckled. "He tried, but I hear Annwyl handled it."

"Does he still have his head?"

"For the moment."

"Sister, I need to ask you something."

"Yes?"

"How did Annwyl survive the flames? Hefaidd-Hen's flames?"

"Uh . . . well, you know . . . um . . ."

Fearghus jumped up and out of the tub, grabbing his sister by her arms and snatching her completely into the tent. "*You let Annwyl face her alone, didn't you?*"

"It was a risk she was willing to take!" Morfyd pulled her arms away and pushed her brother.

"But not a risk that *I* was willing to take! Not with her life!" Fearghus pushed her back.

"I feel no guilt for what I did. I had to protect her, and the family agreed."

"I didn't agree!"

"We didn't *ask* you!" She punched her brother in the chest.

"But Annwyl belongs to me." He slapped his hand over his sister's face and shoved her.

Morfyd stumbled back and glared at him. "No. She doesn't." Morfyd smirked at him. "You haven't Claimed her." Fearghus winced at that. His sister spoke true. Until he performed the Claiming Ceremony, Annwyl was as unshackled as a virgin. "You haven't marked her as your own. So she belongs to no one. Although the way Gwenvael has been looking at her lately, you never know."

The siblings growled at each other. Then Fearghus pulled his sister into a headlock.

"Ow! Let me go, you crazy bastard!"

He ground his knuckles into the top of her head. "You are the most irritating little—"

"Annwyl, I . . ." Fearghus looked up as Brastias entered the tent. But he took one look at the siblings and walked back out.

Fearghus released his sister and shoved her away so she couldn't get in a good kick.

"If anything had happened to her . . ."

"But it didn't. And maybe you didn't notice, but it saved her life!"

With that Morfyd straightened up her robes, pushed her white hair out of her face, stuck her tongue out at her brother, and left.

Fearghus growled, smoke curling out from his nostrils. "Brat."

* * *

Annwyl headed back to her tent. She'd grown tired of pushing Gwenvael's hand off her thigh every ten seconds. Eventually she'd just pulled his fingers back until she heard one of them give a satisfying *snap*. It angered him to no end, but after the past day he really didn't worry her.

She walked past rows of men feasting and celebrating. Still so much more work to do, but she let the men have their time. They earned it. And they would earn more still. Annwyl knew that she must attack Garbhán Isle and take possession of the castle before she would truly be queen. It galled her that she would have to return to a place she held with such contempt, but the seat of power for Dark Plains *was* Garbhán Isle. She had no choice. And once done there she would then have to defeat any and all that might still hold loyalty to her brother. Yes, she had much work to do. But tonight she would celebrate. Tonight was special.

She slowed down to stop and glance at the front of camp. There it stood. Her brother's head on a spike. She smiled, feeling an overwhelming sense of satisfaction.

"Uh . . . Annwyl?" She looked around to see Danelin standing before her. "You're scaring the men."

Annwyl looked at her troops. They'd stopped eating to watch her stare at the remains of her brother. And they did appear a little frightened.

"Sorry." He made to walk past her, but she stopped him. "Nice work today, Danelin."

He smiled proudly, nodded, and moved on.

As she neared her tent, Annwyl realized that no troops guarded it. That could only mean one thing.

As she stepped through the flaps, she saw him lounging decadently in a high-backed chair. A fur spread from the bed wrapped around his long, muscular body. His long black hair, recently washed, partially covering his face and chest. Her breath caught in her throat. She became wet at the mere sight of him.

"Lord Dragon."

"Queen Annwyl."

This was the first she'd seen of him once the battle turned. He'd gone off to help his family finish off the enemy dragons, she to destroy as many of Lorcan's men as her troops could get their hands on. But war and sex had now become one for her. Probably forever. She blazed through men, knowing that the sooner she completed her task, the quicker she could return to Fearghus.

"A bath awaits you." She glanced over at the huge tub. Since she still had her brother's blood in her hair, a bath might be a good idea.

She moved to the middle of her tent and quickly removed the sheathed swords hanging from her back.

"Slowly."

She looked up at Fearghus. He watched her closely with those beautiful black eyes of his. The walls of her womb clenched, and it took all her strength not to launch herself at him. Instead, she slowly removed her surcoat. Pulled off her boots and her chain mail. Unbound her breasts and slipped off the material that covered her sex. When done, she stood there. His eyes roved languidly over her. Taking in not only her body but every wound she now wore on it after the day's battle.

He motioned to the tub with a flick of his eyes. She slipped into it and shivered.

"Cold?"

"A little."

Throwing off the fur covering, he slowly stood and walked toward her. She studied his body as he came to rest beside the tub. Underneath all those long, hard muscles lay the heart and soul of a dragon. *Her* dragon. She licked her lips, her only thought, sucking his sweet cock once again into her willing mouth.

Fearghus crouched down next to her. He placed his hand in the tub between her thighs. She'd hoped he would touch her but he didn't. His hand only rested there until she noticed that the water warmed up, nice and hot. This dragon Magick really did have its uses.

"Relax," he coaxed her gently. And she did just that, leaning back into the tub. Letting her head rest on the rim.

Fearghus poured water over her hair and soaped up her scalp. He washed the blood and sweat of the day from her hair and eventually her body.

"Comfortable?"

"Yes."

"Relaxed?"

"Very."

"Good."

Then Annwyl screamed as Fearghus shoved her head under water. He held her down for several long seconds as she fought to get that piece of steel he called an arm off her head. Eventually he released her and she came coughing and sputtering back to air.

"*What in all that's holy*—"

He took hold of her shoulders and easily lifted her from the tub. "Listen to me clearly, woman. Never face my family again without me! *Ever!* You are never and I mean *never* to risk your life like that again! Are we clear?"

Annwyl pulled away from him and took several stumbling steps back. "No! We are not clear!" She turned on him. "I did what I had to. And I'd do it again! And I'm not afraid of your family!"

"Annwyl," he warned through gritted teeth.

"No! I don't want to hear it!" She fought to get the strands of wet brown hair out of her eyes. "Do you have any idea what I went through today? In just one day I stood in the dragon's flame . . . *twice!*"

"But I—"

"*Quiet!*" He stood there, startled into silence. "I also had to face that cold bitch you call a mother! I took my own brother's head! *And* I was forced to break *your* brother's hand because he wouldn't stop touching me!"

Fearghus broke out in a grin and she stopped her tirade. "What?"

"You broke his hand?" He couldn't help but laugh.

"Well, it was more like a finger. But the way he carried on, you'd think I'd broken his entire arm."

Fearghus laughed. Hard. And, eventually, Annwyl smiled.

What the hell was he going to do? He loved this woman. Loved everything about her. Wanted her as his mate. But she had a kingdom to run. Allies to forge. Enemies to crush. He already saw the fear in the men's eyes. They'd witnessed her "dance" with the dragon's flame. A dance she'd survived. And they all knew she'd taken him as her lover. His presence would do nothing but put her safety at risk.

"What are you thinking, Dragon?"

He shook his head and moved to her. "Nothing," he whispered as he slipped an arm around her waist.

"Still lying, I see." She pulled away from him.

He sighed. "What, Annwyl?"

"You're planning to leave, aren't you?"

How she knew these things, he'd never know. "Look, you have a kingdom to—"

"Horseshit!"

"What?"

"He told me you'd come up with some noble horseshit about me having to defend my kingdom and no one able to accept the two of us."

"Gwenvael," he growled angrily. "Annwyl, it is for your—"

"You have two choices, Dragon," she cut in smoothly.

He crossed his arms in front of his chest. "Do I?"

"Yes. You do."

"And they are?"

"Claim me now. Or let me go forever."

He'd kill his brother for his big mouth.

"You don't even know what that means."

"Yes. I do."

He wanted to Claim her. To make her his own. Yet he planned to wait until she'd secured her reign. And if, after that, she still wanted him. . . . "No. You don't."

"I know I'll not waste my life waiting for you." That stung. More than he wanted to admit.

"I'm not asking you to."

"Really? You're not?"

"No."

"So I can take any man right now and you won't care."

"If that's your wish." He bet a lie that size could kill him.

"Well, any man won't do," she mused softly. "But I think Gwenvael is still here."

She grabbed a fur covering and headed toward the tent flap. Fearghus seized her by her arm and swung her around. "That's not funny," he growled.

"Fearghus, just admit it. You'd kill any man or dragon who came near me."

He wanted to say no. He wanted it to be the truth. But they both knew better.

"I would."

She leaned into him. Her breasts against his forearm. He closed his eyes as her hand ran down his chest, his hips, finally grasping his shaft in her hand. She ran her fingers over the veins and ridges, her thumb circled the head. "Then Claim me."

"No."

She angrily released what had now become a healthy erection. "Why?"

"Because it would be clear to all that you are mine. That your love and loyalty belonged to a dragon."

"And?"

"Could you at least *act* afraid?"

"The only thing I feared has his head on a spike outside my camp. Now my fear is of living the rest of my life without you."

Fearghus stared at Annwyl. Just that morning the woman bravely took the queen's flame. A flame imbued with the most ancient of Magicks. And until her death, Annwyl would always be immune to any dragon's fire. But he knew his mother well enough to know she didn't make it easy on the girl. Annwyl's back and side were completely covered in dark bruises. The old bitch probably knocked her right out of her chamber.

His eyes glanced briefly at the mark clearly defined on her chest; it was burned into the tan skin above her breasts. She now wore the Chain of Beathag as well. And would for the rest of her life. It would always be there, right under her skin. One of the most powerful gods-created items a dragon could bestow upon a human. The Chain of Beathag could extend the life of the wearer but only if her heart remained pure and her love true. Her love for the dragon. Otherwise it would be a fiery and painful death that would last days.

He touched the mark and Annwyl winced, her skin still sensitive. Annwyl loved him. She wouldn't have survived if she hadn't.

Yet he couldn't let that change his plan. He wouldn't put Annwyl at risk until she secured her reign. Of course that didn't mean Annwyl would make it easy on him.

"Annwyl—"

"I grow tired of this . . . and of you." She snatched her arm away from him, taking several long strides to the wood table in the middle of her tent. Already she moved like a queen. The humans would be lucky to have her as their sovereign.

"Claim me now, Dragon." She crossed her arms in front of

her chest, the fur barely covering her at all. "Or go. And never come back."

He knew what he should do. He should walk out of her life forever. He should let some nice human boy take her. Some nice human boy he would have to kill for touching the woman he loved.

With a sigh, Fearghus went and stood in front of her. "You are a mad bitch, Annwyl the Bloody."

"What other woman would put up with you, Fearghus the Destroyer?"

Fearghus leaned down and kissed the top of Annwyl's head to prevent himself from laughing. "You are a strange woman, Queen Annwyl." He brushed his cheek against hers.

"So I've been told." His hands slid under the fur covering, gliding along her waist, her back, her rear. He heard her breath catch as she leaned into him. "Don't make me wait, Dragon. Claim me now or let me go forever."

"Are you sure, Annwyl? Once this is done, there will be no going back."

"I've made my decision, Dragon." She let the fur covering drop to the floor. "But make sure it's what *you* want. Do me no favors."

He gripped her around the waist and easily sat Annwyl on the wood table. He kissed her forehead, then her neck as he grasped both her forearms in his hands. He leaned in and kissed her luscious mouth as his grip on her arms became tighter.

Annwyl stared at Fearghus and wondered what he was doing. He stood quietly, holding onto her forearms as if he were afraid she'd run away. But that wouldn't happen. She wanted this, and him, more than anything. But maybe he'd decided he just didn't want her. That he'd rather spend his long life with a dragon as a mate.

Gwenvael led her on this course, damn him. The drunker the dragon got, the more she realized how much he actually cared for his gruff older brother. Even as he tried to put his hand on her rear. Then Morfyd confirmed it. The two of them planted themselves on either side of Annwyl and told her that if she wanted their brother, she'd best get him to Claim her this night. Otherwise he'd leave, thinking he did it for the right reasons.

But maybe they were wrong. Maybe he didn't want her at all. Not for any length of time anyway.

Annwyl winced. His grip on her arms hadn't tightened, but pain still slashed across her flesh. Her fists rested against his chest and she felt his deep, even breathing against her skin as her agony became more intense. The pain reminded her of when she burned her hand over an open flame or got too close to a bubbling pot. It went through her skin right down to the flesh and bone beneath.

She tried to stifle a yelp of pain, but she just couldn't. It hurt that much. She dropped her head against his chest, praying it wouldn't last much longer, when a warm jolt passed through her body. Her nipples hardened. Her sex became wet. Her breath came out in short gasps. She moaned as her entire body tightened. Fearghus's erection rose against her in response to her body's call.

Annwyl gasped as another pulse of heat passed through her. Her sex clenched. Her legs weakened. She was coming. She didn't know how or why; but she was coming. And when a third wave of heat flashed through her body, she cried out. She came hard, her teeth biting into the flesh of his chest.

Fearghus kissed her then. His mouth brutally claiming hers, his tongue torturing hers with bold strokes.

The pain in her arms receded and her spasms stopped. Fearghus released her and she glanced down at her forearms, saw burned flesh on both. The lingering after-pain made her wonder if they would ever heal.

"That is so every dragon knows you belong to me." He kissed her again as he laid her back against the table. "And this"—he kissed her breasts, her chest, her stomach—"this is for me." He lowered his head between her legs, his tongue swiping the inside flesh of her thigh. She clenched her teeth as a burning pain spread over the area. He did the same to the other thigh and she gripped the table, her fingers digging into the wood. He breathed over the two areas and the pain swept through once again. Annwyl bit her lip to stop herself from screaming but a low moan escaped as her body shook. Then his tongue speared through the folds of her sex, replacing the pain with sweet, deep pleasure. Her back arched off the table, but he gripped her legs and held her as his tongue dipped inside and around the swollen, hungry flesh.

She forgot the pain as Fearghus's talented tongue stroked her over and over again, bringing her closer and closer to release. Her hands clenched into fists, her moans filled the tent. Soon she began to shake as her climax ripped through her, a loud cry torn from her heated body.

Fearghus gently gathered her to him, pulling her off the table, and pressing her still shuddering body against his.

Fearghus whispered softly against her ear, "Are you all right?"

Her arms hurt. The insides of her thighs were sore. And burns permanently marred her body. Yes, Annwyl felt just fine.

She wet her lips and took a deep breath. "Is that all, Dragon?"

Breathing hard, his cock hot and demanding against her, he growled. "Not even close."

"Good. I was about to feel disappointed."

Fearghus's head brushed against hers as he breathed in deeply. "You always smell so good, Annwyl."

"I do?" At least she hoped she said that. She wasn't quite sure. Fearghus slowly rubbing his head against hers, his long hair sliding across her naked body, completely distracted her. An innocent move, it still made her knees weak and her nipples tighten painfully.

"You amaze me, woman."

"Then finish it," she purred as she wrapped her arms around his neck, ignoring the searing pain the move caused her forearms. "And keep me as your own."

Apparently he needed no further prompting. He turned her so she faced the wood table and ran his hands down her back. His lips following close behind. Alternately nipping and sucking her skin. He licked any wounds she had, cleaning them with his tongue. She wanted to order him to get on with it, but she knew he would just make her wait longer. So she placed her hands, palms flat, against the table and wondered when she'd become such a bitch in heat. She'd lost all control around her dragon.

Fearghus wondered how long before she started barking orders at him. He grinned against her flesh. Annwyl reigned absolute as the most demanding female he'd ever met. And every day she surprised him. Already she handled the worst part of the Claiming, the Branding not being for the faint of heart.

Truth be told, he thought as soon as the process began she'd beg him to stop. At the first touch of heat on her arms, she'd panic and run. But he should've known she'd stay. She'd gritted her teeth and faced the challenge.

But he never expected her to climax. Her whole body shook with the force of it and she drew blood when she bit into his chest.

The Claiming differed from pairing-to-pairing—after all these years his parents' notorious Claiming still remained the talk of the court—but he knew what he needed from his Annwyl. And, as always, it would be his pleasure to get it from her.

He pushed her legs apart and deftly entered her from

behind. He wasn't sure, but he thought he heard her mutter "About time." Already wet and so tight, he felt like he might come before he even finished the first stroke. No other female ever made him so desperate. So hungry. He let his cock rest inside of her and he waited. And waited. She lasted about ten seconds before she pushed back into him.

He slapped her rear.

"Oi!"

"This is my Claiming, wench. Not yours. Try that again and we stop . . . for good." He lied, of course. There would be no way he would ever stop taking her. Fucking her any and every way he could. But he loved that growl of annoyance she gave when he taunted her. It made him harder.

For good measure—and really just because he wanted to—he slapped her rear again. She glared at him over her shoulder, but she couldn't hide the rush of moisture or the way her muscles gripped his cock.

She wanted him. Needed him. Which was good. Because this night he would make her his own, so that she'd never forget it.

She knew now that only one male could have ever claimed her. Only one dragon was strong enough to make her his and his alone. Any other male she would have left dead on the wedding sheets. But her Fearghus was brave enough to take her. Brave enough to burn his mark into her flesh. And brave enough to slap her ass.

He never tried to tame her. He loved everything about her, including her rage, and he never tried to change it or make it go away. Fearghus embraced it as he embraced all of her.

He was her perfect match and one day they would rule Garbhán Isle together.

Fearghus moved inside her. Slowly. Taking his time. Making her hungry for it. She cursed him but it came out suspiciously like a moan. But by the gods it felt so good. And she couldn't stop herself from moaning. Gasping. Saying his name. Screaming his name.

He brought his long, hard body over hers and kissed her shoulders, back, and neck. His hands slipped under her body and gripped her breasts, squeezing her nipples tight. She leaned her head back and he kissed her.

He stood, lifting her chest off the table with one hand while the other slowly found its way down to her dripping sex. He massaged her there, avoiding her clit. And she thought briefly that she might possibly have to *kill him*.

She needed release. And she needed it now.

She leaned back against him, her arms going back to wrap around his neck as he hungrily nipped her throat. She again ignored the pain in her forearms as his black hair rasped across the wounds. She didn't care. Because at that very moment, even the pain felt good.

"Finish it, Fearghus," she begged desperately. "Now."

"Tell me what I need to hear first, Annwyl. Tell me."

Somehow, she knew exactly what he wanted. What he *needed*. And she would not delay in telling him. "I love you, Fearghus. I love you and I'm yours. There will be no other. Ever." As if that had ever been an option.

"And I'm yours, Annwyl. Forever."

"Yes. That's wonderful," she barked dismissively. "Now finish it." He laughed, she assumed at the desperation in her voice. His cock thrust smoothly in and out of her as his fingers gripped her clit and firmly stroked the engorged nub. Her fingers dug into Fearghus's hair, gripping the silky strands as the wave of heat spread across her lower back. She moaned desperately as her body began to shake. Heat tore up her spine and her clit throbbed uncontrollably. The moan became a scream as the climax racked her body. He fucked her through her orgasm, but when her cries settled he allowed himself to come with a roar, his seed exploding into her.

The pair laid against the table, tiny spasms rocking their bodies. Until Annwyl looked back at him.

"Fearghus?" He looked asleep. His eyes closed; his breathing even and deep.

"Aye?" he finally answered without opening his eyes.

"So is that it then?"

He smiled. "Yes, Annwyl. That's it."

She looked across the tent to the tub, then back at him. "That tub certainly is far away."

He opened his eyes and glanced over. "Aye. That it is."

"Think we can make it?"

"Leave it to me, woman." He took a deep breath, wrapped his arm around her waist, and lifted her off the floor. He walked over to the tub, carrying her easily, his cock still buried inside her. With his free hand, he reached down and dumped the tub over, the used water splashing across the floor.

"Watch. Learned this from Morfyd."

He spoke an incantation in a language Annwyl never heard before. In moments, the tub filled with steamy water.

"Nice trick."

"I thought so." Fearghus stepped into the tub, still tightly holding Annwyl in his arms. He lowered himself into the hot water and relaxed back. "Of course, somewhere I may have just caused a drought."

"Couldn't be helped."

"Selfish bitch."

He kissed her neck, licked her ear, while his hands roamed slowly over her flesh. His shaft still buried deep inside of her.

"You know, Fearghus, you can let me go now."

"I know," he muttered against her neck. But his body seemed to have a plan of its own, as his hands did nothing but excite her, his cock hard again, growing in response to her moans.

Annwyl smiled. This was going to be a long night.

* * *

Annwyl forced her eyes open. Based on the shadows crawling across the dirt floor, most of the day had already passed. She'd probably missed luncheon.

She didn't reach for Fearghus. There was no point. He was gone. She didn't know when he left, but as soon as she awoke, she felt his absence.

The dragon took possession of her body all night. A few times she'd wake to find him inside of her, making love to her until she climaxed. One time she thought she dreamed that she'd taken him, only to wake up to find herself straddling his hips and riding his cock until he exploded inside of her. But the last time he came to her she knew something was different. He moved slow and gentle inside her. Taking his time, giving her the sweetest experience she ever had.

And she knew that when dawn came, he'd leave her. Tragically, she'd been right.

Annwyl dragged herself up to a sitting position, the fur cover slipping to her waist. She ached all over. And she did mean *all over*. Wounds from the battle littered her body. And her muscles and skin were sore from Fearghus's Claiming of her.

Remembering the Claiming, she glanced down at her forearms and froze.

"*Brastias!*"

In a few moments her head battle lord strode into her tent, his eyes averted from her naked breasts that she didn't bother to cover. "Is Morfyd still here?"

"Aye."

"Fetch her."

He didn't ask questions, he just moved. In a few minutes Morfyd came in, she saw the look on Annwyl's face and immediately became concerned. "What's wrong?"

"Your brother's gone."

Morfyd nodded. "Yes. I saw him this morning."

"Why?"

"He said you needed to do this on your own. You would be

the one ruling these people. It was up to you to earn their loyalty. All he could do was bring their fear."

Of course, he spoke true. *The bastard.*

Annwyl pointed to the marks on her chest. The pain she endured made her hope it had some useful significance and wasn't merely the queen having a bit of fun. "You never gave me a straight answer about this."

"That is the Chain of Beathag. It's now a part of you, like your skin. The marks will never go away. And it has extended your life five . . . maybe six hundred years. Perhaps a bit more or less than that. Hard to tell, really."

Annwyl stared at her friend. "Oh." Well, that might be worth a few minutes of excruciating pain.

She cleared her throat and held out her arms. "And these?"

Morfyd took Annwyl's forearms in her hands and studied them. She smiled. "Fearghus Claimed you last night, I see." Clearly Morfyd slept somewhere else last night, since anyone within a league of the campsite could hear their exhaustive couplings.

"Yes. Now what are these?"

Morfyd shrugged. "He branded you."

Annwyl looked again at the wounds. Last night they had just been areas of burned skin. She assumed that once she healed, scarred flesh would remain. But that's not what she saw now. Instead she saw a dragon brand on each of her forearms. The lines were dark, the dragons clearly defined. Easily seen. Each dragon different from the other, both wrapped around her forearms. Otherwise the flesh on her arms remained healthy and clear.

"He *really* branded you," Morfyd added.

"What does that mean?"

"I've just never seen one so . . . dark before. Except my mother's. These lines are coal black."

"He said it would be clear that my love and loyalty was to the dragon. Your brother was not joking." Annwyl blinked as she remembered all of the Claiming from the previous night. She lifted the fur covering over her legs and sighed. "Oh, honestly!"

Morfyd peeked over the fur covering and snorted out a laugh at the sight of Annwyl's thighs. Dragons, larger than the ones on her forearms, clearly branded on her flesh. "He's more like Bercelak than any of us realized," Morfyd laughed.

"Well, I'll not wear a chain. I'll leave that to the queen."

Morfyd leaned back, her smile revealing what a beautiful woman she was even with the scar. "If you like I could have some gauntlets made that would hide the ones on your arms. If you are feeling unsafe."

Annwyl shook her head. "No. What are a few more scars, brands, burns? Besides, I'll not hide my loyalty to your brother from any man." She stood and headed toward the tub. "And if one of them dares call me a dragon's whore, I'll take his head." She stopped and motioned to the tub. "Now, can you do that trick with the water?"

Chapter 20

Brastias searched the castle for her. She kept disappearing on them. And once they found one hiding place, she would simply find another.

One year had passed since Annwyl took her brother's head and his place as leader of Garbhán Isle and Dark Plains. For six months she squashed rebellions as quickly as they rose.

She also created alliances with other nearby kingdoms that hadn't been in place for almost a century.

But once the battles stopped and Annwyl's kingdom became peaceful, she seemed increasingly unhappy. It didn't take him long to realize that she was a wartime ruler. Her leadership born of blood and struggles for ground. That was all she knew.

But Brastias also knew that if Fearghus had been by her side, she'd be much less restless. Yet the dragon never came for her. And she never returned to Dark Glen to find him.

Morfyd, however, stayed by her side as counsel. With almost two hundred and fifty years of knowledge trapped inside that beautiful body, she helped Annwyl with the decisions involving peace and politics. Brastias did what he could, but it was Morfyd who kept Annwyl from taking nobles' heads on a whim. An amazing dragon, that one.

He'd just passed an unused bedroom when he heard a sound from the other side of the door. The sound of a turning page.

Brastias walked back and pushed open the heavy oak door. He found her reading by a window, a lone candle the only illumination in the room.

"Annwyl?"

"What now?" Her snappish tone increased as the months passed.

"We need you in the main hall."

"Why?"

"Delegations are here to bring you tributes."

"Again?" She sounded so annoyed, he wasn't about to tell her the truth. "Can't you do it, Brastias?"

"I do not rule this land."

"*Fine!*" She threw her book across the room and stormed past him. Once she was too far away to get in a good punch, he sighed quietly in relief and followed her.

He cringed when he saw what she wore. Leather breeches, leather boots, and one of those damned sleeveless chain-mail shirts she insisted on wearing. Her branded forearms exposed for all the court to see. He thought about asking her to cover them with gauntlets, but he really liked his throat uncut and he had every intention of keeping it that way.

He thought of the upcoming evening and hoped that Morfyd had thought out this plan of hers carefully.

Annwyl stalked into the throne room. Some of the nobles began to bow, but seemed to remember how much Annwyl hated it and they stopped themselves. If she weren't so annoyed with the whole process, she would laugh. But she *was* annoyed. Very, very annoyed.

Annwyl threw herself into the high-backed stone chair her brother and father once used as a throne. She hated it. And she only used it for occasions like these.

"Lady Annwyl—" Morfyd began, but Annwyl cut her off.

"Can we just get this over with?"

Morfyd nodded. "As you wish."

Delegations from surrounding kingdoms began to come before her. They offered her a tribute of precious metals or gems. Or presented something that meant a great deal in their land. But Annwyl also began to notice something else. Every last one of the nobles who came before her brought a son. A strong, virile, unmarried male. When the House of Arranz presented three sons, one of them a boy no more than ten and two years of age, she'd had enough.

"Excuse me." She stood up and walked over to Morfyd. "May I speak with you for a moment?"

She didn't give the dragon a chance to answer, but grabbed her arm and dragged her out of the throne room and into a servant's hallway.

"What is this?" Annwyl demanded.

"What do you think? And get off me."

Annwyl silently reminded herself that Morfyd *was* a

dragon. She could decide to shift right now and take the whole castle with her.

"I don't want this."

"No one is saying you have to take any of them as a mate. But you should at least look like you're considering it. If they think one of their sons has a chance at being your consort, we've got a little more bargaining power."

"Bargaining power for what?"

"Grain from Kerezik. Lumber from Madron. The list goes on and on. Do you not listen to our daily meetings about the state of your lands?"

"Of course I don't. They're dead boring."

"Not everything can involve bloodshed, Annwyl."

"Can't you come get me when there is bloodshed? Otherwise just leave me alone to read." Morfyd took Annwyl by the shoulders and none too gently shoved her back into the throne room.

Grudgingly, Annwyl returned to her throne and let the painful procession continue.

Eventually she stopped looking at any of them. She sat sideways in the big chair, her legs thrown over the arm. She responded to each representative politely enough, but she could no longer hide her annoyance at the entire process.

But when the heir to the House of Madron strutted in with his entourage, she knew she'd about hit the end of her tether.

The Madron advisor made the announcement. "Lady Annwyl of Garbhán Isle, the people of Madron bring you their thanks and undying loyalty."

Annwyl glared at Brastias and Morfyd, huddled together in a corner watching her. They both knew her feelings about Hamish Madron. And how Hamish Madron felt about her.

Hamish stepped forward. "Lady Annwyl. It's been so long since we've seen each other."

"Lord Hamish." She gave a wave of her hand and prayed the torture would end soon.

"Perhaps, lady, when you are done here we can dine together and discuss the future of our kingdoms."

Annwyl smirked at the sudden look of panic on Brastias's face. She knew what her old friend feared and she delighted in giving him exactly what he expected.

"No."

A long pause followed as the Madron representatives took in her short, but direct answer.

Hamish pushed. "I'm sorry, lady. Is there something else that keeps your attention this night?"

"No. I just don't like you." Brastias rolled his eyes in exasperation. Poor thing, he didn't realize that the torture had only begun. "You were ready to force me into marrying you. You're lucky I let you keep your lands and your head." Hamish glared at her. "Besides, Lord Hamish, any attempt to seduce me to get my crown would only have my dragon hunting you down and killing you. And I'd let him."

Hamish became very pale and he didn't bother hiding his disgust. "So the rumors are true then? You have mated with a dragon."

"Very true. But, of course, if it bothers you, Lord Hamish . . . please, feel free to come and take my throne from me."

Rhiannon landed and watched the men run for their lives. She really never tired of that moment. The panic on their tiny little faces. The sounds of their screams as they scurried off. She would have laughed and maybe sampled a few of the delicacies, but she had a purpose.

She needed that little human girl to get off her precious throne and return to her son. Any more time apart and there would be war. Already she'd regretted her recent insistence Fearghus come to the court. It cost Kesslene his life. It started with a simple, although admittedly crass, remark on Fearghus's choice of mate. It should have led to a challenge between the two. But this time no challenge came. No warning. Fearghus calmly told him to apologize. Kesslene wondered aloud if he, too, would enjoy bedding the girl. And Fearghus snapped the dragon's neck without a moment's pause. All court activity stopped. True, it wasn't the first time a brutal death happened in her court. Mostly due to Bercelak's rage or parts of Gwenvael being where they should not. But this was the first time that Fearghus had caused the problem. And then Fearghus challenged any and all in the hall to take his rightful place among his clan. After seeing his hearty dispense of Kesslene, no dragon stepped forward. Not even his own kin would approach him.

Later, Rhiannon spoke with her children, asking them about their brother. His siblings expressed worry about their brother's sadness. A word she would never use with Fearghus. He wasn't as exuberant as Éibhear or as lusty as Gwenvael or as cocksure as Briec. He wasn't even brutish and grumpy like her Bercelak. Instead, he lived quietly and calmly. He only became upset when he couldn't have time to himself. He left the court earlier than any of her others because he couldn't stand the noise or his siblings constantly pestering him. And she let him go with her blessings. She prided herself on understanding all her hatchlings. She understood them better than any of them realized. She knew he needed to be alone. And even when he took the throne as king, he'd be the same way still. Nothing would change that. Or him.

Then the chatty little human girl came along. Because of the girl, people now knew dragons could shift into human. Her sweet Éibhear, whom she always had such high hopes for, only spoke of mating for life with a human. A human! And her own daughter, heir to her Magick and power, actually *served* the human female at Garbhán Isle.

In the beginning, Rhiannon became convinced that the girl

seduced her son—and clearly the rest of her family—with her feminine wiles. At least, that's what she thought before she met her. But she quickly realized the girl had absolutely no feminine wiles to speak of. A hard warrior who risked death so she could protect all her tiny human kin. Rhiannon even stopped referring to her as "it" the moment she took her flame. She screamed, true, but mostly because the pain was excruciating. But once the process changed her body, the girl had gone on to take her brother's head, become ruler of all Dark Plains and Garbhán Isle, and still unite with a dragon. *All in the same day*.

That still impressed Rhiannon. But now she had an unhappy son and she blamed the girl. A year had passed. The female tamped down all forms of insurgence with her tiny but mighty fist and now she needed to return to her mate. He'd Claimed her, she now belonged to him. If the girl changed her mind . . . well, it would be in her best interest *not* to change her mind.

Rhiannon's offer to Annwyl was simple. "Return to Fearghus now or suffer my wrath."

She stalked through the castle, her children trailing behind her, Keita desperately trying to cover up her mother's nakedness with a cloak. Her children had arrived a bit earlier and were already dressed. They lived among the humans more than she, and she often forgot how much the humans' own bodies caused them such distress. She paused outside the throne room long enough to pull the cloak on, but stopped and halted her children at the sound of Annwyl's voice.

"So the rumors are true then?" a male voice snapped in disgust. "You have mated with a dragon."

"Very true. But, of course, if it bothers you, Lord Hamish . . . please, feel free to come and take my throne from me."

Rhiannon exchanged glances with her children. Seemed she still might be underestimating the tiny human.

* * *

Annwyl swung her legs off the arm of the stone chair and stood to her full height. She looked in the eye of each and every head of the Houses before her. She tired of games and pretending. With all the Houses present, the time now came to make sure everyone understood her reign and her.

"Perhaps this is as good a time as any to clarify the situation for all. That way there are no misunderstandings. Yes. The rumors are true. My mate is Fearghus the Destroyer, the Black Dragon of Dark Plains. He is my mate and my consort. With him I shall rule. I understand if any of you have a problem with this. And please, feel free to try and take my throne from me." She lowered her voice to a whisper, but it razored across the silent hall like a shout. "Please."

She waited. When none stepped forward she turned her back. But the flicker of Danelin's eyes alerted her. They'd weathered many battles together and sometimes all you had time for was a look or one word. She knew exactly what he needed to tell her and she moved with her usual speed and brutality.

Annwyl pulled the jeweled dagger Fearghus gave her so long ago from her boot and, turning only her upper body, flung it behind her. The blade skewered the throat of a member of the House of Adhamhan who wanted to kill her in the name of his people. A big man in full armor, he wore no helm and Annwyl's blade lodged itself right in his neck. His big body crashed to the floor, causing everyone but Annwyl and her troops to jump.

Annwyl stared at him for a long moment, letting it all settle in for everyone present. Then she looked over the faces of the nobles. "Anyone else?" No one moved. "I guess we are all clear now."

She sat back on the throne, watching as Hamish scurried

to the back of the hall. She glanced at Danelin. "Are we done now?"

He leaned in low so only Annwyl could hear him.

"There were to be three more, but I believe they may have run for their lives."

"That weighs heavy on my heart, Danelin," she muttered under her breath.

He raised an eyebrow. "I can see that, Annwyl." All her original troops from her squire to Brastias still called her by her name only, without the formality of title and she would not have it any other way.

"Annwyl the Bloody!" A voice rang out across the hall, startling Annwyl and Danelin as well as the entire court. "You speak of your mate and yet you are not with him."

Annwyl's eyes narrowed as her rage began to flow through her veins like blood. It must have been on her face as well; Danelin stepped back from her, his hand on his sword, while Brastias and her troops moved in closer. Whether they were worried *for* her or *about* her she did not know.

She stared at the woman who stood at the large wood doors of the hall. Completely covered in a light blue cloak, she was the tallest female Annwyl had ever come across.

"Not sure what business that is of yours, lady." Annwyl wondered whether she would kill her slowly or just outright.

The woman came forward, the cloak swirling around her bare feet. "I've traveled far to meet with you, Lady Annwyl, but I don't like to waste my time or bandy words about."

"And neither do I. So perhaps you should get to your point before I lose my patience."

Annwyl felt a hand grip her shoulder and looked up to see Morfyd beside her. "Annwyl, I'd like to present Queen Rhiannon of the House of Gwalchmai fab Gwyar." Annwyl cringed. What an ugly family name. She would hate to be stuck with something like that. "My mother."

The feeling to bury one's head in a ditch can be an

overwhelming one, but Annwyl fought it all the same. The queen stood in front of her. As human. She snatched back the hood of her cloak. Snow white hair tumbled down around her shoulders and an expression of intense dissatisfaction rippled across her face. She didn't even seem to notice the gasp that went up from the court when they saw the mark of her own Claiming, a black dragon brand that went from her jaw down her neck and disappeared under her cloak.

But now Annwyl understood why all Rhiannon's children were beautiful. As human Rhiannon was absolutely stunning.

Annwyl looked at those who accompanied Rhiannon. A beautiful red-headed female who looked as innocent and sweet as any daddy's girl. And three males who were clearly brothers. All quite beautiful in their own way. The one with silver hair looked as if he appeared before her under protest. The golden-haired one openly leered at her. And the blue-haired one grinned so happily she could do nothing but give him a quick smile back.

"My point, *lady*, is that it is time to take your rightful place beside my son."

Annwyl took a deep, shaky breath. The bitch had just ordered her back to Fearghus. *Ordered her*. Her hands clenched into fists as the rage welled up. She could control the emotion now, but that only made it more deadly. Gwenvael must have seen it. He shut his eyes in resignation.

"And perhaps, *lady*, you should mind your own business." Morfyd's fingers dug deep into her shoulder as warning. A warning she ignored. "What goes on between Fearghus and myself is our concern. Not yours. And you need to remember that."

She noticed Rhiannon's children desperately trying to get her attention while Morfyd came dangerously close to tearing her arm off.

"Perhaps you forget who I am."

"I forget nothing. And pray tell me, lady, how is your mate's tail?"

At that point, Morfyd threw up her hands and walked back to Brastias's side while Rhiannon's sons cringed and the beautiful redhead dropped her head in her hands.

Rhiannon smiled. A disturbing sight to say the least. Unlike her children, her human teeth still resembled fangs more than anything else. "You know, Lady Annwyl, any woman strong enough to impale a dragon as mighty as Bercelak the Great, should be strong enough to go claim what is hers."

Interesting turn from the queen. Annwyl expected her to rip her head off instead. At least she expected her to try. "I appreciate your concern, lady. But I am at a loss as to why your son did not come himself."

And save me from his damn kin!

"He foolishly fears that he will bring great risk to your safety. I now know there is nothing to fear. You are a deadly adversary. I doubt anyone here would dare your wrath. I know I wouldn't."

Annwyl wondered for a moment if Rhiannon spoke these words just for the benefit of the nobles. But she doubted the dragon would be bothered. The female was dangerously honest—foe or friend. "But since my son is such a—"

"Prat?" Gwenvael offered.

"Insidious harpy?" Briec countered.

"Concerned mate," their mother spat out between gritted teeth as she silenced them both with a glare. "I have a gift for you."

Annwyl readied herself. The queen may be honest, but Annwyl still didn't take anything she said at face value. "Gift" could leave her covered in blood and eyeless. "Really?"

"I offer you my loyalty and the loyalty of all dragons in Dark Plains."

Annwyl wasn't sure what that should mean to her. "Oh. That's very . . . um . . . sweet."

Morfyd returned to her side and leaned down to whisper loudly in her ear so all could hear. "In case you didn't know, that means if anyone ever tries to strike out against you or your throne they will bring the entire dragon kingdom of Dark Plains and all our allies down on their heads. It happened once before about one thousand years ago. When the dragons were done, they'd wiped the land clean."

A jolt passed through Annwyl's body as some of the humans in the hall began to inch their way toward the exit. And Hamish couldn't run fast enough. She wondered what he'd originally planned.

Annwyl looked at Fearghus's mother. "You give this loyalty to me? A human?"

"Yes."

"Because of Fearghus?"

"No. I give nothing to my children. It all must be earned. And you have earned this. You've done very well. Without us. And without Fearghus." She gave a bored sigh. "Simply put, you've impressed me, Annwyl the Bloody. And I do not impress easily."

"I . . . uh . . . thank you?" For once Annwyl couldn't think of a thing to say.

Rhiannon waved her hand dismissively. "Yes. Yes." She turned away. "But my son awaits, perhaps you best get that rump of yours moving." Rhiannon headed toward the exit. "I must go. Bercelak, too, awaits and he is so impatient."

"Need to get back to your chain, lady?" Morfyd and Keita coughed in surprise while the brothers simply appeared stunned.

Rhiannon glanced at Annwyl over her shoulder and gave the most sensual smile Annwyl ever witnessed. "Jealous?" Then she was gone.

Gwenvael stepped forward. For the first time Annwyl watched him get angry. "Woman, are you mad?"

"Why does everyone ask me that?"

"Well, you must have impressed her," Keita added. "I thought for sure she would tear out your throat." Annwyl remembered those white talons of the queen quite well. "I kept thinking what are we going to tell Fearghus? Then I thought *who* is going to tell Fearghus? Then I thought we'd make Morfyd do it."

With a vicious hiss, "Excuse me?"

"Would all of you stop!" Annwyl wiped her hands on her leggings and stared down at her knees. She knew what she had to do. She looked up at the dragons. "I need a ride."

Gwenvael smiled. Relief seemed to spread through his entire body. He would never admit it but Annwyl knew the dragon cared much for his brother. "Thought you would. I can take you."

Annwyl raised an eyebrow. "Sure that is wise?"

Gwenvael shrugged. "Good point. Briec will take you."

"I will not! I'll not have her smelling like me when she gets back to him. I *like* my tail."

"I'll take her!" Éibhear offered happily.

"No!" both his brothers snapped.

"Honestly. You three are such idiots." Keita motioned to Annwyl. "Let us go, sister. *I* will take you. I have some . . . uh . . . plans with a few soldiers near the glen."

Annwyl shook her head as Morfyd snorted in disgust. "Um . . . all right." She glanced over her shoulder. "Brastias."

"Yes, Annwyl?" He stood beside Morfyd trying desperately not to smile, and failing miserably.

"I must take care of something, Brastias. Think you and Morfyd can keep that grain and lumber moving until my return?"

"Of course." He grinned. "But we'll let you know immediately if there's any bloodshed."

Annwyl looked at him. "And that's all I've ever asked."

* * *

Fearghus stretched out by his lake, his jaw cupped in one claw, the tip of his tail making swirling patterns in the blue water. He sighed. A year since he'd left her the morning after the final battle with her brother. A year since he'd held her in his arms. A year since he'd kissed her. A year since he'd buried his head between her thighs. A year since she'd punched him in the face.

He sighed again. He truly did miss her. He didn't think he could miss anything or anyone that much. He wanted to go to her. Wanted to take his rightful place by her side. But he feared for her safety. And, more importantly, did she even still want him? What if she'd found someone else? Someone human? Someone who wouldn't cough and accidentally toss a fireball at her in the process?

Did she already forget about him? Did she still love him? And when exactly did he become so insecure?

He sat up. *This is ridiculous.* He would go to Garbhán Isle. He'd retrieve his woman. She belonged to him. He'd Claimed her and nothing would change that.

Besides, he couldn't take it anymore. Everything around his lair reminded him of Annwyl. He could almost smell her. Could almost feel her running up his dragon back, climbing atop his head, and bending her body over him so their eyes could meet.

"Did you miss me?"

"*Annwyl?*"

Fearghus, startled, jerked and Annwyl fell backward, tumbling down his back and tail. She hit the ground with an, "Oaf!"

He spun around and stared at her, unwilling to believe she was really in his lair. As she struggled to her feet, he shifted.

"Well that was quite the greeting . . . oh!"

He grabbed her and dropped both of them to the ground, his arms protecting her head and back. Once he had her on the ground, he kissed her. Her body's response immediate and as strong as always. Then he pinned her arms over her head, holding her body down with his. *"Where the hell have you been?"*

"Where have *I* been? *Where have* you *been?*"

"Here! Waiting for you!"

She tried to yank her arms from his grasp, but he held on tight. He would not let her get away now. "You left me, Fearghus. I woke up and you were gone. What was I supposed to think?"

"That I wanted to protect you."

"Yes. So your sister told me. But why didn't you tell me?"

"Would you have let me go?"

"Don't flatter yourself."

He stared at her . . . hard. She glared back.

"If that's how you feel, then why are you here now, Annwyl?"

"Your mother came for me," she bit out between clenched teeth.

Fearghus stopped. "What?"

"I said that your mother came for me. Told me it was time to take my place beside you."

His mother ordered Annwyl back to him. That couldn't be good. Fearghus was afraid to ask but he had to know. "What did you say to her, Annwyl?"

"I told her to mind her own business."

"Gods, woman!" Fearghus released her so he could use his hands to cover his eyes in exasperation as he sat back on his heels. "Are you mad?"

Annwyl pulled herself out from under him. "Why does everyone keep asking me that?"

"What else?" He looked at her. "What else did you say to her?"

She shrugged. "Let's see . . . well, I asked her how Bercelak's tail was doing?"

Fearghus buried his head in his hands again. "Are you that sure she won't kill you?"

"Oh, no. Not at all. Figured she'd kill me right on the spot." She stated it so nonchalantly he knew she was being completely honest with him.

"And yet you . . ."

"Don't like to be ordered around, Fearghus. You should know that."

"Well, she clearly didn't kill you. So what did she say?"

Again the shrug. "She gave me the loyalty of all dragons." Fearghus stared at Annwyl. Not sure he heard her correctly. His mother handed to a human the loyalty of all dragons? Was he on another plain of existence? Had the gods decided to play tricks on his mind? *What in hell* . . . "Then she said she had to go, and I asked her if she was going back to her chain."

His mother's gift completely forgotten, he tried to look stern, but kept laughing instead. "Tell me you're lying. Please."

Annwyl grinned at him. "Wish I could. But it just flew out of my mouth."

Fearghus grinned back. How could he not? He loved the most difficult woman he'd ever met, and he couldn't imagine his life without her. He eyed her slowly. A bit leaner and a little darker, he guessed from the time she spent in battle and under the two suns. She still had a thin scar across her cheek from her brother's gauntleted hand. And his brands stood out clear and triumphant on her forearms. Ah, Annwyl. Still beautiful. And still his.

"That's a very subtle tunic you're wearing, my love."

Annwyl glanced down at the sleeveless chain-mail shirt she wore. "I had these specially made. I like my arms to be free and comfortable. Easier to take heads."

Fearghus nodded. "Did you miss me?"

Annwyl leaned back, the palms of her hands lying flat against the cave floor. Her body stretched tight. Taunting him.

Tempting him. After all this time he still wanted her so badly he could barely breathe. "Not really."

He tilted his head to the side. "Tell me you missed me, Annwyl."

Annwyl's eyes locked with his own. "No."

He raised an eyebrow. "Tell me now, woman."

She stared at his mouth. "Make me."

"A challenge, *Queen* Annwyl?"

"Not a challenge you'd ever be able to live up to, *Prince* Dragon."

With a snarl he knew only Annwyl would find playful, he seized her ankle and snatched her body to him, dragging her across the cave floor.

"Oi!"

He pulled off her weapons, yanked off her chain-mail shirt, and dragged her leggings from her body, pausing only briefly to lick the brands on the inside of her thighs.

Annwyl pushed at his chest. "You know, I should really beat the living—" He didn't let her finish. Instead he pushed her down and stretched himself across her, covering her mouth in a brutal kiss. She shoved at his shoulders while her legs wrapped around his waist. Still his Annwyl, always fighting to the bitter end while milking him dry. He grabbed her wrists and again pinned her arms above her head. She growled in response as she sucked his tongue deep into her mouth. He settled between her thighs and buried himself inside of her. Slick and ready, her body shook beneath his with barely contained lust. Her moans and cries desperate against his lips. Her hips arched against him and he thrust hard into her in response.

She'd been gone too long from him. Too many nights spent alone, wondering if she were safe. If she were happy. If she missed him. Too much time apart for both of them, and he would never let it happen again.

So he Claimed her. Again. And he made sure she knew it.

* * *

Annwyl wrapped her legs around his waist and wondered how she'd managed so long without having him inside her. Filling her completely, making her think of nothing but him. Wanting nothing but him. A brutal coupling, but one she understood. He was Claiming her. Again. And she wouldn't have it any other way. She needed it as much as he did. To know she belonged to him. And that he belonged to her.

She struggled to loose her arms from his steel grip, knowing that he'd never let go. She wanted to touch him. To feel his skin beneath her fingers. But she loved the fight just as much. He'd never give her an inch. Never let her get away with anything. She would always be his challenge and he would always face it with his usual unquenched vigor.

Annwyl strained against him. Each hard thrust bringing her closer to climax. He kissed her face. Her jaw. Her neck. But when his teeth sank into the flesh below her collarbone, she went over the edge. She screamed in release. A war cry. But he continued ahead. Never stopping until, several minutes later, he tore another scream from her. And that time he came with her. His roar almost drowning out hers.

Fearghus released her arms, laying his head against her chest. She managed a tired smile as she wrapped herself around him. "All right. So I missed you a bit," she finally admitted.

He laughed and she closed her eyes, the feeling of that deep voice sliding through her. She was safe. At home.

"No, no, Annwyl. Please stop. You're drowning me with all your emotion." He chuckled as his hands gently caressed her sweat-covered body. "And just so you know. I missed you too."

"Then why did you not come for me?"

* * *

Fearghus heard the pain in her voice and he hated himself for causing it. "Because I'm an idiot, Annwyl. That's why."

"So long as we understand each other."

He smiled. "We do."

"Well . . . good." He hugged her tight and licked the side of her breast. She gave a soft moan and Fearghus knew that he never wanted to be without that sound ever again.

"And why exactly did your mother come for me, Fearghus?"

"Guess I had her a bit worried."

"Oh? And how did you do that?"

He shrugged. "Well, you know . . ."

"You scared the hell out of everyone, didn't you?"

"Just a bit."

Annwyl gripped him tighter. "Foolish higher beings."

He looked into the face of his mate, stared into those beautiful green eyes. "You should be scared. I'm a dragon, Annwyl. A born hunter and killer. The most ancient of destroyers."

Annwyl burst out laughing. "You are so cute when you try to look scary." She tweaked his nose with her thumb and forefinger.

"What the hell am I going to do with you, wench?"

She ran her hand along his jaw. "Rule with me, Fearghus."

"What?"

"Rule with me."

"You want me to come with you to Garbhán Isle?" And of course he would. He would give up everything to be with her. He had no intention of ever letting her go again. He just wanted to hear her say it.

Annwyl looked off toward the lake. He could see it on her face. She already had a plan; she just needed to figure out how to get him to agree to it. "That's one option."

"And another option is . . ."

"We rule Dark Plains from here."

"No."

"Why? It's perfect."

"Annwyl, I don't think the nobles would feel comfortable being here." And he didn't want them anywhere near his lair.

But Annwyl sneered in disgust. "I don't want those people here!" she barked at him, clearly annoyed he'd even suggest it. "With us! And don't you dare offer!"

"Then what are you saying?"

"Garbhán Isle is not my home, Fearghus. This is. You are."

He thought of the part of his lair he'd made into their home. He'd equipped it with everything he thought a human might need or want and then added the biggest bookshelf and bed he could find. At the time he kept wondering why he would even try. He always thought a queen must have her court with her. But then, Annwyl would never be an ordinary queen.

"I'm guessing, woman, you already have this planned."

Her eyes sparkled with excitement as she sat up, pulling away from him. "I've got it all worked out. The troops can set perimeters outside the glen. That way we'll be protected. And, of course, I'll only use my best and closest men. Morfyd and Brastias can take care of the day-to-day issues at Garbhán Isle. It's all dead boring, anyway. It's all about lumber and grain and . . . yuck! I can't even make myself care." He shook his head and grinned as she continued, "Your family and the other dragons will feel safer here, if they dare visit. And if there is any strike against our throne, Morfyd will be able to let us know. And now that your mother is on our side we can strike down anyone that gets in our way. Crush them like ants!"

She finished the last part off as if she just told him about a beautiful dress she made or new horses she bought. *Not* that she was, actually, discussing an alliance not seen in Dark Plains for more than a thousand years between men and dragons. An alliance she clearly planned to use.

He stared at her, not sure what he should say.

"Come on, Fearghus. You can't tell me that's not bloody brilliant."

He laughed. "Yes, Annwyl. It's *bloody* brilliant." Fearghus leaned in and nuzzled her neck, his fingers brushing her hard nipples.

She giggled as she pushed his face away. "That's not an answer, Dragon!"

"Oh, you actually want an answer. I thought you already had your mind made up."

She shrugged, a less-than-innocent smile on her lips. "I do. I was just being polite."

He stared at her, then shook his head. "No."

"What do you mean, no?"

He stretched out next to her. His hands behind his head. "I mean no. I don't think so."

Annwyl pushed him. "Why not?"

Now he shrugged. "Just don't feel like it."

Annwyl crossed her arms in front of that gorgeous chest he'd never stopped thinking about, "Really?"

"Annwyl, I've been alone for well over a hundred years. I'm used to being on my own. I think it will take some . . . *convincing* on your part."

"Convincing?" She raised an eyebrow. "How much convincing?"

"Well, I am a stubborn dragon. Very stubborn. We're looking at hours, if not days of convincing . . . or years." He looked into her green eyes. "Perhaps a lifetime."

Annwyl stretched out across his chest, her head propped up on one arm. "I guess I best get started then."

"I guess you better, wench."

Annwyl kissed him then. And Fearghus never let her go.

CHAINS
&
FLAMES

Chapter 1

"You demanded my presence, Queen Addiena?"

The queen didn't even look up from her book. "Is it so hard for you to call me Mother?"

Actually . . . yes it was. "You demanded my presence, *Mother?*"

Sighing, the queen laid down her book and looked at her oldest daughter. "How I do love that sneer."

Rhiannon, First Born of the Dragon Queen, First Born Daughter, White Dragonwitch, and heir to the queen's throne, sat back on her haunches. She brushed her long white hair out of her eyes and stared at her red-haired and red-scaled mother. "Can we just get this over with? I have things to do."

"Really? Like what?"

Damn. She really didn't have anything to do; she just didn't want to be here. Rhiannon and her mother had never gotten along. Never learned to tolerate each other. There was even a story passed among the queen's court that when freshly hatched, Rhiannon bit her mother on the neck when she tried to cuddle her new daughter. But Rhiannon didn't believe that for one second. True, she believed she bit her mother, but she didn't believe her mother had tried to cuddle her.

"What I have to do is my own concern. Can we just speed this along?"

"Fine." Her mother moved forward a bit and Rhiannon's entire body tensed at her approach, especially as she watched the queen's guard follow. "I've made a decision."

Rhiannon's eyes narrowed. "About?"

"You. It's time for you to be mated. To be Claimed. And I've chosen your mate. One of my finest warriors. Bercelak the Great."

Snorting a laugh, Rhiannon stared at her mother. "Bercelak the Great? Don't you mean Bercelak the Vengeful? And that low-born lizard is your choice of mate for me?" She laughed louder, harder. "You have gone mad!"

Her mother's blue eyes glittered dangerously in the low-lit chamber. "He's the one I've chosen. He's the one who shall Claim you."

Rhiannon's laughter died in the face of her mother's cold expression. "What? Why?"

When the red dragon only stared at her, Rhiannon exploded. "*You callous, deceitful bitch!*"

Her mind screamed when she thought of Bercelak the Great. A Battle Lord of her mother's court, everyone knew Bercelak as dangerous, mean, and generally unpleasant. In all the years she'd known him, she'd never seen him smile to anyone . . . except her. And it was only once. Constantly he watched her, ignoring the rules of rank, until finally she told him in all honesty to stop staring at her like a horse cooking on a spit or she'd rip the horns from his head. He'd only smiled at her. For the first and only time, he'd smiled. When she'd threatened him. She did not take that as a good sign.

At the time, she'd feared she'd have to protect herself from a forced Claiming. They were rare, but they happened. Then the Dragon Wars began. A battle of dragon against dragon in pursuit of power. As her mother's champion, Bercelak led that war and she hadn't seen him since.

But the wars were over, her mother's reign secure. And apparently, as reward for his loyal service, her mother planned to hand Bercelak *her*.

"I've made up my mind. We'll have a ceremony at the next moon to celebrate your union. You will attend. You will look beautiful. And you will let him have you."

"I know why you're doing this. I know what you're up to." She hated the desperation in her voice. She hated her mother.

When the queen only stared at her, Rhiannon continued. "You fear I'll take your throne before you're ready to give it up. You're afraid if I mate with someone not loyal to you, I can have it all . . . and you'll have nothing. So you hand me over to that piece of trash!"

"Why, Rhiannon. That's a horrible thing for you to believe about your loving mother."

She said it so flippantly that Rhiannon knew she'd been right. Her mother feared her. Feared the loyalty she'd built up among the other dragons and in court. She feared her Magick skills, still weak, but growing excessively—and surprisingly—strong.

Her mother feared *her*. And for that the bitch was willing to hand Rhiannon off like a human slave.

Rage blinding her, Rhiannon lashed out at her mother with one of her claws, but her damn guards, who protected the queen's life as if it were their very own, were there before her forearm barely left her side. They shoved her back. Her! A *princess!*

"You'll not do this to me, you old whore!" she screamed, unable to control herself any longer. The hurt and pain eating away at her like a parasite. "I'll take your throne . . . I'll take your power and your treasure! And I'll leave you to rot!"

Cold, crystal blue eyes stared at her and she knew she'd never find mercy there. Never. "You'll regret this, little bitch."

"Go to hell."

Rhiannon took several steps back until she stood a good distance from her mother and those insane guards of hers. Then she turned and stormed off.

She'd regret nothing. But she would make sure her mother regretted everything.

* * *

Bercelak the Great, Dragonwarrior of the Dragon Queen Throne, Ninth Born Son of Ailean the Slag, Ruling Commander of the Dragon Queen's Armies, and on and on and on, marched through the place he'd grown up in. Unlike most dragons, his first home had not been a cave . . . but a castle.

He stalked through the halls, nodding in greeting to his many siblings as he passed. Including himself, there were fifteen of them. Some mated. Some not. Some already with their own off-spring. Before entering his father's home, he had to shift to human and put on human garb. His father, Ailean, insisted on it. For reasons unknown to any of them, their father loved being human. Not for part of the time, like some of his kin and, at times, even himself. But all the time. He only turned back to dragon to fight or to fly somewhere quickly.

To this day, Bercelak had no idea how his mother, a beau-tiful dragoness of royal blood tolerated the old bastard. He was loud, rude, and crude. Growing up with him had been a horror to every male offspring he had. The females fared much better, but as they came into full age, they found that having a slag as a father worked against them when time to mate came along. Everywhere they went, their father's repu-tation preceded them.

Now Bercelak had to face the old bastard and he didn't know why. Ailean had demanded his presence, sending four of Bercelak's brothers to bring him back. Not wanting to kill his own kin, Bercelak had finally agreed to return to the castle. But he wanted this over with so he could go home. Now that the wars were over he had plans to make and his father was delaying him.

He stormed into his father's study, then winced and turned away. "Think you could get off my mother long enough to tell me why you demanded my presence?"

"When did you get so shy, boy?" Bercelak heard his mother slap his father, which she seemed to do often, then he could hear her getting off the desk Ailean had tossed her up on and pulling her clothes back on. For Ailean, his mother stayed human. Bercelak just didn't know why.

"Put your clothes on!" he heard his mother hiss and he shook his head. The bastard lived to embarrass him. He did a good job of it, too.

His mother's hand rested on his shoulder. "My son."

He turned and looked down into her beautiful face. "Mother." He kissed her on the cheek. "I'm glad to see you."

A corner of her mouth quirked up. "Really? I have to admit that with all of my hatchlings, it's hardest to tell with you."

"Boy." His father, who finally pulled on his leggings, leaned against the desk. Why the old bastard insisted on calling him that, Bercelak would never know. He wasn't human and he was no "boy." But still, his father called him, more than any of his brothers, "boy." Most likely because he knew how much it irritated the living hell out of him.

"Father. You sent for me."

"Aye. Word came from the queen today."

His mother stiffened beside him. She always did that whenever a mention of the queen came up.

"About?"

"Princess Rhiannon."

His heart stopped in his chest. "What about her?" Although he was afraid to ask. The acrimonious relationship between mother and daughter had almost taken on legendary proportions. And Rhiannon was barely a hundred and twenty-five winters. Gods, could the queen have finally done something to her?

"You are to have her."

Bercelak frowned, which seemed amazing even to him since he frowned most of the time. But this made him frown more.

"What does that mean?" his mother asked before he had a chance. "He is to have her?"

"It means that the queen wants you to mate with her daughter."

"*Over my dead—*"

"Shalin," Ailean cut her off. "This isn't your decision. It's the boy's."

"Yes, but—"

"I know how you feel about Addiena, Shalin. But, again, this is Bercelak's decision. Not yours. Not mine. Nor the queen's." Silver eyes focused on him. "If you don't want her, tell me now and I'll fight the queen on this. I haven't seen her in centuries, but I'm sure I can still be quite"—his father grinned—"persuasive."

Shalin snorted and turned away, but his father continued, "But I wanted to give the option to you. What is your decision?"

He had no decision to make. He'd made it long ago the day he saw the white dragoness. He was barely fifty winters and she was already fifty-two. An *older* dragon. He'd never been to court before and he'd accompanied his mother this time. He made his first misstep as soon as he entered the Queen's Hall. He stomped on the snowy white tail of a princess. Her rage was instantaneous and without waiting for an apology, she sent the tip of that tail directly for his eye.

What few knew, but eventually learned, was that all of Ailean's children were raised . . . well . . . *differently* than other hatchlings. Bercelak couldn't remember a day when his father didn't come jumping out of somewhere dark, grab his tail and toss him across the room. Not to be abusive—although it was—but because he wanted his offspring's reflexes to be better than anyone else's. And, to Bercelak's annoyance, it worked. While other dragon warriors were caught off guard or had run from fear during battles, Bercelak never flinched, never feared, and he definitely never ran. Not ever. Instead, he destroyed any and all in his way until they finally gave him the title of Queen's Battle Lord. The highest rank a low-born warrior dragon, such as himself, could hope to obtain.

So, on that day, when he saw that razor-sharp tail point coming for his face, he reacted as he would with any of his kin; he grabbed hold of that tail and swung, flinging the princess and heir to the queen's throne across the Queen's Hall and right past her mother.

As the queen's guard took firm hold of him, he thought for sure he'd die that day. But the Queen . . . she had other plans. And, to be honest, didn't seem to care how he'd treated her daughter.

But he did care. After that, he tried everything to get Rhiannon to forgive him. To get close to her. But when she saw him, she rolled her eyes and went the other way. If he tried to speak to her, she yawned in his face and left him standing there.

Eventually, he left her alone. But he never gave up wanting her. And that hadn't changed. That would never change.

"I'll take her."

His mother gripped his arm. "Bercelak—"

"It's all right, Mother. I know what I'm doing." He looked at his father. "I'll take her."

Ailean grinned. One of those big, toothy grins that annoyed Bercelak to no end. "Somehow I thought that's what you'd say. She'll be waiting for you at your den."

Bercelak and Shalin passed glances. He'd thought for sure he'd have to go get her himself. This was Princess Rhiannon after all. And she never let anyone forget it.

Bercelak tilted his head to the side. "She will?"

Rhiannon took to the air as soon as she walked out of Devenallt Mountain. She flew and flew, determined to make it back to her own den before nightfall. She had much planning to do since she knew her mother would probably plan a counterattack of some kind immediately. But her den was a stronghold. With the help of wizards loyal to her, she'd put up so many Magickal and physical defenses around her cave home, there was no way her mother would ever be able to break through.

She flew past forests and towns. Castles and farms. Few saw her. The ones who did screamed in terror and ran away. Gods, she must be angry. She didn't even go down and snatch a quick meal from one of the villages or simply revel in their screams.

She headed to open sea, moving quickly since the wind was with her. She neared a large mountain when she felt it. A small tickle in her stomach. She knew it was her mother and immediately chanted a spell to raise stronger barriers around her body. But before she could get them in place, the power of the gods passed through her like a flash of lightning . . . and then she was falling.

Desperate, she tried flapping her wings, but nothing. Then she looked down at herself . . . and she screamed in horror.

Human. Her mother had shifted her to human. And she was unable to shift back!

Seconds before she hit the ground, she had one last thought. . . .

Oh, shit.

Bercelak stared at the naked female crumpled in front of his den. White hair, matted with blood and dirt, covered her except for the small odd brand on her bare shoulder.

Leaning in, he sniffed her. No . . . she wasn't born a human. She was in fact a dragon in human form.

Well . . . there goes dinner.

He pushed her with his snout, forcing her onto her back. When he saw her face, his heart stuttered in his chest for a second time this day.

Rhiannon. Princess Rhiannon. *His* Rhiannon.

He looked her over. She was bloody and broken. He looked up at the sky and realized that's where she'd dropped from. No wonder the queen said Rhiannon would be waiting for him at his den. This was where she'd dumped her daughter.

This can't be good.

But it didn't matter. He finally had her. He had his Rhiannon. And he planned to keep her . . . forever.

Screaming. *Why is there all that screaming?*

Rhiannon moved and the screaming became decidedly worse, but she also realized the screaming was in her head.

She put her claws to her forehead, hoping to push back the pain . . . except something didn't feel right. Her head felt different. So did her claws.

By sheer will, she opened her eyes and stared at her talons. Except they weren't her mighty white talons she proudly kept sharpened. They were—she frowned in confusion— they were nails. Human ones. So was the claw those tiny useless nails were attached to. Not her mighty claw, but the claw of a human. A . . . a *hand*.

She looked down at herself and realized she hadn't been dreaming. Human. Her mother had turned her human. She'd shifted to human many times, but only to fool the humans around her . . . well, and to see if her human form was remotely attractive. Otherwise, she lived her life as a dragon and never understood those who didn't. Why anyone would want to be human was beyond her understanding. . . . And damn it all, she was *brilliant!*

Knowing she needed to calm down, Rhiannon took a deep breath and slowly released it. Once she'd cleared her mind and the screaming in her head lessened, she said the chant that would shift her back. Bright colors of Magick sparked off her human body . . . then nothing. Absolutely nothing.

"She took your powers."

Rhiannon turned her head and looked over at the black dragon watching her.

"Bercelak," she sneered. Of course, where else would her mother make sure she dropped but at the feet of the one dragon Rhiannon never wanted to see?

I hate that bitch.

"Rhiannon."

Growling, she forced her human body to sit up. "You will . . . Low Born . . . call me by my title. I'm Princess Rhiannon to you."

He stared at her for a moment with his typical frown—did he have any other expression?—then he snorted. "Princess you may be. But at the moment you are one without powers or claws." He stood up and took several steps toward her. "You are human. No wings. No way to escape me. It was a good thing I recognized you or I might have had a lovely meal of you with some parsley. And potatoes."

Two more steps brought him closer, and Rhiannon ignored the pain in her head and backed up.

"All that soft skin and those breakable bones," he fairly crooned. "We can't let you out in this cruel world so defenseless, Princess. You'll need me to care for you. To protect you. Just as I had to do today. If it hadn't been for the skills my mother gave me and what I learned on the field of battle, I may not have been able to heal you."

"I need nothing from you, Bercelak, son of a slag."

He stopped moving, his cold black eyes locking on her face. "Since I know for a fact your own mother took a turn on my father's cock, excuse me if I'm not truly insulted." One eyebrow raised. "We aren't kin, are we?"

"You . . ." Stunned that anyone dare speak to her in such a manner, Rhiannon forced herself to her feet. The screaming in her head became decidedly worse, but she didn't care. She wouldn't let the arrogant bastard treat her like this. No one . . . absolutely *no one* treated her like this.

"Listen to me well, Low Born, don't think for a second I won't cut your heart from your worthless hide and wear it on my head . . . like a hat."

Bercelak spit out a spell. Flame burst around the dragon and faded, leaving only his human form. And, oh . . . by the dark gods of fire . . . what a human form. Coal black hair reached down his back, sweeping around his narrow hips. Because he was a battle-dragon, his hair was shorter than the royalty he protected. He also had scars. Lots and lots of scars, some in the most interesting of places. One brutal scar was right by his eye. Oh, and his eyes . . . black like his hair. Dark and fathomless, glaring at her from under black brows. But his body . . . she never thought of human bodies as all that pleasing. Especially the male ones. Until now. All those muscles and those big strong shoulders. Everything about him was perfect. His face, his body. His scars.

She stared at him as he marched over to her, forcing her to back up against the cave wall. She winced, the rocks pricking the soft human skin she'd begun to detest. She felt weak, defenseless.

How do you humans live like this?

"Tell me, Princess, do you really think someone is coming here to rescue you from me? I am all you have. Even your mother has deserted you."

"She deserted me a long time ago."

It seemed like his naturally hard expression softened a bit at that. "I know she did. It hurt you."

She gave a short, cruel laugh. "Nothing hurts me, Low Born. Absolutely nothing."

"How is that possible?" And for some reason he sounded as if he truly cared about her answer.

"When you stop feeling anything, you find it quite possible."

One big hand cupped her cheek. "I have no desire to hurt you, Princess. But I do want you to feel. I want you to feel everything when you're with me."

Rolling her eyes, "Oh, please, Low Born. Don't try seducing me." Planting two hands against his chest, she shoved him back and moved away from the wall. "I'm not a child. I've been seduced by the best." She looked him up and down. "Those of *royal* blood. And it pains me to tell you that you are sorely lacking."

He leaned back against the spot she'd just vacated, his arms crossed over that gorgeous chest. "Does my lack of royal blood truly bother you?"

"No. It insults me," she answered honestly. "Are you the best my mother could come up with? I'm not some table scrap to be tossed off to her favorite battle dog. I am of royal blood. The daughter of a king. To be quite honest, I deserve better than *you*. Now, Low Born, you'll escort me to the closest exit."

He moved so fast, she didn't have a chance to jump, much less run. His hands slipped around her neck, holding her in place. She thought he'd try to choke the life from her—unfortunately, it wouldn't be the first time that had happened to her. Instead, he towered over her, staring down into her face. His black eyes locked with hers.

"When I'm done," his low voice said softly while his face still looked so intensely . . . cranky, "you won't be able to imagine your life without me. You'll pine for me, wanting me like you've never wanted anything before in your life. You'll miss me when I'm gone and desire me when I'm right beside you. No other male will ever be good enough. No other male worthy of taking this body and bringing it and you pleasure you've only dreamed of. And when you're coming and screaming my name, begging me to keep you as my own, I'll Claim you. And your heart and soul will belong only to me. But until that time, Princess, you're not going anywhere."

Then he released her and walked away.

She waited until he was far enough away so he couldn't hit her and said, "Oh, yes? You and what army?"

He stopped walking, looking over his shoulder at her. Unable to meet his gaze, she rubbed her eyes with one hand and sighed. "Well that came out terribly wrong."

Chapter 2

Bercelak dropped the cow carcass on the ground and stared at it thoughtfully. Now, if Rhiannon were dragon, he'd merely sear it and they'd feed. But with her being human, at the moment he'd have to adjust. At least until she got her powers back.

So, using his talons carefully, he removed the animal's hide, tossing it aside. Then he put the animal on a spit over the pit fire. He chose some of his best and most precious herbs—obtained from the Desert Lands of Alsandair—and seasoned the cooking meat.

With a sigh, he sat back to watch the flames and think.

Princess Rhiannon was definitely as mean as he remembered, and it only made him want her more. Not surprising. Dragon males liked their females dangerous. It made the mating that much more interesting and intense. Of course, her calling him "low born" was beginning to grate on his nerves.

No one had to remind him of his father.

The other dragon warriors he fought with never understood why Bercelak didn't flinch during battle. Never showed any signs of fear or panic. If they lived the way he had, they wouldn't either. But until you were awoken in the middle of the night with, "*We're under attack!*" and thrown out of bed by your well-meaning but clearly insane father, you didn't know what fear was.

His mother was of royal birth. His father . . . not so much. Which meant no one handed Bercelak a damn thing. He worked for everything he had and he did it with one thing in mind. Crystal blue eyes, long white hair, and a snarl that could scare an army of demons.

The day he met her—when those gorgeous blue eyes locked on him with such hate—he knew he had to have her.

"I want his head!" she'd screeched. And for a minute, he thought she'd get it.

But then he heard, "Oh, leave him be. As usual, my daughter is overreacting."

A red dragon, big and beautiful, walked toward him. "He didn't mean it, Rhiannon."

His mother bowed but he continued to stare at the queen. And he knew it was the queen. Just the way she moved and held herself told him that. He'd been in awe.

She'd motioned for her guards to release him and smiled, showing her fangs. "Shalin's son."

Now free, he immediately bowed. "Yes, my Queen. Bercelak the Black, Son of Ailean."

"Yes. You look very much like him. So handsome." A red claw with pitch-black talons reached out and caressed his jaw. He felt his mother stiffen beside him and knew this was for her benefit more than his. For years Bercelak had heard how the queen had taken one turn in his father's bed and had never forgotten him. Nor had she forgiven him. For the very next morning he'd left the then-future queen to meet with Bercelak's mother and the queen's one-time friend, Shalin. Who, if the story was to be believed, threw an ax at his father's head when Ailean found her.

Up to that day, Bercelak never believed any of the stories. His low-born father with a dragon princess? Not bloody likely, he used to think. Still . . . one look at the female before him and he wondered if perhaps all the stories were true. For she looked at him with something he could not name. Perhaps something he did not want to name. At fifty winters, he was much too young for such deep thoughts. . . .

"Tell me, Son of Ailean, what is your life's dream? Wizard? Warrior? Sword maker? What is it you think of when you lie awake at night?"

He answered honestly, unable to lie to those dark blue eyes. "Of glory and wealth. Of power."

"I see. So you may look like your father, but his aspirations had never been as lofty." She glanced at his mother, but he didn't realize until years later what that look meant. Then she turned and walked off.

"You shall stay here, Son of Ailean," the queen casually tossed over her shoulder. "You shall train to be one of my battle-dragons. You will protect this throne and me and anyone else I deem worthy."

Then she was gone. Up the stairs to her private chambers.

Her daughter stomped her foot and glared at him, before marching off in quite a rage.

Once activity began again in the court, he heard his mother mutter under her breath, "I hate that bitch with every fiber of my being."

Still . . . his mother left him there when she returned home. She had no choice. After that, the queen's daughter treated him like so much trash caught between her talons. And the more she did, the more he knew he'd do anything to win her. The meaner she was, the more deadly he became. Soon, with the moniker of Bercelak the Vengeful firmly in place, he'd led the troops into the war against the lightning dragons . . . the barbarians. Barbarians they may have been, but worthy opponents. The war lasted decades, but when the smoke cleared, Queen Addiena's throne stood secure and she graced him with the new title of Bercelak the Great. Fair enough. He'd earned it and had the scars to prove it.

Now he wore the elaborate armor of Battle Lord, Dragonwarrior Leader, and Queen's Champion. He had the attention of every female from the lowest born to some of the most important royalty. And although he found pleasure among those scales, he knew there was only one whom he wanted for life.

"I must feed. I'm starving."

Pulled from his reverie, he looked at the princess and frowned.

"You put on clothes." She wore a bright blue robe she must have taken from his treasures. It covered her from shoulders to feet. Although the color of her robe brought out her eyes, he liked seeing her naked. Then again . . . hiding those delicious full breasts and gorgeous ass from his view was probably for the best. At least for now.

"This skin is so fragile. . . ." She shook her head. "I don't know how they tolerate it. Being so defenseless. At least forest animals have fangs or claws or, at the very least, good instincts. Humans have none of these things."

He shrugged. "A few do. They vary."

"You like them?" She didn't sound haughty, merely curious.

"Not really. I find them treacherous and painfully annoying. Although made with the right seasoning, they are *very* tasty."

She nodded in agreement. "This is true."

Of course, he'd only been joking.

With a quick shake of his head, he said, "Why, Princess, did you just agree with me?"

Startled, she blinked. "Uh . . . no. No, of course not." She turned away from him, walking over to a boulder. She sat on it and looked at him, her head held high. "I'm hungry. I await food."

He had to give it to her. She certainly didn't let a change in her current circumstances faze her for long. "Then you best get that rump in gear. The potatoes and vegetables are over there. There's a pot to cook them in and fresh water. Good luck."

Her mouth dropped open. "You . . . you expect me to cook food?"

"I did the hard part. I went down to the farm, scared the little farmer, and took his cow. Then I removed its hide, the cow's not the farmer's, placed it on the spit, and now watch it while it cooks. The least you can do is cook some vegetables. We'll eat like humans. With plates and utensils . . . and a table."

"But I don't know how to cook."

"Then you best learn, Princess. I'd hate for you to starve."

She *despised* him. Rude, arrogant, low-born dragon!

Was this to be her life from now on? Trapped in this human body, forced to cook food for an angry-looking peasant?

Couldn't her mother have just killed her instead? Wouldn't it have been kinder?

"I don't see that beautiful ass moving, Princess."

She glared at him, about to tell him to go to hell, when her stomach rumbled. By the gods! What was *that* sound? Was she dying?

She looked down at her stomach, her hands clasped over it, and for the first time ever, she heard Bercelak laugh. Even more shocking . . . she kind of liked the sound of it.

"You are merely hungry, Rhiannon," he said kindly. "Do as I ask and we'll eat soon enough. I promise."

Groaning in annoyance, she slid off the boulder and walked over to the pit fire. As he said, he had potatoes and some other vegetables out beside a large pot filled with water. Another bowl of water beside it. Crouching down, she studied the food in front of her. In fact, she studied the food for about five minutes, until she heard the low born lean his long body over and, his snout right behind her, say, "What, exactly, are you doing?"

She ignored that shudder his low voice elicited in her body. Dammit, she *had* to ignore it! "Deciding my next plan of action."

"To cook potatoes, you need a plan of action?"

"Everything in life needs a plan of action, Low Born. I just don't randomly do things and hope everything turns out all right."

"But where's the excitement in that? The fun?"

"Fun?" She looked at him over her shoulder. "When do *you* ever have fun?"

"I have fun," he snapped. "In fact, I'm a very fun person."

"Really?" She turned and faced him. "And what do you do for fun?"

"Lots of things."

"Do most of those things involve killing something?"

"On occasion," he grumbled.

"Exactly."

"Well what do you do for fun?"

She shrugged. "I enjoy when the villagers near my den run for their lives." She grinned. "All that screaming."

He shook his head, the tip of his snout brushing against her human body. "I guess that's something."

The low born leaned back, returning to the carcass. She had to admit, at least to herself, it smelled delicious. And, dammit, so did he.

"I must say, Princess, I'm surprised you haven't been able to shift back yet."

She shrugged. "My skills have always been weaker than my mother's."

"That seems strange. White dragons are known for their powers."

"Well, apparently I'm the exception to the rule." She stared at the potato. Odd-looking vegetable. "My Magick has always been weaker and I'm much smaller than most dragons. One of the wizards who trained me called me the runt of the litter."

"That's a cruel thing to say. I can kill him for you, if you'd like."

Rhiannon barely bit back her smile of surprise. No one had ever offered to kill another for her—at least no one she ever believed. But she believed Bercelak. "No. No. That's not necessary. He merely spoke the truth."

"Well, there's truth and then there's just being a right bastard."

"You know, you're not . . ." She stopped herself abruptly, but the dragon's black eyes were on her in a second.

"I'm not what?"

"Well . . . you're not quite what I expected."

"And what did you expect?"

"To use your words . . . a right bastard, I guess." Definitely not one who would cook her a meal. And he hadn't yelled at her once. She really expected him to be much more . . . brutal. Brutal and deadly and he wouldn't be happy until she was crying . . . which she would never do.

"That I can be . . . during battle. I don't feel the need to be that way when I'm home."

Squeezing the potato to see if it was juicy like fruit, she muttered, "There are some who say you're cruel. Heartless. And not just to our enemies."

"And who says these things?"

"You want me to tell you so you can go and hunt them down? I have not forgotten that before you were Bercelak the Great you were Bercelak the Vengeful."

"Do you know how I got that name?"

"No." And she shouldn't care, but she was kind of curious.

"Because of Soaic."

Ahh, Soaic. She'd taken a turn with him once. It was all right, but nothing that she'd write down in a diary. Plus, he feared her. They all did. To be truthful, her reputation wasn't much better than Bercelak's, and she had yet to wake up with the dragon she'd gone to sleep with. They slipped out like they feared she'd wake and simply kill them for her amusement.

"Aye. Soaic." She shrugged. "He has had much to say about you."

Bercelak poured liquid over the cooking carcass. "That's what I thought. You know that scar Soaic has on his right hind-quarter? The one that even his scales can't hide?"

"Aye. He received that during the battle of—"

"He received it when I ripped him open from hip to claw."

"Why would you do that?" Not knowing what else to do with the stupid potato in her hand, Rhiannon dropped it into the water.

"Did you clean that first?"

Growling, she stood and turned to face him. "Did you tell me to clean it first?"

"You've truly never cooked for yourself before?"

"Not only am I a princess—so I don't have to—I'm a dragon. There's a universe of cattle at my disposal. Why would I waste time cooking *anything? Ever?*"

"Have you never spent any time around humans? At all?"

"Only when I talk to them before feeding. But I don't do that often. I find when they start sobbing it's harder to have a peaceful meal."

He chuckled at her words. Bercelak had never laughed at anything. At least that was the rumor in court. But she'd gotten him to laugh twice. *She* did. Rhiannon bit the inside of her mouth to stop from smiling with pride.

Bercelak shifted, grabbed a pair of black breeches, and pulled them on.

She frowned, confused at why he was putting on clothes.

He saw her expression and shrugged. "Trust me, Princess. This will be much easier if I'm dressed."

With a sniff of dismissal, she turned away from him. Closing her eyes, Rhiannon worked hard to ignore the beauty of the dragon. And all those battle scars did nothing but enhance it. She'd never reacted this way to any male, dragon or human. Perhaps it was this unruly human body she had to tolerate. She didn't know, but she did know she didn't like it.

"You never told me why you attacked Soaic."

"He spoke ill of my father." He reached around her and pulled the potato out of the boiling water, casually dropping it back on the pile. "I don't allow anyone to speak of my father that way."

"You allowed me." Rhiannon winced. "Well that came out horribly wrong." *What if the big bastard hadn't noticed*?

He gently tugged a strand of her hair. "True, but I had no intention of mating with Soaic."

She slowly turned to face him. Although he didn't touch her, he still stood as close as possible. She could smell him and he smelled quite nice. No perfume like some of the royals. Nor the smell of blood for those who took less care cleaning themselves.

"We, Low Born, are not mating."

"Yes we are."

"No. We're not."

"Why?" And he seemed truly perplexed. "Have you never been—"

"Before you even finish that statement . . . no. I'm not a virgin. Haven't been for quite some time. I leave virginal female royalty to the humans."

"So then I don't understand why you're so set against us being together. We're both attractive and of breeding age. Both extremely intelligent. And quite worthy of each other's company. So I'm not sure what the problem is."

Oh, well when he puts it like that. . . . "Did you think my mother's orders would send me willingly to you?"

He frowned in confusion. "What does your mother have to do with anything?"

"I'm only here because of her."

"True. But you'll stay, Princess, because of me."

She laughed. Dragons were naturally arrogant, but by the dark gods of fire this one made the rest of them look insecure and unsure of themselves.

"Will I now? And why would I do that?" She glanced around his sparse cave fit for a battle-dragon rarely home, but not a princess. "Your grand riches? Your royal standing? Really . . . what reason would I have to stay other than this human body cannot fly?"

She was pushing him. She knew she was and yet she couldn't stop herself. And when he didn't answer right away, she felt a vague sense of disappointment. She truly thought he'd be up to the challenge. Unlike others in her mother's court. Shame she was wrong.

"That's what I thought." She sniffed again and turned, walking off. He could fix his own damn potatoes.

But she never should have turned her back on him. His hand threaded through her hair and snatched her back to his side. She braced her hands against his big chest, but he pulled until she looked up at him.

It wasn't a vicious pull. Or even brutal. It was just . . . in control. And gods be damned . . . it felt so good.

"Don't walk away from me when we're talking." He said it calmly. No trace of anger or rage. Actually, she saw amusement and lust in those dark eyes. Even his frown had faded a bit. "If you're going to ask me a question, you have to give me time to answer."

"Let me go," she snapped.

"No. Not until we're done." His eyes roved over her face as he spoke, like he was drinking in her every detail. "Now, you asked me a question. You asked what I could give you to entice you to stay with me?"

He tugged the strands of hair he had a grip on and she desperately fought the urge to moan out loud.

"What I'll give you is someone worthy of you. Someone who can handle a dragoness such as yourself. I don't fear your rages. I don't fear your acid tongue. In fact, I like you mean. The meaner, the better."

She opened her mouth to say something, but another tug had her growling instead. "Except," he continued, "when we mate. Then you'll give yourself to me . . . completely. You'll let me do whatever I want to this body. Whether human or dragon . . . because we'll play with both, Princess. We'll play a lot." This time he grinned. A full grin showing beautiful white teeth and fangs as well as the handsomest human face she'd ever seen. Immediately her nipples hardened under the robe and a sudden, hot slickness slid down between her legs. "That's not to say you shouldn't put up a fight every once in a while. I don't mind a few battle scars coming from you. But in the end, so to speak, you'll submit to me. Willingly. Happily. And with a smile on this gorgeous face. And when you rule as queen, I'll be by your side. Your consort. Your battle-dragon. I'll protect your throne and you with a fierceness no one has ever known. You'll wear my mark boldly and with utter pride. Together, we'll breed sons and daughters who will make us proud and carry on our bloodline. We'll be a mating to be feared. To be spoken of in whispers. And when we go to meet our ancestors in the next world, we'll spend eternity together. Terrifying those who came before us."

His other hand came up, softly caressing her cheek then slipping down her jaw, her neck, until it slid under her robe and took firm but gentle hold of her breast. "That is what we'll do, Princess. And that is why you'll stay." She panted as his hand squeezed her breast, his fingers playing with her sensitive nipple.

"Because at the end of the day, you're going to love me. I promise you that."

His mouth hovered close to hers and she lifted her chin a bit, waiting for him to kiss her. His lips brushed over hers and then he said, "Now. Let me show you how to make boiled potatoes so we can eat."

He released her. Just like that. She stared at him in shock as he crouched down beside the boiling pot of water. "You see," he said calmly, "first you have to clean off the potato before you cut it up."

And for the first time in Princess Rhiannon's life she didn't know whether to kill or cry. At the moment, she was certain she might do both.

Chapter 3

With a happy sigh, Rhiannon pushed the empty plate away and leaned back against the boulder. "All right," she said while licking grease off each finger, "that was amazing."

Bercelak smiled again and she was amazed his face hadn't cracked. In more than seventy years, she'd never known the dragon to smile at anyone or anything. No matter what awards and treasure her mother bestowed on him or when others may have said something funny. "I'm glad you enjoyed it, Princess."

"What I don't quite understand is . . . well . . ."

"Yes?"

"How you know so much about humans? You can cook like

them. You know what they should eat. How they eat. What utensils to use." They'd forgone the table when Bercelak couldn't remember where he'd put it last.

Pouring more wine into her goblet, Bercelak confessed, "My father."

She gasped. "Good gods, your father's not a human?"

He shook his head. "Now that would be quite a trick . . . since humans and dragons can't breed. No, Princess, he's not human. He just prefers human company."

"He does? Why?"

With a shrug, "I don't know. He just does. He thinks they're interesting. And he loves the females."

Rhiannon shook her head and grinned. "Your father has quite a reputation."

"Aye. That he does. And he's damn proud of it. It'll be interesting when you two meet."

She looked up from her goblet of wine. "Meet? Why would we meet?"

"I have to introduce you to him before I Claim you. He's rather insistent on some of the Old Ways."

"I don't want to be Claimed by you, Low Born."

He growled. Low and deep from his chest. She ignored the odd little bumps that spread across her human skin, praying it wasn't some kind of strange human disease.

"Stop calling me that. I do have a name." For a brief moment, he sounded like a cranky hatchling, rather than a feared Battle Lord.

"Fine. I don't want to be Claimed by *you*, Bercelak. But it's not personal. I don't want to be Claimed by anyone. No one has Claim on me and no one ever will."

"But don't you want to Claim someone? Don't you want someone to breed with and to call your own?"

"No."

"Not at all?"

"No."

"I don't understand. There is so much passion burning inside you. So much desire. I see it in your eyes. You need to release it or you'll become . . ." He stopped speaking abruptly and looked down at his empty plate.

"Like my mother?" His eyes slowly rose up to look at her. "You fear I'll become like her? Trust me, Low Born, I'm making sure I never become like her."

"But you already are. As surely as you sit before me now as human. The more you harden your heart. The more you cut yourself off from everyone and everything. . . ."

"Dragons were meant to be alone."

"No. Dragons are social. We just don't need to spend endless amounts of time with each other like humans. But you . . . they say you go to your den and aren't seen for years at court or anywhere else. You don't see your kin. You've seen no one since the death of your father."

She winced at that. The one being she missed with all her heart was her father. He'd loved her. Cared for her. And protected her from her mother. But with him gone . . . she had no one. Her siblings were petty and only wanted the throne or what they could grab from the queen's treasure. The other royals were not to be trusted. And the unclaimed dragon males did truly fear her.

"You're young, Rhiannon. Much too young to cut yourself off from everyone and everything. What your mother did to you was cruel . . . but perhaps we should see the good in it. It forced you out of your den and into the world. The world you'll one day be queen of."

Finally, she looked Bercelak in the eye and said with all honesty, "Do you truly believe I'll live long enough to be queen?"

Bercelak leaned back against the boulder he sat next to and placed his arm on the knee of his raised leg.

"Why would you say that?"

"She wants me dead. She's always wanted me dead. Why do you think she sent me to you?"

Bercelak didn't know whether to be insulted by that last statement or merely horrified. "What the bloody hell does that mean?"

"Don't be a fool, Low Born! She's testing your loyalty. Once you Claim me, she'll expect you to either drag me back to her court in chains or to kill me."

"That's not true." He shook his head. He refused to believe that could possibly be true.

"What? You think she sent me here because she thought we'd fall in love? That we'd look in each other's eyes and have a beautiful and meaningful Claiming? Try again. I'm in her way. Since my birth, I've been in her way. When I was younger, I was just annoying. Now she despises me and wants me dead. And you . . ." She gave him almost a pitying look. "She thinks of you as her pet. A well-trained warhorse. Or some oversized battle dog. And she's dropped me right in front of that dog, completely defenseless, and left me. Hopefully, to die."

"And you actually believe I'd kill you on your mother's orders?"

"No." She looked weary. Exhausted. "But I wouldn't put it past you to try and break me."

"You're not a horse, Rhiannon."

"I know that."

"Then why would you even think that?"

She let out a long breath. "Your reputation precedes you, Bercelak."

His frown deepened. "Now what the hell does *that* mean?"

"Rumors of what you do to females once you have them here have circulated the court for years. I hear everything."

He raised an eyebrow, even more intrigued. "Oh? And what are those rumors?"

"Forget it. This conversation is getting uncomfortable."

"Forget nothing, Princess. Tell me what you've heard. And I'll tell you if they're true."

"Fine." She stared him straight in the eye and he adored how she didn't back down from a fight. "Banallan the Gold said you kept her chained here for days."

Bercelak grinned. He couldn't help himself. "I did."

Rhiannon's body flinched the smallest bit and her brows pulled down into a brutal frown.

"But she wasn't forced if that's what concerns you. If memory serves, she enjoyed every second of it . . . immensely."

Rolling her eyes, she snorted in disgust.

"What else, Princess? What else has you so concerned?"

"Derowen the Silver."

He really had to search his brain for that one. Derowen the Silver? Gods, it had been ages since he lay with a silver. "Oh. Do you mean old Gobrien's daughter?"

"Yes. *That* silver."

My, what was that tone in her voice? "Yes, I remember her. What about her?"

"One of my mother's guards said he could hear her screaming from nearly a quarter league away."

"Aye. She was a noisy one. Fun . . . but noisy."

"He said she sounded in pain."

"Well, there's pain . . . and then there's pain." He grinned at the expression on her face. "Anything else?"

"I heard what you did to the Argraff twins."

"Yes. But I only had one. My brother had the other. Don't ask me which. They both look exactly alike. Imagine coming from the same egg."

She looked at him in horror. "Dark gods! You're as bad as your father."

Bercelak laughed outright at that. He hadn't laughed so much in his entire life. Always so serious and intense, with much on his mind, this was the first time he ever felt he could relax. "Not in a million ages. There aren't enough dragons in the universe to compete with him. No, I'd be forced to involve humans, elves, and, rumor has it, centaurs."

"I'm done with this conversation." She stood up but he reached over and grabbed her wrist.

"Tell me, Princess, what truly bothers you?"

"Nothing. But if you think you'll chain me here and turn me into some broken dragon available at your beck and call, you're as insane as my mother. I bend for no male, Low Born."

"I have no desire to break you, Rhiannon. I like you mean." He growled that last part and her breathing sped up. As, it seemed, did her desire to get away from him. She tried to yank her arm from his grasp, but he didn't let her go.

Bercelak sat up until he rested on his knees in front of her. "Perhaps it's time to set up some rules."

"Rules?"

"Aye." He tugged her until she grudgingly knelt down in front of him. "So that you feel more comfortable."

She watched him with narrow eyes, but she did relax a tiny bit. "All right."

"If there's anything you don't want me to do when we're together . . . say no."

She stared at him for a long time, then shook her head. "That's it?"

"That's it."

"All I have to do is say no?"

"Aye. You say no . . . and I stop."

"That sounds very odd to me."

"Why?" He leaned over and gently kissed her neck.

"I . . . I don't know. It just does."

He kissed a spot under her ear. "Let me explain it to you this way—You say 'don't,' I will. If you say 'stop,' I won't. If you really want me to stop, you'll have to say 'no.'" While keeping a tight rein on her left wrist with one hand, he used the other to wrap around her waist and pull her closer to him. "You can beg me, Rhiannon. Beg and plead for me to stop, and I won't. Because between us, there will be only one word that will stop me. And it's 'no.' Now do you understand?"

Her body melted against his, her head tipping so he had better access to her neck. "Aye. I understand."

"Good." He slapped her ass. "Now you should go to bed."

It took her a moment, but suddenly she pulled away from him. "What?"

"To bed, love. You look exhausted. I've fixed a place for you down the cavern and to the left. It has a bed and everything. Until you can shift back to dragon, no floors for you."

As hard as it was, he pushed her away and stood up, dragging her with him. "Besides, tomorrow we travel into Kerezik."

A bit dazed, she pulled herself up. "Why?"

He didn't want to answer that, at least not honestly, so he dragged his hand along her cheek. "Are you all right? You look a bit . . . ow!"

She punched him. Right in the face. And the female had a right hook that could destroy the jaw of a strong human male.

"*What the hell was that for?*"

"You play games with the wrong female, Low Born," she snarled. She walked away from him, her robes swirling around her. "Do you think I'm like one of those stupid whores you had here before? Do you think you can toy with me?"

Rubbing his jaw, he looked at her. "I don't know what you're talking about."

"Liar. You know exactly what I'm talking about. You hope to leave me wet and wanting so that I'll come begging for your affections like some dog looking for food."

Damn. She was right on that. He was.

He stepped toward her. "Rhiannon . . ."

"No. Say nothing," she growled.

His eyes narrowed. Why was she so angry? Angrier than he'd expect since she figured him out quick enough.

Of course, it could be . . .

"Are you already wet for me, Rhiannon?"

She turned on him like a coiled snake. "*What*?"

"You heard me, Princess." He walked toward her and immediately she stumbled back away from him. "If I put my hand on your pussy right this second, will it be dry like the deserts of Alsandair or wet and desperate like the Kennis River?"

She slammed into the far wall and immediately Bercelak placed his hands on either side of her head, caging her in. She looked caged in, too. Like a wild animal about to snap.

"Perhaps I should find out."

"Get away from me, Low Born!"

"Now, Rhiannon," he gently admonished as he used one hand to yank off the belt holding her robe together, "you know those aren't the right words."

She was gorgeously naked underneath. Bercelak placed his hand against her breast and squeezed before moving down her body, past her hips, only to slip his fingers between her trembling thighs.

"Wait."

"Still not right," he muttered low, unable to turn away from the sight of his hand disappearing between her legs. As soon as two of his fingers slid inside her they both let out a low moan.

So wet and hot. Like a volcano. Just thinking of having his cock buried there for several days or years was making him shake like a young one.

He started shafting her with his fingers and she groaned in response, her eyes shut and her teeth biting into her bottom lip. Leaning in close he kissed her cheek and couldn't help but mutter, "Mine, Rhiannon. You're mine."

And that's when he felt her claws slash across his face.

Yanking his hand out of her and away, he stumbled back. He could feel and smell the blood dripping down his jaw.

"I belong to no one, Low Born. And if you hope to trap me with this game, you are sadly mistaken."

He didn't even wipe the blood away as he stared at her. As they stared at each other. Their eyes locked in silent battle.

"What are you talking about?"

"You force me into a Claiming, and I can fight you with the Elders. And we both know it." Aye. He did know that. "But if I let you willingly take me . . . fuck me . . . I have very little room to argue, now do I?"

She pulled her robe together and knotted the tie around it. "You'll have to work a little harder than that, Bercelak the Vengeful, to ever hope of Claiming *me*."

Rhiannon walked past him, her shoulder brushing his as she stalked out. "I will be Claimed by no one, Low Born," she said over her shoulder. "But especially not by you."

She disappeared around the corner and although his cock was so hard it hurt, he couldn't help but smile. Because she didn't even realize . . . she still never said the word, "No."

Once a good distance away from him, Rhiannon stopped and slid down the wall. She glanced at her hand. For several seconds it had returned to claw. Promising. She may be able to reverse this spell yet. But she couldn't worry about it at the moment. Not when thoughts of a black-eyed dragon kept playing through her head. Just with his fingers he'd managed to make her feel . . . full. For those few seconds she was his.

Gods, could she be any weaker? What kind of queen would she be if she couldn't keep the local riffraff from her pussy?

But was it really that simple? She'd let Bercelak get away with more in the few hours she'd been with him than with any other dragon she'd ever met. And, she had to admit, it wasn't merely because her mother had trapped her in this weak, human body. No, it was worse than that. She liked Bercelak's touch. She liked having his hands on her. She was, in fact, beginning to like *him*.

And she absolutely *hated* him for it.

Chapter 4

Rhiannon spent the hour before dawn trying to undo whatever her mother had done to her so she could shift back to dragon. But to no avail.

She missed her dragon self. She missed her wings and her talons. She missed being able to take a horse for a quick meal.

But most importantly, she felt unsafe in this human body. She poked at her skin and it hurt. She dug her nail into her forearm and it bled. By the gods! *How do these humans live like this?*

And then there was Bercelak. She thought for sure he'd come to her last night. He'd come to Claim her. And she'd been prepared, too. Ready to challenge him as human. Ready to die if he'd come as dragon. But he didn't come at all. And, in the end, neither did she.

Damn him! She'd never had a male, any male, make her feel so . . . so . . . needy. And not for food or safety or any of those important things. But for sex. She wanted a lusty ride from that bastard and she hated him for making her feel this way. Especially when she'd been so comfortable with not feeling anything at all.

"Are you ready?"

She looked away from the early-morning two suns to the dragon standing beside her. They stood at the mouth of his den, leagues above the earth. If she fell from here now, she'd die. Perhaps that was what her mother had hoped for. That her human form would crumple and Bercelak would be forced to deal with the remains.

"I'm still waiting for you to explain to me why we are going to Kerezik."

She pulled at the collar of the dress she wore. It wasn't in any way high. In fact, it scooped dangerously low across her breasts. Much more and her nipples would show. She hated wearing clothes, but she felt terribly bare without them, and felt suffocated when she had them on.

"We are, in fact, going to the valley between the grand mountains of Kerezik."

"Fascinating. Still waiting on why."

He looked at her and his scales barely hid where she'd ripped into his flesh. She didn't bother to hide her smirk at that.

"And you'll continue to wait," he growled. "Now get on, dragoness. Or I'll bring you there in my claw."

Without another word, she hoisted herself onto his back. "I haven't ridden on the back of another dragon since I was no more than a hatchling. This might prove to be fun."

To emphasize that point, she dragged her hands through his hair before taking a firm hold. She heard his stifled moan and bit her lip to keep from laughing. There was only so much mocking any dragon could take.

Without another word, Bercelak hit the skies and headed toward Kerezik . . . and whatever was in Kerezik.

"And you remember my mother."

Rhiannon barely held her growl in as Bercelak introduced her to all his kin. An extremely large, handsome brood who all felt the need to be human on this day. Even Bercelak brought a change of clothes with him. Chain-mail leggings and shirt and a dark blue surcoat with the crest of humans destroyed by the queen's army long ago.

He introduced her to all his kin as the female he intended to Claim.

Bastard!

His mother briefly bowed her head, but she saw the hate in the woman's eyes. "Princess."

"Mistress."

Gold eyes turned to Bercelak. "May I speak with you a moment, my son?"

"Of course." He nodded at her. "I'll be right back."

"As you like," Rhiannon muttered, wishing she'd ripped his throat out the night before.

Someone, she had no idea who, placed a goblet of wine into her hand while she leaned against a large dining table already laid out in preparation of a feast.

"I'm Maelona."

"I remember," Rhiannon sighed, unable to hide her annoyance at her current situation.

"Bercelak's youngest sister."

Rhiannon fought her urge to say, "So?"

"I'm a witch, too."

Now Rhiannon looked at the female in surprise. A petite green dragon with Bercelak's black eyes, she was extremely pretty as human with her dark green hair. And she probably glittered like emeralds when dragon. She leaned against the table beside Rhiannon.

"Witch? Me? My skills are . . ." Rhiannon shrugged. "Weak." Embarrassingly so.

"Really?" Another sister, Ghleanna or something, leaned against the table on the other side of Rhiannon. "That's surprising. A white dragon with no Magick at all? Doesn't sound right."

Was anything right at the moment?

"Perhaps."

"Ever wonder why?"

"Ever wonder why what?"

"Why your Magick seems to be lacking?"

"No. I just assumed I was born that way."

Ghleanna, a black dragon and several decades older than Bercelak, raised one glossy black brow. "Perhaps."

"What does that mean?" Rhiannon had no patience for word games with the lower classes.

Instead of answering the question, Ghleanna asked one of her own. "You do know that your mother was with our father . . . long before any of us were born, of course."

"Ghleanna!" her younger sister admonished.

"What? I don't think it's a secret."

"It's not." Rhiannon sipped her wine. "From what I understand there are few of a certain age who have not lain with your father."

"True enough," Ghleanna laughed. "My father has a way with all females. It's in his blood."

"And passed down to all of you, I suppose?"

"A couple of our brothers. And one of our sisters."

"And Bercelak."

Both sisters spit out their wine.

Rhiannon looked between the two women, one eyebrow raised. "Something I said?"

"Bercelak who?" Ghleanna demanded as she wiped her chin.

"*Our* Bercelak?" Maelona asked in surprise.

"Well . . . yes."

"He's *nothing* like Father."

"Father's very jovial and happy," Maelona explained. "Whereas Bercelak is very . . . um . . ."

"Sour and impossibly cranky?"

"That's not fair, sister." Maelona looked at Rhiannon. "He's always been nice to me."

"He's been nice to me, too," Ghleanna interrupted. "But he's still not exactly the life of anyone's party. I don't think I've ever seen him smile."

"Mother said he used to smile . . . you know . . . until Father," she shrugged, "well . . . you know."

Ghleanna took another gulp of wine. "Father's way of raising us differs from most."

"You do learn to stay on your guard. I've never been captured or harmed during battle."

"Aye. That's true."

Curious at what their reactions might be, Rhiannon admitted, "Bercelak smiles at me."

Both sisters froze at Rhiannon's words. Then they slowly turned to face her.

"He smiled? At you?" Ghleanna asked softly.

"Aye. A few times yesterday. And once before many years ago."

Ghleanna's eyes narrowed. "Are you sure it was Bercelak?"

"I think I'd know. I've only been held captive by one black dragon these days."

Maelona shook her head in wonder. "That's fascinating. I'm not sure any of us have seen him smile . . . ever."

"I thought he was physically incapable."

Rhiannon frowned at Ghleanna's words. "Well he's not," she snapped.

Wait. What was she doing? Why did she feel the need to defend the bastard? Gods! She was pathetic!

With a growl, Rhiannon walked away from the two females, leaving them to chatter to each other in low whispers.

* * *

Bercelak took his mother's hands. "Please. Trust me."

"I trust you, son." His mother's gold eyes shifted to the female of his dreams. "It's she I do not trust."

She pulled one hand away and her cool fingers carefully slid along her son's jaw. Right where Rhiannon had clawed him the previous eve. Healing nicely, it still felt a bit sore. "What is this? Did she do this to you?"

"I angered her."

"Is this going to be your life? Praying you don't anger the crazy bitch because you fear she'll kill you in your sleep?"

Bercelak looked at his mother in mock surprise. "Why, Mother. I'm shocked at your words."

"You sound like your father." She went up on her toes to get a better look at his wound. "I won't tolerate her hurting you, my son. I'll kill the bitch first."

"Weren't you the one who tried to cut Father's throat before he Claimed you?"

"He deserved it. You, however, do not."

"How do you know that?"

"I know my son. I know all my hatchlings." And she protected all of them. Even from their mad father. "Can't we get you someone else? Someone . . . kinder?"

"I don't want kinder. I want Rhiannon."

They both watched as Rhiannon walked across the room, a goblet of wine in her hand. A large dog ran up to her and she crouched beside it. She ran a hand over its hide and then leaned in and sniffed it.

"Rhiannon?" he called out softly. She glanced at him over her shoulder. "No."

"No what?"

"He's a pet. Not a treat."

She frowned. "Pet?" She let out an annoyed sigh and stood up, walking around the beast.

He smiled at her confusion over human living and he heard his mother gasp.

"What?" he asked, looking down into her beautiful face.

"She made you smile."

"Aye. Rhiannon always makes me smile."

Shalin dropped her head against her son's chest. "Dark gods, I've lost you forever."

Bercelak rolled his eyes. "I think, Mother, that's a tad extreme."

Sipping her wine, Rhiannon looked around the hall she stood in. Bercelak didn't take her to some mountain fortress to meet his kin. Ailean kept his family in a castle. A gorgeous castle nestled in a valley between the Taaffe Mountains of Kerezik. But this seemed a strange way for any dragon to live. The only way to enter the building was to shift to human. No one in dragon-form could get through the doors.

Rhiannon had heard many tales about Bercelak's father, Ailean the Wicked. In fact, details about his many, many, *many* loves and conquests filled volume after volume of books her own father would never let her read. She'd always heard he preferred to live among the humans, but she never realized to what extent until now.

He even had human servants who seemed to have no fear of the dragons they served.

Strange.

"Well, well, well," a great voice boomed behind her. "My son's female." Before Rhiannon had a chance to argue that particular point, a large hand slapped her on the back as way of greeting. She stumbled forward, thankfully right into Bercelak's arms; otherwise she would have ended up face-down on the marble floor.

Bercelak helped steady her. "Are you all right?"

"Aye."

"Fragile little thing, isn't she?"

Growling, Rhiannon turned around to face the one behind her, but she froze on the spot and stared.

By the dark gods of fire, he's gorgeous!

This had to be Ailean. Built much like Bercelak and all Bercelak's brothers, the dragon had blue hair streaked with the white of age that reached down his back and swept across the floor. His sharp silver eyes looked back at her with curiosity as sinfully full lips tilted into a smirk that made her knees weak. All this explained why his offspring were so beautiful—their father was that and so much more.

No wonder her mother had taken a tumble in this dragon's bed. He had to be at least in his fifth or six hundredth winter and yet he was strong, powerful, and deadly attractive still.

When she didn't say anything, simply stared at him, Bercelak nudged her shoulder.

"Say something," he near snarled between his teeth.

So she did. To his father. "You are absolutely gorgeous."

Ailean grinned and looked at his son. "Well, at least we know she has damn good taste."

"Excuse us."

Then Bercelak was dragging her from the room, but she continued to stare at Ailean until a door slamming shut in front of her cut off her view.

This wasn't the first time a female he was intimate with stared at his father with such keen interest. Before he'd never cared. But this was Rhiannon . . . *his* Rhiannon. And jealousy was fairly choking him to death at the moment.

He turned her to look at him, both hands gripping her upper arms. "Could you have been more obvious?"

She blinked in confusion. "Obvious about what?"

"Your blatant admiration of my father."

"Well even you have to admit he's bloody gorgeous!"

He didn't have to admit a damn thing.

She winced. "Oooh. Well that came out terribly wrong. What I mean is . . . I suddenly understand my mother a little better." She grabbed onto the arms holding her. "If he looks like that as human, what by the dark gods does his dragon-form look like? It must be magnificent!"

He couldn't take any more. Hearing her talk about his father like that filled him with a territorial need he'd never had with any female before.

The grip he had on her arms tightened as he pushed her against the far wall. She only had time to let out a gasp before his mouth covered hers. She struggled, her arms trying to yank away from his hands, but he refused to let her go. Instead he tilted his head to the side, getting a better angle, his tongue thrusting between her lips and into her warm mouth.

He felt her move her leg and not wanting her to shove her knee in his groin, Bercelak pushed his hips forward, trapping her lower body with his own.

She gasped again and his rational mind demanded he release her. But her hips tipped forward the tiniest bit, pushing herself against his rapidly growing erection. He stilled, afraid he might be misreading her, but then her tongue gently rubbed against his.

That was all he needed. He released her arms so he could dig his hands into her hair, holding her head still for his kiss. Her arms, now free, wrapped around his neck and pulled him closer. Her response, nearly explosive in its carnality, had his legs shaking from lust. His control broken, Bercelak thrust his hips against hers. She groaned into his mouth and his hips thrust again, determined to give them both release.

But a banging on the door stopped him.

"Oi! Brother!" He could hear his brothers laughing hysterically from the other side of the door. "Father begs your attendance at dinner, O mighty battle-dragon, defender of the queen's throne!"

"And defender of the queen's daughter!" one of his sister's yelled as well.

He went to pull away, but Rhiannon clung to his neck with a grip bordering on painful.

"No. Don't stop," she panted.

Gods, he'd gotten the spoiled little brat to beg. Well that gave him a nice bit of hope he didn't have the previous eve.

"Sorry, Princess," he gasped out. He wondered if she had any idea that no female, dragon or human, had ever made him this desperate before. "My family awaits. And unless you'd like an audience for this, I suggest we go."

He pulled away, letting his hands slowly fall away from her body. What he wouldn't give to be able to rip that dress off her body and take her until the two suns rose . . . several weeks from now. But he'd do that if he only wanted her for a night or a few days. This game they played was for the rest of their lives. Winner take all.

His heart belonged to this dragoness, whether she wanted it or not.

And she damn well better want it.

Chapter 5

"So how's your mother?"

The entire table froze, all eyes not on Ailean or Rhiannon, but on Bercelak's mother, Shalin, who'd asked the question.

Rhiannon cleared her throat. "She's fine. Although I pray for her death every night, mistress."

Well, that refocused everyone's attention back on her.

"Should we guess you're not close to your mother then?" Ghleanna asked as she expertly used the human utensils to eat the seared flesh on her plate. Starving, Rhiannon wished she could just pick the meat on her plate up with her fingers, but decorum instructed she follow the lead of those whose den it was.

"She detests the ground I walk on. But it's a mutual dislike."

"She fears your power," Maelona offered as she kindly showed Rhiannon which utensils to use without letting on to the rest of them.

Giving a small nod of thanks, Rhiannon followed her example. "My power is nothing compared to hers. And she knows it." She cut the meat on her plate, her mouth already watering.

"You're incorrect," Shalin said softly. "You have much power. Much more than your mother's. The Magick's all around you. I can see it."

Rhiannon chewed on her food. She found herself enjoying these cooked meats almost as much as the raw stuff she normally ate.

Except . . . she did miss the screaming. Although not the sobbing.

After swallowing, Rhiannon said, "I was just discussing this with your daughters. I've had many teachers, mistress. And all of them said I was quite the sad failure."

Ghleanna swirled her wine-filled goblet while one foot rested up on the chair, the hand holding the goblet braced against it. "I've thought about this a bit since we spoke, Princess. And I think they lied to you."

Rhiannon's eyes looked up at the female sitting across from her. Ghleanna did not waste time wearing dresses or any other human feminine trappings. She wore black breeches, black shirt, and high black boots. She kept her thick hair short, which Rhiannon had never seen before on a dragon.

"Why do you say that?"

"You're a white dragon. The power you have was born within you. Like the barbarian Kyvwich witches from the north or the Nolwenn witches from the Desert lands. Your power flows through your veins and nothing your mother does can take that away for good."

Rhiannon swallowed another bit of beef. "Then why are my skills so lacking? Why can I do so little?"

"It took me a bit but I think I finally figured it out. When you trained you were always dragon, weren't you?"

"Of course."

"So they would have never seen it because of your scales."

"Seen what?"

Ghleanna motioned to Rhiannon's shoulder with a gesture, bare where the dress dipped down. "That brand you wear."

Glancing down at it, Rhiannon shrugged. "Aye. All my siblings bear this mark. To be honest, I forgot it was there."

"Well, it's that mark that keeps you from your true strength, Princess. And I'd bet my treasure your mother knew it when she had it placed on you."

Frowning, Rhiannon looked down at the mark on her shoulder.

Bercelak should have paid more attention to the females' ongoing conversation. Instead, he sent threatening looks to his two youngest brothers and several of his oldest when they leered at Rhiannon.

Then his baby sister gasped in shock and he turned in time to see his female take her eating knife to the small brand she had on her shoulder.

"Rhiannon!" But it was too late. She'd already shoved the point into the flesh around the brand and dug under it, flicking out a chunk of skin and muscle.

His kin burst into surprise gasps and comments as he

pushed himself away from the table and went immediately to her side.

She stared down at the wound gushing blood. "I feel nothing."

Crouching down beside her, Bercelak took a cloth from off the table and placed it over the wound. "Nothing? You feel no pain?"

"Oh. I feel pain. Lots of pain. But nothing else."

He worked hard to understand her words, but failed miserably. "What are you talking about?"

She grabbed hold of the cloth and stood up. Holding it against her arm, she walked away from the table, his entire family watching her.

"Nothing's changed." She turned and faced them. "Are you sure about that brand?"

"It was a guess," Ghleanna answered, her eyes wide with shock.

"A guess? That would have been nice to know before I cut it out of my arm."

"Well, you mad cow, how were any of us to know you were going to do that?"

"What did you expect me to do? You tell me . . ." Rhiannon abruptly stopped talking.

Bercelak stood up as her blue eyes locked onto his. "Gods, Bercelak. It hurts. It hurts," she whispered. Then her arms flung out and her body lifted off the floor.

"*Rhiannon!*" He moved toward her, but two of his sisters grabbed hold of him.

"*Let me go!*"

"No, brother. Leave her be," Ghleanna ordered against his ear. "You can't help her."

Bercelak watched as the Magick of his kind tore through Rhiannon's body, looping around her limbs, cutting through her chest and stomach, pouring off her like rain water.

"*Do something!*" he roared, unwilling to watch her writhe in pain. "We can't leave her like this."

"Naught we can do, but wait until the gods are done with her," Maelona whispered.

As soon as Maelona said the words, Rhiannon's body slowly rose up toward the ceiling. In fascinated silence, he and his family watched her rise and rise.

Then . . . she dropped. As if one of the gods slammed her with his mighty claws. But the force behind it was so great, Rhiannon's body slammed through the floor of the Great Hall, disappearing from their sight.

"Gods!"

"The dungeon! She's gone to the dungeon!"

"We have a dungeon?"

Bercelak's father led the way into the rarely used lower floors of the castle. Cobwebs hung everywhere and they could hear the noises of small, frightened animals scurrying through the dank place. They found her right where she'd landed.

Bercelak ran to her side. "Rhiannon?" Ghleanna and Maelona crouched next to her.

Leaning over Rhiannon's body, Maelona let out a deep sigh. "She breathes."

Angry and unable to take it out on anyone else, Bercelak pushed Ghleanna's shoulder. "Why did you have to tell her that?"

Growling, Ghleanna pushed him back. "How was I supposed to know she'd do something that bloody stupid?"

"Stop it."

They both looked down to find Rhiannon's eyes open and staring at them. "Stop fighting."

"Rhiannon, are you all right?"

She blinked. "My head hurts a bit." She licked her lips and Bercelak hated himself for wanting to kiss her again as opposed to taking care of her. "And every part of my body's on fire."

"Not surprising," Ghleanna offered. "When that much

Magick goes through you, Princess, you can expect a large bit of pain."

Rhiannon turned those blue eyes to Bercelak's sister. "That, too, would have been wonderful to know *before I did this!*" she ended on a healthy yell.

With a shake of his head, Bercelak carefully slipped his arms under Rhiannon's neck and knees, lifting her off the floor as he stood. "Let's get you back upstairs, Princess."

"I'm still hungry, Low Born," she muttered.

But before he could promise her food, she was snoring.

Rhiannon yawned and stretched. She felt amazing. Alive with power. She could hear things . . . sense things she'd never been able to before. She could actually see tendrils of Magick swirling around her.

She watched one small pink one twirl and twirl and twirl. She turned over, her eyes following it until she realized Bercelak lay next to her in the bed. Awake, his head propped up on one arm, he watched her with warmth, which did nothing but cause her the highest level of anxiety.

Then she realized that, except for the thin animal skin covering them, they were both quite naked. As dragon, this would mean nothing. But in human form. . . .

"Ow!" he snapped as her fist made contact with his hard chest.

"Why are we in bed together? What have you done?" She went to punch him again but he grabbed both her wrists, pushing her onto her back.

"Stop hitting me!"

"Get off me!"

"Not until you calm down!"

Very hard to calm down, though, when Bercelak's warm, heavy body lay directly on top of hers. Part of her would like nothing more than to open her legs to him. All that Magick running through her system had done nothing but increase her overwhelming desire to have this dragon fuck her . . . hard, long, and with absolutely no mercy.

Aye. That's what she wanted.

Good gods! What have I done to myself?

"Calm down, Rhiannon, and I'll let you go."

He spoke calmly, soothingly. Like he were trying to coax a yummy mare over to him before taking her off to be a snack.

Rhiannon had no choice but to comply. As human she was still so weak compared to him.

Taking a deep breath, she forced herself through sheer will of effort to relax. It worked, but instead of releasing her, Bercelak stared at her face. Specifically her mouth.

"Bercelak?"

"Mhmm?"

"Let me go."

"Are you sure?" And he looked at her with such desperate longing she smiled.

"Aye. I'm sure."

With a groaned sigh of resignation, he released her wrists and rolled onto his back. Still, she had to bite her lip to stop herself from laughing at the sight of his erection creating a nice tent with the bedding.

"You're too cruel to me," he groaned.

"Why? Because I won't let you have your vile way with me?"

"Yes. That's exactly why."

He sounded so wounded, it forced Rhiannon's smile into a brutal grin. "Poor thing. How you've suffered so."

"Don't mock me, wench." His arm slipped around her waist and pulled her over so she rested against his chest. "You seem to enjoy teasing me and I was so worried about you."

He was worried about her? "Really?"

"Aye, Rhiannon. I feared I lost you. Especially when you went through the floor . . . it's marble, you know. Thick, un-yielding marble."

She blinked. "Oh. I . . . I guess the gods protected me."

"I guess." He paused a moment, then said, "Can you shift back now?"

She reached inside herself but after a few moments, she knew. "No. I can't."

"Perhaps soon, though."

"Perhaps." Or, perhaps she'd be trapped like this forever. Stuck in this weak body until her ancestors called her home. But one look at her human body and they'd most likely send her away in disgust.

"Don't worry, Rhiannon. I promise we'll fix this. Soon you'll learn to manage the Magick that flows through you, and then nothing will stop you."

"You seem so sure."

"'Cause I am sure. Now," he kissed her forehead, then her cheek as he moved down her body, "let's no longer talk."

She pushed against his chest, but even she had to admit it was a very halfhearted effort. But what could she do? Especially with him nibbling under her chin and his hands roaming over her body.

"Bercelak," she panted, "stop."

He chuckled seconds before his mouth closed over one hard nipple and sucked. His "rules" came rushing back to her and she realized he wouldn't stop. If she wanted him to stop, she'd have to say "no."

She said, "Don't."

A deep groan reverberated through her breast from his mouth while one of his big hands slid up the back of her leg, settling between her thighs. One of Bercelak's large fingers slid inside her and Rhiannon heard herself whimper. Gods, the beast had her whimpering like some weak human.

Still, it felt so damn good. His fingers making her body go wild. His tongue and lips teasing her nipples.

Rhiannon wanted release. Preferably now. But she would never ask. So, instead, she said, "Bercelak . . . we mustn't."

Like that she was flat on her back, Bercelak's hard body pressing down on her, pushing her into the mattress.

Oh, she enjoyed these rules of his. She didn't have to act like the slag she currently was. Instead, she could pretend this was all beyond her control when, in fact, he'd given her complete control. How did he know all this would turn her into a ball of flame? How did he know her so well? She'd never spent any time with him. Barely spoke to him unless her mother was around and she didn't want to hear her telling her she was a horrible bitch.

Or was it that they were merely well matched? Dragons believed that their true mate waited "out there" for them. The one meant to be theirs until their ancestors called them home.

Could her true mate truly be this overbearing, cranky, arrogant bastard?

He moved down her body, his tongue leading the way, until his big shoulders pushed her legs apart and he settled his face between her thighs.

For the moment, she answered her own question out loud. Actually, she screamed her answer. "*Yes! Gods, yes!*"

Hearing her scream out in lust nearly sent Bercelak over the edge. He gripped her thighs tighter and delved deeper inside her tight pussy. She groaned and bucked under him, her hands digging into his hair.

Gods, she tasted good. Smelled even better.

This was the Rhiannon he always knew existed. The one he knew would be his forever. He'd wanted to wait until they'd returned to his den before taking her since he had no doubts he'd *never* be able to wait until their Claiming. Which, due to her royal lineage, must take place at the full of the moon . . . four very long days away.

Still, he never planned to do this here, in his father's house.

But he couldn't help it. Especially with her goading him. That "we mustn't" nearly killed him. She knew exactly how to entice him. She understood him better than anyone; she just hadn't realized it yet. She would. Soon she'd understand everything.

She'd realize that apart they were strong . . . but together they were unstoppable.

One of her hands released his hair and grabbed hold of the headboard. She writhed beneath him, unable to move her hips because he'd pinned her lower half to the bed while his tongue tormented her toward release.

"Bercelak," she whispered his name and his entire body clenched. "Gods, Bercelak . . ." She probably didn't even realize she'd said it out loud, but it was all he needed to hear.

He closed his mouth over her clit, suckling. Rhiannon's entire body bowed and she let out a shattering groan. He felt her toes curl and uncurl where they rested by his shoulders and he feared she'd break the headboard with the way she was holding it.

Finally, she settled down and Bercelak moved back up her body until he hovered over her. He took firm hold of both her hands—after prying one of them from the headboard and the other from his hair—and pinned them over her head.

Then he waited.

After a few moments, Rhiannon's eyes slowly opened and he smiled down into her face.

"Feel better?"

Giving a wicked grin he prayed he'd be able to keep on her face the majority of the time they were together, she nodded. "Aye."

"Good." His grip tightened on her wrists, pushing them down onto the mattress. She raised an eyebrow in question.

"My turn," he answered as he slammed his hard cock inside her, letting her delicious roar of surprise wash over him.

Chapter 6

Finally, her mind cleared and she could again see straight. But by then it was too late.

She felt his cock push inside her with no warning, no preamble . . . and it felt delicious. It also meant she'd have little grounds to refuse his right to Claim her. If he hadn't made his intentions clear in the beginning, she could have used him until the two suns burned away and the oceans disappeared and he'd still never be able to have her without her agreeing. Yet she knew his intentions, and without any force whatsoever, he'd taken her . . . and she let him.

The dragon Elders would have little patience for her denials of his Claiming now.

Damn him!

"Rhiannon," he whispered in her ear and her entire body melted. "I'm going to fuck you, Rhiannon. I'm going to make you come . . . again." She rolled her eyes at that and she felt his smile against her cheek. "It will always be this way with us, you know. Always."

She doubted that, but then he started moving and she stopped thinking about much of anything except how good he felt inside her.

Bercelak held onto her arms, but her legs were free. She wrapped them around his waist, her heels digging into his ass. He growled at that and kissed her while his hips continued to move against her, his big cock powering into her over and over again.

Her tongue met his and she cried out in desperation. Amazing that after what she'd just experienced, she now wanted more. So much more.

Kissing her cheek, licking her chin and throat, Bercelak continued to push her toward another blinding climax. She tried to pull her hands away, but he took a tighter grip and pushed them deeper into the mattress.

He won't let me go, she thought to herself and that's when his mouth clamped over her breast again, sucking hard on her nipple.

Her release hit with brutal swiftness, tearing through Rhiannon's entire body the way the Magick had, only this time no pain. Just pleasure. Wonderful pleasure.

Panting and trying to focus, she realized Bercelak had come inside her and now lay collapsed atop her.

That's when she had to admit—at least to herself—that it didn't feel too bad to have him there.

"Rhiannon?" It felt like ages until he could get up enough energy to say that. But when she didn't answer him, Bercelak became seriously concerned. Scared he may have accidentally hurt her, he pushed himself up on one elbow, looking down at her.

"Rhiannon?" he said again, louder.

"Mhmmm?"

She sounded sated.

Bercelak couldn't help but smile. It felt nice to smile. "Are you all right?"

Slowly, her eyes opened, staring at him in wonder. Then, just as quickly, her eyebrows pulled down into a brutal frown. "This changes nothing, Low Born."

Bercelak laughed out loud and that felt even better than smiling. "Sorry, Princess. This changes *everything*. And we both know it."

Growling, she tried to pull away from him, but he caught hold of her waist.

"You're not going anywhere."

"Let me go."

"No. I want to talk first."

"Talk?" She looked absolutely horrified at the idea.

"Aye. Talk. Make sure we are both clear on a few things."

She relaxed back, but watched him warily. "Clear on what things?"

"The next full moon is in four days. At that time I'll Claim you."

"Wait—"

"No. I won't wait, Rhiannon. You're mine as I am yours. Nothing will change that."

Angry, she pulled away from him, scrambling across the bed. "This isn't fair. It was the Magick . . . it changed . . ."

He shook his head. "Try another tack, Princess. I won't believe the Magick made you, of all dragons, do anything you didn't want to do."

"But—"

Frustrated, he barked, "No! No more excuses. No more denials." He pulled his body up and, on all fours, moved toward her.

Eyes wide, Rhiannon moved back away from him. The bed was big, but it wasn't that big.

Her back leg slid off the bed, almost tumbling her onto the floor. But Bercelak grasped tight hold of her wrist.

"Wait—"

He ignored her plea, yanking her onto the bed.

As he placed his body over hers, she snarled, "I'll never love you, Low Born! Never!"

His heart stuttered to a stop. He wanted her love. Needed it, even. This wasn't about taking a royal as his mate. This was about Rhiannon and only Rhiannon. He'd loved her since he saw her and, he had admitted to himself years ago, he would always love her. No female would ever compare with her. And now that he'd actually been inside her, had actually heard her cries of passion and felt her lust, he wanted no other female in his arms. Only Rhiannon. Always Rhiannon.

But from what he knew of his Rhiannon, no "sensitive" male would ever live in her bed . . . *own* her bed. So, the side that wished to care for her—that wanted to make her laugh as well as see her smile—he pushed aside. He would bury it until he'd Claimed her. Even if he missed the next full moon, he'd only Claim Rhiannon if she loved him. Nothing was worse than being with someone who didn't love you and never would. Dragons lived many years and that was too long to live without a true mate to care for you.

So he buried the part of him that cared and brought out the warrior. The merciless battle-dragon who had destroyed more dragon kingdoms than he could remember.

He dug his hand into her hair and snatched her head back. One of her hands reached up and gripped his shoulder, trying to push him off.

"Perhaps we should understand each other, Princess. I will have you. I will make you mine until the end of time. Challenge me if you wish, but you'll lose in this battle. I promise that you'll lose."

Clear blue eyes glared at him but he also saw the heat in them. With her hatred came her lust. Just as he knew it would.

He pulled her head back a little farther and the hand on his shoulder dug into his flesh.

"I think it's time you understand how things will work between us, Princess. I think it's time I *show* you."

Bercelak banged on his older brother's door again. Finally, Addolgar pulled the heavy oak door open.

"What?"

"I need your chains, brother."

Addolgar stared at him for several long seconds. "Should I ask why?" he finally said.

"No."

"The cuffs only, or the collar as well?"

"All of it."

With a shrug, Addolgar went back into his room. He heard his brother speaking to his mate. Bercelak shook his head when he heard her snap, "Where do you think you're going with our chains?"

"It's for a good cause," Addolgar said over his shoulder as he handed the chains to his kin. "It's brought me luck, brother. Perhaps it will work the same for you."

He fucked me to sleep, she thought as she forced herself awake. The suns showed brightly through the narrow windows and she knew it was late in the morning.

The last thing she remembered at all was him bathing her, against her muttered protests, in fact.

Rhiannon shook her head to clear her exhausted mind, but the sounds of heavy chains froze her. She went to touch her throat, but her hands would only move so far. She turned her head and saw that metal cuffs held her wrists, the chain tightened so her arms didn't stray too far from the headboard. She couldn't see or touch the collar around her neck, but she felt it well enough. Heavy metal weighing down on her shoulders. Even her feet were shackled, the chains securely locked to the end board.

"*Bastard!*"

"Oh, good. You're awake."

"Release me! *Now!*"

He smiled and she took very little comfort from it. "I think not. I like having you at my disposal. All wet and ready to fuck when I so choose."

She'd spit at him if he were any closer. Especially when she felt her body respond so immediately. Her nipples peaked and wetness seeped from between her legs. He saw it, too, and his grin grew wider.

She fought the chains again. "I'll scream for help."

"I wouldn't bother. Remember whose family this is. Ailean the Wicked. Somehow he managed to woo my mother who, I've been told, tried to kill him more than once before their Claiming. So, I seriously doubt he'll find this such an extreme form of courtship."

"I am a princess," she argued, "you can't treat me—"

"You are a princess," he cut in. "A beautiful princess who belongs to me."

He finally walked over to her and she stared hard at the human body before her. *Gods, why did he have to be so beautiful?*

"Tell me you're mine, Rhiannon, and I'll let you go."

Angry and lustful all in one turn, Rhiannon turned her face away.

"Tell me, Rhiannon." His fingers slid up her calf, teasing the skin with just the tips of his fingers. "Tell me"—fingers slid between her thighs, soft kisses followed—"or I'll be forced to get it out of you . . . somehow."

She shuddered and, to her shame, it wasn't from fear or anger. But lust. Her weakness sickened her. How could she ever hope to be queen, when she couldn't even tell this bastard "no"?

Kisses turned to licks that trailed over her sex and across her lower belly.

"Such simple words, Rhiannon. 'I belong to you, Bercelak.' Say them and let's be done with all this."

As she turned her neck, the collar bit into her flesh a bit. She closed her eyes in horror when she realized how much she liked it.

"I won't," she choked out, while his tongue was teasing the very tip of her nipple. "I won't say it."

"Fine. Then I guess we'll have to do this the hard way." He pulled away from her and she briefly wondered what the "hard way" was? She couldn't imagine Bercelak hurting her. At least not without some proper begging involved. He stretched out beside her, his head in her lap. She watched through narrowed eyes as he kissed her sex, his tongue pushing in to tease her clit the tiniest bit.

She groaned, her eyes closing and her body tightening. Then he stopped, pulled back and blew on her. Gently.

Her eyes snapped open and he gave her that gorgeous smile. For someone who rarely smiled, he seemed to be doing it a lot all of a sudden. Because of her?

"Give me what I want, Rhiannon, and I'll give you what you want."

Refusing to speak, she shook her head. The collar, warm from her body heat, felt wonderful resting against her flesh.

"As you wish." He leaned down and began teasing her again. Growling, she looked away, only to see his engorged cock bobbing there, Bercelak's hand gripping it firmly, stroking it slowly.

Unable to stop herself, she growled with wanting and Bercelak's mouth stopped moving. He lifted his head and looked at her. They stared at each other for several long moments, then Rhiannon licked her lips.

Bercelak groaned and growled all at the same time while he easily pushed himself up until he rested on his knees. He moved toward her, his cock leading the way. She no longer looked at him, but at *it*.

Straddling her chest, Bercelak slid his hand behind her neck and gently lifted her head up. She opened her mouth and he slid his cock inside her. They both closed their eyes with a moan as Rhiannon sucked on him, loving the way his body shook as she took possession of him.

"Gods, Rhiannon," he whispered. "Gods, that feels good."

She thought about torturing him the way he'd been torturing her, but she didn't want to. She liked having his big cock in her mouth. She liked having him over her. She felt no fear, no sense of dread, wondering when he'd prove what a bastard he was. So she sucked and she licked.

His hands tightened in her hair, holding her head still as his cock moved in and out of her mouth as he neared release. Finally, he pushed into her one last time. She nearly gagged as his seed filled her mouth, bursting into the back of her throat. But she swallowed it and sucked until he pulled away from her and dropped down on the bed.

Feeling smug, she licked her lips again and watched him panting, a light sheen of sweat over his body.

Now he wouldn't be able to resist her. Now he'd rip these chains off her and fuck her until they both passed out.

That's what she waited for. And she kept waiting.

Eventually, Bercelak gave one big satisfied sigh, then leaned back against the bed, his hands behind his head, his legs crossed at the ankles. The legs currently resting by her head.

He looked up at the ceiling. "So which would you prefer, Rhiannon? A male hatchling first? Or a female?"

Her eyes widened in annoyance. "Wha-what?"

"For our first. Male or female? I like the idea of a female. I've always wanted a daughter." He smiled at her and it was the warmest smile anyone had ever given her. "I want her to look like you." Then his eyes returned to the ceiling as if he could see their entire future—their entire future *together*—playing out above their heads. "But a male offspring would also be nice, too, don't you think? He could take care of his younger siblings. Now I don't think we have to have as many as my parents. Fifteen is excessive, but . . . definitely more than two or three, don't you think?"

Unable to look at him anymore without screaming, Rhiannon stared out the window and debated the logic of flinging herself from the ledge . . . *after* he released her, of course.

With a pathetic roll of her eyes, Rhiannon sighed but it came out more like a sob.

Chapter 7

He finally released her arms and legs, and allowed her enough chain to get to the chamber pot and the bath. Other than that, he kept her tied to the bed for the remainder of the day and well into the night.

Rhiannon really wished she could say she hated him. Hating him would make this so easy. She would promise him whatever he asked, wait until he untied her, and then she'd cut his currently human throat with a jagged piece of glass . . . or simply rip his throat out with her teeth. Whatever was convenient.

But she didn't hate him. And she hated herself for not hating him.

Pathetic female.

She yanked her chain again. When Bercelak decided to leave her alone for a bit, he quickly realized that the headboard wouldn't last two seconds against her strength and rage. So he wrapped the chain around a pillar and locked it. With an annoyingly happy smile, he kissed her on the cheek with promises of returning and walked out.

That had been nearly an hour ago and he still had not returned.

A soft knock at the door had her grabbing an animal fur from the floor and wrapping it around her body since these human servants reacted so dramatically to any kind of nakedness. Why they would react that way over their own bodies with someone they didn't lust for, she had no idea.

"Come." Might as well since clearly she wouldn't be for quite awhile.

The door pushed open and Ghleanna and Shalin walked in. Gleanna held a tray of food, the smell bringing Rhiannon's stomach to growling life, and her mother followed with a goblet and decanter.

Rhiannon prayed that was wine she had with her, because she needed to numb her brain before she began destroying things around her for her own amusement.

"We thought you might be hungry."

"I'd like the key even more."

The two females looked at each other but, not surprisingly, it was Ghleanna who spoke, "You've lost your mind, Princess, if you think we're about to get between you and my brother on this."

"Fine!"

She turned, the chain winding around her throat, and stalked back across the room.

"Now, now," Bercelak's mother soothed. "No need to get angry. Everything will be fine. I promise."

"Your son is unreasonable."

"My son is in love."

At Shalin's words, Rhiannon spun around, but the chain pulled tight around her throat, snapping her head back.

"*Ack!*"

* * *

Bercelak watched one of his younger brothers pass out and drop to the floor. All that wine . . . he should have known better. His father's wine could kill an elephant.

His father's hand slapped him on the back. Anyone else, even dragon, would go flying. But all of Ailean's children learned to have sturdy backs and good balance.

"Don't worry, son. You'll break her."

Rolling his eyes, "I don't want to break her. If I wanted that, I'd have chosen one of those insipid royals."

"But you didn't choose her," his brother Caerwyn felt the need to say.

"Her mother may have thrown her to me, but I'd chosen Rhiannon long ago. Everything I've done, every battle I've won, every rank I've earned has been for her. To be worthy of her."

"You *are* worthy of her." His father sat down in a chair, putting his feet up on the table. "You're my son."

"Oh, yes. *That's* been quite helpful."

His brothers and two of his hard-drinking sisters laughed in agreement, but his father looked at his brood in confusion.

"What does that mean?"

"Come on. You can't tell me you don't know. Your name follows us around like the stink on a dog."

"Everyone knows you, Father," one of his sisters offered up. "And what they know isn't good."

His father, always jovial and smiling, looked suddenly angry. "So you're saying . . ."

"That you're an embarrassment? Yes." Bercelak didn't mean to be cruel, but he wondered if his time with Rhiannon wouldn't have been a tad easier if his father hadn't been known throughout Dark Plains as Ailean the Slag.

"I'm still your father, *boy*! So watch how you speak to me! It's not my fault you can't get the little bitch to submit. Perhaps if you were more like me, this wouldn't be a problem."

If it hadn't been for his siblings grabbing hold of him, Bercelak would have torn the old bastard apart.

"Oh, I tried to kill him twice. Almost succeeded that one time." Rhiannon watched as Bercelak's sweet mother made a line across her throat with one finger. "Sliced his throat from here to here. But he shifted to dragon before I could finish. His scales prevented him from bleeding to death."

Rhiannon glanced at Ghleanna, who looked bored and unimpressed. "Why . . . that's a lovely tale, mistress."

"No. It's not. But it is to say that the males of this brood are not looking for shy, retiring mates. The more you fight my son, the more he wants you. After I cut Ailean's throat, he Claimed me one moon later."

"Do you . . ." Rhiannon looked away from Shalin's steady gaze.

"Do I what?"

"Well . . . ever regret being with him?"

Shalin leaned back in her chair, a soft smile on her lips. "No. I've never regretted being with him and I can't even imagine my life without him. I do, however, regret how hard his reputation is on our offspring."

Ghleanna snorted as she stared out the window. "That's a bit of an understatement." She looked at Rhiannon. "Where my brothers have done well by our father's reputation, his female offspring have not. I've beaten more than my fair share of dragons nearly to death who thought I was some kind of whore they could treat as they liked."

"Now she sees no one."

"I won't be treated like trash, Mother. I love my father . . . with all my heart, but there's not a day that goes by that I forget I'm the daughter of Ailean the Wicked."

"Your father has done the best for his offspring, Ghleanna.

You included. Between you and me, you are one of his favorites. It would hurt him to know this was how you feel."

"And it hurts me to be alone. And yet, we all must endure."

If she'd not been chained to the spot, Rhiannon would have left mother and daughter to finish this discussion on their own. If for no other reason than that she felt a bit jealous. A very large bit jealous. Her arguments with her mother were nothing like these. If it hadn't been for the protection of her father, Addiena probably would have killed her long ago. That was why every new moon she sent a prayer to the gods in honor of her father. Because he above all others loved her.

Now Shalin wanted her to believe that Bercelak loved her. Could he? Could anyone? She wasn't exactly the easiest being to get along with.

Bercelak's mother reached over and grasped her daughter's hand. "We're here for you, love. If you let me, I can help you," she said to Ghleanna.

Ghleanna shook her head and looked out the window, but her grip tightened on her mother's hand. But they were startled from their silent moment when the bedroom door opened and Bercelak entered.

Rhiannon stood up as soon as she saw his face. "Gods, what happened to you?"

"Nothing," he grumbled as he walked across the room. "Just a little discussion with my father."

"You promised me you wouldn't fight with him anymore," his mother accused, standing up so she could get a closer look at her extremely tall son.

"I didn't. I was arguing with someone else and he decided to end it."

Rhiannon reached up and touched the black-and-blue mark around Bercelak's eye. It startled him, and he turned to her so quickly she snatched her hand back and turned away from him.

"Um . . . we best be going," Shalin said as she made a hasty retreat. "Come along, Ghleanna."

Rhiannon heard mother and daughter leave and it took all her strength not to demand they stay.

"Rhiannon?"

"She's very sweet, your mother."

"I know."

"She brought me food and wine. Made sure the collar wasn't too tight." Gods, she was babbling.

"Rhiannon—"

"Ghleanna can actually talk to her mother. That must be nice."

"Rhiannon." He turned her around to face him. "Stop."

"Stop what?"

"Avoiding me."

"I'm not." Yet she wouldn't look him in the eye. Really . . . exactly how was she supposed to rule a kingdom?

Bercelak's big hand gripped her chin and lifted her face.

"What's wrong?"

"Nothing.

"Then why are you looking at me like that?"

Finally, she couldn't stand it anymore. Her hand reached up and she gently ran her fingers over his wounded eye. He stared down at her in wary shock, but she couldn't stop herself.

"Are you sure you're all right?"

Gods!

What had the bastard done to her?

This had to be some sort of trick. Some sort of grand trick she thought she could play on him for her own amusement. But her eyes looked so sincere, and her fingers on his face were gentle and so careful.

Gods, was she actually concerned about his welfare?

About his health? This had to be progress. Yet, she looked appalled at herself for even asking.

"I'll be all right. I've taken worse hits. Growing up in this family, you learn to deal with surprise attacks."

She pulled her hand away. "Good. Yes, very good."

Rhiannon tried to turn away, but he pulled her back around again. "Aren't you going to greet me?"

"Greet you?"

He nodded and leaned down until his lips hovered over hers. "Anytime I return from defending your throne you should make sure to greet me like this so that the entire court knows you care for me."

"I don't care—" But he cut off her denials with a kiss.

Gods, for someone who didn't spend much time as human, Rhiannon truly knew how to kiss like one. Her warm tongue teased his, her throaty groans slowly destroying his control.

Somehow, he pulled away from her and Rhiannon looked up with absolute frustration. "*What now?*"

Bercelak pulled the thin silver chain he currently wore around his neck out from under his shirt. He kept the key to Rhiannon's bondage on it. He unlocked the collar at her throat while she watched him with narrow eyes.

"What is this? What are you up to?"

Taking her hand, he pulled her onto the bed with him. "One of my brothers told me he got word from one of his friends at court . . ." Gods, how did he tell her this? He looked into Rhiannon's clear blue eyes. They stared at him, waiting. No. There would be no delicate words for his female. She deserved nothing but absolute truth.

"Rumors are flying around court, Rhiannon."

"Rumors? What kind of rumors?"

"Some are saying your mother wants you dead."

She shrugged. "I already knew that."

Rhiannon said it so nonchalantly. Whereas his kin would never believe in a million lifetimes Shalin would ever harm them in any way, Rhiannon took it for granted her mother would.

"You are handling this much better than I did." That was actually how he got the black eye. His brother told him the news. He called him a liar. They pushed, they shoved, they yelled, and then the hitting started. It wasn't until their father, who tolerated no fighting among his offspring, jumped in. With one punch he snapped Bercelak out of his rage, and with one solid backhand across the face, Ailean controlled his younger son.

"What's there to handle? This is the way of my life. Always has been. My father warned me long ago this time would come. That's why he made sure I was trained."

"Trained?"

"Aye. Whether human or dragon I can handle sword, mace, dagger, bow, and whip. I also know many forms of hand-to-hand combat." She smiled and he saw pride light up her eyes. "And I can do things with flame that would amaze even you."

He wondered if she even realized he still held her hands while they talked. "Amaze even me, eh?"

"Well . . . as a battle-dragon you must have seen many amazing things."

Rubbing the back of her knuckles with his thumbs, he said, "Nothing as amazing as you, Rhiannon."

Startled, she cleared her throat and looked away from him. "So what does this change?"

"Maelona knows a witch who may be able to help you now that you have your full powers. Tomorrow we'll go see her together."

"I don't need you babysitting me, Bercelak. I think I can talk to a witch on my own."

"She's a very old dragon, Rhiannon, who will no longer shift to human. And I'll not risk you." Old dragons could be a bit unstable. Catch them on the wrong day and they would rip the scales from your body without a second's thought. And what they were known for doing to humans. . . ."

Sighing, she nodded. "Fine."

"We'll go in the morning." Bercelak finally released her hands so he could push the fur from her shoulders. "Tonight I have other plans."

She tried to hide her smile, but she didn't do a very good job. "And I wonder what plans those could be."

Chapter 8

"A white dragon, too. Haven't seen your kind around in a bit."

Rhiannon sighed heavily, mostly from boredom, as Bercelak stood in front of her, trying to get the old bitch to help them.

Donnfhlaidh, an *old* brown dragon—*I didn't even know their kind still existed*—had been keeping her waiting for nearly half the hour.

"Mistress," Bercelak tried again with a patience Rhiannon had become well acquainted with, "we truly need your help."

"She can't shift back to dragon, can she?"

"No. She can't."

"Well, I can't help her with that."

"Fine!" Rhiannon's patience ran out. She stormed around Bercelak. "If you won't help me, I'll find someone who will!" she yelled up at her.

The old dragon cackled hysterically. "Gods, Bercelak! Do you know what you're getting yourself into with this one?"

Rhiannon, uncaring she had no protective scales, growled and moved forward. But something grabbed hold of the back of her gown and she turned to see that the tip of Bercelak's tail had caught hold of the thick material and held her in place. She glared up at him and he winked.

She really should hate him, except he looked so regal in his full battle-dragon armor worn to impress the old bitch dragon. The metal breastplate, used to protect not only a dragon's chest but his vulnerable underbelly during battle, fairly glowed with the fire coming from the pit. Bercelak's was an intricate design of past battles. The detail of the work showed his rank. Then there were the scars covering a good portion of his body. . . .

Gods! What had he done to her? When did she become one of those lovesick females? How did she allow this to happen?

"Mistress, I ask you again . . . will you help us?"

"I can't change her mother's spell, Bercelak. The queen either has to die or your lady love will have to reverse it on her own."

"And how do I do that?" Rhiannon sighed dramatically.

"Try this." The old witch lobbed a book at her. Written by dragons, the book was enormous and with Bercelak's tail holding her in place, she could only cringe as it neared her head. But one black claw reached out and snatched the book from the air.

"Ahh. Thank you, mistress."

"Keep it. Soon I'll need none of this any longer." The dragon slowly turned and headed back deeper into her lair, but over her shoulder she said, "You do know that you two are well matched, don't you? You, Princess, allow him to be kind rather than just a killer. And Bercelak allows you the ability to be a right bitch whenever you want.

"Aye," she continued, her voice echoing in the cavern as she disappeared into the darkness. "You two are perfect together. And one day . . . one day your children will change *everything*."

Bercelak watched his sister and mother work with Rhiannon to find the spell that would break the queen's hold.

They'd been at it for hours, and he could see his female's patience begin to wane.

When she literally roared in frustration, shaking the table they were all working on, he knew she badly needed a break.

"*This is useless!*"

"Come, Rhiannon." He grabbed hold of her wrist and dragged her toward the exit. "Mother? You'll be all right?"

"Go, go." His mother didn't even look up as she shooed them away. Except for one other brother, his poor mother was the only scholar of the clan. Deciphering ancient text was the kind of thing she lived for. "I'll be fine."

Using that to his advantage, Bercelak dragged Rhiannon from the castle and toward the woods.

"Where are we going?"

"You are dangerously tense, my love. I fear for my family's safety."

She dug her heels into the soft ground and he turned to look at her. "What?"

"Don't say that again."

"I know you'd never hurt my family, Rhiannon."

"Not that. Never call me your 'love' again. None of that."

"You're unbelievable, Princess." He headed back off, yanking her along behind him. "You argue the most insane things."

"I think not. I need none of those insipid endearments from you."

"Oh, you'd prefer them from another?"

"There is no other."

He stopped again and looked at her. "And it will stay that way, Princess. There will only be me. There will only be you."

Shaking her head, "I don't understand you, Bercelak. Truth told, you could have anyone. Low-born or royal. Do you truly wish to be consort to a queen so badly?"

"I don't want 'anyone,' Rhiannon. I only want you. Since I saw you that first time I've only wanted you. That has never changed. That never will change. Whether you take your mother's throne or leave it to one of your siblings, it won't change how I feel about you . . . and I think you know that. I think you fear it."

She pulled her arm out of his grasp and took several steps away. "I may never be dragon again. I may be trapped in this weak human body forever. I may never be queen. I may never rule. And one day you may have to choose between my mother and me. One day she'll *make* you choose."

"There is no choice. It will always be you, Rhiannon. You will always be my first and only choice. Your well-being is all I care about. Human or dragon, queen or low-born . . . I will make it my life's work to protect you and any offspring we have. I will not let anything harm our family. And I will defnitely not let anything harm you."

He grabbed hold of her hand again, bringing it to his mouth so he could kiss her knuckles.

"My heart belongs to you, Rhiannon. It will always belong to you."

Frowning, she looked away, then down at the ground.

He knew she'd reject him again. That fear of her feelings would make her run, but he was willing to wait for her. He had no choice. No other female would ever do.

Then, to his shock, she slowly reached her free hand out for him while she kept her eyes on the ground. He grasped it and gave a small tug. She shuddered once, then she was against him. Her arms wrapped tight around his waist, her head on his chest.

He closed his eyes and sent up a silent prayer to the dragon gods who protected him in battle and life.

* * *

Big hands smoothed up and down her back. He didn't speak. He made no triumphant proclamations. He merely held her tight and let her be part of him.

She let his strength flow through her. He gave it to her gladly, with no regrets and without asking for anything in return.

When the silence became too much for her, she said, "Where were you taking me?"

"Come. I'll show you."

Gently, he unwrapped her arms from his body and, taking possessive hold of her hand, again guided her away from the castle. After several minutes, she heard the sound of rushing water and her heartbeat sped up. Soon they came upon a river, the water not so rough a human could not use it.

"Water," she sighed. "It's been ages since I bathed in anything but a tub."

"I know. I meant to bring you here yesterday, but I became sidetracked by that chain."

She smiled while Bercelak moved behind her. There was no surprise when his hands came around and began to untie her bodice. "You know, Bercelak, my hands work quite well."

"I'm sure they do. But one thing they teach warriors of all breeds is how to tie and untie knots."

He made quick work of the ribbon holding her bodice together and soon his hands slid across her exposed breasts.

Rhiannon sighed again and leaned back into Bercelak's hard body.

"You know, Princess, I think your being so tense is what has made banishing your mother's spell that much harder."

"Oh, you do, do you? And where did that tenseness come from? Perhaps because some mad bastard had me chained inside a bedroom for hours?"

"No. That's not why."

She grinned. He really was mad. And, apparently, all hers.

"I think that's what we should work on today. Getting you to relax."

The dress slipped off her body and down her legs, pooling at her feet.

"Is that right?"

"Aye. I want you relaxed and calm. The Magick will probably just flow from you then."

She had to admire his ability to spin centaur shit into fine gold.

Soft lips kissed her neck. Strong teeth nibbled the flesh beneath her ear. Large calloused hands kneaded her breasts before slipping down her body, rubbing soft circles into her skin.

"One day, Rhiannon, you'll be dragon again. I won't stop until we make you whole once more."

Pulling from his arms, she smiled up into his handsome face. "We'll worry about that later. There's a river waiting for us." This time, she took his hand and brought him to the river's edge. She pulled off his shirt and unlaced his breeches. He toed off his boots while she dragged his pants down his legs. She teased his screaming erection with the tip of her nose and he groaned.

"You truly are evil."

She laughed. Bercelak was the only living being she could name who made her laugh *with him* as opposed to *at him*.

Dragging her hands along his powerful thighs, she stood up. Leaning in she kissed his bare chest. Bercelak sighed and muttered her name. His arms again wrapped around her, pulling her tight against him. She had to admit, she did like feeling his naked human flesh against her own.

Rhiannon dragged her hands down his lower back and across his ass. Her fingers dug into the flesh of his cheeks and gripped him tight. Chuckling low, he grabbed her shoulders and held her away from him.

"You don't play fair, Princess."

"I didn't know I was supposed to."

"Good point." He lifted her up easily, tossing her over his shoulder. "I truly hope you can swim with that human body of yours, Princess."

"I can learn."

They swam for a good while. Rhiannon continued to tease him, torment him. She seemed to enjoy it. She actually smiled. He loved seeing her smile.

When she moved up behind him in the cold, clean water and took firm hold of his balls, he'd had enough. He dragged her out of the water and into the trees. Laying her out on the ground, he stretched out beside her.

"It's time I teach you who's in charge."

"That would be me."

"So sure are you?"

Her hand reached out and took firm hold of his cock. Bercelak groaned, his head dropping forward and rubbing against her.

"Yes," she muttered smugly. "I am sure."

But two could play this game of hers.

While she slowly stroked his cock, he eased his hand down to her sex. He slid a single finger inside her and she arched into his hand.

Grinning, he watched as she bit her lip and pumped her hips against his hand.

"Want more?"

She nodded, a small whimper coming from her throat.

He thrust another finger inside her and she cried out. He continued to fuck her with his hand while his mouth wrapped around her breast, his tongue teasing the nipple.

Rhiannon's strokes on his raging hard cock became a little more fitful, not nearly as graceful as before, but she didn't release him. She stroked him with one hand and dug the other into his hair, clutching the back of his head, holding him to her.

They both continued touching and rubbing each other, pushing each other to come. When her legs began to shake, Bercelak thrust harder and teased her clit with his thumb. Her hand gripped him tighter, stroking and stroking until they came together, writhing and grinding.

When they finally released each other, he looked into her eyes and together they said, "You're absolutely mad about me."

She burst out in delightful laughter, but he covered her mouth with his hand, his body tensing at the smell of human flesh nearby.

Rhiannon's blue eyes watched him, but she said nothing. She didn't fight him.

They waited and he wasn't surprised when human soldiers stepped into view. Thankfully, they were so deep into the trees that none of the men could see them.

There were a lot of them—at least a battalion—and they had two large catapults equipped with long, thick spears. Perfect for taking down a dragon. This wasn't the first time humans came to his parents' home in the hopes of capturing or killing one of his kind for sport. Nor would it be the last.

Leaning into Rhiannon, he whispered in her ear, "They've come to hunt us. You need to get back to the castle. Get my father. My brothers and sisters."

Again, she didn't argue. Merely nodded her head and brushed her hand against his jaw.

"Wait until I challenge them . . . then run. Understand?"

She nodded once more.

He kissed her forehead and stood up. He moved away from her and shifted, knocking down trees and startling the soldiers.

They attacked immediately, but he still took a quick moment to make sure she'd followed his orders. She had. He could see her long body darting through the trees. Knowing his family would protect her, he turned his attentions back to the soldiers moving on him.

Rhiannon had barely cleared the trees when big arms wrapped around her and yanked her back into a large, armored body.

"Gotcha!"

There were four of them and she was naked and unable to change. Nay. Not good.

"Willing to whore yourself out to a dragon. So I guess you'll be willing to take us on as well, eh?"

The one holding her threw her to the ground. She kicked out, nailing one in the groin. When he doubled over, she slammed her fist into his jaw. She felt bone shatter under her knuckles. Her father would be proud.

The soldier stumbled away, staring at her as Rhiannon scrambled to her feet.

"Gods, she broke his jaw," one of them said in awe.

She truly did detest them. Humans. Vile, horrid creatures that smelled awful and seemed averse to general bathing.

The three still-undamaged men, stood around her now. Surrounded her. But before they moved a roar from the river's edge caught all of their attention.

Rhiannon turned in time to see some human twisting a broadsword into Bercelak's back. Others had ropes around his snout and neck.

"No." She didn't know she said it out loud until she screamed, "*No!*"

But before she could run back to the castle for help, the men surrounding her attacked. One slamming his fist into her stomach, another grabbing hold of her hair. Yet it was the one who slapped her face that caused her the most anger. The rage swept through her and she roared.

Humans. *Humans* were treating her like this!

"Look at her!" one of those insipid little humans yelled, and Rhiannon turned toward them. It took her several moments to realize she now glared *down* at them. And with a quick glance at herself, she saw that she was dragon again.

Grinning, she watched the men who had been so ready to beat and rape her run for their lives. She snapped one up, biting him in half. Another one she backhanded into the trees, loving the sound of his spine snapping as he hit a sturdy trunk. But the one who slapped her . . . him she picked up in her claw and bathed in his screams as she ground him to pulp.

Once done, she headed back toward Bercelak, determined to help him now that she actually could. But as soon as she burst from the trees, they screamed warnings and suddenly ropes wrapped around her throat.

"A pair," one of them screamed. "A breeding pair! Bring 'em back alive."

Chapter 9

Bring them back alive? Well that was unacceptable. No one was bringing her or Bercelak anywhere.

But the ropes around her neck cut into her throat in such a way she couldn't breathe fire. Whoever sent them knew how to hunt dragons.

Still, Rhiannon had other talents.

The power buried inside her for so long now soared through her body, and she used it to full advantage.

She flicked the talons on her right claw and the line of men beside her flew back. With a flip of her claw, she set another line of soldiers on fire without even needing to open her jaw or speak a chant out loud.

Her ability to harm them without doing much more than *think* in their direction confused the men, which allowed her to pull on the ropes holding her. She dragged the soldiers over to her in the process and as they got close she stepped on them, enjoying the little squishy sounds they made.

While she finished off the few who'd targeted her, Bercelak destroyed the others. The broadsword still protruded from his back, but he no longer seemed to notice or care.

Yanking the rope off her throat, Rhiannon finished off the few soldiers running from her with a blast of her flame. Showing off for Bercelak, she let it whip out and around trees. Circling around until it leaped out in front of them, enveloping them in fire.

She looked at Bercelak and smiled. "Not bad, eh?"

"I thought I told you to go back to the castle? Was I not clear?"

He was angry, which made her defensive. "I did what I had to do. I'd do it again. And I don't owe you, Low Born, an explanation for anything I do!"

"So," he barked while struggling to reach the broadsword sticking out of his back, "I cannot rely on you to follow simple instructions? That's what you're telling me."

"What I'm telling you . . . oh!" She stormed around him and, without an ounce of mercy, yanked the steel from his back.

His pained roar rang out over the valley.

She tossed the weapon down. "What I'm telling you is I did what I thought was right. I'll always do what I think is right. Including protecting you if I deem it necessary!"

"*I don't need your protection!*"

"*And I don't need you!*"

She went to walk around him and out of the valley, but his tail caught hold of hers, yanking her back.

"Rhiannon, wait."

"No!" But with their tails locked together, she couldn't leave. And Bercelak wouldn't let her go. "Release me, Low Born!"

"Stop calling me that!"

"Then stop acting like it!"

Both crouching down now, their tails locked, they circled each other. Both ready to attack at a second's notice.

"You make everything so difficult, Princess."

"No. I don't. I don't need you to baby me, Bercelak. To always protect me. I can't be queen if you're constantly stepping in and telling me what to do."

He stopped moving. "I was only trying to protect you. It's my job to keep you safe."

"No. It's not. If I'm ever queen, I'll have guards for that. They will protect me from enemies. But I'll not bed them."

His black eyes focused on her face. "You better not."

She finally chuckled. "I hadn't planned on it."

"Good," he grumbled while he took several steps toward her. "I'd hate to kill all those guards for no reason."

Rhiannon grinned and moved around him, their bodies getting closer and closer. "I will always listen to your counsel, Bercelak. But you must trust me to make the best decisions I deem necessary."

He stared at her body, but didn't respond.

"Bercelak?"

"What?"

"I'd actually like an answer on that one."

He turned back to her face. "An answer on what?"

"Your attention seems to be waning."

"Not really." His eyes again roamed over her dragon-form. "You're dragon, Rhiannon."

"Aye, Bercelak. I am."

"Then come to me. I plan to take you as dragon."

She knew how this game was played, although she'd never found anyone worthy. Until now.

With a shake of her head, her white hair falling around her, "You'll have to catch me first, Low Born."

Then she took to the darkening skies, her lover hot on her tail.

It was her screaming that woke him the next morning. Bercelak scrambled up and searched the area for more soldiers. But all he saw was a screeching Rhiannon.

A screeching *human* Rhiannon.

"*Look at me! What happened?*"

He had no idea. When they'd finally worn themselves out after finding many more uses for their tails, they'd nearly passed out more than fallen asleep, exhaustion of the day and night finally catching up with them.

But when they'd slept, Rhiannon the dragon lay curled against his side, her light sleep-growls making him feel more content than he ever had before.

Yet here she was before him in the harsh light of the two suns. As human. It didn't matter to him whether Rhiannon was human or dragon. As long as she was his. But he knew it bothered her, which meant he had to fix this.

"Rhiannon—"

"Look at these spindly things!" Her arms flailed wildly over her head. "And all this soft, useless flesh!"

If she were trying to get him hard and lusty, she was succeeding quite nicely.

She turned and pointed at her ass. "And I could be wrong, but I think this thing is even bigger than is normal for a human my size. *How is that acceptable?*"

Quickly, Bercelak shifted. "Rhiannon, calm—"

"*Don't tell me to calm down*! That bitch did this to me, and I'll make her pay for it!"

She stormed off and Bercelak had a hell of a time keeping up with her. Anyone else, he'd assume they were merely spouting centaur shit about challenging the queen. But he would put nothing past Rhiannon, especially when she was this angry. Yet she could not face her mother now. Forget the guards who never left the queen's side. Rhiannon was still human—and clearly would remain that way as long as the spell remained unbroken—her powers not nearly as strong as when she was dragon. And since he'd never seen the queen shift to human in all the decades he'd been at her court, he somehow doubted she'd do it now if her daughter issued a challenge. In fact, he felt relatively certain nothing could get the queen to shift to human while Rhiannon still breathed.

"I wish you'd stop for a second so we can talk."

"Talk? About what?"

"About what we need to do next."

"Besides kill my mother? I have no idea."

Grabbing hold of her arm, Bercelak pulled her up short and turned her to face him. "We're in this together, Rhiannon. You and me. What hurts you, affects me the same way."

"You don't understand."

He gripped her other arm gently and pulled her close. "Then explain it to me."

Rhiannon took a deep breath and stared at the ground. "She knew how much this would hurt me. How much not being dragon would . . . would eat away at me until there was nothing of me left." She looked up into his face. "I know you don't see it. I know you don't see my mother's true intent. You've always had a blind spot when it came to her. But she won't be happy until she's destroyed me, Bercelak. Until she's taken every last bit of me. Your family . . . they love each other. Your mother protects all of you, and your father . . . he'd die before he let anything happen to one of you. But I don't have that with my mother or my siblings. I never have and I never will."

She took a deep breath and pulled out of his grasp. "She will make you choose, Bercelak. I know you don't believe it. But trust me on this."

With one sad, long look at him that completely destroyed his heart, she turned and walked off. Back to the castle and the safety of his kin.

Rhiannon sat on the slanted ledge outside her room, staring out over the battlements of Ailean's castle and lands as the two suns faded to make room for the night. All that kept her from falling was her sturdy foothold on the slats.

She wondered what she'd do next. Wondered where this particular path was going. She knew now she loved Bercelak. She knew it because she'd risked her life for him and because seeing the hurt look on his face had ripped the heart from her feeble human chest. She loved him, but she could only bring him pain. Her mother would make sure of that.

Gods, how she hated that female. Her own mother. No matter what humans thought, dragons were not the godless creatures they believed her kind to be. They loved, they despaired. They felt joy and pain. They experienced all those things humans thought only *their* kind could feel.

For more than eighty years, Rhiannon had cut off her heart. She didn't allow herself to feel much of anything, but still her mother found a way to hurt her. Not really surprising, though, since only a mother knew how to truly hurt or enhance children. Where Bercelak's mother always had a kind word or a soft touch for her lawless brood, Addiena only had derision and complaint for hers.

Rhiannon didn't realize how much she'd missed having her mother's love until she came here. Until she watched Bercelak's kin with each other.

Part of her wanted to hate them. Hate them for giving her hope she could one day feel as safe as they all did. That one day, she'd have a family that fought and screamed and generally annoyed each other nearly to death, but who still loved and protected each other as if it were their right.

But no . . . she'd never have that. She'd never have that life.

She sighed and debated whether to go back in when Maelona screamed, "Don't jump!" It startled her and Rhiannon felt her body slip on the smooth tiles, her balance gone. She slid down, her hands scrabbling for something to grab onto. Her human body would never survive this fall and she had no idea how to stop herself without wings.

Her legs flailed over the side of the ledge and she slid into nothingness.

Bercelak, leaning back in his father's favorite chair, took the goblet of wine his mother offered him. He glanced at her and she smiled.

"Don't worry. It's not your father's. It's mine."

Nodding, he took a long drink.

Her hand slid over his face, cupping his jaw. It was something she did often because she could.

"Mother?"

"Hhmm?"

"Have you ever regretted being with my father?"

"Why does everyone keep asking me that question?"

"Sorry?"

"Nothing." She sat down at the table across from him, her hands sliding through her gold hair. "That is not an easy question to answer, my son. At least not to you."

"Why?"

"Because you're not as easily put off as your kin." She gave a delicate shrug. "Look, there are sacrifices all mates must make for each other. And you do it willingly because you love them."

"You hate spending so much time being human, don't you?"

She was quiet for a long moment, then said, "I miss my cave. I miss my privacy. I've learned to tolerate this body because . . ." She gave a soft smile and her son held his hand up.

"I understand." If there was one thing he and the rest of the universe knew about his father was that the bastard knew how to pleasure a female. But Ailean took special delight in exploring a woman's body. "So you have given up much."

"No. I still have my cave. I go there when your father leaves for war or to travel. When I'm alone, I am always dragon and I revel in it. But nothing, absolutely nothing brings me as much joy as your father."

"He's loud and obnoxious."

"He's hilarious and passionate and *your* father."

"More's the pity."

His mother's hand slamming down hard on the oak table caused Bercelak to jump even though Bercelak didn't jump . . . ever.

"Your father loves you, brat. He would die to protect you and only wants you to be happy. I never saw a dragon look as proud as he did the day he saw your frowning face look up at him the first time. Even then he knew you were special. Different. So don't think for a second that you can dismiss him, and definitely don't think you can put him down to me. I won't tolerate it."

Bercelak bowed his head. "I'm sorry."

He heard his mother take in a deep breath. Then another. Finally, she said, "It's all right. I know you're frustrated and unsure what to do. But I know you'll do the right thing."

"I hope you're right."

The study door opened and his father walked in, stopping short as soon as he saw the pair of them looking so serious.

"Oh, sorry. I'm not . . . uh . . . interrupting something that will make me uncomfortable, am I?"

Shalin laughed. "No, you old bear. You're not. Just talking with our hatchling."

Ailean nodded his head. "Good. Good." He walked up to his mate, but spoke to his son. "Nice work with those soldiers out there, by the way."

"Thank you, Father."

"Your female did a nice job as well. I'm impressed she's not some vapid princess."

"She protected me."

"Good. Good." His father scooped his mother up, sat in the chair, and then repositioned her on his lap, holding her close like he always did. "I like her, if that means anything. She's a bit rough around the edges, but I think that's because she had no choice with that bitch of a mother she was cursed with."

"I agree," Bercelak replied solemnly. "I just don't know how to make her happy."

"You'll learn that in time. Of course, you may want to see if she hit the ground or not. I just saw her sliding off the ledge under her window."

Bercelak's head snapped up. "*What?*"

A strong hand grabbed hold of her wrist. "Gotcha!"

Rhiannon looked up to see Ghleanna smiling down at her. "Almost lost you there."

"Your sister scared the centaur shit out of me!"

Ghleanna easily hauled Rhiannon back into her room window. "She's as skittish as a colt, that one. Thought you were leaping to your death."

"I haven't become *that* human."

"I'm very glad to hear it."

Maelona shrugged. "Sorry. I had a moment of panic."

"She has lots of those," her sister joked.

"No I don't! I just saw her sitting out there and became worried."

Kicked open, the door slammed against the wall and Bercelak strode in. "*Why were you hanging off the ledge?*"

Glancing at Ghleanna, Rhiannon said with forced seriousness, "I couldn't take it anymore. I decided to end it all."

He frowned in confusion. "What?"

Ghleanna grabbed Maelona and pulled her from the room. "We'll just leave you to it, eh?"

The door closed and Rhiannon looked at Bercelak. "Do you really think I'd do something stupid? Do you think so little of me?"

"All my father said was that he saw you falling off the building."

"If he saw me, why didn't he help?"

Bercelak snorted. "My father? Do you have any idea how many times the old bastard's thrown me off the roof while I was human? For him that's a test of courage and speed."

"Your father is . . ."

"Frightening? Horrifying? Disturbed?"

"Interesting."

Bercelak rolled his eyes and gave a short shake of his head. "Forget him." His voice dropped impossibly lower as his black eyes locked on her. "Come to me, Rhiannon."

Stepping around the bed so that it stood between them, she murmured. "Why should I?"

"Because I ordered you to."

Rhiannon laughed out loud. "As if *that* means anything."

Picking up the cuff still chained to the bedpost, he held it up to her. "I see it will be the hard way again this eve."

"You'll have to get that on me first, Low Born. And I don't think you can manage."

He grinned, apparently more than eager to take her up on her challenge, but another knock at the door had him cursing instead.

"What?"

One of Bercelak's brothers pushed the door open and looked in. "We need you downstairs, brother."

"What is it?"

"The queen's guards are here to speak with you."

Rhiannon held herself still, unwilling to react to this news, but she saw the color drain from Bercelak's face. It wasn't fear for himself but for her that brought that reaction.

"Tell them I'll be right down."

His brother nodded and left.

Bercelak turned to Rhiannon. "Come to me, Rhiannon."

She did without question this time and he put his arms around her, holding her tight. "Stay here until one of my kin comes for you."

She nodded and felt his lips brush against her forehead.

Then he released her and was gone.

Chapter 10

The full moon had come and gone and still Bercelak had not returned to her.

She knew he'd intended to Claim her on the night of the full moon as custom dictated, but she'd spent the night alone in her room, staring out at the battlements and praying to the dragon gods for her lover's safety.

His family had done what they could to keep her spirits

high, but even she could see how they'd begun to worry as the days passed. Even his father had begun to look serious.

Now she sat in their dining hall, a book in her lap but unread while she stared blankly across the room. Bercelak's kin kept themselves busy by sharpening weapons, reading, talking, or setting things on fire with small bursts of flame. Still, they always stayed close to her, protecting her as they no doubt had promised Bercelak before he left.

Shalin sat near her studying the book the old dragonwitch had given them, but as far as Rhiannon knew, she still hadn't found any way to reverse the queen's spell. Although Shalin did think she'd found the spell the old bitch used on Rhiannon in the first place. At the moment it looked as if Rhiannon might have to kill Addiena in order to break the spell . . . like she had a chance in hell of that. Not with her human and her mother surrounded by her damn guards.

Part of her had given up hope she'd ever be able to shift into dragon again. But that concern paled against her fear of what may have happened to Bercelak.

"Lord Bercelak has returned!" one of the human servants yelled from the courtyard.

Rhiannon stood up so fast, she knocked her chair back, the book falling from her lap, completely forgotten. She pushed past Bercelak's kin as they all made their way to the dining hall doorway. As dragon, Bercelak released his battle armor so that it clattered loudly to the ground. He stepped over it and shifted to human without missing a step.

Her knees weakened at the sight of him alive and seemingly unmarked. But she saw the look on his face. Something was wrong and she could only guess what.

Naked, Bercelak took the steps leading to the hall two at a time. With only a brief nod to his mother, he took tight hold of Rhiannon's hand and dragged her toward the stairs. Glancing back at his confused family, she followed because she had no choice. He led her up the stairs and back to their room. He pulled her inside, closing the door behind them.

Once inside, he released her and strode to the window. He stood where she'd stood night after night waiting for his return. She'd even slept in a chair because she couldn't bring herself to return to the bed without him.

He clasped his hands behind his back, his legs braced apart.

For many minutes, Bercelak said nothing and she waited while staring at his human body. She'd never seen his muscles so tight and tense before, even when he was fucking her.

Finally, he said, "You were right. About your mother. And, apparently, about my reputation among most of her court."

She still didn't speak, letting him get this out in his own way.

"She wants me to break you, and then . . . I'm certain . . . she's going to demand I kill you. To prove my allegiance to her. And," he choked out, "she seems to think I will."

Bercelak cleared his throat, then went on. "The first thing she asked me was whether I Claimed you already and when I said no, she seemed relieved. She knows it would be hard for any dragon to kill their mate. That's why she kept coming up with excuses to keep me there so that the full moon would pass. From what I could tell among the court gossip, she thought the fall would kill you." He looked over his shoulder at her and Rhiannon saw the love and pain in those beautiful black eyes. With a soft smile, he said, "She underestimated your will to survive, I think."

He turned back to again look out the window. "She wants me to bring you to court in three days' time. Broken and chained. I think then she'll expect me to kill you."

Rhiannon walked up to Bercelak. She ran her hands across his strong shoulders and down his back, enjoying the feel of his flesh and muscle. Leaning forward, she kissed him between his shoulder blades. Sighing, Rhiannon wrapped her arms around his waist and rested against him.

"I'll go back tomorrow. One of your brothers can—"

Bercelak turned around so fast, she almost fell flat on her ass.

"You'll do no such thing!" Grasping her upper arms, he pulled Rhiannon hard against him. "You'll stay here with my family is what you'll do! I'll take care of your mother."

"No! She'll destroy your family just to get to me and I won't allow that!"

Lifting her so that she had to go on tiptoes, Bercelak leaned in close. "Who said I was giving you an option, Princess?"

"Who said you had to, Low Born?" she snarled in return. "This is my problem to deal with. Not yours. And definitely not your family's!"

"Unless we decide it's our problem."

Startled by the presence of a third, the pair pulled apart and looked at Ailean. He stood in the open doorway, leaning casually against the frame with his arms crossed over his massive chest.

"Neither of you will face that old bitch on your own."

"This isn't your problem, Father."

Bercelak was using all his control to hold in the rage he felt. It had been growing day by day, especially as he played the oblivious fool for that bitch queen. All that kept him going was the thought of getting back to his Rhiannon and making sure she was safe.

Now, with his father staring at him and acting like all this was some meaningless diversion, he didn't know how much longer he could keep this up before he snapped like so much dry wood.

"You're my son," he said calmly. "That makes this my problem."

"Actually," Rhiannon interrupted, "she's neither of your problems. She's mine. And I'll deal with her."

"Like hell you will!"

"Don't bark at me!"

"You'll do as I tell you!"

"Like hell I will!"

The lash of flame came out so quickly, they almost missed moving in time. But Bercelak pulled back, his arms around Rhiannon, and the flame slammed into the wall behind them.

"*What the hell are you doing?*" Bercelak yelled at his father, his control gone.

"*Getting fed up with both of you!*" Ailean yelled back, stunning Bercelak into silence. His father *never* yelled. Ever. He never had to. He found it much more annoying to mock people than to yell. Only one being ever forced him to yell . . . Bercelak's mother.

"I hate to break this to the both of you, but this has very little to do with either of you. True," he motioned to Rhiannon, "she wants you dead all right. But she could have done that at any time. And the way her court fears her, no one would dare question it. And you," now he motioned to Bercelak, "she doesn't use to get to her daughter. She's using you to get to me. And dumb ass that you are, you fell right into it. I've been telling you for years to watch your back with that bitch and you refused to listen. Now she's found a way in. And she knows if she hurts you, if she destroys you, she destroys me. Because, as much as it pains me to admit it, you're *my* son."

Ailean took a deep breath, closing his eyes briefly. He let it out and that silver gaze focused back on Bercelak's face. "She's right. Whether you go to her or Rhiannon goes, whether you kill her or not, they'll come here to destroy the rest of us. And I plan to lose none of my offspring to that slag bitch or any other. Have I made myself clear?"

Rhiannon opened her mouth to speak, but Bercelak covered it with his hand while his other hand held her in place. He nodded at his father. "Aye. You have."

"Good. Now, you've got tonight. Fuck until you're both raw, but when the two suns rise, we decide how we handle this. Together. As family. You've got some of the meanest, scariest, battle-ready minds at your disposal, *boy*. Use them." He turned and headed to the door. "I'll have food sent up. I'll see you in the morning."

The door slammed shut behind him.

Rhiannon pulled Bercelak's hand off her mouth. "Well, that was . . . interesting."

Bercelak's eyes narrowed as he stared down at the top of Rhiannon's head.

Rhiannon glared at Bercelak. "Why did you put this back on me?"

Bercelak fingered the collar around her throat and she punched his hand off. How dare he!

"I don't want you to do anything stupid. I don't want to wake up in the morning and find you gone. Off to martyr yourself to that bitch."

She pulled at the chain, but it was as strong as the pillar Bercelak had wrapped it around. "This is ridiculous! Let me go!"

"You heard my father's orders. We are to fuck." He grabbed her around the waist and tossed her onto the bed. "It's best we obey him. You saw how angry he was."

"You son of a—"

"Ah, ah, ah. Watch what you say to me." He grabbed her hips and flipped her over onto her stomach. She heard his sharp intake of breath, felt his fingers tighten on her body. "I've been thinking about this ass for days now."

The flat of that palm slammed across her rear and she froze. Good gods! Some low-born dragon had just slapped her ass.

And she had enjoyed it!

As if to prove it, Bercelak's big palm came down on her other cheek.

She kicked out, trying to strike the big bastard in the balls, but he pinned her legs down with his own.

"I can't believe you tried to kick me. Your lord and master."

"My . . . oh, you insane bastard!"

Another slap rang off her ass and she squealed. Like some weak human, she squealed!

"Be nice to me, Princess."

"Get off me!"

"Interesting. I'm not actually hearing the right word. I wonder why?" His hand slid under her body, and his index finger slid inside of her. She bit her lip to keep from moaning, but Bercelak chuckled anyway.

"Why, Princess. You're dripping wet!" Teeth nipped her backside. "I guess you like me slapping your ass then."

"I do not!"

Another slap bounced off her cheeks and, unable to stop herself, Rhiannon moaned.

"Oh, yes, Rhiannon," he whispered in her ear. "I love when you moan like that."

"Let me go."

"Not yet, Princess. I don't think you're nearly wet enough." His hand returned to her pussy and Rhiannon squirmed as his fingers played with her clit.

Fingers circled and circled and circled. One more touch and she'd come all over his hand, and that's when he pulled away.

"No!"

"Oh. You want me to stop?"

"No!" She took a deep breath. "I mean . . . don't stop."

"All right then." He slapped her ass again.

"*Ow!* That wasn't what I meant!"

"It isn't up to you, Princess. Your pleasure, like your safety, is up to me. Once we make you queen, you'll have bigger concerns. Like making sure the dragon kingdom is safe from enemies and controlling the Elders. You'll negotiate with the kings of other races and destroy those who would dare question your reign." He leaned in close, his tongue flicking her ear while his finger went back to caressing her clit. "But when you come to our sleeping place, when you lie beside me at night . . . then you'll belong to me. The worries of your day will be left outside because you will give yourself over to me and I will make you scream in pleasure until all of Devenallt Mountain thinks I must be killing you.

"Do you understand me, Princess?"

She nodded, unable to speak as she desperately sought the release he kept just out of her reach.

"That's not a clear answer, Princess."

Another slap on her ass had her screaming into the pillow, "*Yes! I understand, damn you! Yes!*"

He said nothing else as he flipped her onto her back and buried his face between her thighs. As soon as his tongue touched her clit, Rhiannon screamed in release. Her entire body shaking at the strength of her orgasm. But Bercelak didn't stop. He sent her over and over again and again, until she was sure she'd die from the pleasure of it. Then he was over her, his hard, throbbing cock shoved inside her.

He slammed into her, making sure—she knew—that her sore ass rubbed against the animal skins covering their bed. He fucked her with powerful, forceful strokes until she sobbed in absolute joy. Then her Bercelak roared as he came deep inside her.

* * *

"Son?"

Bercelak forced his eyes open. His mother stood at the foot of the bed, looking much too sweet to have ever spent a night—much less hundreds of years—in his father's bed.

"Aye?"

"We're waiting for you two downstairs." She smiled as Rhiannon stirred awake next to him. "I think we have a plan."

Chapter 11

Bercelak, in his finest dragon armor, led a still-human Rhiannon to stand before her mother, while Queen Addiena watched them in smug silence. As always, her dragon guards hovered close, watching the pair with wary eyes.

A collar around her neck, and cuffs around her wrists and ankles, with a silver chain running through the loop on each and clasped firmly in his claw, kept her in complete control.

Bercelak bowed low before the queen, resisting his urge to look at Rhiannon. The family had decided that any eye contact between the lovers would be a bad idea. They said the couple's feelings for each other showed too brightly to hide from Addiena.

"My Queen. I present to you, Princess Rhiannon."

"Ahhhh," the queen sighed out while staring coldly at her own daughter. "I knew you'd be the right one for her, Bercelak. Look how she's finally learned her place."

"No female comes to my bed, Majesty, without learning that I am master."

Rhiannon's head dipped even lower and he knew she was doing her best to hold in the laughter. *Mad bitch*, he thought with a hidden smile.

"Good. Good." She walked closer to the pair. "I knew you'd never disappoint me, Battle Lord."

The queen slithered closer—and it was a "slither," Bercelak noted—causing Rhiannon's body to tense up.

"We have much to discuss, you and I, Bercelak."

"Of course, my Queen. But first, as tradition dictates, I've brought my father with me to meet my intended mate's . . . kin." Gods, he'd almost said "victim."

At his words, Addiena's head snapped up and her eyes found Ailean immediately. Human, the older dragon wore a lush, blue cape that covered him from head to toe and matched his hair color.

Once the old bitch saw him, she couldn't turn away. She was mesmerized by him and Bercelak realized then that his father had been right . . . all of this had very little to do with him and Rhiannon and everything to do with the love one dragon had for another.

He understood that feeling. He had it for Rhiannon. The only difference . . . Rhiannon returned that love. Ailean had love only for Bercelak's mother, which was why Addiena hated them all.

Rhiannon peeked up from under her hair and watched her mother walk around them to face Ailean.

"Ailean."

With a small bow of his head, "My Queen."

"Now, now, Ailean. Is that title necessary between old friends? I'll always be Addiena to you, yes?"

Unable to help herself, Rhiannon rolled her eyes and

Bercelak gave a sharp tug on her chain to remind her that at the moment she was all contriteness and submission. It wasn't easy, though. Especially when all she really wanted to do was punch her mother in the face.

"You know, Addiena, I had to take this opportunity to see you again. It's been so long."

Her mother practically melted at Ailean's words and Rhiannon's heart went out to her long-dead father. She could only hope he had or would meet his true life mate in the next world since clearly he hadn't in this one.

"I've missed seeing you, Addiena," Ailean continued. His voice was like the sweetest honey. Low and deep, making anyone listening think about fucking. Lots and lots of fucking. "Gods, you're still so beautiful. But . . ."

"But? But what?" And Rhiannon could hear the desperation in her mother's voice.

"Would you shift for me? Would you show me your human form once again? I did always love looking at you as human."

Rhiannon didn't turn around, but she felt the flames heralding her mother's shift. Now she was as human as Rhiannon, shocking her daughter. It may have been centuries since last the bitch shifted to human.

The guards, clearly also concerned by this sudden event, moved closer to their queen.

"I thought you'd come to see me much sooner than this, Ailean."

"I know. But with fifteen offspring to raise, I lacked time. My mate needed me."

Addiena snarled and suddenly her mother moved in Rhiannon's line of sight. Gods, the old bitch was beautiful as human. Perhaps even more beautiful than Shalin . . . and how that must have nettled her mother no end.

"Ah, yes. Your *mate*," she sneered. "How is dear Shalin?"

"She is well. And very happy."

Addiena's eyes narrowed dangerously and Rhiannon knew they were quickly running out of time. "Is she?"

"Aye." Ailean stepped in front of the queen. His big hands reached out and gently caressed her face, her neck, and although her mother did her best to keep her growing anger hot, apparently she couldn't ignore how those hands stroking her made her feel.

Rhiannon watched silently as Ailean kissed her mother's forehead, her cheeks, her nose while he slowly stepped forward. Lost to the feel of him, Addiena didn't even pay attention to where he led her.

"You know, Addiena, Shalin always regretted how the two of you ended your friendship."

Friendship? What bloody friendship? Damn! And things were just getting interesting!

"That was her choice, Ailean. How was I to know she wanted you for herself?"

"That no longer matters, my dearest. But she did send you a gift."

Leaning her head back so that Ailean could kiss her throat, "Gift? What gift?" she moaned.

Leaning forward now that Ailean had maneuvered the female directly in front of her, Rhiannon whispered, "Why, my Queen"—the chain held tightly in both hands, Rhiannon wrapped the heavy silver around her mother's throat and yanked her close—"*this gift!*"

The guards attacked immediately but Ailean shifted and he and Bercelak faced them together.

Flames rose up from her mother, but immediately sputtered out.

Using nearly the same spell Addiena used on Rhiannon, Shalin imbued the chain so that the bitch couldn't shift.

Her mother knew it, too, based on the sudden and brutal fight she put up, clawing at her daughter's arms and face.

Growling, Rhiannon pulled her away from the fighting

dragons and over to a corner. "Come, Mother, let us discuss this in private."

Bercelak had to hand it to his father. The man could seduce the dragon gods out of their gold if he set his mind to it. He'd thought it was a long shot that Ailean would still be able to affect the queen as he once did. But he did all he'd promised. He'd gotten Addiena to shift to human and had maneuvered her close enough to Rhiannon so that she could use the chain his mother had given them just that morning.

When his mother had woken them up yesterday morning with words of "a plan," Bercelak had felt a little wary. Left to their own devices, who knew what crazy nonsense his kin would come up with. And when he heard the plan, he thought, "See . . . crazy kin means crazy plan." Yet it had worked. His father's seductive ways still held true. Thank the gods.

While the guards stayed focused on the three of them and the queen, they never saw his siblings slip into the Queen's Hall, using the shadows to their advantage. Prepared for battle, they moved as soon as Rhiannon wrapped that chain around the queen's throat.

The queen's guards, some of them his own comrades, really thought they could beat the low-born family with their well-trained ways. Bercelak snorted at the idea as he twisted one dragon's head around until the bones cracked, breaking into pieces, while his tail impaled another dragon, attempting to sneak up behind him, under the chin. Growing up with Ailean the Wicked as a father prepared all of his offspring for any kind of battle. He'd trained each of them at hatching to fight any and all in their way. And even though his sisters were definitely a little more gently treated than the males of his kin, they were much more brutal and Bercelak winced when two of his sisters ripped a dragon to pieces between the two of them.

He turned and searched for Rhiannon. He trusted his mother's Magicks, but he didn't know how strong or weak her skills in comparison to the queen's.

Quickly, he located his mate and her mother over in a corner. Rhiannon still had the bitch by the throat with that chain, which meant she still couldn't shift. But five of the queen's guards were advancing quickly and Rhiannon couldn't fight them off or run with her mother in her arms. Besides, he knew his Rhiannon . . . she'd never run.

Storming across the hall, Bercelak batted bigger dragons out of his way like they were toys. Nothing would keep him from reaching Rhiannon.

He grabbed two guards around the neck, yanking them back and throwing them at his brothers who'd followed him over. He went for two others, but suddenly a small troop of battle-dragons attacked him, swarming over him en masse.

Desperately he fought, trying to get to Rhiannon. He saw the queen's guards begin to move again and the grim determination on her face. Then her arms jerked to the right, the sounds of bones cracking reaching Bercelak's ears. As the dragons approached her, Rhiannon suddenly let out a sigh. For a brief moment, he thought one of them had run her through with the tip of his tail. But flames, bright white flames, swirled around her and then Rhiannon was Rhiannon the White Dragonwitch. Most powerful dragonwitch in the land. And now . . . Queen Rhiannon.

Her power fully free, her dragon-form back, she lifted her head and, with a powerful roar, unleashed a line of flame that singed the rocky ceiling above her head.

Everyone stopped fighting and all eyes focused on her.

She kicked out with her front claw and her mother's limp human body, the neck broken, flew across the hall floor and slammed into the opposite wall.

Bercelak's cock stirred as Rhiannon's blue eyes met on the eyes of her court.

Rhiannon had never felt so strong, so alive before. Power, power of the gods, flowed through her veins when it never had before. Even her dragon-form was bigger. All these years she thought she was just tiny, a runt. No. Clearly her mother had been holding her back . . . but no longer.

She stared at the dragons of her court. She was Queen now. It was now her turn to rule.

But first. . . .

With a short chant, she released a line of white flame imbued with powerful Magicks. Like a snake, it slid around the hall, avoiding Bercelak and all of his kin until it reached each of the old queen's guards. With lightninglike precision, she tore into them, leaving nothing but a pile of ash and some burnt scales.

The others, the ones whose loyalty was to the current queen, rather than to Addiena herself, watched in horror, most likely waiting for her to go after them next. But she had no intention of killing those loyal to the throne. They just needed to remember who the throne now belonged to.

"My mother is dead," she said flatly to the survivors. "I am your queen. Bow to me now and show me your undying allegiance or leave Devenallt Mountain and Dark Plains forever and hope I never see you again in this life."

She thought there would be moments of waiting while people decided. There wasn't. As one, they all bowed before her.

All except one.

Bercelak stood tall and stared at her, not bothering to hide his smile. She motioned for him to kneel, trying her best to look suitably haughty. He smirked in return. So, with everyone else's head bowed in supplication, she took a moment to stick her tongue out at him.

He laughed loud and long, scaring everyone else—even his family—nearly to death.

Bercelak walked with his father, now in dragon-form, for the trip down to the entrance of Devenallt Mountain. "Sure you won't stay for a while?"

"No, lad. Your mother waits." He grinned. "And I don't like to keep her waiting . . . much."

Shaking his head, Bercelak mirrored his father's grin. "Gods forbid you leave a female waiting."

"Only one female now. Just like you." His father glanced back into the cave as if to assure they were truly alone. "Although I wouldn't wait too long, boy. She is still unclaimed and there were many who watched her with eager eyes."

"She's beautiful, so I'm not surprised. But I'll not give her up."

"Of that I have no doubt. Your lust comes off you in great waves when she's around."

"True. But still, tradition dictates I wait until the next full moon."

"Don't be a fool, boy. She's queen. You two *make* tradition. So do what you like, eh?"

Bercelak nodded in agreement, then took a large breath and said, "Thank you, Father. For all your help today."

His father waved his words off with his claw. "You're my offspring, Bercelak. No words of thanks are ever needed."

"Well, I'll say this then . . . I no longer detest you."

Laughing, his father slammed his claw against his son's back. Anyone else would have toppled from the mountain with a snapped spine but Bercelak, as always, stood strong. If for no other reason, he'd rather not hear his father's mocking laughter following him down. "Now that's good news indeed! Your mother, at least, will be very happy."

"But you . . ."

"Could care less. I only want my children strong enough to survive these times." The old dragon grinned and Bercelak saw his rows and rows of fangs that grew as age came upon them all. "And since you are now consort to the queen, I'd say I've done my job, wouldn't you?"

Bercelak nodded. "Aye. That you have."

"Then, my strong son . . . you best Claim that deadly wench of yours or lose her forever."

With those words, Ailean the Wicked took to the air and back to Bercelak's mother. Shalin . . . the Tamer of Ailean the Wicked.

Bercelak turned and headed back to the Queen's Hall. As he passed other dragons, they greeted him but none challenged him. Instead they kept their eyes turned away. Except for some of the females who openly showed their lust. Apparently the fact that he hadn't Claimed Rhiannon caught their interests as well.

Many of his brothers and sisters waited for him in the Hall. They would stay until Rhiannon's reign was secure. The best fighters of his kin, including Ghleanna, had gone off to confront Rhiannon's siblings. They would not wait for them to come to her.

"Everything all right?" he asked his remaining siblings.

They all nodded, but Addolgar motioned up the many stairs that led to what would now be Rhiannon's bedchamber . . . *his* bedchamber.

"She's gone up. Lots of activity with the servants since she went up there, too."

Bercelak nodded as he stared up that long corridor. Strange how he suddenly felt a little . . . well, nervous. A Battle Lord who'd faced death on many, many occasions made nervous by one white dragon?

Then again . . . what if she'd changed her mind? True, they'd already been lovers but she *could*, in theory, make a case with the Elders. The thought that she may have changed her mind chilled the blood in his veins. He couldn't lose her now.

Of course there was only one way to find out what she thought. And that was to face her head-on, as his father had trained them all to do with every challenge.

"Worried she changed her mind?" Addolgar asked.

"It's not an unreasonable thought."

"Aye. Perhaps. But you'll never know until . . ."

"I know. Until I face her."

"The worse she can do, brother, is turn you to ash."

Bercelak looked at his kin and his brother merely smiled.

"Bastard."

With that last word, Bercelak headed up the stairs to his future.

Chapter 12

Bercelak walked into the queen's chamber only to find it empty. Completely empty. Which seemed strange. He figured Addiena would at least have a treasure to rest upon.

Personally, he found lying on gold and jewels rather uncomfortable.

"Ah, my lord . . . the queen has moved chambers."

Bercelak turned to look at who spoke to him, but he didn't see anyone.

"Down here, my lord."

He looked down and his eyes widened in surprise. This was no dragon in human form, but a human . . . sort of. It was actually a centaur. A female. Quite pretty—although she smelled like horse. Which made him a tad hungry.

"And you are?"

"I am attendant to the throne, my lord."

"I've never seen you before."

"I often stay in the shadows . . . as you can imagine, my lord." She glanced at her hindquarter which was . . . well . . . a *horse's* hindquarter. "It is much safer for me that way."

With an understanding smile, Bercelak nodded his head. "I understand."

"Please, my lord. Follow me. She's waiting for you."

"Is she armed?"

The centaur's head tilted to the side. "I'm sorry?"

"Never mind." He motioned to her. "Go. I will follow."

She did and he admired the beauty of Rhiannon's servant. Her hair and hide were a dark brown, but her eyes were a startling blue. Her long hair covered her chest, so she wore nothing but her skin and hide. How he'd never seen her before, he'd never know. But centaurs had strong Magicks, so perhaps she could protect herself from the dragons' keen senses.

She stopped outside a smaller but still enormous chamber. "She is inside, my lord."

"Thank you."

With a small smile, the centaur said, "I will make sure no one disturbs you at least until morn."

Bercelak chuckled and said again with much sincerity, "Thank you."

Then she was gone. Just like that. Bercelak looked around but he couldn't see her anywhere.

Interesting, but of no real concern. Besides, he had bigger issues at the moment.

With a deep intake of breath, Bercelak entered the new queen's chamber.

"Rhiannon?"

He couldn't see her anywhere. But he did see the enormous bed she had set up in one corner. That made him smile. Seemed his princess had come to enjoy the benefits of a human body.

On a whim, he shifted to human and walked toward the bed. "Rhiannon? Where are you?"

He reached the bed and looked down at the animal skins covering it. He felt his cock harden at the thoughts of what he planned to do to his princess in this bed. What he planned to do to her for hundreds of years if all went as planned.

"Rhiannon?" he called again.

Suddenly she slammed into his back, her arms around his neck, her legs around his waist. She was human and deliciously naked.

"Ha!"

It took him a moment, but he realized Rhiannon was . . . well . . . *attacking* him.

Grunting, she had firm hold of his neck and actually tried to throw him on his back.

"What in bloody hell are you doing?" He wasn't angry. Just greatly perplexed.

"What?" she panted as she did her best to drop him to the floor. "You thought this Claiming would be easy? You'll have to fight for me!"

The fact she couldn't get him to budge or even wind him, seemed to irritate her as she growled in his ear. Of course, the sound only made his cock pulse in time to his heart and lust.

Crossing his arms over his chest and bracing his feet apart, "Didn't I just fight for you?"

"No. You fought for your queen, who is me. But in order to Claim Rhiannon the dragoness . . . you'll have to fight *me*."

"Oh. Is that right?"

"Well, you didn't think I'd just roll over, did you?"

"Actually I was hoping for an on-all-fours sort of thing."

"You'll have to do more than hope, Low Born."

"Are you sure?"

"Of course I'm sure!" she said with her usual dose of arrogance.

With a smile, Bercelak reached back with one arm, his forearm stretching over her and his fingers taking tight hold of her under her armpit. With a smile, he flipped her over his shoulder and slammed her onto the bed.

"I win!" he cheered.

Bastard!

She should have been much sneakier. She forgot the stories his siblings told her about Ailean's way of raising his offspring. When she slammed into his back, although she knew he never sensed her coming, the big ox never even moved. She could have been a fairy or a piece of dust from the way she affected him.

Gods, she loved him.

She looked up into his smiling face. He'd knocked the wind out of her by slamming her on the bed so hard, but she really had no one to blame but herself.

He moved closer but his big feet hit something under the bed and he glanced down only to look back at her with a huge grin. He did that a lot now, and she loved it.

"I'm guessing my sisters helped you get your chamber set up, eh, Rhiannon?"

He reached down and when he stood tall again, he held those damn chains in his hands. "I love how my kin cares for me so."

"Dammit!" She tried to scramble away from him, but as strong as he was, he was also unbelievably fast. He caught hold of her around the waist and slammed her back to the bed.

"Oh, no, no, my love. You wanted me to Claim you properly. Then Claim you I shall. So that *everyone* knows it."

Gods, what did *that* mean?

The collar snapped around her neck and she growled in protest.

"Don't complain. You know you love it."

She did, but she wasn't about to admit that.

Once he had the collar on securely and the chain that ran from it in his hand, he pulled her up the bed until her head nearly touched the headboard. Then the bastard clamped cuffs on her wrists and chained her arms to the bedpost.

And his sisters suggested this bloody bedpost! *I'll have to thank them later*, she thought happily to herself.

Now it was true she could, finally, shift back to dragon at any time, but then . . . so could he. Besides, where would be the fun in that? Bercelak stood up and stared at her with both her arms bound.

Gods, the heat in his eyes made her wet and needy. As it always did. No one had ever looked at her like that. True, she'd seen lust before, but never so mingled with love.

He glanced at her legs. "Hhhm. I'd hate for you to kick me," he muttered to himself.

"Don't you dare!"

Which, of course, meant he would dare.

Bercelak's big fingers dragged along her body as he slowly walked to the foot of the bed. He stopped long enough to gently grip a nipple between thumb and forefinger and squeeze. She barely stopped that moan in time, but he saw her struggle and grinned.

Then he was moving again. Once he reached the end of the bed, he locked a chain to the tall bedpost and then grabbed hold of her foot, cuffing it.

He walked to the other side, the whole time staring at her.

"Gods, Rhiannon, you are beautiful. Whether as dragon or human . . . you're beautiful."

She'd had other males say similar words to her in the past, but never with such passion and, because Bercelak wanted only her and not her crown, those words meant so much more than anything anyone had said before.

Her other foot locked to the bedpost, she now lay spread eagle and open for his pleasure. She couldn't wait.

Instead of taking her, though, he stared at her for long moments and finally she couldn't stand the silence anymore.

"What? What are you staring at?"

"I'm thinking about what I'm going to do to you. I want everyone to know that you belong to me, Rhiannon. Everyone. Tell me now if that's not what you want."

Ooh. This was going to hurt. But it would be a short-lived pain and she wanted all to know she belonged to him. She wanted dragons from far and wide to know that to even look at her was to risk her mate's wrath.

"No more words, Low Born. Don't waste my time. Just do what you intend or let me go."

He nodded once and then he was on the bed, his mouth over her human foot. Right by that oddly shaped "big toe." Bercelak's talented tongue slid across her toe and down the top of her foot. And where his tongue went, a brutal pain followed as he burned her. Most dragon mates marked a shoulder or wrist. Some a breast or, the ones with senses of humor, the ass. But Bercelak was his father's son and when he took a woman he wanted everyone to know he'd Claimed her. Kin or enemy. Friend or foe. They would all know.

She bit her lip to keep in the screams of pain she wanted to unleash as Bercelak's tongue wound its way across her exposed body. And where his tongue couldn't reach, he let out a lash of Magick-imbued flame to do the job for him. But even as the pain grew worse and worse, so did the feeling that was growing steadily along her spine and in her pussy.

As she fought to keep her cries of pain in, she also fought to keep in her screams of lust. By the time his tongue slid across her belly, she arched her back and screamed out her climax. But he didn't stop. Not her Bercelak. He kept going, his tongue moving up her body, across her ribs, and around one breast to lash across a nipple. That's when another climax racked her. Still, he wasn't done. His tongue slid across her upper chest and collarbone, then across her neck, finally stopping as he stroked her jaw.

For a moment she thought he'd splash it across her face, but he'd hate to give her any more scars than he already had.

"Does it hurt?" he whispered in her ear.

"Aye."

"Do you care?"

"Nay."

"Do you want me to fuck you now, Princess?"

It should insult her that he still called her by that title, but she wanted him to call her that until they were gray Elders. She wanted to always be his princess because she had thousands who would see her as their queen.

"Get on with it, Low Born," she snarled.

And she saw her Bercelak smile just before his mouth slammed down on hers. He kissed her hard, snatching the breath from her lungs and her ability to think or reason. Then he was on top of her. His flesh pressing against hers. She cried out from the pain of his skin rubbing against her fresh burns, but the sound was lost inside his mouth. Then he was inside her and she immediately climaxed before he finished the first stroke.

He slammed into her, forcing his hard cock into her body again and again, as words tumbled from his mouth and it took her a moment to understand what he kept chanting over and over against her ear.

"I love you, Rhiannon. I'll always love you. I'll always love you."

Bercelak came with a roar, pouring his seed into her hot, tight body as she came yet again, this time screaming his name.

Collapsing on top of her, Bercelak wrapped his arms around her and held Rhiannon tight. She was his now and every dragon would know it.

She gasped for air beside him and he realized he couldn't keep lying on top of her like this. As dragon they were now of equal size. But as human, she was still smaller than him . . . although taller than most human males.

Using his arms to push himself off her body, he rolled over and lay beside her, his head cradled in the curve of her still bound arm.

"I love you, Rhiannon," he whispered as if others could hear.

She whispered back, "I love you, Bercelak." He'd waited so long to hear that . . . and it felt even better than he used to imagine it would.

He reached up and unshackled her. He glanced down at her feet, temporary exhaustion weighing him down. "Think you can take care of those?"

"Aye."

Her hand waved tiredly in the air and the shackles unlocked and dropped from her feet.

"You know, love, your new skills could get in the way of our mutual enjoyment of your being bound."

She smiled, her white hair plastered to her sweat-covered forehead. "Only if we let it."

He grinned and turned over, lying on his stomach. "All right, then, Princess. Your turn."

She stared at him in confusion. "My turn what?"

"To Claim me. I'd like you to avoid the face, though. I think I have enough scars there, don't you?"

She stared at him in surprise. It wasn't that females didn't mark their mates, but it rarely happened in the beginning. Most males needed to show their dominance and did it with the Claiming. Years later, after all had settled down, did the females finally mark them.

"Are . . . are you sure?" She couldn't seem to get that look of shock off her face. It made him smile. She usually hid her surprise so well.

"Am I sure that I want everyone to know I belong to you as you belong to me? Oh, yes, love. I'm very sure. Now," he settled down, his head resting on his crossed arms, "what was it you said to me? Oh, yes . . . No more words, Princess. Don't waste my time. Just do what you intend or let me go."

Before he could say another word, Rhiannon straddled his ass and he just *knew* this was going to hurt.

"My lord."

Bercelak forced his eyes open to find the centaur standing beside him. She leaned in and whispered. "I'm sorry to awaken you, my lord. But your kin have asked to speak with you."

He glanced around, his eyes still trying to focus. "Is it morning?"

The centaur smiled, most likely remembering her promise from the night before. "Yes, my lord. *Late* morning."

"Tell them I'll be right there."

Without another word, she bowed and left.

Rhiannon, still human as was he, was pushed up tight against his side, her head nearly buried in his armpit. She slept deep and looked beautiful doing it.

He smiled as he remembered their Claiming from the night before. With all that screaming and roaring and snarling, the whole court must have thought they were killing each other. He kissed her forehead and dragged himself out of bed.

Without even thinking about it, as human he went to the Queen's Hall. He had every intention of getting right back into bed and enjoying Rhiannon—*his* Rhiannon—even more before first meal. Then he'd spend the rest of the day and eve taking her as dragon.

Several of his brothers and Ghleanna, all those who went to track down Rhiannon's kin, waited for him.

One of his younger brothers whistled. "Gods, Bercelak. What did that female do to you?"

"What is it?" he barked, his arms crossed over his chest and his feet braced apart. He was in no mood for his siblings' antics when he had the woman of his dreams waiting for him back in their bedchamber.

Ghleanna answered, "By the time we arrived, her three brothers and that viper sister of hers were long gone. Word is that two of her brothers went into the Northlands."

"Northlands?" he scoffed. "The lightning dragons will eat them alive. What else?"

"While the sister and the other brother went to the desert lands of Alsandair. Those dragons might help them."

Addolgar stepped forward. "There's no guarantee the lightning dragons won't help them either. They may be barbarians, but they are greedy ones. They'd love to have this territory."

"And they'll never get it."

At the sound of Rhiannon's voice, they all turned except Bercelak. When around others he would never turn away from those who may harm her. Now that she was queen, even with her mother dead, Rhiannon was in more danger than she had been before. So, instead, he gave a quick glance at her over his shoulder. She stood before them as human, completely naked, the marks of her Claiming pitch black against her skin and the collar and chain still around her neck.

Bercelak had never loved her more.

"Gods, Bercelak!" his sister exclaimed. "What the hell did you do?"

He knew what she meant. He'd branded a dragon the entire length of Rhiannon's body, the tail starting at the very tip of her foot and reaching up one leg, across her stomach, around her back and across her ass, then back around and up her rib cage, across her breast, then upper chest and collarbone, until it rested across her neck and stopped at the right side of her jaw.

But even though he knew what his sister meant, he didn't

answer her. Their Claiming was their Claiming and no one, even his nosy kin, had any say in it whatsoever.

He spoke to Rhiannon without turning around, "What do you want us to do? Do we follow them?"

"No. I'll not send out troops to bring back four dragons," she stated with confidence. "But that doesn't mean we won't be prepared for them. If they come back here, with or without dragons from other regions, we'll rip the scales from their body and tear their flesh apart."

Bercelak bit back his smile as the entire hall fell silent at Rhiannon's casually dropped words. He knew she meant it, but it was the coldness that frightened the rest of them. It didn't frighten him, though. He knew she'd make a wonderful queen. He never had a doubt.

"We have things to do right here first," she continued. "My kin can wait until they do something stupid."

She grew silent and he could feel her eyes boring into his back, examining her own mark. A dragon burned into his human flesh covered his entire back and, to his amusement, his ass as well. His body grew tight while his cock grew hard at the thought that his female wanted him as much as he wanted her. And he didn't bother to hide his reaction. Let them see. Let them see it all.

"My bed grows cold, mate," she murmured behind him. "Don't leave me waiting."

With that she turned and walked back to her bedchamber. Her chain dragging behind her.

Bercelak focused on his family. "We leave them for now as she said, but we'll be ready for them should they return."

His brothers nodded as did his sister. They were all part of Rhiannon's court now. No longer the low-borns . . . but royalty.

With a nod, he turned and walked back up the stairs. He heard one of the other dragons, not his kin, mutter to a comrade beside him, the voice filled with disgust, "She's marked him already. Look at his back." The dragon snorted. "Well, we see who has the cock in that family."

Bercelak kept walking, even as he sensed his kin silently backing away from the one who spoke. As he reached one of the weapon stands at the edge of the hall, he grasped a long pike, turned, and threw it with unerring aim.

The pike slammed through the dragon's neck, yanking him back, and impaling him against the marble wall behind him.

Bercelak turned to the rest of the court who watched him in fear. All except his kin. They looked down at their feet or at the ceiling. Because they knew if they looked at each other they'd burst out laughing. Which would definitely destroy the terror thing they were all striving for at the moment.

He smiled, which seemed to scare the royals even more. "I didn't hear him. What did he say?"

No one answered. No one dared.

"That's what I thought."

With that last bit sneered at those too weak to challenge him, he went back to his bedchamber and made his mate scream his name for the remainder of the morning . . . and well into the afternoon.

Epilogue

195 years later . . .

Snarling, Rhiannon marched back toward the family's cave. While Devenallt Mountain held her throne, it was this cave where she raised her hatchlings. And what spoiled, rotten little hatchlings they were!

Without even thinking, she stormed past her mate, busy with his kin looking at attack plans. Her throne was at risk and they would be going to war. Already her two eldest had been given the armor of battle dragons. She didn't want them to go, but they were old enough now to make their own choices.

Bercelak's claw grabbed her upper forearm, holding her in place. "What's wrong?"

"Nothing." She tried to pull away, but his grip was like a vice.

"Leave us," he commanded the dragons in the room. And, without hesitation, they did.

"What's wrong, Rhiannon? Tell me."

She yanked her forearm away and glared at her mate. "Your," and she punctuated that "your" with the tip of her tail in his face, "viper offspring cut off his tail!"

Bercelak shook his head in confusion. "Cut off whose tail?"

"Gwenvael's!" she shouted, so angry, she could barely see straight.

But instead of Bercelak demanding his offspring's presence so he could tell them what horrible little bastards they were, he burst out laughing.

"I'm sure he deserved it."

Her tail slapped him across the neck. "This isn't funny!"

"Oh, Rhiannon, just repair it. You baby him too much."

She slammed her foot down, shaking the cave walls. "I can't!"

"Why not?"

"When I caught them, I yelled right as Fearghus was throwing it to Briec. He was so startled that it slipped past his hands and into the river . . . they have not been able to find it."

Bercelak cleared his throat and worked hard to keep his face straight. "It's an easy enough thing to happen, my love."

Her tail slammed into Bercelak's chest, which didn't even

budge him. "You raised them very much as your father raised you, *my love.* Those little bastards don't *get* startled!"

Unable to hold it back anymore, Bercelak once again burst out laughing. "*I know!*"

"Oh!" Rhiannon turned and started to storm away, but Bercelak's forearms wrapped around her and he pulled her dragon body tight against his own.

"Don't be angry, love. Please. I'm sorry." He gave a valiant try at not laughing.

"It was horrible, Bercelak. Blood was flying everywhere, and he just kept swinging that tail around."

With one snort, Bercelak started laughing again.

"You know," she growled, "you wouldn't think this was so funny if it were your precious Morfyd or Keita."

As she knew, that sobered him immediately. "No, I would not."

"Well that's how I feel about my Gwenvael."

"Again . . . you baby him too much."

"And you're too hard on him because he reminds you of your father."

"From the time he was twenty winters I kept finding him with my father's kitchen staff."

"He's lusty."

"He's a whore."

"Oh!" She pulled out of his arms. "I won't discuss this anymore. You're irritating me, Low Born."

She turned to walk away from him, but his voice stopped her.

"Don't walk away from me, Rhiannon." There was no threat in his voice. Only delicious promise.

"Shift," he ordered with a low purr.

"Why should I?"

"Because I told you to."

She did her best to hide the shudder that went through her body and shifted to human. In seconds, his human arms wrapped around her from behind, then his low voice muttered in her ear, "You are much too tense, Princess."

"Think you can help me relax then?"

"Oh, aye. I know I can."

His hands on her breasts, he pulled her back until she knew they were right by the table with all its elaborate battle plans and maps. And that's right where he tossed her.

Stepping between her legs, Bercelak's head lowered until his mouth covered her breast.

Moaning, she leaned back, her legs wrapped around his waist, her hands buried in his silky black hair. After all this time, he still felt so very good.

But they kept forgetting one small thing . . . actually, five not-so-small things . . .

"Gods!" Their eldest son barked. "Can you two not find a private alcove or, at the very least, a bed?"

Rhiannon looked over to see her children at the entrance. Her eldest, Fearghus, slapped his claws around the eyes of her two youngest, Keita and Éibhear. Morfyd looked appalled and embarrassed, Briec looked bored and Gwenvael, of course, applauded.

"It's nice to see old dragons fucking, isn't it?" he cheered. And she suddenly wished that *she'd* taken his tail.

Bercelak lifted his head and roared, "Out, you little bastards! *Out!*"

Morfyd couldn't move fast enough. She practically sprinted from the room, white hair flying behind her. *I really will have to find a way to toughen that little dragoness up.* Briec snorted and walked away, reaching back to grab Gwenvael's wounded tail and drag the cheeky little bastard, yelling and threatening and still bleeding, from the room. Fearghus lifted up his young kin and walked out while Keita tried to remove her brother's hand so she could get a better look, and Rhiannon's sweet Éibhear just kept saying, "What? What am I missing? *What?*"

Once they'd left, Bercelak focused those black eyes on her. Eyes that her eldest son had.

"*You* wanted hatchlings."

"I know. I just didn't want *those* hatchlings. Personally, I blame your father."

Bercelak's eyes grew wide. "Excuse me?"

On a burst of laughter, she exclaimed, "Well that came out horribly wrong!"

"Oh, that's it, Princess. You've got to make it up to me now."

With that, he lifted her up and tossed her over his shoulder.

"Where are we going?" she demanded, even as she kept laughing and he stalked off deep into the cave.

"Where do you think?"

And, laughing, they said together, "To get the chains!"

A TALE OF
TWO DRAGONS

Chapter 1

"Oy! Addolgar!" they yelled into his human face. "*Oyyyyyyyyyyyyyyy!* You awake?"

Idiots. Every one of his brothers and sisters were utter idiots. Even these two—Ghleanna, his older sister; and Bercelak, his younger brother—who he believed to be the smartest of his kin, were still . . . idiots.

"Maybe he's dead then," Bercelak suggested.

"Nah. I think he's breathing. He just sleeps like the dead, is all."

An elbow, probably Ghleanna's, rammed across his jaw. "*Addolgar!*" she screamed. "You awake?"

His jaw throbbing, Addolgar knew he couldn't keep ignoring his siblings or he risked losing part of his face.

He slowly opened his eyes. "What?"

"See?" Ghleanna said to Bercelak. "He's not dead."

"Such a relief. Mum would have had a fit if he'd turned up dead."

"Your concern overwhelms me, brother." Addolgar cracked his neck. "So what do you want?"

His brother and sister, also in their human forms, stood tall, hands on hips, staring down at him. The two of them looked the most alike of their siblings. Black hair, black eyes, rude natures. Bercelak had the nastiest attitude, but really he was only the most focused. He had big plans. He didn't just want to be a warrior; he wanted to lead the Queen's Army. It was a lofty goal, especially for one of the low-born Cadwaladr Clan, but if any of them could do it, it would be Bercelak.

Ghleanna was more like Addolgar. They battled because they liked it and were good at it. They loved the armor, the weapons, the blood, the death. When the Queen had no wars, Addolgar and Ghleanna found human wars to fight. They were always fun and good training.

But still, could Addolgar not get a few minutes to himself? He'd just wanted to have a meal and get a little nap before heading back to the human troops he'd been fighting with. As always, though, with his kin . . . that apparently wasn't possible.

"Why are you two bothering me?"

"Her *Majesty*," Ghleanna sneered, "wants to see us."

Addolgar smirked. His sister didn't even bother trying to hide her dislike of the current monarch, Dragon Queen Addiena. She'd taken over for her mother, the much-loved Queen Ganieda, nearly a century ago, and Ghleanna still barely accepted Addiena as their ruler. True, she'd protect her as the monarch of their people, but that was as far as Ghleanna the Black was willing to go.

Curious as to what was going on, Addolgar asked, "She wants to see us for what?"

"You don't question," Bercelak snapped. "You come when called."

"When did we become pets?" Addolgar asked his brother. Ghleanna snorted.

"Don't anger me, brother. We serve the Queen—without question, without delay. Now get off your fat ass and let's get going."

Knowing quite well that his ass was perfect, Addolgar was getting ready to argue, for no other reason than to annoy his brother, when Ghleanna cleared her throat and motioned behind her. A group of humans were running toward them, all of them poorly armed with pitchforks and rusty swords and pikes.

"I'll handle—" Bercelak began, but Ghleanna quickly stepped in front of him.

"No," she told him. "You'll keep your mouth shut."

The humans quickly crossed the open field until they reached them, the one out front stopping in front of Ghleanna. "Did ya see him, soldier?" he demanded. "Did ya see the dragon?"

Ghleanna nodded. "We have troops searching for the bastard now. We'll find him. And we'll kill him."

"He destroyed my cattle!" one of the men yelled. "Look at this!"

They did. All those bones, sucked clean of meat, fat, and marrow. It wasn't the entire herd that Addolgar had eaten but at least half. He'd been hungry, though. Very hungry.

"That bastard," Ghleanna snarled. "We'll wipe the land of him, I promise you that."

The humans looked at Addolgar. "What's wrong with him then?" the leader asked.

"He . . . was attacked by that dragon." Ghleanna nodded at Addolgar.

With a sigh and a barely suppressed eye roll, Addolgar raised his arm and weakly stated, "Don't mind me. I'm just slowly bleeding to death from the attack." All that cow's blood smeared over his human flesh helped with that lie. Of course, he'd been dragon when the blood had splattered, the human herder running off, screaming hysterically and pissing himself. And after Addolgar had finished eating, he'd shifted to human so he could relax with his back against a sturdy tree and his long human legs stretched out in front of him.

One of the humans studied Addolgar and asked, "Why's he naked?"

The three of them blinked and then Bercelak lied, "Because it'll be easier to carry his dead body back to the troops with no armor."

"Won't he need his armor for the funeral?" asked another curious human.

Addolgar and Ghleanna looked at Bercelak, waiting to see what their younger brother would come up with next.

"Uh . . . yes. You're right, of course. Um . . . but we all hated him. So we're stripping him of any honor at his death."

"But he's still alive," said a horrified woman.

That's when Addolgar bit the inside of his mouth to prevent the laughter threatening to come out; Ghleanna, always short on patience, had had enough.

"Here," Ghleanna said to the humans. "Take this." She held out her hand to Bercelak. He glanced at her open hand and back at her face.

"What?"

Ghleanna tilted her head the tiniest bit, and Addolgar read that move for exactly what it was. A threat.

Growling a bit, Bercelak ripped the coin pouch he had tied to his sword belt off and handed it to Ghleanna. She, in turn, handed it over to the humans. "For your cattle."

"You'll take care of the dragon, though, yeah?"

"Our troops are moving on him as we speak. Have no fear. He'll not be back."

"Lizards," the human spit out. "Hate them all."

With that, the humans turned around and headed back to their homes.

"I should have eaten them," Bercelak sneered.

"What is wrong with you?" Ghleanna demanded.

"They made me angry." He paused a moment, then admitted, "And they smell really good. I'm so hungry."

Addolgar pointed to a nearby meadow. "There's more cows over there. And I could eat again."

Ghleanna shook her head and rubbed her fingers against her temples. "You two are such idiots."

Addolgar laughed. "I was just thinking the same thing about you lot!"

* * *

Braith of the Darkness, Daughter of the House of Penard-dun, so named by the western city she'd destroyed when they'd sent an army to her cave to hunt her as if she were some common bear in the woods, landed on the side of Devenallt Mountain.

The seat of power for the Dragon Queen of the Southlands, Devenallt Mountain was the one place Braith loathed going. As a royal, there were certain times of the year she was expected to come and spend time among other royals, but she hated it. She had nothing in common with . . . well . . . anyone. She had nothing to say. At least nothing that would interest anyone. So she mostly just stood around, holding a chalice of wine she never drank, and waited until she could sneak out without being noticed.

Unfortunately, she wasn't here for a specific royal event but because she'd been sent for by her father. Something that frightened her more than she'd ever admit out loud. She wasn't close to her father. Never had been. Her father had always made it clear that, to him, she was nothing more than "your mother's daughter," which was fine with Braith. She didn't need her father and didn't want to be around him, and he had always seemed to feel the same. So why he was summoning her to Devenallt Mountain, she had no idea.

Determined to get this over with, she tossed back her blue hair and headed into the mountain stronghold.

Moving out of one cavern and into another, Braith stopped when she saw one of the Queen's offspring, Princess Rhiannon. Of all the Queen's offspring, Rhiannon was the only one whom Braith managed to tolerate, which was probably as close to a friendship as either of them had ever had.

"My lady," Braith said to the royal, dipping her head a bit out of respect.

"Braith of the Darkness. You look well."

"Thank you, my lady."

Those who dismissed Rhiannon as another vapid royal truly did not know her, and they didn't want to know her. And with reason. Queen Addiena, a being to be feared, loathed her daughter more than Braith's father loathed her. While Braith's father ignored her, Queen Addiena seemed to take pleasure in making Rhiannon's life miserable. The current ruler of the Southlands was a cold, heartless, and petty cow who wielded hate and revenge with knifelike precision.

"What brings you here to Happy Mountain?" Rhiannon asked Braith.

"I've been summoned by my father."

The princess cringed in a rather unroyal manner. "Poor you."

"I know."

"It could be worse. You could have been summoned by that bi—gods!" the princess suddenly squealed, quickly turning her back to the entrance. "It's *him*."

Braith looked and saw Major Bercelak the Unpleasant—a name, it was rumored, that had been given to him by his own troops—making his way toward them. His gaze was locked on Rhiannon like a jungle cat's on a wounded deer.

In the mood to sacrifice herself for the greater good, Braith stepped around so that she stood between the pair. "Make a run for it, my lady. I'll protect your back."

"I'll not forget this, Braith of the Darkness."

Then Rhiannon took off, all that long white hair flowing behind her.

Bercelak marched up to Braith, trying to see around her. "Where'd she go?"

"Who, Major?"

Painfully black eyes locked on Braith. "Princess Rhiannon."

"Oh. I haven't seen her."

"She was just standing behind you." The black dragon

glowered at Braith. "But maybe with that large ass of yours I just missed—"

"Bercelak!" the dragon's sister, Ghleanna, snarled as she stepped up behind him.

"She got in my way!" he barked.

"I don't care if she shaved your hair off. *Be nice!*" The black She-dragon nodded at Braith. "Lady Braith."

"Lieutenant."

Now second lieutenant, Ghleanna might not outrank her brother in the Queen's Dragon Army, but she was his older sister and rank meant nothing when kin was involved.

"Sorry about my brother."

"You don't have to apologize for me," Bercelak snapped.

"*Someone does!*" she bellowed back, one of the few who showed no fear at the constantly snarling, glowering bear of a dragon. He had to be the most unpleasant bastard in the Southland territories, but, Braith could admit, he was very good at what he did, which was protecting the Southland borders.

"Oy," another voice said. "Did you lot hear?"

Then he was there. As tall as his brother, but wider. Like a mountain of granite inside the mountain fortress.

"Hear what?" Ghleanna asked while still glaring at Bercelak.

"About Davon the Elegant."

Ghleanna faced her handsome brother. "What about her?"

"Lightnings snatched her from her father's cave."

"What?" Ghleanna gasped, clearly shocked.

"Word is it was the Olgeirsson Horde."

"We should have killed that bastard Olgeir long ago," Bercelak growled. "The fact that he still breathes offends me."

"Did you hear of this, Lady Braith?" Ghleanna asked Braith.

"I had not."

But Braith wasn't exactly surprised. The Northland dragons did not breed many females, so they were often forced to steal She-dragons from other regions. But She-dragons weren't helpless victims waiting to be kidnapped, so the Lightnings usually cut off one wing when they took a female so that she could not fly away. And some She-dragons were so shamed by it, they ended up staying in the north with little to no fight. It was the kind of fear that could keep a She-dragon up at night and one of the reasons few knew where Braith lived. In fact, her father believed her cave was nearly fifty leagues away from where it actually was located. Not that she didn't trust him but . . . no. She was lying. She didn't trust him.

"Perhaps that's why the Queen's asked us here," Ghleanna suggested. "So that we can track the bastards down and cut their hearts out."

"I want Olgeir dead as much as you," Bercelak complained, "but it annoys me that once again we need to run in and rescue the weak royals because they can't protect themselves."

Ghleanna rolled her eyes and rammed her fist into her younger brother's shoulder.

"Ow! What was that for?"

Ghleanna motioned to Braith. "We're standing next to a royal, you idiot."

"Does she really count?"

That's when Bercelak's brother took notice and cheered, "Braith of the Darkness! You're looking well!"

I am?

"She is?" Bercelak asked, which got him a shot to the neck from his sister's tail. He pushed Ghleanna back and the two began fighting. Addolgar ignored them both to focus on Braith.

"It's been a long time. How have you been doing?"

I'm fine. How are you? You're looking very handsome today, Addolgar the Handsome, lord of my loins.

At least that was what she'd like to say to him, but instead she came out with, "Yeah, hi."

Even worse, she said that into her chest because she couldn't bear to look into those lovely brown eyes. Her tail curled into a circle like a snake caught under the hot sun and her claws curled into tight fists.

Gods, he was handsome. She'd never known such a handsome dragon. His dark silver scales shiny. His fangs bright white and long. His dark silver hair reaching past massive shoulders to powerful muscled forearms.

Handsome!

And what was she? Her lip almost curled. She was nothing but Braith of the Darkness. Destroyer of a single city that no dragon had ever heard of.

How was that impressive to someone like Addolgar? Revered Dragonwarrior. Loved by his army comrades— dragon and human—and considered one of the "nice" Cadwaladrs of their Clan. The only other nice Cadwaladr was Addolgar's father, Ailean the Wicked.

Truth be told, it was Addolgar's good nature that warmed Braith's hard heart more than anything else. Not only because he was kind to her when even her own father was not, but also because he was kind to all he was not against in war.

Glancing over at his battling siblings, Addolgar said low, "Sorry about my brother, Braith. He can be a bit of a prat."

"Yeah," she said into her chest. "I know."

"What did he come over here for anyway?" Since, apparently, they both knew he'd never walk this way to see Braith.

"Rhiannon, I believe."

"Ahhhh. I see." Addolgar laughed. "His obsession with her is so ridiculous. That royal would cut his throat while he slept and laugh while he bled out."

Braith wished she could defend the princess on that . . . but it was probably true.

"You two friends then?" he asked.

"Not really."

"Just royal politeness. I get it."

"Guess you could say that." Braith cleared her throat, studied her claws against the stone ground, and wondered when this nightmare of awkwardness would end.

"Oy! Addolgar!" his sister called out, now that she had Bercelak in a headlock.

"Looks like I've gotta go," Addolgar said.

"Of course."

"It was nice seeing you again, Lady Braith."

"You, too."

He walked around her and Braith let out a breath, grateful that was over. She hated that she seemed to be such a ridiculous mess around that dragon.

"You. Girl," her father's cold voice snapped at her from one of the chambers.

Braith turned toward her father. Perhaps if she could get this over with quickly, she could head home to her quiet, hidden cave with some cattle she could steal from the local farmers.

"Father," she said as coldly as he'd called to her. "You summoned me?"

Chapter 2

"You didn't torment her, did you?"

Addolgar stared down at his sister while they waited in the crowded hall for their turn to speak with the Queen. "Torment who?"

"Braith."

"Torment her? No." He liked that big-boned dragoness. She seemed sweet, if a little shy.

"She's not bad-looking."

Addolgar shrugged and answered honestly, "I wouldn't know. She never looks at me."

"Do you have any idea why?" Ghleanna asked.

He grinned. "No. Why?"

Ghleanna sighed and looked away. "Pathetic."

"Who me?"

"I don't like her," Bercelak complained.

"I think the feeling is mutual, little brother," Ghleanna replied. "She looked like she was seconds from tearing your eyes out."

"I don't know why," Bercelak replied. "I'm known throughout the land to be so friendly."

Addolgar and Ghleanna faced their younger brother . . . and stared at him.

"What?" he asked drily. "Everyone knows I'm like happy puppies in a meadow on a sunny day."

There was a long pause after that proclamation and then both Addolgar and Ghleanna exploded into laughter, Bercelak almost cracking a smile.

Braith's father led her to a quiet alcove. When he finally stopped and faced her, it was like he looked right through her. "The Queen," he said, "will request that you be the companion to Lady Katarina when she's returned to her home in the west."

"Me?" Braith asked, shocked. No one had ever asked her to be anyone's companion. A royal she might be, but she wasn't charming or elegant or schooled in any of the finer arts. In fact, royal dragons mostly found her uninteresting and she prided herself on that. Because it wasn't easy to do as little as possible to elicit as little interest as possible.

"Yes, you. And you'll accept the offer."

"But—"

"There is no arguing here. Do as you're told."

"I guess I'm just surprised that the Queen—"

"Yes. She's your queen and you'll follow her directive without question. Understand?"

She wanted to punch her father in his snout, but she wouldn't. He was her father after all. True, a father whose funeral rite she planned to dance at and toast with ale, but her father just the same.

"Yes. I understand."

"Good. Now go to the throne room. She's requested your presence there."

Her father walked off, his tail following behind him. She was so tempted to step on it, just to see him yank back or fall on his face. Either would make her feel better.

"Hello, hello," Addolgar growled. "Who's that then?"

Ghleanna looked around him and rolled her eyes. "So typical."

"What?"

"A royal. You're as bad as the idiot over here."

Bercelak blinked, looked away from the Queen as she spoke to her Dragon's Maids. "Do you mean me?"

"Yes. You. Both of you. Always going for these simpering weak royals. Where did you get that from anyway?"

"Dad?" Addolgar asked.

"Don't insult our mother. She may be a royal, but she's hardly weak and she definitely doesn't simper."

"Who says this one simpers?" Addolgar studied the royal She-dragon speaking to the Queen. A pretty, gold dragoness with long, luxurious hair and light gold eyes. "Her legs are sturdy enough."

"Bloody twigs, if you ask me."

"I didn't ask you. I just wanted to know who she is."

"She's Lady Katarina from the Western Mountain territories. Her father is Lord Berg."

"Addiena hates Berg," Bercelak reminded them.

Addolgar felt a quick bolt of panic. "Gods, we don't have to kill her, do we?"

"No."

"Good. 'Cause she's cute."

Ghleanna sighed. "Idiots."

"Why am *I* an idiot?" Bercelak wanted to know.

"Let me count the ways," a voice muttered from behind them.

Surprised at that retort coming from Braith, Addolgar and Ghleanna laughed, but Bercelak turned around, faced the Elder's daughter.

Braith blinked and asked, "Did I say that out loud?"

"You did," Bercelak growled.

She gave a small shrug of good-sized shoulders for such a supposedly weak royal female. "Sorry."

"Lady Braith!" Queen Addiena called out from her throne. "Perfect timing, my dear! Come forward. Come forward. I have someone for you to meet."

"Yes, my Queen," Braith said.

And that's when Addolgar noticed something. The few times Addolgar had met Braith, the royal had never looked him in the eye, but she didn't seem to have that same problem with Bercelak. In fact, as she walked around him, she held Bercelak's gaze, almost challenging him. Perhaps she had more bite with those fangs than any of them had realized.

"What are you smirking at?" Bercelak barked at him.

"I didn't know I was," Addolgar replied.

"Well, you were."

The brothers were silent for nearly a minute until Addolgar noted, "You're awfully tense."

"Shut up."

"Braith, I don't think you've met Lady Katarina. Lord Berg's daughter."

Braith nodded at the fellow royal.

"Now," the Queen went on, "I thought you would be perfect to travel with Lady Katarina on her way back to the Western Mountains."

Braith and Katarina locked gazes, and Braith knew in that moment that she was not alone in not wanting to go on this trip. . . . Katarina didn't want her to go either. Braith had no idea why Katarina felt that, nor did she care to know since, in the end, they both had the same desire.

The problem was Addiena. How to handle her?

"Your Majesty," Braith tried, "I truly appreciate this honor, but I'm not sure I'm the best one for such a role."

"And I'm sure you are. Your father suggested you himself."

Braith tried not to frown, but it was hard. "*My* father suggested me for this? Really? *My* father."

The Queen laughed. "Oh, Lady Braith. You're so adorable. See, Lady Katarina? You'll be entertained by Lady Braith's humor all the way home. Won't that be fun?"

Katarina gave a reluctant nod. "Of course, Your Majesty. She seems quite entertaining."

"Now I'm sure you have," Addiena sneered, "*very* important things to do, Lady Braith. We all know how busy you are." And no, her sarcasm wasn't lost on Braith or anyone else standing within a twenty-league radius. "But I'd really like Lady Katarina to have a female companion along for this trip. She'll be simply surrounded by males and you know how those Western Mountain dragons are about their females." Did she mean the Western Mountain dragons that were, in fact, Southland dragons? Then yes, Braith knew the Western Mountain dragons because they were just like every other bloody fire-breathing dragon in the Southlands.

Gods, this She-dragon!

"But—"

"Now, if you're concerned that you'll be at risk on this trip because of those horrible Lightnings and what they did to poor Lady Davon, please, both of you, don't worry. You'll be protected by my *best* escorts. Your father chose them himself, Lady Braith."

Was that really supposed to mean something to Braith? Because, ya know . . . it didn't.

"Of course, Your Majesty."

"Tell me, my Queen," Katarina asked softly, "will you be sending your troops into the Northlands to retrieve Lady Davon? As you know, the Northlanders do not kill our She-dragons, just force them into a Claiming."

"I know," the Queen said, sadly shaking her head. "It's truly horrible what these Lightnings do to our poor sisters. But sending my army into Northland territory would be seen as an act of aggression with the Hordes and I'm . . . just not sure we're ready for war."

Ready for war over one meaningless She-dragon was what the Queen really meant. Because if there was one thing they all knew, her dragon army was *always* ready for war. They thrived on it the way the Sea dragons thrived on water. Still, the Queen would do nothing until she was ready.

"So we're agreed?" the Queen asked, although they all knew she wasn't asking a damn thing. To be honest, Braith would rather her just make it an order. Playing these constant political games with the female did nothing but chafe the bloody scales off Braith's ass.

* * *

Addolgar smiled at his brother's announcement. "I'd love to," he announced.

"Of course you would." Bercelak glared at his brother. "But this isn't a time for you to be trying to get under some royal's tail. You have a duty to our Queen. Do not fail her because you're busy trying to fuck Berg's daughter."

Placing his claw against his chest, Addolgar reared back and gasped, "Brother! How could you say such a thing? How could you question my—"

"Oh, shut up."

Addolgar chuckled. "I don't know why you're getting so upset about this. She won't be the first royal I've ever escorted."

"I'm not upset. But I'm concerned. Something . . ."

"Something what?"

Bercelak shook his head. "I don't know. But watch your back, brother. With gods-damn Lightnings coming over our borders to snatch our females, we don't exactly have time to be battling bloody Thracius and the Iron dragons in the west as well. And this is Berg's daughter we're talking about. So this is no time to be lazy."

Addolgar understood that. Lady Katarina's father and his dragon army kept the Iron dragons, who lived—and plotted—on the other side of the Western Mountains, from trying to invade Dark Plains at every possible opportunity.

Of course, the reason that Katarina had been at Devenallt Mountain for nearly a year was because the Queen had been reminding Lord Berg of her power. Although she'd welcomed Berg's daughter with open claws, no one was fooled into thinking Addiena cared for her. At least no one but Bercelak, who continued to believe that Addiena was a wonderful queen who just liked to invite royal females to Devenallt Mountain for fun. But anyone not blinded by the Queen's beauty or, more importantly, the beauty of the Queen's daughter, knew this was simply a power play by the cold-hearted royal.

Politically, though, it did make sense after what had happened during the Great Battle of Aricia, when the Iron dragon Overlord Thracius had taken the Queen's consort and had him crucified in Quintilian Provinces. Something that had not bothered the Queen nearly as much as it had bothered the Queen's offspring. Especially Princess Rhiannon, who'd always been close to—and protected by—her father. Yet her consort's death had brought her throne under threat, because some Southland dragons didn't believe she was worthy of her position as their queen if she couldn't keep her kin safe. That had put Addiena into action, involving Lord Berg and his vast army. But not trusting his loyalty to her or her throne, Addiena had taken his beloved daughter Lady Katarina as security until the borders were secure and her point made.

The word "hostage" was never used, but it didn't need to be.

Still, no point in mentioning any of that to Bercelak. He was blindly loyal to the Queen.

"I am not lazy," Addolgar informed his brother. "I'm many things, but lazy is not one of them. But have no fear, Ghleanna told me that we will have a small squad with us and Lady Braith as well."

"Lady Braith," Bercelak sneered, his distaste for the royal more than evident. "Why is she going? What use is she?"

"Well—"

"None! That I can see," his brother cut in, which only made Addolgar laugh.

"Don't be such a bastard, little brother. She'll keep the royal entertained."

"Braith will keep the royal entertained? *Braith* of the Darkness?"

"She's nice. I don't know what you have against her."

"She does nothing."

"What do you expect her to do?"

"She's one of the Penarddun bloodline. You'd think she'd do *something*," Bercelak complained.

"Her mother may have been a Penarddun but her father has gone out of his way to ensure his daughter was not by raising her himself after her mother's death."

"With those shoulders and arms? Even that neck. It's a waste! The least she could do for the army is move some trees so the troops can get through."

"Is there anyone you don't think should be working for our precious army?"

"No."

"I'm leaving," Addolgar stated, giving up.

"Just be careful, idiot," his brother called out to him.

Addolgar headed off to find the lovely Lady Katarina, throwing a wave over his shoulder. "I'll do that, brother. I'll do that."

Chapter 3

"I am sorry about this, Lady Braith."

Braith looked down at the diminutive She-dragon, forced a smile. "It's all right, Lady Katarina. I know this isn't your fault."

"Just Katarina." She stepped aside as one of their escorts hustled by. "I'll be glad to return home so I have to worry less about all these titles."

"Well, you need not worry about mine at all."

Braith studied the soldiers that had been chosen for this trip. She recognized a few. They were soldiers loyal to her father. She didn't know why that bothered her, but it did. She didn't like this.

"Something wrong, Braith?" Katarina asked.

"Uh . . ." She focused back on the royal. "No. Nothing. Just thinking. Wasn't really planning on a trip."

"And I wasn't really planning to come here." She raised, then lowered her front claws. "Yet here I am."

Braith felt bad for her. This was just a few days out of Braith's life. Yet Katarina had spent a year as nothing more than a well-treated hostage.

Placing one claw on the royal's shoulder—and ignoring how she dwarfed the She-dragon like a bloody ogre—Braith said softly, "Do not worry, Katarina. We will return you to your loved ones safely."

"I know you will."

Braith smiled at the royal, trying her best to put her at ease.

"There you are!" a cheerful, low voice said from behind her.

Braith's claw tightened on Katarina's shoulder, and she knew her eyes had widened in panic.

No. He couldn't be on this trip. Not him. Ghleanna. Or Bercelak. Gods, even Braith's own father, she would rather travel with! Anyone but . . .

The panic must have been clearly on her face because Katarina suddenly moved around Braith, distracting the Silver.

"And you are?" Katarina asked.

"Sergeant Addolgar of the Fifth Legion, my lady."

It took Braith a few seconds to get control of her initial reaction. Of all the dragons who could be going with them, why did it have to be him? Her one weakness. Her one very handsome, very thick-tailed weakness.

"So, Sergeant Addolgar," Katarina continued as Braith finally faced them both. "Why were you looking for us?"

"I'll be your military escort for this trip."

"Oh, I thought these dragons were. . . ."

Addolgar glanced over at the soldiers. "These lads mostly guard Devenallt Mountain and the Elders. Good, solid soldiers," he quickly added, never wanting to insult anyone—unlike his younger brother. "But I've been through the Western Mountains. Fought a few battles there. So, it was a good decision on my brother's part."

Figures! Gods-damn Bercelak! She should have known! Bastard.

"Now I don't want either of you to worry. I'm here to protect you both." Grinning, he nodded at the waiting soldiers. "Let me check on these lads and then we can get on our way."

He walked off and Katarina faced her again.

"Sorry about that—" Braith began, but Katarina shook her head.

"No need to worry. I understand that feeling. Felt it myself not too long ago."

"Well, if we could just keep it between us, I'd appreciate it."

"Because there are those here who use weakness as currency?"

After living at the royal court, it seemed Katarina understood the Queen as well as anyone.

"You might say."

"Don't worry, Braith. Your secret is safe with me."

"You two ready?" Addolgar asked. "Have everything you need?" When they both nodded, he gave that adorable, wide grin of his, showing all those perfect fangs, and swung his forearm out from his body. "Then after you, my ladies."

Determined to get through this somehow without embarrassing herself, Braith nodded and walked on, Katarina right behind her.

Then Braith realized something. . . . She had no idea how

far away the Western Mountains actually were. A couple of days' travel? Gods. Hopefully not more than that.

Early on the fourth day of their trip, they camped for the night in a small grove. They still had at least another three-day flight before reaching the Western Mountains, but so far they'd made good time, considering it was nearing winter and the winds were beginning to howl.

Yet today's trip had ended early when Lady Katarina, who had been doing so well, with few to no complaints so far, suddenly announced she was getting tired. Addolgar understood; she seemed a frail thing. At least by dragon standards, she seemed frail.

So they'd settled here for the night. It was nice. Lots of trees, a lake nearby, and some tasty-looking oxen a few miles away. Addolgar never needed much more than that.

He settled down beside a large oak, his back pressed against the trunk so that his wings could get a good stretch. He'd rest for a while before searching out that oxen so he could eat, then take night watch.

Just as Addolgar began to get comfortable, Lady Katarina softly stepped up beside him.

"Lord Addolgar," she greeted.

"Just sergeant, I'm afraid, Lady."

"An *earned* title," she mused. "Much more admirable, I assure you."

Enjoying the compliment, Addolgar asked, "Do you need something, my lady? Or Lady Braith?"

"Oh, she's fine. A little fed up with this traveling. I think she believed this to be a much shorter trip, but she'll probably go down to the lake in a bit to relax. Actually, though, I'm about to make some tea. Would you like some?"

A royal? Making something for a low-born Cadwaladr? Who would have thought? "That would be lovely."

"Give me a few minutes then."

"Of course."

Feeling elated by the obvious attention of Lady Katarina—she was making him tea!—Addolgar relaxed back and let out a contented sigh. As he waited, watching the lovely Lady Katarina move around the campfire, he noticed Braith heading off into the woods toward the nearby lake. She had her head down as she silently eased away. No one noticed, which he expected was what she wanted.

Braith sat down by the river. Her back legs stretched out in front of her, her claws resting on her knees, and her wings stretching out from her body.

She'd admit, she couldn't stand to watch another second. By the gods, the fawning. The fawning!

It was all so easy for them, wasn't it? The pretty ones. It was as if the males felt an inherent need to coddle the pretty ones. Did their beauty make them somehow weaker?

Nor did it help that Lady Katarina was inherently sweet. It would be easier if she were a right bitch like most royals. But instead, she was polite, charming, and damn pretty.

Braith wanted to hate her, but she just couldn't. The bitch.

She heard movement in the trees, and Braith stood on her haunches and raised her claws, curling them into fists. Addolgar the Cheerful lumbered out of the trees, stopping when he saw her raised fists. He blinked hard.

"A bit nervous?" he asked.

"Aren't you?"

"No." Addolgar glanced off, silent for a moment, then asked, "Should I be?"

"Can you honestly tell me you feel comfortable here?"

"Oh. Do you think we should travel as human?"

Braith took a breath and reminded herself that this was Addolgar. He wasn't quite like his brother Bercelak. Although that could be why she actually liked him, because he *wasn't* his brother Bercelak.

"That's not what I meant." She turned her body a bit so she could see Addolgar clearly. "I don't trust these guards."

Addolgar stepped closer. "Why not?"

Braith did not answer right away. She might be attracted to Addolgar, but that didn't mean she could trust him. In fact, Braith trusted few, which was why she spent most of her time alone in her cave. It was safer.

Addolgar knelt down on one knee, one forearm resting on his massive thigh.

"What is it, Braith?" When she still didn't answer: "You can trust me."

Perhaps she could, but Braith had been protecting herself *by* herself for more than a century, since the death of her beloved mother, when her mother's kin had sent her a letter saying they wanted nothing to do with her because she had her father's blood coursing through her veins. So no, she wouldn't suddenly confide in Addolgar the Cheerful, but what she would say was, "Watch the guards. They are loyal to my father, not to the Queen."

Addolgar's head tipped to the side. "But your father's loyal to the Queen, is he not?"

"My father is loyal to my father. I have always made sure never to forget that."

From the camp they could hear Lady Katarina calling out to Addolgar. Something about tea. Braith hated tea.

"We'll be eating soon," Addolgar said.

"I'll be there in a bit," Braith replied, turning her body back around to face the lake.

Addolgar stood and began to head back to camp. But he stopped just before stepping into the trees. "Want me to save you some ox?" he asked kindly. Why did he have to be so bloody nice?

Braith didn't even bother to turn around. "No, thank you."

She heard him walk off, which wasn't really hard since he stomped like a moose. Once she knew she was alone, she let out a long sigh.

Briefly, she entertained the thought of breaking her oath to the Queen and just flying off. It would be easy enough; no one really cared that she was here. No one cared about her at all. But she knew she couldn't do that—her oath was her bond. Just as her mother had taught her.

After allowing herself to really wallow in all that self-pity, Braith decided to head back to camp. But as she stood, she knew dragons were near again. Once more, she brought up her fists and spun around, ready to fight.

Strong claws covered handsome faces because they, if no one else, knew what those fists could truly do.

"A little nervous, sister?" her brother asked from behind his raised claws.

"Always a little nervous," her other brother said.

And once Braith saw her older brothers standing in front of her, in the middle of nowhere, she knew she'd been right— her father was going to betray the Queen.

By the time Addolgar returned to the campsite, Lady Katarina was waiting for him with fresh tea and biscuits. She smiled at him as he approached.

"I was afraid you'd abandoned me, Sergeant."

"No, no. Not at all. Just checking on Lady Braith."

"She doesn't seem very happy," she murmured.

"Oh, she always looks like that." Addolgar sat down by the fire and took the tea from Lady Katarina, holding the metal cup between both claws. He sipped it, forced himself not to wince at the bitter flavor. He'd never been a fan of tea. He preferred water . . . or just plain ale. He really liked ale. "She just has a lot on her mind."

"I'm sure she does. In fact, I think she has *you* on her mind."

"Me?" Addolgar chuckled. "Doubt that, Lady."

"Why would you say that?"

"She's never shown me the least bit of interest. I doubt she'd start now."

She held out a tin of biscuits and Addolgar picked one up with the tips of two claws, nibbled it, rather than shoving it into his mouth before grabbing a handful more. He worried he'd have to eat the oxen like this as well. All polite nibbles and patient rendering, rather than tearing and ripping until he could get to the steamy insides like he usually did at mealtime.

She motioned to the tea, apparently done with the topic of Braith of the Darkness. "Drink up. The bitterness will go away in a bit."

Addolgar nodded and took another gulp of the tea.

He didn't think Lady Katarina was right, though, because he couldn't imagine the tea tasting better anytime soon.

Lady Katarina sat down beside Addolgar. "You're very . . . sweet, Sergeant Addolgar."

Addolgar couldn't help but smile. "You mean . . . compared to my family?"

"Oh, no, no—"

"It's all right, Lady." He shrugged. "I'm a Cadwaladr. I have no shame about that. No . . . insecurities."

"You're proud of them."

"Of course I am. They're my kin."

"And they'll be there for you? No matter what?"

Addolgar frowned, confused by the question. "Why wouldn't they be?"

"I'd heard they can be"—she thought a moment—"harsh. To each other, I mean."

"Some might say. But no more than any one of us can handle. And usually not more than any one of us deserves."

"Good." Her smile was soft . . . and a little sad. "I'm glad."

"I'm glad you're glad."

Unable to tolerate any more of the horrid tea, Addolgar went to put the cup down, but it tumbled from his claw, tea splattering across the ground.

"Huh." He looked at Lady Katarina. "I'm a bit of a fumble-claws tonight. Guess I'm more tired than I realized."

"Go to sleep. It's all right."

"All right. Just have the lads wake me up in a few hours so I can take night watch."

"Of course," she said, her voice seeming to fade to Addolgar's ears. "And thank you, Sergeant."

Addolgar stretched out, trying to keep himself raised on his elbow, but his forearm gave out and he ended up crashing to the ground.

He tried not to look as clumsy as he felt and asked, "What for, Lady Katarina?"

"For being ever so kind."

"You're welcome," he said, grinning.

Lady Katarina's image dimmed, and he briefly thought about spitting in an attempt to get the bitter taste of that awful tea out of his mouth. But, unfortunately, everything went black before he had the chance.

"What are you two doing here?" Braith asked her brothers, hoping to sound as vapid as they believed her to be. As confused. Like their father, they gave her very little credit.

"To take Lady Katarina."

"Against her will?"

Meical scoffed, rolling his eyes. "Of course not. She's as involved in this as the rest of us."

"The rest of us?"

Afanen said with a dismissive shrug, "The soldiers

here. They're loyal to Father. Well . . . except for that big Cadwaladr oaf."

"Good thing they sent him and not Bercelak," Meical noted. "Or Ghleanna. That would have been messy."

"Do you really think he's just going to let her go without a fight?" Braith asked, her mind already racing.

"No need for all that." Meical stepped back as Lady Katarina came through the trees, three of the soldiers with her.

"It's done," Katarina announced, her eyes on Braith. Locked on Braith.

"Good, my lady," Meical said. "Then we should be off quickly."

Katarina kept her eyes on Braith and, for a few brief seconds, she thought the female was challenging her. But then Braith realized . . . she wasn't. She was, however, trying to tell her something.

Braith cleared her throat. "Uh . . . what about Addolgar?"

"He's been handled," Meical insisted.

"And if he's not," Afanen told her, "the rest of the soldiers will ensure he is before they follow us."

"You lot go then," Braith said brusquely. "I'll make sure he's taken care of."

"Braith—"

"We don't want to get this bit wrong, brothers. Father will have *your* asses if we do."

"She's right," Meical agreed. "Go. Make sure he's done, then follow the soldiers to our next location. They know where to go. Understand?"

"Of course."

Katarina nodded at Braith, her eyes widening a bit before she turned from her and took to the air.

Braith waited until her brothers and the three soldiers followed before she turned and charged back toward the campsite.

She found the remaining guards surrounding Addolgar's

body. They glanced at her as she burst through the trees, but quickly refocused on Addolgar.

"I don't think he's dead yet," said one.

"Should we wait?" asked another.

"No," he said, and Braith began to panic. "Kill him. Let's be done with it and go."

He was only unconscious for a bit, but Addolgar had quickly figured out that Lady Katarina had poisoned him, though she clearly hadn't given him enough to kill him. One of his cousins liked poisons and understanding how much poison to use based on weight and gender and age was something all good poisoners learned. True, Katarina might be a bad poisoner, but if she'd been really trying to murder him, she most likely would have overcompensated, giving him enough to kill him instantly and with great pain and blood.

No. He was certain she'd known what she was doing, but she probably hadn't counted on these soldiers hanging back to make sure he was dead. They probably wouldn't have bothered for anyone else, either, but they would never take a chance on a Cadwaladr surviving. That was something a royal like Lady Katarina would not understand.

Addolgar could move, but he was weaker than normal and so he waited, pretending to be unconscious, hoping that he'd get a chance to use the element of surprise to his advantage.

While he waited, he used his mind to call to his sister, a skill all immediate kin had with each other.

Ghleanna.

Addolgar? What is it?

Trouble. I need you. Where are you?

Ten minutes away.

What?

Did you really think Bercelak trusted bloody Berg? Do what you must, brother. I'm coming for you.

Addolgar should have known his brother had sent someone to shadow them, but he would be forever grateful. Still. Ten minutes could be a lifetime if he couldn't stop these bastards before they hacked him to death. Yet before he could come up with a plan, Addolgar heard Braith's voice. Gods, was she part of this, too? No. He couldn't imagine that. Not Braith. There was something about her that seemed . . . well . . . she seemed not to care about much of anything. He couldn't imagine she would bother betraying the Queen. So he refused to think she'd start now. Especially when she'd been the one to warn him about her father's handpicked soldiers.

"You lot go on," Braith ordered, and Addolgar opened his eyes just a bit so he had a good idea of where everyone was standing . . . and what his odds were. "I'll finish him," she said, holding up an eating dagger sharp enough to cut his throat.

The soldiers nodded and began to move away . . . except one. That one, a big Red, held up his claw, halting the others. His blue eyes narrowed on Braith and, after a moment, he said, "That's all right, Lady Braith. Your father's orders were clear. We kill the Cadwaladr and then we go. This isn't something you need to worry about."

With a jerk of his head toward Addolgar, the soldiers turned back to him, all of them pulling out their swords. Behind them, Braith let out a sigh, her head momentarily dropping. Perhaps her father's control over her was greater than Addolgar had thought. It seemed valid. He was clearly a dragon to fear.

But then she raised bright green eyes, her gaze locking on the soldiers. Fascinated, Addolgar couldn't even focus his attention on his imminent death. Instead, he continued to watch Braith.

Watched as she grabbed two of the guards by their hair with her talons, using one forearm for each. She yanked them back, flipped *both* of them up at the same time, and then brought them down hard, their necks snapping in the process. Before dying, the two males cried out, startled at the attack, and the remaining soldiers spun around to face her.

The Red snarled, smoke coming from his nostrils. "Your father warned us we might have to kill you. Guess he was right."

The Red raised his sword and charged, and Braith punched. She punched him in the snout. A punch so hard that Addolgar heard bone shatter, saw blood splatter the others. The Red stumbled back, landed on his ass. His snout was pushed back so far, he couldn't speak and he had to breathe through his open mouth.

The others charged, and Braith caught the forearm of one, yanked him forward, and broke it over her other forearm. While still holding him, she brought up her now-free fist and hit the soldier behind her in the face, spun, and punched him in the gut. She grabbed the one whose arm she'd broken and yanked his head to the side, breaking his neck.

By the time Braith faced the last standing soldier, the dragon's sword was arcing down toward her. Braith quickly reached up and caught the dragon's forearms in her claws, held them. The pair struggled against each other. The soldier was strong, but to Addolgar and the soldier's surprise, Braith was much stronger.

She yanked the soldier's forearms apart so his sword dropped to the ground. Then she dragged the guard closer, rammed her head against his. Once. Twice. Until he was dazed, nearly out cold. That's when she went behind him and grabbed his head. Addolgar thought she'd snap his neck like the others, but instead she forced her claws between his jaws and pried them open—and she kept prying until she'd broken the soldier's jaws away from his head.

She dropped the body, picked up her dagger, and ran toward Addolgar. As she did, she passed the Red and she didn't even stop as she charged by the still-breathing-but-clearly-dying dragon, cutting his throat as she moved and letting him bleed out while she came to Addolgar's side.

Addolgar closed his eyes again, continued to feign unconsciousness. He felt her stroke his hair. "Addolgar? Addolgar?" She pressed two claws against his throat, felt for signs of life. When she found them, she let out a sigh.

"Thank the gods," she whispered. "I'm so sorry, Addolgar. I had no idea he would ever . . ." She swallowed. "Don't worry. We'll get you help and then I'll go straight to the Queen. I'll tell her everything. My father will pay for this betrayal."

Yes. Her father would pay. And so would Braith. As one of Elder Emyr's offspring, she would suffer the fate of her kin for no other reason than that she shared their bloodline. Addiena would want revenge *now*. Not when they eventually tracked Emyr down. And Addolgar realized he couldn't let that happen. It wasn't fair. Addolgar would hate to be held responsible for some of the stupid centaur shit his kin did on a daily basis. So why should Braith suffer for her father's treachery?

Yet he now understood Braith's sense of honor. Not that people talked about it as they talked about Bercelak's triumphs in battle or Ghleanna's fearsome reputation among enemies. No. He hadn't heard about it, he just saw it. In what she'd just done. Using her bare claws, she'd fought for his life and saved it. So Addolgar knew her honor existed. Knew it was powerful, which meant she wouldn't listen to reason. She wouldn't believe that Queen Addiena would hold against Braith what had clearly been plotted and executed by her father.

Addolgar wouldn't let that happen.

So when Braith got to her claws and turned away from him to, he assumed, figure out her next step, Addolgar did the only thing he could think of. He forced himself to his claws, ignored how dizzy he felt, and grabbed the back of Braith's head, slamming her right into the tree he'd passed out beside.

She went down hard, and was definitely out cold.

Panting, exhausted just from that little burst of energy, Addolgar stumbled and landed on his ass. He let out a sigh, glad to be sitting since standing wasn't working well for him at the moment. He patted Braith on her now-bleeding head.

"Don't worry, Braith of the Darkness. I won't let you get yourself into trouble. No. I'm going to save you from yourself just as you saved me from those bloody treacherous bastards. That's what friends do for each other. And since you saved my life . . . we're friends, you and me." He grinned despite the pain in his head and the need to vomit whatever he'd eaten earlier in the day. "Friends! Because look at the great way I take care of you!"

Chapter 4

Addolgar smiled and waved at his sister and one of his older brothers, Rhys the Hammer. The pair landed and stared at Addolgar, their wings retracting against their bodies, their heads tilting to the side in curiosity.

Ghleanna went back on her haunches and placed her claws on her hips. "What the bloody hells happened?"

"I've been poisoned."

"By Braith of the Darkness?"

"No. She saved me life."

"So the soldiers killed her?"

"She's alive."

Ghleanna looked around at the soldiers' bodies. "So they beat her *before* you killed them?"

"Oh, I didn't kill them."

"Then who did?"

"Braith."

Ghleanna frowned. "Braith . . . who?"

"Braith of the Darkness." He pointed at the prone She-dragon. "That Braith."

Ghleanna looked over the dead soldiers again. "Braith of the Darkness killed all these soldiers? With poison and then you beat them up after they died?"

Addolgar, known for his patience, was running out of it. "Braith didn't poison anyone. *I* was poisoned and these soldiers were going to finish me off. Braith killed them all, with her bare claws, and saved me. Which I found quite impressive."

"But the soldiers beat her up first?"

"No one beat her."

Ghleanna looked at Rhys, but their older brother could only shrug.

"Okay," Ghleanna said. "Then what did happen to Braith?"

"Oh! I rammed her head into the tree to stop her from leaving."

Rhys the Hammer, third born to Ailean the Wicked and nearly a hundred years older than Addolgar, shook his head and reminded him, "That is not how you keep a female. Even one that impresses you, Addolgar. Because when she wakes up . . . she's going to hurt you."

"I did it for her own good."

Rhys rolled his eyes. "You all say that, but—"

"No, no. Really. I was saving her."

"From?"

"Herself."

Ghleanna and Rhys again looked at each other before Rhys asked her, "You brought me here for this?"

"You'd never believe me if I just told you these things. You must see. So you can understand what I go through."

"Would you two stop?" Addolgar ordered. "I don't feel well."

"Because you beat up Braith of the Darkness?"

"I didn't beat up anyone, Rhys. Because I've been poisoned."

"Is that why you're sweating between your scales?" Ghleanna asked, appearing slightly disgusted.

"Probably."

"Who did poison you then?"

"Lady Katarina."

"Lady Katarina poisoned you and Braith of the Darkness killed all these soldiers?" Ghleanna abruptly shook her head and demanded, "Addolgar, what the holy fucks has happened here?"

He shrugged. "You're not going to like it, I'm afraid."

"Well . . . to be honest, I don't like anything."

Rhys, who had been poisoned by more than one female over the years before he'd met and mated with the perfect She-dragon for him, mixed up something to calm Addolgar's stomach and get him back on his feet.

Addolgar was grateful. The poison Katarina had fed him might not have killed him, but it had made him feel like ox shit. Now, however, he was standing over a still-unconscious Braith and explaining to his sister and brother exactly what had happened.

And what was at stake.

When he was done, Ghleanna looked him right in the eyes and said, "She'd be better off if you kill her now."

"I am not killing her, Ghleanna."

"So you'll let Addiena do it? Because we both know the

Queen will. We both know she'll enjoy doing it. She'll take her time with that one, make sure she gets lots of screams."

"Stop. I don't want to hear this. I'm going to help Braith. It's up to you whether you help me."

"So what do you want to do?" Rhys asked. "Hide her in your cave?"

"I think I should take her home."

Rhys frowned. "To your *cave*?" And it was more a strong suggestion than a question.

"To Mum and Da's house."

"Have you lost your mind?" Ghleanna snapped. "You can't take this bitch to Mum and Da's."

"She's not a bitch."

Braith moaned and her head rolled from one side to another, letting them know she was waking up. So Ghleanna slammed her back claw against the poor She-dragon's head, knocking her out for a second time. "You'd put our parents at risk for some piece of tail?" Ghleanna demanded.

"She saved my life."

"You can fight your own battles!"

"Not when I'm knocked out on my ass!"

"You mean knocked out on your *fat* ass!"

"*My ass, like the rest of me, is perfection!*"

"You two!" Rhys bellowed. "With the yelling! *Cut it out!*"

Annoyed with each other, Addolgar and Ghleanna folded their forearms over their chests and glared off in different directions.

Rhys sighed, and without even looking at him, Addolgar knew his brother was crossing his eyes. It was probably the same expression he always had on his face when he'd been forced to watch the pair of them when they were just hatchlings. He'd finally told their mother it wasn't remotely fair. "They'd be better off with demons watching them. At least the demons would have a fighting chance!"

"We take her back to Mum and Da's," Rhys said.

"What is wrong with you two?" Ghleanna snarled.

"Do you think Da would make a different decision on this?"

"I love our father," Ghleanna told them, "but he can be an irrational idiot. I won't expose our mother to this."

"She definitely wouldn't make a different decision."

"Because she hates Addiena. Loathes her. From years ago. The only time she's ever irrational is when the Queen's name comes up."

"It doesn't matter," Rhys decided. "We take her with us and let Mum and Da decide. If they're fine with her staying, she stays. If not, she goes."

"Fine," Ghleanna growled. "But if this goes bad—I'm blaming *you*, Addolgar."

Well . . . Addolgar had expected that last bit.

Chapter 5

Braith brought her claws to her head and quickly realized her claws were now hands and that she was on a bed in what appeared to be a castle.

"That *idiot*," she muttered. Because only a Cadwaladr could make this situation *worse*.

Braith sat up, tossing her legs over the side of the bed. But as soon as her feet touched the cold stone floor, she fell back on the bed, waiting for the spinning to stop.

She gingerly touched her forehead, felt where her head

had been split open. Why . . . why would that big idiot ram her into a tree? If it was because he thought she'd been part of her father's treachery, she would be in the Queen's pits right now, awaiting execution. Instead, she was in a human bed, in human form—how he'd managed that, she had no idea—and trying desperately not to pass out again.

While lying there, Braith moved her jaw around. It, too, was swollen, although there was no lump. Somehow she doubted Addolgar had done that to her, but she wouldn't put it past one of his siblings.

Siblings who were probably all over this castle.

She knew that was where she was. In a castle, where the scent of fire dragons was in every nook and corner, which meant only one thing. . . .

Because there was only one dragon she knew of who not only had a castle but actually lived in it rather than on it. And that dragon was Ailean the Wicked.

It made sense, though, didn't it? Anytime Ailean's offspring were concerned or confused or had done something that might get them put to death, they returned here for advice from their mother, Shalin the Innocent, or help from their father and the rest of the Cadwaladr Clan. But to Braith, coming here meant putting two very kind dragons at risk. Something she'd been trying to avoid from the beginning. She didn't want any more innocents hurt because of her father.

The room finally stopped spinning, and Braith was able to sit up. When she felt strong enough, she stood. She took a few tentative steps, and since that felt good, she walked to the door and opened it. The servant standing in the hallway gasped at the sight of Braith. Quickly closing the door, Braith proceeded to look for something to wear. Since she only intended to be human until she made it to a clearing, she pulled a long cotton shirt out of a trunk and drew it over her head. It reached her knees, and she decided that would cover enough of her for the sensitive humans.

She went back to the door and again opened it. The servant was still there, cleaning up after one of the dogs running around. Head held high, Braith walked down the hallway and then down the stairs until she reached the first floor and the Main Hall.

As one of the main dining areas for the extensive Cadwaladr Clan, there were many tables, but only one was occupied. That's where Addolgar and his parents sat eating their breakfast of meat and bread. Braith decided to forgo common courtesy and headed straight toward the open front doors.

She had barely passed the table when she heard, "Oy!"

Braith kept walking, not looking back, not answering. She merely had to get to the open double doors. She did, too. Making it outside and going down the stone steps. But as her bare feet stepped onto the courtyard, Ghleanna stood there, waiting for her.

"Going somewhere, Lady Braith?" Ghleanna asked.

"I have somewhere to be. So move."

"Wait, wait." Addolgar jogged down the steps, stopping by Braith's side. "You can't leave."

"I can't stay, Addolgar. You are putting your kin at risk. You know what the Queen will do—"

"Exactly," he cut in. "I know what the Queen will do even though you did nothing wrong."

"Then that's what I'll tell her."

"Oh, please," Ghleanna scoffed. "Do you really think that female will listen to you?"

"*That* female is our Queen. Now get out of my way."

Braith pushed past Ghleanna, but the She-dragon caught her wrist, held her in place.

Letting out a sigh, Braith looked over her shoulder at Ghleanna.

"Perhaps," Ghleanna murmured, "I wasn't clear."

"Actually," Braith admitted, "you were."

* * *

"Oy. Boy."

Addolgar looked behind him and saw his father gesturing to him with his hand.

"But, Da—"

"Up here *now.*"

With a frustrated sigh, Addolgar jogged back up the stairs until he stood by his father's side.

After Rhys had headed out to see if he could find out any more information about what all of Emyr's plans might be while not alerting the Queen to what had already happened, Addolgar had sat down with his parents to talk about what their options were. What he hadn't expected was to see Braith walking out of his parents' home with, he was sure, the intention of turning herself in to the Queen.

"What is it, Da?" he asked Ailean, anxious to get Braith back inside.

"Just moving you out of the way, boy."

"What are you talking—"

Before Addolgar could finish the question, his sister flipped up the steps, her back ramming into the hard stone. Snarling, Ghleanna pushed her short, black hair off her face before charging back down the stairs toward Braith. Addolgar began to follow, but his father quickly caught hold of his arm and held it.

"You don't want to do that, boy."

Addolgar didn't understand. Ghleanna was a great soldier, but when she lost her temper . . . well, he just knew his sister, and Ailean knew his daughter. So he didn't understand why his father would stop him from protecting Braith—until he saw Braith protecting herself.

It wasn't Braith's skills that stopped him in his tracks but her strength, her power.

Ghleanna, a true battle-hardened soldier, didn't bother to

play by the dragon rules of fighting etiquette. Instead, she just swung her fist—and Braith caught it. Easily. Shocking even Ghleanna, who couldn't pull her hand away. After a moment of silence and intense glaring, Braith yanked Ghleanna forward at the same time she swung her free fist. Her knuckles slammed into Ghleanna's face, blood splattered, and after Braith released Ghleanna's hand, Addolgar's sister crashed to the ground. She was out cold, her nose broken from the looks of it.

Unfortunately, the other Cadwaladrs that were lurking nearby, most likely using the courtyard to sleep off last night's drink, were now awake and moving forward. As one, as they'd been trained to move since hatching, they surrounded Braith. One of their own had been harmed. No matter the situation, Cadwaladrs always protected their own, whether it was from humans or other dragons or bloody centaurs. They prided themselves on their loyalty to blood and kin.

And Braith was neither.

Braith slowly looked over those surrounding her, then cracked her neck. It must have been the sound of those bones grinding that panicked one of his younger cousins. She moved first, coming at Braith quick and hard, but she barely got within three feet of her before Braith's forearm hit her with such force, she sent the young She-dragon flying back and *through* the wall of one of the courtyard buildings. That's when the others moved, Addolgar's kin descending on Braith like the battle dogs the royals called them.

But, wearing only his shirt and with no weapons, Braith stood her ground as he'd never seen anyone stand their ground before. She wasn't graceful. She wasn't a proper soldier. No. Braith of the Darkness was simply brutal . . . vicious . . . like a powerful pit dog. There wasn't one part of her body she wasn't willing to risk in order to harm her opponent. Yet her innate strength seemed to protect her, and she used that strength without pity, without regret.

"Gods," Addolgar breathed.

"I know." Ailean glanced behind him before softly admitting, "Just like her mum, that one. I knew her mum long ago. Before she met Emyr."

"Is there anyone you hadn't fucked before you mated with Mum?"

"One or two," his father teased. "Of course, those were girls that," he felt the need to add, "really didn't like males in the first place."

Addolgar rolled his eyes, unwilling to discuss his father's past conquests further, which was when he noticed that Braith still stood—while the rest of his family did not.

He glanced at his father. "It was like watching one big dog massacre a gang of smaller, weaker dogs."

"Like I said, she's truly her mum's offspring. That female had massive arms and a thick neck. But a lovely long tail," he added with a sigh.

"I don't know how Mum tolerates you."

"She knows that my heart and soul belong only to her. But me past is me own."

Braith looked back at Addolgar, sneering at him, one side of her top lip rising a bit to illustrate her true disgust. Then she stepped over his kin and headed off.

But as Braith walked, she didn't bother to acknowledge the extremely old She-dragon walking toward her in human form, a long, hooded robe covering her from head to booted feet. She moved slowly, leaning heavily on a long walking stick.

Braith had just passed her when the She-dragon's free hand came up and her fingers curled into a fist.

Braith stopped, her own hands reaching for her throat, and began to gasp. Her fingers pawed at what was not there, her body struggling against what no one could see.

The old She-dragon kept walking forward, her hand still in a fist, and as she moved, Braith was dragged along with her. She still struggled, still tried to free herself from the invisible grip, but it was useless.

Addolgar tried to go to help her, but his father's grip tightened, and now with no humor in his usually mirth-filled face, Ailean the Wicked gave a quick shake of his head. "Not this time, boy. This you don't do. This you don't *ever* do."

Ailean looked over his shoulder and called out, "Shalin. We need you. Now."

By the time Addolgar's mother reached Ailean, the old She-dragon stood in front of the castle stairs and Braith's human face was beginning to turn blue.

"The shame," a voice said from deep inside that hooded robe. "The shame of seein' me own kin getting bounced around like toys by this bit of a lizard."

Brigida the Foul, a more than nine-hundred-year-old Cadwaladr Elder, glared up the stairs at Ailean. Her hood finally fell back, revealing a human face that had been through much over the years and long, white hair. Not the white hair of age— Brigida had been blessed by the gods with that mane of hair since hatching. She was one of the rare White Dragonwitches and feared—for good reason—throughout the Southlands and beyond.

Everyone, even the Cadwaladrs, kept waiting for her to die . . . but she simply wouldn't. She wouldn't!

"Hello, Great-Aunt Brigida," Shalin cheerfully greeted. "What a surprise to see you here. It's been much too long."

"Always so cheery, now that you've got the idiot here plowing ya on the regular."

Addolgar's mother smiled in the face of that appalling insult and said, "Would you like me to show you an available room? I think your favorite is—"

"Quiet, girl! With all that chattering! It annoys me." Brigida glanced at the still-struggling Braith. "Who is this?"

Ailean opened his mouth, but Brigida cut him off with a curt, "I'm talking to the boy."

Addolgar realized she was talking to *him*. "Uh . . ." Addolgar cleared his throat. "This is Braith of the Darkness."

"Who is her kin, boy? I care not for her name."

"She's a Daughter of the House of Penarddun."

His great-great-aunt made a sound that some generous soul might call a laugh. "Well then . . . that explains so much."

"She's here under my protection, Great-Aunt."

"Is she?" Brigida sneered. "Well, you're doing a bang-up job since she just beat up your kin and almost walked out of here to wherever she was headed."

"It's all a misunderstanding. I just need time to speak to her. So could you please . . . unhinge?"

"You'll need some chains," she replied.

"Chains?"

Brigida lifted her fist, and Braith's body rose from the ground at the same time. Then Brigida dropped her fist hard and Braith slammed into the ground, knocked out completely from the impact.

Poor thing. If she wasn't being thrown into trees or attacked by his kin, she was being mystically flung to the ground by his old, terrifying great-great-aunt.

It was really going to be impossible to talk to Braith in a rational, calm manner after all this.

Addolgar looked at his father. "Uncle Arranz leave those chains of his around?"

"Check our room, dear," Shalin suggested. A suggestion that had Addolgar and Brigida staring at her while his father grinned and gazed off across the courtyard. Shalin's pale, freckled face flushed a deep, extremely bright, red.

His poor mother lifted her skirt so it didn't drag on the ground and quickly said to Brigida, "Why don't I get your room ready, Great-Aunt?" She spun and practically ran off.

Brigida shook her head at Ailean, her white hair whipping around her brutally scarred face. "Another poor female you've turned into a whore, Ailean the Slag."

Ailean didn't have the decency to be a little humble. Instead, his grin stretched into an outright leer and the old witch sucked her tongue against her teeth before slowly walking up the stairs, refusing Addolgar's offer of assistance.

"Get your bit of lizard, Addolgar the Cheerful. Let's get her secured before she wakes up and tears the walls of this ridiculous place down around us."

And based on what Addolgar had already seen . . . Braith was the one dragon who could do just that with very little effort.

Oh, and as for his battling kin? They were already starting to wake up, which meant the complaining would come soon enough because none of them liked to lose. Especially when they lost to a bloody royal.

Chapter 6

Braith opened her eyes and screamed at what hovered above her, "Gods! *Death comes for me!*"

The horrifying face of death curled its lip at her and growled, "Well, that's charmin'." Death sat back in its chair, hands resting on its knees. "This face is not me fault, ya know?" Death looked off, thought a moment. Its finger traced one of the deep gouges across its jaw. "This one actually is kind of me fault." She pointed at the other side of her face, where part of her chin was missing. "And this one. A bit of barney at the pub."

Braith studied the beast sitting next to her bed. There were so many scars on that face and neck. Gouges. One eye was crystal blue, but the other was a milky white and grey. But that was the eye she felt saw beyond scale and flesh to soul . . . so that it could steal it right from the body.

"What are you?"

That milky white and grey eye quickly locked on Braith, the blue one slowly coming along for the ride, sizing her up. "Don't you mean *who* am I?"

"No."

Those disturbing eyes narrowed and that damaged top lip curled. But before further words were spoken, the bedroom door pushed open and Addolgar—that idiot!—rushed in.

"What's going on?"

"She asked me what am I."

Addolgar's brown eyes widened in what appeared to be panic.

"I'm sure she didn't mean that," he said quickly. "It was . . . it was the hit on her head," he offered, nodding desperately at Braith. "She's mad from that. You should ignore her."

Death growled a bit, then stood. "I'll be downstairs with your father," it told him as it slowly made its way across the room. "Sort this out, boy. The Cadwaladrs don't need anyone's problems but their own. Understand?"

"I do."

"Good."

Death walked out of the room, slamming the door behind it and Addolgar let out a breath, shoulders slumping, arms hanging down.

"What the hells was that thing?" Braith demanded. "Why are you sending death to my room?"

Addolgar glanced back at the door, his hands lifting, indicating for her to keep her voice down. "That was not death," he whispered. "That was our Great-Aunt Brigida."

"Brigida? Brigida the Foul?" He nodded. "I thought she was dead."

Addolgar shook his head and whispered, "She just won't *die*."

"I heard that, boy!" Brigida's voice rang down the hall, and Addolgar's pale human face turned paler. Braith did find it disturbing someone that old could hear a whispered comment behind a thick wooden door, but honestly, at the moment, Braith had other issues to deal with.

"Addolgar?"

He looked up at her, tried to smile. "Aye?"

She lifted her hands. "What are these?"

"Chains."

"Why am I wearing them?"

"To protect you from yourself." He seemed to calm down, his uncomfortable smile turning bright and cheerful. "See? I'm here to take care of you!"

Braith sighed. "Addolgar the Cheerful . . . you are *such* an idiot."

Addolgar walked across the room and sat on his bed. The bed that Braith of the Darkness was currently on. She looked surprisingly cute on his bed, wearing his shirt and his uncle's chains, and sporting that big lump on her forehead.

"I know you're angry," he told her.

"You threw me into a tree."

"I had to."

"You *had* to? And why did you have to do that?"

"Because if I'd stopped to discuss the situation with you instead, Braith, we'd still be there . . . *talking*. I didn't have time for that. I didn't know if your brothers would be coming back to look for you or if I'd be strong enough to fight them."

"Addolgar, I'm trying to protect you and, unfortunately, now all of your kin."

"The kin you just slapped around?"

"They're still breathing, aren't they? Because, usually, I don't allow for that last part. I was just trying to leave. Your family decided to keep me here."

"Because I'm trying to protect you."

"I don't need your protection, you git!"

"And I don't need yours, brat, but here we are!" Addolgar folded his arms across his chest and suddenly realized something. "You've made me angry."

"I've been angry for hours now."

"We're not talking about you. You're Braith of the Darkness. *I'm* Addolgar the Cheerful. I've earned this name, and you're ruining it by being unreasonable."

"You throw me into a tree—"

"That was for your own good."

"—have me attacked by your kin—"

"You brought that on yourself."

"—and leave me alone with Brigida the Foul, of all She-dragons—"

"She got away from us. Normally none of us would have done that. Not even to our worst enemy."

"—and *I'm* being unreasonable."

Addolgar nodded. "See? You do understand."

Eyes closing, Braith sighed once more, her head dropping into her open hands. "I can't believe I once thought you were adorable."

"Really?" Addolgar grinned. "You think I'm adorable?"

That's when Braith dropped to the bed, using a pillow to cover her face.

"Wait. Does that mean 'Yes, I think you're adorable' or 'No, I don't think you're adorable'?"

When Addolgar pulled that pillow off her, she refused to open her eyes. She didn't want to see his handsome face. This whole thing was ridiculous. She didn't understand what she was doing. What he was doing. What anyone was doing!

"Well?" Addolgar asked her.

Braith finally opened her eyes and found Addolgar leaning right over her. "Well what?"

"Do you really think I'm adorable?"

Braith raised her manacled hands, gripping his chain-mail shirt with her fingers. She lifted her body up by pulling herself closer to his face. Then, while trying to rein in her anger, and failing, she snarled, "I am *trying* to help you!"

"I know," he said simply. "We're trying to help each other. Like friends."

"Friends?"

"Aye. We're friends now."

"Are we?"

"Of course we are!" he replied cheerfully—just like his name. "Why wouldn't we be friends?"

"Because you threw me into a tree?"

"To *help* you. You keep forgetting that part."

Unsure what else to do, Braith released her grip on his shirt and dropped back to the bed.

"So are you just going to keep me here? Locked in chains like some human prisoner?" She studied him. "Maybe I should just shift to dragon and be done with all this."

"You wouldn't do that," he told her with what seemed to be an astounding amount of confidence, considering what they'd recently been through. "I know you wouldn't harm innocent humans, nor destroy my father's property."

Damn the bastard, but he was right.

"Look, Braith, once I'm sure you're not going to do anything incredibly stupid, I'll release you. And going to the Queen to tell her about your father—incredibly stupid."

"So is hiding from her."

"You're not hiding. You're trying to fix the problem. *We're* trying to fix the problem. And we will."

"This isn't your fight, Addolgar."

"It's more my fight than yours. It was me they'd planned to kill. That alone will bring every Cadwaladr within a thousand leagues to exact revenge. Trust me when I say you don't want to be in the middle of that shit storm."

"What does it matter? Your family already hates me."

Addolgar gazed at her for several moments before asking, "Why would you say that?"

"Because they attacked me in your father's courtyard?"

"Only because you battered Ghleanna. And she only tried to stop you because of me. Actually . . . my kin was quite impressed. Once we wrapped up their wounds and snapped bones back into place. Where did you learn to fight like that?"

"My mother. And she learned from her mother. The females on my mother's side are, what my father has always called when he was feeling nice, hearty."

"Hearty's good. The Cadwaladrs respect hearty."

Braith couldn't help but snort a little laugh at that while she tried to figure out where to put her damn hands with these damn manacles and chains on them.

"What's so funny?" Addolgar asked.

"Lady Katarina wasn't exactly what I'd call hearty . . . and you didn't seem to have any problems with her."

"Well . . . no. She wasn't hearty. Not like you." And Braith briefly entertained using the chains to choke the life from the big idiot. "But she's a nice lass."

"Addolgar, she poisoned you."

"But she didn't kill me. That's what's important."

Her mother had been right, all those years ago, when she'd told Braith, "Males will always make excuses for the pretty." It was too bad, really. Braith had always hoped Addolgar wasn't like most males. But in the end, they were all the same, weren't they?

"You're sneering at me," Addolgar noted.

"Am I?"

"Your lip is curled, so it does look like you're sneering."

"I don't mean to." She really didn't. "I just don't know how we're going to fix this. My father . . . he's destroyed my life, the honor of my bloodline. He's destroyed everything. And for what?" she asked. "To take the throne of Addiena?"

"That seems like a foolish goal. He'd have to get rid of Addiena, which is near impossible with her Royal Guard protecting her. And then there's her offspring, two of which are witches." He shrugged massive shoulders. "In other words, the House of Gwalchmai fab Gwyar is not to be fucked with, I'm afraid."

"Perhaps my father's raised an army."

"Wouldn't you know if he had? Wouldn't he discuss it with you first?"

"My father and I aren't . . . close. We never have been. He wanted two things when he chose my mother as his mate: sons and her royal title. I was never part of his plan and I mean nothing to him."

"Then why did he involve you in this at all?"

Braith admitted the sad truth. "Because he hates me. Always has. He knew I'd never go along with this. I'm a Daughter of the House of Penarddun, and our oath is our bond. He's never had the guts to outright kill me, so he was hoping I'd go along, put up a fight, and one of the soldiers would do the nasty job for him. This way he keeps his talons clean and he still has his precious sons."

She saw a very dark frown on Addolgar's face, and he said, "Or you could have just gone along with his plan."

"The honor of my mother's bloodline means everything to me," she snapped, "just as it meant everything to her and to all our female ancestors who came before us. You may be from the Cadwaladr Clan, Addolgar the Cheerful, but I'm a direct bloodline from the House of Penarddun. A *Daughter*. That means something to us. So, I'd rather be executed knowing I'd kept our honor than live a millennium in shame."

Addolgar said nothing as he gazed into her face. She didn't know what he was looking for or what he expected to find. Instead, she held his gaze until a voice at the doorway said, "Then we'd best figure out how to get your granite fists out of this, Braith of the Darkness."

It was Ghleanna. She leaned against the door frame, a wet cloth held to her swollen cheek. Her nose had already been put back into place by kinder hands than the one that had knocked it out of joint.

"I don't understand," Braith admitted. "Why are you all trying to help me?"

The She-dragon shrugged, smirked. "Maybe because it's nice to finally know a female with shoulders wider than mine." She motioned toward the stairs with a tilt of her head. "Come on then, you two. We'd better start figuring out what we're going to do before the rest of these idiots begin drinking again. They'll be useless once the ale comes out."

Ghleanna walked away, and Braith simply couldn't help herself. She lowered her chin to her chest and tried to see how wide her shoulders truly were.

"Don't worry," Addolgar cheered as he grabbed her hands and pulled her up from the bed, the chains obscenely rattling. "Ghleanna actually meant that as a compliment. She *loves* her giant shoulders."

Once on her feet, Braith looked up at the big, good-natured idiot. He grinned at her and all Braith could do was sigh, shake her head, and walk out of the room . . . her chains rattling along as she did.

"What?" Addolgar asked from behind her. "What did I say?"

Chapter 7

Addolgar walked past Braith and went to the table where most of his kin had assembled. He pulled out a chair for her next to his mother and turned. Behind him, he could see Braith walking from the stairs to the Main Hall. She had her head down as she walked, her focus on the chains between the cuffs that were on her wrists. So she was unaware of Bercelak walking up behind her, pulling his sword from the sheath at his side, his face a mask of rage and hatred.

Word of what had happened was spreading among their kin, it seemed, and Bercelak had clearly made up his mind that Braith had betrayed his precious Queen. And for Bercelak the Unpleasant there was only one way to deal with a traitor to the throne.

Addolgar opened his mouth to yell a warning at Braith, but Ghleanna slapped her hand around his mouth, silencing him. He tried to run forward, but one of his good-sized cousins caught hold of him and held him back.

"Shhhh," Ghleanna whispered against his ear. "We've all got gold on this."

Addolgar rolled his eyes, disgusted by all his kin . . . and the fact that he hadn't gotten in on the betting.

Bercelak was near Braith by now, his human body moving silently, the sword raised in one hand. If he moved fast enough and severed the spine at the base of Braith's neck, it would be the fastest way to kill her, or any dragon, in human form.

Suddenly Braith's head came up, and without missing a step, she turned and swung. Bercelak was close behind her now so that the chains didn't stop her from making contact with his face.

Bercelak blinked, stumbled a step, blinked again, and fell straight back, crashing to the stone floor.

Shaking out her hand, Braith faced them. She stood there, staring, as the Cadwaladrs stared back. Until Ailean barked, "You lot owe me. Pay up!"

With groans and growls of disappointment, Addolgar's kin began tossing gold coins on the table in front of his father.

Disgusted, Addolgar faced Ailean. "You bet against your own son?"

"Just like you, the boy doesn't pay attention. And seeing that she's just like her mother, he didn't stand a chance against Braith of the Darkness."

"Mum?" Addolgar said to his mother.

"Because I love him," she reminded them all as she'd been doing for centuries. "That's what I'm doing with your father. I love him. So, honestly—just let it go already."

Holding a wet cloth to his head, Bercelak was helped into a chair by his younger sister Maelona.

Maelona wasn't much like the rest of her siblings. Sweet and lithe in her human form, she took more after her mother than her father. A healer rather than a warrior. Which was good—a healer was clearly something this group needed.

"You bet against me?" Bercelak demanded of his father, completely ignoring Braith, who sat across from him.

"You seem surprised," Ailean replied, busy counting his freshly earned gold.

"And explain to me," Bercelak snarled at the rest of his kin, "why this traitor to our Queen is still breathing?"

"Perhaps we think she's too pretty to kill?" one of the cousins suggested with a smile.

"We don't have time for your jokes, Kel," Bercelak snapped back.

"Thank you," Braith mumbled as she again focused on the ridiculous chains. "Thank you very much."

"This isn't Braith's fault," Shalin told her son. "It's her father's."

"And I guess she wants to protect him as well."

Braith shrugged. "Eh."

"We're not going to hold against Braith what her father has done."

"Done with her help, I'd wager."

"She wasn't part of it," Addolgar cut in. "And she saved my life."

"Who cares about *your* life?" Bercelak demanded.

Addolgar was silent for a moment before he replied, "I do."

Braith studied the dragon who sat next to her. "You had to think about that reply?"

"Wanted to make sure it wasn't a trick question, didn't I?"

"If she lives, chances are high we all die," Bercelak reminded them.

"Not all of us," another cousin reasoned. "Probably just you lot."

"And that suits you, then, does it?"

The cousin shrugged. "No, but you should be clear."

Bercelak closed his eyes, a long sigh escaping his lips. "Why do I bother with any of you sorry bastards?"

"See?" Addolgar said to Braith. "That could be a trick question."

"Would you stop fooling around?" Bercelak snapped, his typically short temper even shorter. In fact, there were newborn mice that were longer than his brother's temper. "This is serious. The Queen will want her head."

"And we will not give that bitch anything." Shalin looked around the table. "Why are you all staring at me?"

Maybe because Shalin only let her anger out when it came to the current queen. Addiena and Shalin had a past revolving around Addolgar's father, and it was something they all understood but rarely discussed. They all knew about Ailean the Slag's past, but discussing it was something not to be done. Some, like Addolgar, merely snickered at the details of their father's past. But Ghleanna and Bercelak felt there was nothing funny about the way Ailean had lived his life before making their mother his all those years ago.

"Mum," Bercelak kindly said, their mother being one of the few dragons he showed any true respect for. "We can't just dismiss this. Whether it was Addiena or her mother, this is something that would be considered treachery by any who held the throne."

"He's right," Braith said softly, her gaze now on Shalin. "I don't know why my father did this, whether he has intentions of taking the throne for himself or for someone who has offered him more than Addiena. But whatever his reason, this cannot be ignored. It has to be dealt with."

"Aye, it does," Brigida announced as she made her slow way back into the hall. She had her walking stick in one hand and a jug of Ailean's ale in the other.

"And what do you suggest, Auntie Brigida?" Ghleanna asked.

Brigida stopped by Bercelak's side and began to tap him on the head with her walking stick. With an annoyed growl, Bercelak got the hint and moved out of the chair and into another one while Brigida took his place and slowly settled her ancient human body at the table.

"I don't know. But I think until we come up with something, we need to stash Lady Fisticuffs away some place safe."

"What about your own kin, female?" Bercelak asked Braith.

"You mean the kin who just turned on the Queen and made

me into a walking target?" Braith asked, her attention still on those chains.

"No. I was thinking more your mother—"

"Is dead."

"I know," Bercelak snarled. "But if I recall, your mother has sisters, aunts—"

"No. Going to my Penarddun kin is not an option," she said simply.

Shalin leaned forward. "Braith, dear, why ever not? The Penarddun She-dragons are very loyal . . . to their daughters."

"My mother's kin made it perfectly clear to me after she died that they wanted nothing to do with me."

"Did you ever tell them how you feel?" Shalin asked her.

Braith winced. "I'm not good at that sort of thing."

"Your mother passed years ago," Bercelak told Braith. "Are you trying to tell me that in this instance they won't—"

"Yes. I'm telling you they won't . . . ahaaaaaaa!" she abruptly crowed, startling everyone at the table. She held up her still-cuffed hands, but now the chain between the cuffs was in two distinct pieces. "Got it!"

She'd pulled the steel chains with her fingers until she'd broken them apart. Something that amazed every Cadwaladr in the room.

Addolgar looked at a shocked Ghleanna and Bercelak, then back at a smiling Braith. "You do know that dwarves made those chains, don't you?" he asked.

Braith studied the chains she'd separated with her bare hands. "So?"

"So?" Bercelak snapped, his head wound briefly forgotten. "Dwarves, female. The ones who share the caves with the Volcano dragons. They make chains that can't be broken by anyone, *especially* dragons."

"Well, these are pretty old."

"It's dwarf steel. It doesn't matter if it was made at the time the gods were born."

"Your point?" Braith demanded of Bercelak.

"*I don't know what my point is!*" Bercelak exploded, but he immediately seemed to regret it, his hand going to his head. "Gods, my head hurts."

"Sorry about that," Braith muttered, cringing at his wound.

Bercelak stared at Braith for several long moments until he said, "Arranz."

Addolgar nodded. "Aye," he said to Braith. "Those are Arranz's chains. He won't be happy you broke them."

"Not the chains, you twit!" Bercelak yelled. "What is wrong with you?"

"Nothing." Addolgar thought a moment and added, "I don't think."

Maelona put another cool cloth against Bercelak's head and that seemed to calm him.

"Take her to Uncle Arranz's cave is what I'm trying to tell you."

"Oh. Oh! That's an excellent idea, brother."

"No, Addolgar." Braith looked at Bercelak. "I appreciate what you're all trying to do, but I can't let any of you get more involved than you already are."

Addolgar was reaching for the back of Braith's head when Ghleanna snapped, "Addolgar! Don't you dare do that again!"

Braith looked over just in time to see Addolgar snatch his hand away. "Really? You were going to do that again?"

"You're not being logical."

"So you ram my head into the table?"

"If necessary!"

"You can't help what your father has done, lass," Brigida noted, almost kindly.

"Who said I want to?"

"It's plain on your human face," Brigida said. "But you can't let your loyalty to blood stop you. Your mother wouldn't."

"What do you know of my mother?" Braith snapped.

Addolgar leaned in and said very low, "Careful here. She turned one of our cousins into a lizard once when he questioned her at a family gathering."

"I knew your mother," Brigida stated. "Knew your grandmother, too. Strong females, like you. With a streak of honor leagues wide. And you're just like them. You let your father get away with this and you'll never forgive yourself."

"Who said I was letting my father get away with anything?"

"You will be if you go to the Queen yourself. She'll take your head and won't even bother to look for your father because she'll have gotten her revenge."

"How? He feels nothing for me."

"Do you think Addiena will care?"

"Why are we bothering with all this?" Bercelak demanded, his forehead still swelling. "If she's not going to listen to reason, then let's take her back to the Queen as she wants and let *her* deal with it!"

Brigida's head snapped around, her steely gaze locking on Bercelak. Black smoke snaked from her nostrils, and Bercelak immediately threw up his hands.

"Fine. Fine," he said quickly. "Do whatever you want."

Braith briefly closed her eyes. "Please don't bicker about this."

"We will if you don't let us help you," Addolgar promised. "At least let us take you to Arranz. He's no big fan of the Queen either, so he'll be more than happy to help."

"You'll be safe there," Ghleanna added. "His cave is like a maze and our cousins enjoy tormenting anyone who tries to enter. You'll have no fear of anyone tracking you down there."

"This doesn't seem right," Braith hedged.

"It's all we can do right now, child," Brigida explained. "At least until we come up with something else or we track your father down."

"Which I will do," Addolgar promised. "He tried to kill me. It's the least I can do for him."

Finally, Braith relented. "All right. I'll do as you ask."

"Good," Brigida said with a nod. "Now, you'll need one of Arranz's kin to accompany you. Take that one with you." She motioned to Addolgar. "And the one with the thick neck over there."

Ghleanna's hand went to her throat. "Me neck isn't thick."

"Thick like a tree trunk," Brigida muttered.

"It's graceful. This neck is long and graceful." Powerful legs landed on the table and Ghleanna crossed her arms over her chest. "Graceful," she growled, appearing to fight an instinct to yell.

Addolgar shrugged at Braith. "Me sister's graceful."

"Yes," Braith replied, her eyes briefly crossing. "I can see that."

Chapter 8

With the chains broken, there was no point in forcing Braith to sit around at dinner with the cuffs still on, so Addolgar removed them.

She rubbed her wrists and nodded a thanks while food was brought out from the kitchens.

Addolgar retrieved wine from the side table and poured Braith a chalice full. He sat down while she sipped it and watched his kin eat, argue, and laugh at dinner.

"You all right?" he asked.

"I'm fine."

"Everything will work out, Braith. I promise."

She gave him a smile that was clearly forced and said, "I know it will. I'm just tired."

"You must be hungry, too."

Braith studied the platters of meats, roasted potatoes, and still-warm crusty bread. "No. I'm not."

"Addolgar," his mother said to him, her small hand resting on his shoulder. "Why don't you take Braith upstairs to get some sleep? It's been a long day for both of you."

When he looked into his mother's face, she frowned a bit and motioned to the back hallway with a tilt of her head.

Taking the hint, Addolgar stood and waited for Braith to follow. She placed her chalice on the table, thanked his mother, and followed him up several flights of stairs to his room. He held the door open for her and Braith stepped in.

"I'll see you in the morning."

Braith did no more than nod before she crawled onto the bed, dropped her head to the pillow, and closed her eyes.

Worried, Addolgar watched her for several moments before he stepped out of the room, carefully closing the door behind him. He turned around, but took a surprised step back when he found his mother standing there. His shoulders hit the bedroom door hard.

"Hello?" a sleepy-sounding Braith called out.

"It's all right, Braith," he told her through the door. "Go back to sleep."

Addolgar took his mother's arm and led her down the hallway.

"What are you doing up here?" he asked, keeping his voice low.

"You'll need to keep an eye on her. She says very little, that one, but I can tell—there's all sorts of things going on in her head."

"You don't trust her either?"

"I don't trust her not to throw her poor, foolish ass on the altar of her mother's honor. She's a Penarddun, Addolgar. They are . . . a special kind of royal. I met her aunts when I lived in Devenallt Mountain, and . . . well . . . honor means everything to them. Which I do appreciate, but this girl is trusting that bitch Addiena to do what is right, which is the stupidest thing she could ever do. So don't let her sneak away from you on this trip."

"I won't, Mum."

"Good." Frowning hard, she studied the floor. He knew his mother was thinking about something, but he didn't expect what she said next. "I like her."

"You do?"

"I do. And I know exactly what she's doing. I used to do it, too, when I was forced to spend time with Addiena. There're all these things you *want* to say but you keep to yourself out of fear or guilt or whatever."

"Because of Addiena?"

"No. Not for Braith. It's that father of hers." She lowered her voice to a whisper. "I've never liked him. Not at all. But he *is* dangerous. Maybe not physically to you, but he's not above using others to get what he wants. Keep that in mind."

"I will. And I'll stay outside her door to make sure she doesn't sneak away from here during the night."

"Excellent plan. I'll bring you some food so you can eat up here."

"Thanks, Mum."

Finally smiling, Shalin went up on her toes, then stretched her arm up so that she could pet Addolgar's cheek. "My handsome son."

She winked at him and went down the stairs

"Don't let that compliment go to your head, brother," Bercelak said from behind Addolgar, and it took all of Addolgar's training not to scream and run away. Did the dragon *ever* make a sound? The big, overbearing bastard. "Mum says the same thing to all her sons."

Addolgar faced his brother. "What are you doing up here?"

"Can't I spend time with my own brother just to catch up and talk about old times?"

Thinking on that, Addolgar finally answered, "No."

Braith was allowed to sleep in Addolgar's room for the night. She didn't mind. His room smelled nice. But she had no delusions she was trusted. Not with Bercelak pacing the hallway outside her door while Addolgar rested against it all night long. The brothers never said a word to each other, but they never left either—although for different reasons she was sure. Bercelak, because he still saw her as a traitor even if it had been his suggestion to take her to Arranz's home deep in the Black Woods about fifty leagues from here. And Addolgar, because he was afraid she would still leave this place in the middle of the night to turn herself over to the Queen.

She would have, too, but there would be no getting past the Cadwaladrs undetected. She did not have the skills for sneaking around. She didn't lumber as some dragons did, but one could definitely hear her coming and going.

So, instead of fretting about it all, Braith slept until she heard a soft knock on the door. She immediately sat up and Addolgar stuck his head in. He smiled at her, looking surprisingly refreshed since he'd spent the entire night on the floor outside the door.

"We'll be leaving in about fifteen minutes. That enough time for you?"

Braith nodded. She didn't primp like some females did. "Are we going as human or dragon?"

"Dragon to start. But bring clothes and a bag for human travel. Just in case, Ghleanna left some clothes for you on that chair over there."

"And my father?"

"Brigida thinks he may have headed north."

"North?" Braith let out a breath, horrified. "He's heading toward the Northlands? To the Lightnings?"

"Perhaps. But don't worry about that now."

Easier said than done. Had her father actually joined forces with the Lightning dragons of the Northlands? The vilest, most brutal dragons and one of their greatest enemies until the Iron dragons had reared their curled-horned heads not too long ago.

Braith threw off the fur covering and swung her legs over the side of the bed. She stood, stretched. And that's when she realized that Addolgar was still standing there . . . watching her.

"Anything else?" she asked.

"No. You got nice legs, though."

Braith looked down at her legs. Human legs that she'd always thought were rather thin and weak-looking compared to her legs when she was in her natural form.

"Uh . . . thanks?"

When Addolgar continued to stand there, staring at her legs, Braith pushed, "Addolgar?"

"Huh?" he asked, looking up at her.

"Fifteen minutes, right?"

"Right! Right." He nodded. "I'll leave you to it, then."

"Thanks."

The dragon stood there a few seconds longer before he seemed to snap out of whatever haze he was in. But before he could move away from the door, a big shoulder rammed into him, knocking Addolgar's entire body into the wall beside the door.

"*Da!*" Addolgar exploded at his father.

"You need to pay attention, boy! You can't let a good set of legs and a pretty smile distract you from what's going on at all times. That's how you get your head taken off. And then

your mother will cry and I hate when she cries." Ailean
smiled at Braith and winked at her before walking off.

Eyes down, his human face red from embarrassment,
Addolgar nodded at her and muttered, "Downstairs then,"
before he stepped back into the hall and closed the door
behind him.

With a shake of her head, Braith went about getting her
things organized. "The whole lot of 'em," she softly said to
herself. "The whole lot of 'em are just daft."

Addolgar was heading down the stairs when Bercelak
caught up to him.

"I don't like this," his brother told him as they walked
down the stairs.

"You don't like anything. I've heard you complain about
the air."

"It irritates me when it whistles. But that's not what I'm
talking about. When did Brigida become so helpful?"

"I have no idea because I avoid her like the plague I once
heard she vindictively spread in that little town near the
Desert Lands."

"Just be careful, brother."

"I'll have Ghleanna with me. She and her thick neck will
keep me safe until we get Braith to Arranz's."

"Her neck *is* thick, isn't it?"

"It runs in the family. Only Maelona has been spared the
Cadwaladr thick neck because she takes after Mum."

They went down another set of steps.

"What are you going to do?" Addolgar asked his brother.
"Head back to your troops?"

"No. I'm going to see the Queen. See if I can head this
off at the pass."

"You haven't told her anything?"

"Of course not. As soon as I heard what happened, I came to make sure you were okay."

Addolgar stopped and focused on his brother. "You do care about me!"

"Oh, shut up!"

They made it to the courtyard and that's where they met Ghleanna. She had on chain mail and the surcoat of an army she and Addolgar had long ago destroyed. A large bag hung off her shoulder and nearly to the ground. It would be much smaller when she was in her dragon-form, but once she untied the knot at the top, it would fit around her dragon shoulders just as well, allowing her to carry clothes and human weapons, along with food and other supplies for her dragon-form.

"Where is she?" Ghleanna demanded.

"She's coming."

"Keep an eye on her," Bercelak warned Ghleanna. "I still don't trust her. And make sure Arranz is completely apprised of this entire situation so he and our cousins know what to do."

"Of course you don't trust Braith. You don't trust anybody," Ghleanna reminded their brother. "You don't trust the air."

"Because it tends to become unseasonably chilly when I'd prefer it to be warm. It's as if it does it on purpose."

Ghleanna closed her eyes, shook her head.

Braith stepped out of the Main Hall and onto the courtyard steps. She wore nothing but one of Addolgar's shirts, showing off those lovely human legs of hers. But she had a bag similar to Ghleanna's over her shoulder.

Once she stood next to them, Addolgar asked her, "You ready?"

"As ready as I'll—"

Braith's words were cut off as Shalin rushed out of the Main Hall. "Addolgar!"

At his mother's barked words, Addolgar, Ghleanna, and

Bercelak dropped their travel bags and pulled their weapons. They instantly surrounded a confused Braith.

From the sky they dropped, the Queen's Royal Guard, surrounding the small group.

Ailean came out of the front door, pushing Shalin and Maelona back inside. Once the doors were closed, he pulled out his sword, resting the tip on the top stone step while his hand loosely clasped the pommel.

"Can we help you?" he asked . . . kindly.

"We've come for her," the leader said, his claw pointing at Braith. "Give her to us and we leave you and yours in peace, Ailean the Wicked."

Ailean laughed. "Peace? Cadwaladrs know little of peace, I'm afraid."

On his words, shadows moved and then the Queen's Guards, who were surrounding Addolgar, Ghleanna, and Bercelak, who were surrounding Braith, were now surrounded themselves . . . by Addolgar's kin. Most of them were just waking up from a hard night of even harder drinking, but it was one of the first things that every Cadwaladr learned . . . to be ready for battle at anytime, anywhere, with the understanding that once they were done killing, more drinking could begin!

Now uneasy, as the Cadwaladr reputation was always in the forefront of any Southland dragon's mind, the guards slowly pulled their weapons, their bodies tensing in preparation for a fight.

"No, no!"

Braith easily muscled her way past Bercelak and Ghleanna, shocking them both since few had ever managed that before. "This isn't going to happen because of me."

"Braith—"

"No, Addolgar!" She let out a sigh, faced him. "I appreciate everything you've done, but no. This is where it stops."

Braith faced the Guard leader. "I'll come with you. Just leave the Cadwaladrs out of it."

Pretending not to be as relieved as he was, the leader nodded and stepped back, gesturing for her to move ahead.

Braith looked over her shoulder at Addolgar. "Thank you for everything, Addolgar. To you and your kin. I truly appreciate all you've done and tried to do." She smiled at him and Addolgar felt his gut tighten at the sight of it.

"Braith, please—"

"It's all right. I'll be fine."

But Addolgar knew she wouldn't be fine. It was her damn honor that was leading her down this road. Her damn honor that was making her take on what he would consider a suicide mission. It was her damn honor that would ensure she'd never listen to reason.

He watched her walk away until she had enough room to remove his shirt and shift to her natural form. She shook out her long, blue hair and blue wings before taking to the skies with the Queen's Guard at her back.

Once they were gone, it was deadly silent all around him as if everyone was giving Addolgar a moment to mourn—

"Owwwwww!" Addolgar roared after Ghleanna's hard hand slapped him in the back of the head. "*What was that for?*"

"Are you just letting her go?"

"She told me to. *Owwwww!*" Addolgar now glared at Bercelak, who had also slapped him in the back of his already sore head. "*What the hells?*"

"She *told* you to?" Bercelak barked. "What are you? A well-trained dog?"

"Last night you were ready to cut her down in Da's hall."

"That was last night. Today is different! And we're not talking about me, we're talking about *you, you idiot!*"

"Big-headed Bercelak is right!" one of their cousins called out, earning a glower from Bercelak. "We should follow those Queen's Guards and slaughter them all!"

Addolgar's kin cheered in agreement, but a calmly spoken, "No," stopped them from doing just that.

Ailean still stood at the top of the stairs, staring down at them all. "We will not slaughter anyone."

"So we just let them take her?" Ghleanna asked.

Ailean grinned. "I didn't say that either."

Chapter 9

Braith would admit, she'd expected rougher treatment from the Queen's Guard as they entered Devenallt Mountain. But the Guards were actually quite . . . kind. Perhaps they appreciated her preventing a battle between them and the Cadwaladr Clan. Because they all knew—it would have been a battle the Guards would have lost even though their brothers-in-arms would have eventually avenged them.

In the end, though, Braith had simply not seen the point of all those dragons fighting and dying. Her father was a traitor. And getting the Guards killed would have only turned the Cadwaladrs into traitors as well. It was something Braith was not willing to put into motion.

So, she did what her mother would have done—faced the Queen.

The Guards led her to the Queen's throne room, the royals watching Braith from the shadows. There were no curses tossed at her. No threats of retribution for her father's betrayal. They just watched her and said nothing. She didn't know how to take that, so she didn't bother to think on it.

When she stood before the Queen's throne, she sat back on her haunches and briefly bowed her head. "My Queen."

Addiena's cold blue eyes slowly turned toward Braith.

"Well, well," the Queen said softly. "The traitor's daughter."

Addolgar leaned around the corner and saw the guards standing outside the Queen's throne room. He pulled back and faced his siblings. "We'll never get past those guards without killing them," he whispered.

Ghleanna shrugged and began to pull out her sword, but Bercelak slapped her claw with his own. "We're not killing the Queen's Guards. We're part of her army."

"Then what do you suggest?"

"Father said we need to buy him time."

"For what?" Addolgar asked. He still didn't know what his father was up to. And based on the way both his siblings shrugged . . . they didn't know either.

"Let's just do what he asks and hope for the best," Ghleanna suggested.

"But how?"

"We could start a brawl. We're always good at that."

"Or . . . ," Bercelak began, but then his voice trailed off and Addolgar realized his brother had caught sight of one of the Queen's daughters. Princess Rhiannon. Everyone in the family knew of Bercelak's never-ending—and fruitless—obsession with the meanest royal in all of the Southlands.

She was walking by when Bercelak quickly stepped in front of her—completely forgetting about poor Braith!

"Princess Rhiannon," he said.

The white She-dragon looked up at him, her lip curling back over bright white fangs. "Low Born."

"It's good to see you too."

Ghleanna's eyes crossed in exasperation—Rhiannon was their brother's one and only true weakness—while Addolgar stamped his claw and snarled at his brother, "What are you doing? We're running out of time!"

Rhiannon suddenly focused on Addolgar and he had to admit—he didn't really like it.

"Running out of time for what?" Her eyes narrowed. "Are you planning to kidnap me?"

"Can we?" Bercelak asked.

Ghleanna slapped the back of Bercelak's head and Addolgar admitted the truth: "We're trying to stop an execution."

"An execution? Oh. You mean poor Braith of the Darkness," she said casually. "Oh, yes. My mother will definitely have her dead in the next five minutes."

"Well, I don't want that," Addolgar said, horrified.

"Why do you care?"

"I just do!"

"She saved his life," Ghleanna explained.

"And like the loyal fight dogs that you are, you feel the need to rush in and rescue her from the scary demon dragoness?"

"You mean your *mother?*" Ghleanna asked.

"There's no proof of that."

"You have her eyes."

"It's like you want me to have you killed," the princess snapped back at Ghleanna.

"This isn't helping Braith!" Addolgar exploded. "We just need to buy some time."

Rhiannon sighed dramatically, eyes rolling. She glanced around, reached into a small group of young males, and pulled one out.

"Bram, my dearest friend. These low borns need your help. Introduce yourselves, all, because I'll not remember you, much less this conversation in the next five minutes."

"Bercelak. Addolgar." The young dragon greeted them, his gaze lingering a little long on Addolgar's sister. "Ghleanna."

Bercelak frowned. "Do we know you?"

"I'm Bram," the dragon said, appearing confused. "I stayed with your parents last summer."

"Oh." Ghleanna glanced at them. "Right. Uh . . . Brogue."

"Bram."

"Right. Bram. Bram the . . . Friendly?"

"Merciful."

"Of course!" Ghleanna smiled, patted his shoulder. "Bram the Merciful. My father speaks quite highly of you."

"Really? What did he say?"

"Uh . . ."

"We don't have time for this!" Addolgar pushed Ghleanna out of the way and grabbed the young dragon's forearm. "Just go in there and do something, whoever you are."

"Do what?"

"They're trying to stop the execution of Braith of the Darkness," Rhiannon stated, still calmly.

"Well, that execution's practically written in stone."

"Then unwrite it!" Addolgar barked. "Or I'll go in there and lay waste to everyone!"

Not liking that response, Bercelak snarled, so Addolgar added, "Everyone but the Queen."

"Then you're of no use to me," the princess muttered.

"Rhiannon," the young, unknown dragon chastised. "Remember our discussion about things to say out loud and things to keep in one's head? This is a keeper."

Bercelak suddenly stepped into the young dragon. "You seem awfully familiar with Princess Rhiannon."

Blinking up at Bercelak, the dragon stuttered, "Uh . . . well . . . uh . . ."

"Gods, Bercelak." Ghleanna shoved Bercelak aside and caught hold of the young male. "Go in there, Bram, and do whatever is necessary to get us some time. Can you handle that?"

"Aye."

"Good. Now go."

Bram the Whatever rushed off toward the throne room.

"Where's Da?" Addolgar demanded.

"He'll be here. But you need to calm down," his sister warned.

Bercelak, uninterested in any of this, faced the princess again. He smiled and she, in turn, sneered. "Low borns. I have absolutely no use for them." However, she did nod at Addolgar. "Good luck saving Braith's life, Cadwaladr. You probably won't, but . . . good luck just the same."

She turned, the sharp tip of her white tail nearly slicing Bercelak's snout in two before she disappeared into a nearby chamber.

"You do realize you don't have a chance with her, don't you?" Ghleanna asked their younger brother.

"Shut up before I remove your scales."

"Your father's betrayal," the Queen went on, "does not sit well with me, Braith of the Darkness."

And Braith didn't bother replying to that or anything else the Queen said. What was the point? Braith could tell by the way this was going that nothing would save her, and speaking out would probably only make it worse. In fact, she hoped if she kept silent the end would be quick. So she kept her eyes lowered and waited for it all to be over.

"Uh . . . excuse me, Your Majesty?" a voice said from behind Braith.

She didn't turn around, but she could hear another dragon moving up behind her.

"What is it, Bram?" the Queen testily asked.

"I'm sorry to interrupt, Your Majesty, but I was hoping to involve myself in this."

"Involve yourself?"

"Uh . . . yes. Involve myself. With Braith's defense."

"Defense?"

"Why, yes, Your Majesty. Braith will get a defense, won't she? Since the accusation has been against her father and not actually Braith herself. Correct?"

There was a long, painful pause, and Braith expected the Queen to order her guards to just cleave off Braith's head. No one would exactly be surprised if she did, and the way the entire chamber became quiet . . .

Braith simply closed her eyes and waited, but in the silence, she heard something. The sound of wood striking stone and it kept moving closer.

It was curious how everyone became *so* silent, even the Queen. Unable to wait any longer, Braith looked over her shoulder. And that's when she saw Brigida the Foul slowly moving across the throne room, her dragon body leaning heavily on her wooden walking stick, her left back claw dragging behind her as if unable to function at all.

As she moved forward, *everyone* stepped out of her way. Royals, guards . . . everyone. Braith had never seen anything quite like it.

Brigida was a Cadwaladr. Not mated into the Clan but born into it like Ailean and Addolgar and all the rest. She was, as far as Southland royalty was concerned . . . a low-born dragon. And royals didn't move back from low-born dragons unless they needed the low borns to remove a half-eaten carcass. Yet no one approached Brigida. No one stopped her. And the Queen gazed at her with something that Braith truly believed to be fear.

"Gods," Bram whispered to her. "*This* was Ailean's idea to save you?"

Braith could only shrug, because she had no idea what the Cadwaladrs were planning. Which, at the moment, was the most horrifying thing about all this.

* * *

Addolgar looked at his siblings, but all they could do was shrug helplessly. Why their father would send Brigida to help Braith, he didn't know. The Queen was not a fan of witches in general, and seemed to loathe White Dragon-witches specifically. No one knew why, but many suspected it had to do with her daughter, Rhiannon. Rhiannon was a white She-dragon after all. But she did not seem to have the same level of mystical power that Brigida or the few other White Dragonwitches of the Southlands had.

But, honestly, none of that mattered. Not with Braith's life on the line.

"Come on," Ghleanna said, tugging at Addolgar's forearm. She headed inside the chamber, Addolgar and Bercelak following. The guards let them by, but watched closely.

Brigida was still making her very slow way across the chamber toward the Queen.

Addolgar was about to storm around her one way while Bercelak went the other, but Ghleanna caught them both by the hair and yanked them back.

"But—" Addolgar began.

"We follow," Ghleanna whispered.

"She's moving like a snail," Bercelak grumbled.

"We *follow*," Ghleanna insisted.

So they did . . . very slowly. Painfully slowly. Addolgar hadn't known anything could move that slowly and still be moving.

Even stranger, though, was the fact that everyone waited for Brigida. They watched. They waited. They moved out of her way. The She-dragon was clearly feared by one and all in this hall.

Except Braith, he realized. She'd been the only one he'd ever met, even among his kin, willing to brazenly, as Brigida called it, "back talk" her.

He found something rather endearing about that. Well . . . maybe not endearing. But charming. No. Not charming.

Cute. It was cute. She was cute. Very, very cute.

"Stop staring at her!" Ghleanna whispered.

"Huh?"

"At Braith," she continued to whisper. "Stop staring at her like you're planning to kill her yourself."

"Was I?"

"What's wrong with you?"

"That is such an open-ended question," Bercelak scoffed.

"Nothing," Addolgar replied. "I was just thinking."

"About what?"

"How cute she is," he answered honestly.

Bercelak stopped. "*Brigida?*"

Addolgar thought on that a moment. "I don't know if I'd call Brigida cute. Would you, Ghleanna?"

Ghleanna stopped, covered her eyes with her claws. "You two have to be the dumbest centaur-fuckers *ever*."

"Gods, you are so hostile," Bercelak complained.

"I was thinking that," Addolgar agreed.

Braith didn't know what Ailean's offspring were doing. They kept stopping and bickering. Stopping and bickering. Even worse, they kept whispering—but they were in a cave chamber . . . *everyone* could hear them.

And, at first, Braith thought that Addolgar was suggesting she was cute but then Bercelak mentioned Brigida . . . ?

Was this really how the end of her life would look? Really?

"You must have faith," Bram said low, his voice managing *not* to carry.

"Faith? In what?"

His smile was small but there. "In them."

Perhaps Bram the Merciful was right. The Cadwaladrs were known to successfully manage two things—fix things completely or make them a thousand times worse.

And since she didn't see how any of this could get worse . . .

"My Queen!" Brigida greeted Addiena when she finally arrived before her throne. "How good to see you looking so well."

"And you . . . you look . . ." Addiena let out a breath. "So what brings you here, dear Brigida the White?" Only the title one received at hatching was used while in the Queen's chamber. But Braith was sure everyone was thinking "foul."

"Ahh, my dear sweet Majesty. I've come here to offer my assistance in such a trying time."

"Trying time?" the Queen asked.

"The betrayal of Elder Emyr. How horrifying for you. That such betrayal was going on here, right under your beautiful snout."

The Queen's eyes narrowed into slits and Braith began wondering again if anyone would actually claim her headless corpse or if it would be tossed off the side of Devenallt Mountain.

"Even his poor daughter, Braith here, has no idea why her father did this. Or that he was about to do it. She was trapped in his horrible web of deceit and lies." Brigida reached over and patted Braith on the shoulder. She'd flinched away, but a claw on her opposite side from Bram kept her from moving anywhere. "He's betrayed us all, my lady."

"And what do you suggest we do about that?"

"He must be caught and brought back for trial as soon as possible. There is no other way. You must try and *convict* Elder Lord Emyr. No one else can do it but you, Your Majesty . . . and Elder Lord Emyr *himself* must know the true wrath of your domain." Brigida's head tilted to the side and the entire chamber cringed at the sounds coming from her old neck. "Don't you agree, Your Majesty?"

The Queen studied Brigida for a long moment, her mind turning, searching—desperately, by the looks of it—for a way out of this. She wanted an execution and she wanted one now. But Brigida the Foul had made a very good point. To execute

Emyr's daughter—who hadn't been caught while escaping with her kin, but debating what to do next with the loyal Cadwaladrs—rather than Emyr himself, would put a dark stain on Queen Addiena's reign.

Since, Braith was guessing, there would be many dark stains Addiena had to worry about during her reign, she was most likely weighing whether having Braith's head now would be worth it later.

Braith, however, wouldn't bother to get her hopes up. She had no faith in . . . anything at the moment. So she just stood there, waiting for the ax to fall—literally and figuratively—until she felt something brush against her spine. She glanced behind her and saw Addolgar. He gave her a small wink and the tiniest smile, and, Braith would be forced to admit, she'd never felt so . . . safe before. Not safe in the sense that her head would not go rolling across the chamber floor, but just that someone, other than herself or her still-missed mother, actually cared for her. That someone was watching out for her.

And that someone was Addolgar.

"You have a very good point, Brigida the White," Addiena finally stated. "But what will I do with Braith the Blue?"

"My liege," Brigida practically purred, "that's very simple." She focused those cold, dead eyes at Braith, sending a chill down her spine. "We send Braith the Blue to bring back her father—dead or alive."

Addolgar had his claw on Braith's back so he felt her entire body go rigid at Brigida's words. And he understood why. He wouldn't want to have to hunt down his father either. Mostly because his father scared him a little and Addolgar was quite sure the old dragon would kick his ass, but still . . .

"Me?" Braith said. "You want me to hunt my father?"

It was the perfect reaction, wasn't it? The perfect reaction for the Queen. To see Braith's fear, her absolute horror at the prospect. If she'd been eager, the Queen would have immediately said no. But there was no eagerness there—and the Queen loved it. She lived on others' misery.

"Aye," the Queen said, her smile so wide, her bright white fangs nearly blinding everyone in the entire chamber. "You will hunt your father. Hunt him down and bring him to me. Or," she added for good measure, "I'll assume you were part of all this."

The Queen leaned in a bit, the tip of her tail eagerly scratching against the stone flooring. "That you were a part of it . . . and anyone who may have helped you was part of it as well."

Braith's mouth dropped open in shock that the Queen was openly threatening all the Cadwaladrs who'd been at Ailean's castle during her stay, and she immediately looked to Addolgar, then Ghleanna. She glanced at Bercelak, but quickly sneered, before moving her gaze back to Addolgar. She stared at him for several seconds before focusing again on the Queen.

"Your Majesty—" Braith began.

"She'll do it," Addolgar quickly said for her, terrified she was going to do something stupid and "honorable."

Braith glowered at Addolgar. "What are you doing?" she demanded between clenched fangs.

"Stopping you from being an idiot." He grinned at the Queen. "She'll do it, Your Majesty. And I'll go with her to assist in bringing this traitor to justice."

"I cannot hunt down my own—"

Braith's eyes grew wide, her claws reaching for her throat.

"Aunt Brigida?" Addolgar pushed.

The old She-dragon smirked while Braith tried desperately to breathe. "Yes, dear?"

* * *

The invisible binding around her throat disappeared, and Braith took in big gulps of air. She really hated when Brigida did that to her.

"Aye," the Queen said, her grin even wider than before. "This is all a *very* good idea."

Cruel, heartless bitch. No wonder Princess Rhiannon hated her mother. Now Braith hated Rhiannon's mother, too.

Bad enough asking her to hunt down her own father but to threaten the Cadwaladrs merely for helping Braith . . . where was the honor in that? Braith's mum would have asked.

"Glad I could be of service to you, my Queen," Brigida replied, her grin showing several rows of fangs, proving she had to be one of the oldest mortal She-dragons living.

"But wait," the Queen said when Brigida began to slowly turn to leave. "You know, I think I'd feel better if I had a little extra protection."

"*Extra* protection?" Brigida asked, casting her gaze over the armed and well-trained Queen's Guard that surrounded the Queen and filled the chamber.

"Aye!" She pointed. "Ghleanna can stay. She can help keep me safe." She lowered her head, those blue eyes on Braith. "Keep me confident."

"Ghleanna?" Addolgar asked. "Yeah. All right."

Braith faced him. "Are you mad?"

"Mad at what?"

She briefly gritted her fangs. "You cannot leave your *sister* here, Addolgar."

"Why not?" He looked at Ghleanna. "You don't mind, do you?"

Ghleanna shrugged. "Nah."

"See? She doesn't mind."

"I don't care if she minds. We're not—" Braith stopped to yank the walking stick from Brigida's claw. "Choke me again, old hag, and I will *beat you to death with this thing!*" She turned back to Addolgar. "Now, we are all leaving here together or I'm—"

"Just go," Ghleanna pushed. "I'll be fine."

"Yes, but—"

"If you're worried," Bercelak sighed out, "*I* can stay with her."

Ghleanna blinked. "I don't need you to stay with me."

"I didn't *ask* if I could stay with you. But I'm staying with you."

"Piss off," Ghleanna told her brother.

"You piss off."

That's when Ghleanna pushed Bercelak. Who pushed her back. So she punched his shoulder. Bercelak went to punch her shoulder, but Ghleanna caught him by the wrist and twisted his forearm around his back. He reached back with his free forearm and caught her by the hair. Then they were a rolling, pummeling mass of black dragon scales thundering across the throne room floor.

Brigida snatched back her walking stick from Braith and headed toward the exit. "Come along, you two," she called back. "We have much work to do."

"Wait!" the Queen called out. "You can't leave us alone with two battling Cadwaladrs!"

"Don't worry, Your Majesty," Addolgar explained while gripping Braith's forearm and dragging her toward the exit. "Once they knock each other out, you'll have *hours* of quiet before they start again."

"Before they . . . *what?*"

Addolgar pulled Braith out of the chamber and around a corner. Even from there, he could still hear his siblings fighting in the throne room. He didn't know why they bothered. Everyone knew that Ghleanna would beat Bercelak within an inch of his life. . . . She never bothered to fight fair when it came to her siblings.

After a time, Brigida came around the corner.

"Come along, you two," she said again.

Addolgar quickly noticed that now that Brigida was out of the Queen's sight, her limp seemed to have lessened so much that it was nearly nonexistent. And her entire body moved much more fluidly . . . as if she were considerably younger.

They walked in silence until they neared the mountain's exit. That was when Braith finally spoke up.

"I can't do this," she said.

"You can and you will," Brigida told her. "You'll find that old bastard and you'll drag his lizard ass back here."

"He's my father."

Brigida stopped and spun around, her dragon body powerful and strong as if she were centuries younger. Even Addolgar's parents didn't move that easy.

"I don't give a shit, Braith of the Darkness. He's a traitor to this Queen's reign and a danger. You don't need to kill him, but you do need to bring him here." She leaned in close and he saw Braith's claws curl into fists. "Think of it as a matter of honor. Your father may be doomed, but the honor of your family line won't be *if* you return him. And isn't that what matters for the memory of your dear . . . mum?" she finished on a whisper.

Addolgar, claws quick after being raised among his kin, caught Braith before she could attempt to rip Brigida's head off and end up a sad little frog or pet chicken.

"Good," Brigida said with a big smile. "Glad we've agreed."

She moved around Braith and stepped out of the mountain and onto the ledge. "You'll track your father down. He and your brothers and that female who tried to kill Addolgar are heading toward the Northlands. He's taking a longer, safer route than flying over the sea, so you do have a bit of time, but not much. You'll want to grab him before he reaches the Northlands."

"What about Ghleanna?" Braith asked, her voice filled with concern for a She-dragon who only yesterday had physically fought her.

"What about her?"

"I don't feel right leaving her with the Queen as a hostage. Even with Bercelak here—"

"Bercelak?" Brigida laughed a little before unfurling her wings and heading up to the top of Devenallt Mountain.

Addolgar motioned to Braith and together they followed her.

This high up, it was cold on the mountaintop. There was ice and snow. And there were Cadwaladrs. They dotted the mountain like crows on a tree. And more kept landing. One after another after another.

Brigida faced Addolgar and Braith. "You see," she said. "Ghleanna is not alone. A Cadwaladr is never alone." The old She-dragon moved in closer, pressed the top part of her walking stick against the middle of Braith's chest. "And you don't have to be alone either. But we all make our own choices, Braith of the Darkness. And I've made mine. Now track down your father and bring him here." Brigida stepped back, her forearms lifting away from her body. "Or you alone will be responsible for the civil war between the Cadwaladrs and the Queen's Guard when we tear this place apart to get dear, sweet, defenseless Ghleanna from the bowels of Devenallt Mountain."

"Dear sweet, *defenseless* Ghleanna?" one of the Cadwaladrs called out. "Since when did centaurs fly?"

Then all the Cadwaladrs laughed, including Addolgar. Because it was funny.

But the way Braith was gawking at him . . . he sensed she didn't see the humor.

Chapter 10

They flew for about an hour before Braith indicated she wanted to land. She pointed at the ground and Addolgar quickly found a goòd, safe spot for them. They dived and landed hard in a clearing surrounded by trees.

Addolgar took off his travel bag, dropping it to the ground, and shook out his wings. He grinned at Braith. "We'll make good time, as fast as you fly."

She nodded and pushed her blue hair off her face.

"You all right?" he asked.

"Aye. I'm fine. Any water?"

"There's a lake right over there."

Braith stared off in the direction Addolgar had pointed out, but she seemed . . . confused. It had been an overwhelming day for her. True, she seemed invincible to Addolgar, but a bit of polite behavior couldn't hurt. She was a royal after all, probably used to getting everything she needed handed to her and all that.

"You wait here," he told her. "I'll be right back."

She nodded and looked off like she'd already forgotten about him.

Addolgar headed into the trees but quickly realized he'd forgotten his travel bags and the water flask he had inside. He turned back around and headed to where he'd left everything, but as he approached, he slowed down, his gaze on Braith. She was still staring off, but he realized she was breathing heavily. So heavily that, suddenly, she dropped to her knees, her front claws digging into the dirt.

Addolgar sprinted to her side, his forearms reaching around her.

"Braith? What is it?"

Panting, barely able to breathe, it seemed, she stuttered out, "I . . . I . . . I almost died. I almost died. I almost died."

Then it hit him—she wasn't invincible at all. She was, however, one of the strongest females he'd ever known. Because she'd lasted this long without having a full-on panic attack, and that was much longer than he would have lasted if he'd been in her place. Much longer.

Braith didn't care that she was making a fool of herself. She didn't care that she couldn't breathe, that she was babbling, that she was wrapping her forearms around Addolgar the Cheerful and holding him tight. She didn't care.

Because an hour ago . . . she'd thought her life would end on a cold stone floor in the Queen's throne room.

Big claws stroked her back and hair, while he held her tight against his warm body, where she felt safe. It was the safest she'd felt since her father had summoned her a few days ago.

When Braith's panting calmed down enough that she could hear again, she realized Addolgar was speaking to her.

"You're going to be all right, Braith. We're going to get through this together. I promise."

Gods, he was trying to make *her* feel better. His sister was being held hostage, his entire family was about to start a civil war that could get them all killed, and he was being forced to track down a traitor outside of Southland borders with a panicking, pathetic female—and he was trying to make *her* feel better.

Appalled, Braith quickly pulled away from him.

"I'm so sorry, Addolgar."

"Sorry? For what?"

"For being . . . pathetic. Weak. I'm of the Penarddun bloodline and I should have been strong—"

Braith's words were cut off because Addolgar had wrapped his claw around her snout, keeping it closed.

"Pathetic?" he asked. "Weak? You? After what you've just been through? You held your head up the entire time. You never showed Addiena or Brigida your fear. A fear you had every right to have. So don't talk centaur shit to me about you being pathetic or weak. I won't hear it. I won't tolerate it. And once you understand that, you and I will get along just fine."

He released her snout. "Now what do you have to say?"

"I . . . um . . ." She swallowed tears of gratitude, unwilling to be even more of a mess in front of Addolgar. "I'm thirsty."

He grinned. "So am I. Let's get some water from the lake and figure out what our next steps should be. Sound like a plan to you?"

Braith nodded. "A very good plan."

"Excellent!" He gripped her claw in his and pulled her toward the lake. "And I stole some oxen jerky out of Bercelak's bag. He makes the best oxen jerky."

"Bercelak the Vengeful *cooks*?"

"Aye. And he's surprisingly good at it, too!"

They traveled late into the night until they could go no farther. Exhausted, they finally stopped near a town. Addolgar would prefer to stay in the woods for the night, but they were in a more densely populated area, filled with humans. So whether they stayed in the woods or not, they'd have to do it as human or risk some farmer or late-traveling merchant stumbling across two sleeping dragons. It was not a good way to start the day, in his estimation. Burning a bunch of humans crispy for nothing more than being in the wrong place at the wrong time. True, Bercelak would do it, but he had little to no tolerance when it came to humans. He thought they should all burn. Or, at the very least, be nothing more than cattle for dragon meals.

They shifted to their human forms and dug into their travel bags for their clothes.

With a comical little expression on her face, Braith pulled out the clothes Ghleanna had put together for her. She held them up for Addolgar to see.

"Your sister seems to have a love of chain mail."

Addolgar chuckled. "She's Cadwaladr. All my sisters love chain mail except Maelona, who has no desire to pick up a blade or an ax. Never has." He studied her as she slipped the clothes on. They fit her, but barely. Especially around the shoulders. She moved her arms, trying to stretch the material out a bit.

"Have you thought about getting in some military training?" he asked as he pulled on his own clothes.

She shrugged. "Actually . . . I have. But my father was against it. He said royals shouldn't lower themselves to being a military force."

"Some of the best kings and queens the Southland dragons have had fought in battle. Addiena's mother was a battle mage for many years before she took the throne."

"I don't disagree with you, but—"

"Your father no longer matters in your future, Braith. Once we're done with this, it'll be all down to you."

She sighed. "I still don't know how I'm going to do this, Addolgar. Turn in my own father?"

"I'll be right by your side." He tugged on his boots, then added, "In fact, let's think of this a different way."

"And what way is that?"

"Instead of you bringing in your father . . . you're retrieving Lady Katarina, while *I'm* bringing in your father."

"And what does that word play actually *do*, Addolgar?"

"Take the pressure off. You think too much of words," he explained while he stood. "They have all this meaning for you." Addolgar reached down and grasped her hands, lifting her to her feet. "So use all that meaning to your benefit. I'll bring in your father while you'll bring in Katarina. Now, what about your brothers?"

"What about them?"

"We should probably bring them in, too, or Addiena will just send us out again."

"Don't worry. Where my father goes, my brothers will go. They've never been able to think on their own."

"That's sad."

"My mum tried to help them, but since hatching they've been loyal to my father. Plus they're rather stupid."

"And you've been loyal to your mum."

"From the beginning to the end of time, I'll be loyal to my mum."

"I don't blame you. She did a good job teaching you to fight."

"She did?"

"Braith, you may not be ready to ride into battle"—*yet*— "but you've got basic hand-to-hand combat techniques down pretty well from what I've seen. You took out Bercelak." He leaned down until their noses nearly touched. "*Bercelak.* Only Ghleanna and a few of our older sisters can take him in a fight."

"He doesn't like fighting females?"

"Bercelak will fight anyone. But my sisters are like you. Strong, fierce . . . a little heartless."

"He started it." She glanced down. "You going to let my hands go, Addolgar?"

"If you insist."

She looked off, thought a moment. "Well, you should keep holding at least one. I wouldn't want to get lost on the way into town." She briefly chewed her lip, still wouldn't look him in the eye. "I've never been here before."

Doing his best not to smile too widely at that, Addolgar

released her left hand but kept hold of her right. And, without much else said, they headed into town, hand in hand.

They walked into the pub. A dark, dastardly-looking place that Braith normally wouldn't do more than tear apart with her claws.

Even worse, as soon as they stepped inside, the entire place fell silent, all eyes turning toward them, watching them with suspicion.

Braith pulled her hand out of Addolgar's and curled both hands into fists beneath her fur cloak, ready to battle her way out of here if necessary. But then Addolgar pulled the hood of his own cloak back, tossed his silver hair off his face, and the entire room went up in a cheer.

"Addolgar!"

"Hello, all!" Addolgar called out in return.

He took Braith's hand again, his fingers easily separating hers so that she no longer had a fist, and led her into the pub. There were more greetings all around. Cheerful pats on the back, and hugs from the females, a few handshakes as they passed through.

Addolgar finally stopped by a table. He stepped behind Braith and took off her cloak, placing it on the bench beside her. He took off his own and then sat on the other side. A barmaid walked up to the table with four big mugs of ale. She slammed them down on the table. "From your fans," she giggled, winking at him.

Grinning, Addolgar pulled three ales closer to himself and pushed one toward Braith.

"We have Mum's stew tonight," the barmaid said.

"Say no more," Addolgar told her.

"And bread?"

"You have to ask?"

The barmaid winked at him again and focused on Braith. "You as well, miss?"

"Aye, please."

She nodded and walked off. Braith watched the girl for a bit before looking at everyone else.

"We're safe here, Braith. You can stop looking so worried."

"You spend a lot of time here?"

He shrugged and gulped from one of the mugs of ale. "I've been here over the years. I travel a lot."

"Yes, but they seem to . . . know you so well."

"I like meeting strangers. You never know what you'll learn. What you'll discover."

She leaned in. "But all these humans?"

"You don't like humans?"

"I don't *dis*like them. But I don't trust them either."

That made Addolgar laugh. "I don't trust anybody except me own kin. But that doesn't mean you can't enjoy others' company. Everyone has a fascinating tale to tell if you're willing to listen."

The barmaid returned, placing large bowls of delicious-smelling stew in front of them along with several platters of fresh, warm bread.

"Need anything else, you just let me know."

"Thanks, Mary." Addolgar ripped off a large chunk of bread and began devouring that first bowl of stew. He didn't speak while he ate. He just ate. And before he'd even finished that first bowl, Mary brought another, and then another. All of which Addolgar ate. More bread was brought and he devoured that as well.

Braith, however, was satisfied with two of the large bowls of stew and one large loaf of bread to appease her human appetite.

By the time she finished her second bowl, Addolgar had finished his fourth and was leaning back to sigh contentedly.

"Good, eh?" he asked, that smile on his face.

"Very."

"Mary's mum runs this place. She makes the best stew. Ale's good too." To prove that, he finished off his third mug of ale, only for Mary to bring four more.

"Dessert?" Mary asked.

"What ya got?"

"Me mum's raisin and ale cake."

"Bring it."

Laughing, Mary walked off and Addolgar rested his elbow on the table and his chin in the palm of his hand.

"You all right?" he asked her.

"I'm fine. I was hungrier than I thought."

"You haven't eaten in a couple of days. And it's been a rough couple of days."

Braith placed her hands on the table and leaned in a bit. "Addolgar."

"Hhmm?" he asked, smiling down at the desserts Mary placed in front of them. "You should try this," he told Braith. "Mary's mum makes a great raisin and ale cake."

Braith glanced down at the cake—it did look good—and back at Addolgar.

"Addolgar . . . I don't know how I can thank you."

"Thank me? For what?" he asked around a mouthful of cake.

"Putting your family at risk? Helping me with the Queen? Protecting me from Bercelak?"

"You protected yourself from Bercelak."

"Addolgar," she felt the need to remind him, "the Queen is holding your sister hostage."

Addolgar blinked, nodded. "Uh-huh."

Braith frowned. "Yet you don't seem too worried about her."

"If it were Maelona, I'd never have allowed it. I'd have torn the walls of Devenallt Mountain down before I let her take Maelona. So would the rest of my kin."

"But Ghleanna . . . ?"

"If the Queen wants to have Ghleanna and Bercelak

staying at Devenallt Mountain while you and I track your father down—that's her decision. And I wish her much luck with it." He pointed at Braith's cake with his spoon. "You going to eat that?"

Chapter 11

"You staying here for the night, Addolgar?" Mary asked. "Me mum wants to know."

"Aye," he said, after glancing at an exhausted-looking Braith. "We'll take a room. Is the one on the top floor open?"

"It is. But it's extra."

"We'll take it."

"Let me check it first, make sure it's been cleaned right. I'll let you know when you can come up."

"Thanks, Mary."

Mary headed to the back stairs and Addolgar again focused on Braith. "Stop worrying," he ordered her.

"Who says I'm worrying?"

He rolled his eyes in answer and Braith gave a small sigh.

"I can't help it," she finally admitted. "I can't believe my father has done this. And for what? He could never rule the Southland dragons. Not as a monarch. Being an Elder was the most he could ever hope to be. And he should be proud of that."

"Perhaps he thinks he's saving his people. There are many who don't feel right with Addiena on the throne."

"But she is. And she has been for nearly a century." Braith rested both her arms on the table. "What I can't figure out, though, is what Lady Katarina has to do with any of this."

"Perhaps he hopes to use her father's army to challenge Addiena. It would be a bold move, but her father's army is strong. They have to be since they are all that lies between us and the Irons."

"I thought the fear was that he'd side with the Irons."

"He could, but he'd be foolish to try. The Irons see themselves as superior to everyone. In their minds, they only answer to the gods. So betraying Lord Berg would mean nothing to them. And he knows that."

"But if Lord Berg challenges Addiena, won't he have to face the Cadwaladrs in battle? I've always heard that's what keeps many challengers for the throne from our borders."

"Using our name will stop those who talk a lot about claiming the throne but really have no true heart for it. But those who truly want it, like Overlord Thracius in the West or the Horde leaders in the Northlands . . . the Cadwaladrs are merely something to figure out how to defeat. All we manage to do with the likes of them is keep them back until they have enough forces to move."

Braith placed the palms of her hands against her eyes, her exhaustion and frustration beginning to grow. "I just wish I knew what he was doing. Who he was working with. My father does nothing on his own." She dropped her hands and looked Addolgar straight in the face. "He's not a brave dragon."

"What about your mum?"

"The bravest I knew."

Addolgar finally asked the question that had been bothering him for most of the day. "Why are you not close to your mum's kin?"

"My mother saw me as a Penarddun, but her kin see me as my father's daughter. And they want even less to do with *him*." She shook her head, glanced off. "As always, I'm on my own."

"Not anymore you're not. You have the force of the Cadwaladr Clan behind you. That's more than most will ever be able to say."

"I still wish we hadn't involved your family. If one of them gets hurt or . . . if anything happens to your kin, Addolgar . . ."

"Nothing will happen. And you seem to think you've somehow forced us into this. Or as if we're doing it out of pity. The Cadwaladrs don't feel pity. Not for each other. Not for anyone."

"Then why are any of you helping me?"

"My father's doing it because you won him lots of money. Ghleanna's doing it because she likes knowing another female near her age who can't quite wear her clothes. Bercelak will say he's doing it to protect Ghleanna, but really he wants to spend time around Princess Rhiannon, even though we all know he doesn't have a shot in all the hells with that one."

"And you?" she asked, before Addolgar could list the reasons *all* of his kin would be involved in this. "Why are you doing this?"

"That's easy. Because I like you." He grinned. "I like you a lot."

"Why?"

"Because you make me smile."

"You're Addolgar the Cheerful. *Everything* makes you smile."

"Not everything. And if I want to like you, Braith of the Darkness, I get to like you. Whether you want me to or not."

"Why wouldn't I want you to?"

"I don't know. Maybe because I'm not a royal?"

"Is there anything about me, Addolgar, that says I embrace being a royal? That I live my life as a royal? Anything?"

Addolgar thought on that a moment before replying, "Not really."

"The Penardduns may be royals, but you don't find any of them living in Devenallt Mountain or attending any of the parties or rituals. My mum hated that stuff. Didn't see the purpose of it at all. And I have to agree with her. I only attended royal events to keep my father off my back."

"So, when this is all over, if Addiena strips you of your title—"

"As long as I get to go back to my cave and be left alone, I won't give a flying centaur shit."

Addolgar glanced up and saw Mary wave to him from the stairwell. "Come on." He took Braith's hand and led her from the table and to the stairs. They went up the three flights and walked down the hallway to the last room. Mary held the door open for them.

"Think you'll be needing anything else tonight, Addolgar?"

"No. We're fine. But we'll be up early tomorrow. We'll need food before our trip. And if you have any bread and meat that can go with us, I'd appreciate that."

"Of course. Me and Mum will take care of it."

"Thanks, luv."

Mary nodded at Braith and walked out, closing the door behind her. Addolgar led Braith across the large room to the fireplace. She immediately held out her hands to warm them and Addolgar took her cloak from her.

"I'll make sure to keep the fire going tonight."

"All right."

"Why don't you get some sleep, Braith?"

"I will."

He stepped behind her. "I meant now."

"I don't know how you expect me to get any sleep with so much on my mind."

"You need to sleep if we hope to get any real traveling done tomorrow."

"The territory between here and the Northlands is enormous, Addolgar. My father could be anywhere."

"I know his route."

Braith faced him. "What do you mean, you know his route?"

He shrugged. "I heard from Brigida." He pointed at his forehead. "Up here." Although he should only be able to do that with his siblings and parents, those rules had never stopped Brigida from popping into anyone's head whenever she damn well felt like it, no matter her relation to them. Many believed it was because of her powers as a White Dragonwitch that she was able to do so with such ease. Others believed she was a demon who could burrow into anyone's soul. Addolgar decided to believe the White Dragonwitch angle so he could sleep at night.

"From here, we head west to the borders between the Southland and Outer Plains. She says we'll find him there."

"Dense forests in those parts. We'll have to be careful."

"You know the area?"

In answer, Braith only shrugged and walked toward the bed. She stopped before reaching it, spun around, and asked, "Are you sure we shouldn't leave now to find—"

Addolgar placed his hand over Braith's face. He had big hands and he covered almost all of her face. "You need sleep. I need sleep. We will not be traveling anywhere tonight."

"You," she said behind his hand, "don't have to keep doing this when you don't like what I have to say."

"Apparently I do. Otherwise you wouldn't keep saying those things."

He dropped his hand, gazed down into her face. "I'm by your side on this, Braith. We're in this together. Stop worrying about things that are already in motion. Already said and done. Our focus should be on our goal. Getting your father and bringing him back for the Queen to deal with. Don't let anything else drag you down."

"I just feel so guilty."

"For the actions of your father? No wonder you and Ghleanna

get along so well. Whatever your father has done or will do, it has nothing to do with you. Just as my father's *illustrious* past has nothing to do with Ghleanna or any of his offspring."

Braith shrugged. "Well . . . I could see how your father's past could follow—" Braith sighed deeply from behind Addolgar's hand. "You did it again."

"You were saying something I didn't want to hear."

She slapped his hand off.

"Ow!" he barked while laughing. "What was that for?"

"I'll get some sleep," she replied. And with that, she got on the large bed and stretched out. Then, stiff as a board, with her arms by her sides, Braith lay there.

"Good gods, female," Addolgar muttered. "What did you do with yourself before I came into your life?"

"I lived quietly alone in my cave," she snapped back. "And I was quite happy there, too."

Addolgar stood over her, hands on his narrow hips. "How can you be comfortable all stiff like this? With your clothes on?"

"I'm cold," she reminded him, desperate not to take her clothes off. Her human body was not something poets would ever write about, so she wasn't about to get naked in front of Addolgar, of all dragons.

"That's what the fur covers are for. You'll get under them and with the fire going, you'll be fine."

"I'm fine as I am right now."

"At least take your boots off."

To appease the big ox, Braith sat up, but before she could touch the leather of her boots, Addolgar was there.

"I'll do it," he said cheerfully, smiling at her.

He tugged off first one boot, then the other. He then pulled off her socks and lifted her feet, studying them.

"I thought they'd be bigger."

"How is that not an insult?"

"It's not an insult. Or a compliment. Just an observation." He thought a moment. "But your feet are cute, and that is a compliment."

Laughing, Braith pulled her feet out of his grasp. "My boots are off. Can I go to sleep now?"

"I don't think so."

"Why not?"

"You're not relaxed. Who can sleep when they're not relaxed?"

"I'll relax eventually."

"At least take your leggings off."

"I will do no such thing."

"You're being as silly as humans about this."

"That's my choice."

"Well," Addolgar said, "*my* choice is for you to be comfortable."

And that's when he grabbed the bottom of her leggings and began to yank them off.

"Addolgar!"

"You'll thank me when I'm done."

No, she wouldn't!

Braith tried to scramble away, but she only managed to assist him in getting her leggings off while, at the same time, flipping herself off the blasted bed.

Growling, she got to her knees and rested her arms on the bed. She glowered up at the beast. "Give me back those leggings!"

"I'm trying to help you."

"I don't know what you're doing, but I'm sure there are laws about it!"

"I don't know why you're being so shy." He paused a moment, then asked, "Do I make you nervous?"

"Yes!" Braith replied honestly.

"Why?"

G.A. Aiken

442

"I just . . . look, just . . . I mean . . ." She slammed her fist against the bed. "Give me my blasted leggings!"

Addolgar studied her for a bit before he surmised, "You don't want me to see you naked."

"Leggings."

"Do you think I've never seen a human body before?"

"Leggings."

"Do you have a few scars you don't want me to see?"

"*Leggings!*"

"Fine." Addolgar tossed her precious leggings behind him and began to toe off his boots.

"What are you doing?" she asked.

"Getting naked."

"What the hells for?"

"So you can be comfortable getting naked, too, so we can get some sleep."

"How would that make me feel comfortable? In what universe would that make me feel comfortable?"

"You can see my scars."

"I don't want to see your scars!"

"There's no shame in scars. The more scars you have, the more respect you get from the Cadwaladrs."

"Addolgar—" she began, but her words were cut off when his chain-mail shirt hit her in the face.

"Dammit!" she barked, yanking the shirt off and tossing it to the floor. But before she could get her bearings, Addolgar's leggings swiftly followed. They were heavier and nearly knocked her on her ass, but she managed to keep her balance and toss them away too.

"See?" he asked when she looked up at him. "I'm just like you."

Braith could only shake her head and reply, "You have to be the biggest idiot, I've *ever* known."

Confused, he looked down at himself, then back at her.

"What?" Addolgar asked. "Is it me thighs?" He cringed a bit. "They're too big for the rest of me, ain't they?"

Unable to look at him a moment longer, Braith buried her head into the fur covering and sighed, long and deep.

The biggest idiot . . . *ever*.

Addolgar knelt on the other side of the bed and studied the top of Braith's head. All that thick, blue hair spread around her, covering her arms, and reaching to the floor. He couldn't help himself—his fingers were running through it before he even realized it.

That's when Braith's head slowly came up. He didn't quite understand the look on her face. Was she angry? Insulted? Disgusted? He didn't know her well enough to know what she was thinking at the moment. So Addolgar did what he always did in these situations. He asked.

"I can't tell. Are you pissed? Or just appalled?"

"Confused," she said softly, her expression unchanging.

"Confused about what?"

"Why did you touch me? To be kind?"

"Kind?" He thought about that word for a moment before admitting, "Braith, I'm not kind."

"You've been kind to me."

"I like you."

"Me? I thought royals like Lady Katarina were more to your taste, Addolgar."

They usually were. But there was just something about Braith. . . .

Addolgar took a risk and reached his hand over again, gently pushing stray blue hairs out of her eyes. "The more time I spend with you, Braith, the more I like you."

"I'm not really likeable."

"Who told you that?"

She shrugged. "Everyone. But I don't need anyone to feel sorry for me about that."

"Braith, no one as strong as you gets anyone's pity. And you certainly don't have mine."

"Then what is it?"

"I'm drawn to you, Braith of the Darkness. You make my scales itch."

Her eyes grew wide. She no longer had that hard-to-read expression; instead she just looked overwhelmed. "*I* do?"

"There's just something about you." He placed his hands on the bed, then pulled them closer so that she wouldn't feel threatened. "But that's just how I feel. You don't have to feel the same way. I know what I am."

"What you are?"

"A Cadwaladr. For some we're a challenge. For others, we're to be avoided like the plague. I understand both sides."

"I envy you your family, Addolgar. Their loyalty to each other is something to be cherished."

"I do. But I also understand how we must appear to outsiders."

"None of that means anything to me," she said.

"I know. You're all about honor and loyalty."

"It's how my mother taught me. It meant the world to her and it means the world to me." She ran her hand through her hair and Addolgar had to bury his fingers in the fur covering so that he didn't do the same. "I keep thinking about what she'd tell me. Right now. She was a direct dragoness. Not like most royals at all."

"And what would she tell you?"

"I think she'd tell me to remember my bloodline. My *Penarddun* bloodline. She didn't think much of my father's." Her lips suddenly curled into a small smile. "And she'd remind me of the strength in that bloodline. The confidence."

Her head dropped forward and then Braith was pushing

herself away from the bed and easily getting to her feet. She stepped back and, with a deep breath, she used both hands to push her hair off her face and behind her back.

Braith stood there, her gaze on Addolgar's—and that's when he understood what this was. What she was risking. For him.

Dragons were never more vulnerable than when they were human, except when they first hatched. Humans had no scales, no claws, no spiked tail, no flame. All they had were their ability to run fast, their interesting human form, and their devious minds. Otherwise, they were as weak and frail as rabbits.

Yet here Braith was, at her most vulnerable, and she was leaving herself open—for him.

Addolgar stood, ready to move to her side, to take her gently in his arms and softly tell her how beautiful she was and—

"Oooof!" he barely managed as Braith suddenly ran over the bed and threw herself into Addolgar's arms.

"Too eager?" she asked, grimacing as he quickly tightened his arms around her so that she didn't fall to the floor. Then again, the way she had her legs around his waist and her arms around his shoulders, she could probably just keep herself up there without his help.

"I like eager," he admitted.

"I just . . . it's just . . ." She gazed down at him, and Addolgar didn't know exactly what to make of this current expression.

"Braith, it's okay if—"

That's when she kissed him. Hard. Her arms moving to his neck and wrapping tight, her lips against his, her tongue pressing into his mouth.

It startled Addolgar at first. He usually had to work harder than this. Much harder. Unlike his father, he didn't have females throwing themselves at him. And yet . . . that's exactly what Braith had done. She'd thrown all the usual centaur shit away, all the promises and lies and ridiculousness, and she'd just . . . given herself to him. Freely. And with hunger.

Making him perhaps the happiest dragon in the land.

Chapter 12

Addolgar walked them over to the bed, turned, and dropped back against it, Braith still wrapped around him like a shameless snake.

But she couldn't help herself. He was so handsome and charming and a tad goofy that she couldn't resist him just standing there . . . naked. Wonderfully, wonderfully naked.

She'd never really found human bodies interesting one way or the other—until she'd seen Addolgar as human. Human and naked. He should always be naked. Just running around naked. Naked, naked, naked!

And now she had that perfect human *naked* body beneath her and, in a moment, on top of her as Addolgar flipped her and himself over.

Their kiss seemed to go on forever and she enjoyed every second of it. Every second of his taste, the feel of his tongue, the stroke of his fingers against her human skin.

She heard groaning and she realized it was her!

It was rather hard to believe that Braith of the Darkness, who was fazed by little, was groaning at the touch of . . . anyone. But it felt so good.

Addolgar pulled out of their kiss so he could lick and nibble her neck.

That drove her crazy, made her legs tighten around his waist.

His hands on her sides, he kissed his way down her throat, across her shoulder, down to her breast. His tongue curled around her nipple, tugged. She was grateful Addolgar's heavy body was on top of her or she would have flipped off the bed. He tugged again and Braith dug her fingers into his shoulders and back. Her human fingers had no long nails, which was good because she would have torn the weak, human flesh from him.

After tormenting her other breast, he began kissing his way farther down. Braith raised her head, briefly wondered where he was go—oh. Oh! He was going there.

She reached up for the headboard as Addolgar's tongue slipped inside her. Unfortunately, there was no headboard to grab so Braith flattened her hands against the wall and bit down on her lip, barely remembering there were others in the building trying to sleep. But she couldn't stop the groans or the growls as Addolgar held on to her hips and explored her pussy with what she considered wild abandon.

Braith's eyes crossed and her toes curled. She didn't think she could take much more. Then the tip of Addolgar's tongue circled her clit, taking her higher and higher until he suddenly gripped it between his lips and suckled.

Braith exploded, her body shaking, her hands tearing at the wall behind her. She cried out even though she tried not to, and fell back on the bed, barely able to breathe.

When she finally opened her eyes, Addolgar was above her, his arms braced on either side of her. He studied her for a long minute, his gaze moving over her face, until he asked with all sincerity, "Are you all right?"

She brought her hands up to clasp either side of his face and pressed her forehead against his chin. That's when she realized her human body was no longer cold; instead she was sweating.

"I'd be much better," she admitted, "with you inside me."

Addolgar slid his hands down and behind Braith's knees. He lifted her legs up and spread them before pressing his cock against her and slowly pushing it inside her.

Braith gasped out, her smile wide. A smile he realized he rarely saw from her. But she was smiling now and nothing felt better.

At least that's what he thought until he went in deeper and Braith tightened down on his cock. Now he gasped, his entire body shuddering.

"Gods, female," he laughed. He kissed her. Once. Twice. "You feel incredible, Braith. Amazing."

She kissed his neck, shoulders. "So do you. So good."

He pulled out, drove back in. They both groaned, holding on to each other.

"What are you doing to me?" he asked, confused.

"What are you talking about?" Braith arched into him. "I'm not doing anything."

He drove in again and it felt better than the last time. Gods, he didn't care what she was doing as long as she didn't stop doing it. He couldn't even talk anymore; his body taking over.

Addolgar raised himself up, again bracing his arms on either side of Braith, and then he powered into her. He knew the female's strength now. Understood she was physically strong. So he didn't hold back. He just took her as he wanted to and the smile that lit up her face told him it was the right choice.

Thank the gods, because he wasn't sure he could stop. If nothing else, he knew he didn't *want* to stop. Between her sweet moans and the way her body easily met him thrust for thrust, Addolgar was in heaven.

Braith suddenly gasped, her hands slapping hard against his shoulders. Her back arched and she came, beautifully, her entire body tightening around him. When her pussy clamped down on his cock, Addolgar came with her, his head thrown back, his hands gripping the fur covering beneath her.

When she'd wrung him dry, he fell off to the side, crashing next to her on the bed. They lay there, staring up at the ceiling and panting until at the same time, they looked at each other. They stared for a long moment, then looked back at the ceiling and continued panting.

The door opened and Addolgar came in with one hand holding the fur covering around his waist and the other holding a tray of bread, meat, and cheese.

"Thank the gods," Braith sighed out, reaching for the tray. "I'm starving!"

"Aye. So am I."

She placed the tray on the bed and Addolgar brought over the water jug and two chalices. He sat down across from her, with the tray between them, and they dove into the food as if they hadn't eaten for days. They mostly ate in silence—except for the grunts—until they'd finished off everything.

Braith picked up a few remaining crumbs with her finger and sucked them off, sighing in satisfaction.

"Cheese and bread has never tasted so good."

"Don't forget the meat," Addolgar reminded her.

Grinning, Braith teased, "Didn't get much of that after you got your hands on it."

"I was hungry . . . and did most of the work."

Braith laughed outright at that. "If you do say so yourself."

Addolgar moved the empty tray, water jug, and chalices onto the floor. Then he stretched out on the bed and rested his head in Braith's lap.

"You don't smile," he suddenly stated.

"What?"

"You don't smile. Not often." He took hold of her hand and placed it on his head. That's how she knew he wanted her to stroke his hair. Since he'd taken such good care of her . . . how could she turn him down?

"I guess I don't," she admitted while slowly dragging her fingers through his lovely silver hair. "Never thought about it much."

"You should smile."

"Why?"

"It makes you look happy. I enjoy seeing you happy."

Braith could say in all honestly that no one had ever said that to her. Her father could not have cared less if she were happy and had told her as much. Which, coming soon after her mother's death, had most likely been when she'd stopped smiling.

"What are you missing, Braith?"

She really had no idea where this conversation was going. "Missing? I'm not missing anything."

"You are. I can tell. We need to find out what that is so you can have it and be happy." He grinned at her. "I enjoy seeing you happy."

"You do? Then kiss me," she ordered, leaning down, her mouth hovering over his, "and I can promise you without a doubt that I'll be as happy as you want me to be."

Chapter 13

Braith awoke in Addolgar's arms. They were facing each other, her forehead pressed against his, her hands resting against his shoulders.

She felt unbelievably comfortable, in a way she normally didn't feel comfortable unless she was alone in her cave. So much so, she didn't want to get up. She didn't want to face the day and the challenge of hunting down her father. But as soon as the suns peeked through the wooden slats of the window shutters, Addolgar's eyes opened.

A true soldier.

Addolgar saw her eyes on him and he instantly smiled in a smooth, easy way that told her it was genuine. He was glad to see her. Glad to have her here. The realization warmed her more than she could have thought.

"Good morn to you," he murmured, his low voice rolling seductively down her spine.

"Good morn."

"We have to get up."

"I know."

"I don't want to."

"Me either," she agreed. "But we have to, don't we?"

"Think of it this way . . . we finish this quickly, and then we can go to my cave and spend as much time rolling around my floor as we like."

"Your cave?"

"Or we can go to yours. Although mine is surprisingly nice. My brother Rhys decorated it."

"Rhys? Rhys the *Hammer* decorated your cave?"

"He has a skill. The family tries not to judge."

"So," she couldn't help but ask, "after this is all over, you and I—"

"Will be rolling around my or your cave floor. Was I not clear?"

Braith laughed. "No, no. You were quite clear."

"You still look happy."

"I am." She hugged him. "I'm very happy."

His arms tightened around her and he whispered into her neck, "Then let's go track down that bastard father of yours and get this done with."

They traveled for nearly three days, pushing their way toward the border. They took only short breaks for food and quick naps. Thankfully, the wind was on their side, helping them move fast.

Addolgar would admit—if he'd been asked—that his reasons for all this were quite selfish. Unlike his brother Bercelak, Addolgar didn't give his all to the Queen. He gave his all to the battle. So finding a snotty-nosed traitor and returning him for whatever punishment the Queen had planned really didn't interest him much. He was a warrior, not a pet dog to run errands.

But for Addolgar, this wasn't about the Queen or her throne or anything but Braith. And he couldn't help but feel that once her father was captured and handed over, things might change for her. Because right now, it seemed as if something was missing. He couldn't explain why he felt this way. Couldn't explain why he knew that whatever was missing had nothing to do *with* her father but what her father was keeping from her. Her true freedom, perhaps? Addolgar didn't know, but he'd always trusted his instincts. Those instincts kept him alive in battle and relatively unharmed when home with his father. So he wouldn't doubt them now. Instead, he'd follow them and get this job done, so he could focus on Braith and what she needed.

Addolgar simply couldn't help himself. He wanted her to be happy. Whether she spent another second with him when this was all done or went off on her merry way without him, he wanted to know that wherever she was, she was happy. And right now, as much as he was sure she enjoyed her time with him, she was far from truly happy.

The suns had set and they'd just passed the border that separated the Southlands from the Outer Plains. He turned and dived, landing outside a mountain that Brigida had told him about. Braith landed beside him and they walked until he found the entrance. A pass that cut right through the heart of the mountain.

Addolgar stopped Braith before she could go farther. "Take this," he said, handing her his sword.

She turned the weapon over in her claws. "Don't you need this?"

"I have me ax and hammer. Don't need much more than that in a fight."

She shrugged. "I don't know this weapon, Addolgar."

"That's all right." He took the weapon back from her and proceeded to wrap the leather belt around her waist. The scabbard hung at her side and she smiled up at him. "Feels good, doesn't it?" he asked.

"It does. Doesn't make me a soldier, though."

"We'll see," he murmured, nodding. "Ready then?"

"Ready."

Together, they flew through the mountain passage and the farther they went, the more Braith realized that Brigida was right. Her father had come this way. Recently. Braith could scent him.

When they neared the end of that passage, and the night sky was easy to see in the distance, Braith landed, with Addolgar right behind her. He placed one raised silver claw to his snout and Braith nodded.

Moving silently, they headed down the last of the passage until they reached a natural ledge jutting from the mountain. They both eased to their bellies, drew their wings in tight, and crawled to the end of the ledge. They peeked over the side and that's when Braith saw her father, along with both of her brothers. Lady Katarina stood next to Emyr and looked upset, busy wringing her claws while Braith's father talked to a dragon she did not recognize. A purple dragon. A Lightning.

Braith turned her head to see if Addolgar had realized what this situation had just become when a flash of steel from the corner of her eye caught her attention. But before she could scream a word of warning, the tip of the spear rammed into the ankle of Addolgar's back claw. Blood gushed from the wound and Braith expected to hear a scream of pain from the dragon, but all Addolgar did was grit his fangs and turn murderous, glowering eyes on his attacker.

There were two Lightnings standing behind them with grins on their faces. But those grins faded when they saw Addolgar's expression, and then watched the silver dragon stand to his full height, the spear still jutting from his back leg.

Addolgar grabbed the one who'd attacked him by the snout and easily shoved him to his knees and held him there. The other Lightning raised his own spear to fight Addolgar, but Braith caught the weapon. The Lightning tried to rip the spear from her grip, but she held on. She wouldn't let them hurt Addolgar any more than they already had. The Lightning pulled again and, annoyed, Braith tore the weapon from his grasp. She pointed the spear at his face.

"You're no warrior," the Lightning snarled at her.

"I know," Braith replied before she rammed the spear through the Lightning's eye. Unlike Addolgar, he did scream.

Addolgar, taking her cue, gripped the other Lightning's jaws and yanked them apart and kept yanking until the bottom part tore away from the Lightning's face. He dropped the gurgling but dying dragon to the ground, and Braith turned to where she'd last seen her father. He still stood there even as her brothers and the other Lightning dragged Lady Katarina away.

"Treacherous female," Emyr hissed.

And, in reply, Braith lifted two talons and flicked them at her father.

Braith's brother Meical returned to grab hold of their father's forearm and pull him away. They'd hit the skies soon.

"Go," Addolgar told her. "Go after them."

Braith shook her head and faced Addolgar. "I'll not leave you."

"Braith—"

"I'll not leave you. In fact"—she crouched down and looked at the spear jutting from his leg—"I need to get you to a healer before you bleed to death. I think an artery was hit, Addolgar."

"But your father—"

"Can wait to face his death. You're more important right now."

Addolgar sighed. "Gods-dammit."

"What?"

"The old bastard."

"My father," she assumed as she put Addolgar's forearm over her shoulder and helped him step over the bodies of the Lightnings.

"No," Addolgar corrected. "*Mine!* The old bastard was right. I need to pay attention to what's going on around me at all times. I *can't* let a good set of legs and a pretty smile distract me."

"Yes, yes," Braith complained. "Katarina has very nice legs."

"I don't mean Katarina, brat. I'm talking about *you*."

"Oh." Braith worked hard not to smile, considering the

current situation they were in. "Well, then . . . we definitely have to get you to a healer so that I can continue to enjoy these sorts of compliments."

"I don't know any healers in the Outer Plains, Braith."

"If I can get you over the border . . . I think I know those who can help us."

"You don't look very happy about it."

"Only because I know they have no desire to see me. But that means nothing to me right now."

"Uh . . . shouldn't we take this spear out before we head off?"

"We take that spear out, Addolgar, and you'll be dead before we get out of this passage."

"Oh," he replied softly. "All right. Guess we'll leave it in then."

Chapter 14

Braith practically had to hold him up the last few leagues of their flight. He could feel his life ebbing from him as every mile passed. But Braith wouldn't let him go. She wouldn't allow him to keep telling her to go after her father, or for her to go on ahead of him. Instead, she kept him steady and kept talking to him. He'd never known she could be so chatty before. Then he realized that she wanted to make sure he didn't pass out.

"Here," she yelled over the wind they were pushing against. "We're landing here."

Addolgar nodded, not in the mood to say anything. They landed in front of a cave opening buried deep in the woods a few leagues from the Southland borders. With his forearm still around her shoulders, Braith led him inside.

"You can rest now," she said, helping him to a boulder and pushing him against it until he could relax and slide down to the ground.

"I'll be right back, Addolgar," she told him, clinging tight to his front claws. "You hold on for me."

"I have to. I refuse to die with this stupid spear sticking out of my leg."

She nuzzled his cheek and stood, releasing his claws. He watched her walk off down a passage. And, a few seconds later, he watched several dragons covered in fur from head to claw silently follow right behind her.

Addolgar opened his snout to warn her, but one of the dragons stopped, focused on him, and waved a single talon at him.

At that point, all Addolgar could do was wait. As far as he was concerned, it was the strangers' funeral pyre because he *knew* what they would be facing.

Braith hadn't gotten far from where she'd left Addolgar when she knew that someone was behind her. She sensed the presence because she heard nothing. Felt only the air move as a weapon was brought down toward her.

She followed her instincts and dropped into a crouch, spun with her tail lashing wildly behind her. The one right behind her was tossed onto her back, blue hair tumbling out from under a fur cape, bright green eyes glaring up at Braith. The female never lost her weapon, though. Nor was she alone.

There were three others. All young, female, armed, and ready to fight.

Then again, so was Braith.

She reared back and raised her fists. The four females glanced at each other, then dropped their weapons, tossed off their capes, reared back, and raised their fists.

Grinning, Braith nodded—and threw the first punch.

Addolgar heard the familiar sounds of a brawl and opened his eyes to see Braith tossed out of the passage. But she got back to her claws and was ready when the first She-dragon ran at her. Then another. And another. Four altogether attacking Braith. Yet . . . she didn't seem to mind. She seemed to be having fun. In fact, if he didn't know better . . . he'd think she'd forgotten about him completely.

She caught a wrist, twisted, and caught a back claw aimed for her face. She yanked both in the opposite direction, and still managed to block a tail to the neck, and a fist to the spine.

Even bleeding to death, Addolgar was impressed.

Braith unleashed her wings and went up to the ceiling holding on to a tail and a fist. Using her wings, she spun in the air, taking the She-dragons with her, and dropped them when she had some speed. Both She-dragons went flying, and Braith landed hard on the ground, panting and grinning—until she saw Addolgar. And the way her grin faded, Addolgar realized something. . . .

"Piss and shit . . . she *did* forget all about me."

Gods! What had she done! The only dragon she'd ever wanted to be with and she'd forgotten he was out here . . . dying! Because she had a chance to brawl against She-dragons just as strong and ridiculous as she was!

She was horrible! She was a horrible, horrible She-dragon!

She wasn't even a dragon. No. At this moment, she was like a human. A worthless, pathetic, weak human! Her mother would be so ashamed!

Well . . . her mum would be ashamed of how she'd forgotten about poor Addolgar. But her mother wouldn't be ashamed of the way Braith slammed her back claw down, catching hold of the tail trying to trip her to the floor while she was busy worrying about poor Addolgar.

Braith reached down, grabbed that tail, and began to ram the She-dragon it was attached to against the cave wall until a voice bellowed out, "*What in all of damnation is going on here!*"

Startled, Braith released the tail and the She-dragon she'd been battering and faced that bellowing voice.

Another blue She-dragon. Older. Green eyes widening at the sight of Braith.

"Gods. Braith? Little Braith?"

"Hello, Aunt Crystin," Braith greeted.

Beside her, one of her cousins stood, looked Braith over, and demanded of Crystin, "*Little?*"

Indignant, Braith glowered at the She-dragon and demanded, "Throwing boulders from that glass cave are we?"

Kin. Now he understood. They were all kin. He could see it now that the fur capes were off and he had nearly ten She-dragons with blue hair, wide shoulders, and startling green eyes, staring intently at him.

"I think he's already dead," one of the younger ones observed.

"He is *not* dead," Braith snapped.

"Everyone calm down." An older one carefully examined his wounded leg. "This spear nicked an artery." She glanced at Braith. "You were smart not to remove this."

"I was hoping I'd made the right decision. He was in so much pain."

"He looks familiar to my eyes," another older She-dragon noted. "Do we know him?"

"He's Addolgar the Cheerful," Braith answered. "Of the Cadwaladr Clan."

The one called Crystin gasped. "Gods. One of Ailean's offspring?"

Then, in unison, the four older She-dragons sighed out, "Ailean."

Braith's back straightened, understanding the smile on her older kin's faces far too well.

"All of you?" she asked. Actually, it was more a demand.

"Not all at the same time," the one examining his wound stated. "That would have been wrong."

"And disgusting," one of the younger ones muttered.

"He looks quite a bit like his father," another older one stated. "In the face. Similar snout. Don't you think, Crystin?"

"I do. But there was just something about that dragon, wasn't there, sister? Something . . . delicious."

"You know my father's not dead, Mum?" one of the younger ones complained. "He may not be here, but you could at least show a bit of respect around his favorite daughter."

Another young one looked at the first. "Daddy never said you were his favorite."

"But I know I am."

"We should move him," his healer stated, resting back on her haunches. "He needs warmth from a fire, and it'll take me some time to get this out without killing him in the process."

Addolgar didn't know if Braith made a sound or an expression that he missed, but the older one quickly soothed her with, "Do not worry so, Braith. This won't be the first time I've fixed this kind of wound. And all those who've come to me have survived. We just need to take care. And I need you to be strong. Understand?"

"I do."

She nodded. "You have your mother's strength, child.

You'll be fine." The healer looked at Addolgar. "I'm Owena. I'll be taking care of you. And you'll be fine. Understand, Addolgar?"

"That's what's been missing," Addolgar noted, raising his talon and weakly pointing at Braith.

"Missing?" Owena asked him.

"With Braith. I see it now," he told them, wanting them to understand, should Owena have her first failure with this type of wound. "She's home now. It was never her father." He smiled up at Braith, took her claw in his. "You're home now."

Addolgar had other things to say, but he was so tired and everything was going sort of black anyway. It made more sense to close his eyes and stop worrying. So he did.

Braith gripped Addolgar's claw. "He's dead," she gasped.

"He's not dead," Aunt Owena told her.

"He looks dead," one of her cousins muttered.

"Shut up, Heledd." Owena motioned to them. "Let's get him inside."

Together, they all lifted Addolgar—not an easy feat even for them—and carried him deep into the lair of the Penard-duns. They placed him in a cavern with a blazing pit fire and a chest filled with Owena's healing tools.

Braith's mother had once told her that Owena was more fighter than healer, but someone among them had to do it and Braith's grandmother had decided it would be Owena.

Once they had Addolgar facedown on a fur bedroll, Owena again examined his wounds and ordered two of the younger females to pull together clean cloth, water, and tools while Crystin grabbed Braith's forearm.

"Come with me. Now."

Braith knew what was about to happen. She'd come here out of desperation. That was all. But she'd face anything to save Addolgar. She truly would.

Crystin pulled Braith out of one chamber and into a much larger one. There was an enormous table surrounded by chairs that she assumed were used when the Penardduns were in their human forms. Another aunt, Aledwen, if Braith remembered correctly, walked in from a separate passageway, her eyes widening at the sight of Braith, just as Crystin's had done.

Aledwen put her claw to her chest. "Gods. For a moment . . ."

"I know, sister," Crystin said, her gaze on Braith. "I also thought our beloved sister had returned to us. You look so much like your mother, Braith." Crystin straightened up a bit. "And you came here when you needed help—"

"I'm sorry about that," Braith quickly cut in. "I know this wasn't what you wanted, but you were the closest and Addolgar needed help now."

"Not what we wanted?" Crystin glanced back at her sister. "Who told you that, Braith?"

"You did. I was considered my father's child, not a Penarddun. Your letter after my mother died made it clear how you all felt."

Crystin sighed, shook her head, while Aledwen turned away.

"What?" Braith asked.

Crystin shrugged. "I never wrote you a letter, Braith."

"It was your dragon script, Crystin. I know it."

"I never wrote it."

Tragically, Braith wouldn't put it past her father to have someone copy Crystin's style of dragon script, but that didn't explain anything else.

"Whether you wrote the letter or not, you never came to see me after Mum's death. You never . . ." She choked back tears threatening to come. "You never came for the Ritual of Ashes. You never came just to see me."

"You're right. We didn't. We stayed as far away from you as we possibly could. Didn't even come to Devenallt Mountain when invited, took the role of protectors of our borders when necessary. You're absolutely right. We did all that."

"Well," Braith said, knowing she sounded bitter but unable to help it, "glad we got that cleared up."

She turned, ready to go back to Addolgar's side, when Aledwen suddenly blurted out, "He threatened to kill you."

Braith stopped. "What?" she asked, without looking at either aunt.

"He threatened to kill you."

"Eventually," Crystin added. "First, he threatened to take your title and any fortune our sister left you. But he quickly realized that threat held no meaning to a Penarddun. But then he said if we made any attempt to contact you again, he'd have you killed. He knew poisoners. 'The best in the land,' he said. That he could do it, even while you were safe here. And that, child, was when we believed him."

Braith slowly faced her aunts, studied their faces, and quickly saw the truth in their eyes.

"To be honest," Crystin went on, "we thought you'd come to us. So we waited rather than risk your life. But we should have known your father had found a way around that as well."

"But why?" Braith asked. "He has no use for me. No love. Why would he care if I was here with you or alone in my cave?"

"The Penardduns are matriarchal, child. His first threat didn't work with us because anything and everything your mother had, including title, was passed down to you. I honestly think that at first, he was just being his usual, vindictive self when he kept you from us."

"We used to openly mock his weak arms and that tiny little neck of his," Aledwen said, grinning. "He hated that."

"But once he understood the true power of our line, he understood that without you, Emyr and his idiot sons risked losing all of their standing among those court royals who actually give an ox's shit about all that as well as your mother's fortune—and *that* he would not stand for."

"But he wouldn't have lost his Elder status."

"Do you really think your father cares about being an Elder?" Crystin asked.

Aledwen gave a hard laugh. "Do you think he would have even gotten *that* had it not been for your mother?"

"Emyr has always had much bigger goals than to be a mere Elder."

"Like taking the throne?" Braith asked.

"Well—" Aledwen began, but Crystin held up her claw, her gaze on Braith.

"Gods, child," Crystin said with a sigh. "What has that ridiculous asshole done now?"

Addolgar opened his eyes and smiled into the face staring down at him. "Braith . . . you've aged beautifully."

Old Braith grinned. "Thank you. But I'm Braith's aunt. Remember? Owena?"

"Oh. Right. You fucked me dad."

"Aw, dear." Owena patted his shoulder. "Everyone's fucked your dad."

"I know. He's quite proud of that. Am I going to die, Lady Owena?"

"Just Owena. And no. You've got your father's constitution and your mother's will to live. Because how that She-dragon survived her time as bitch Addiena's companion, we have yet to figure out."

"Now, now. That's treasonous talk."

"I like to live on the edge." She winked at him while wiping blood from her hands with a big cloth. That's when Addolgar realized he was in his human form.

"Hey. I'm naked!"

Owena laughed. "You are. And I realize that my sister was

right. How like your father you are, sweet Addolgar." She leaned in and whispered, "I see why our little Braith likes you."

"Does she?"

"Can't you tell?"

"I'm male. I have no idea what you females are thinking."

Owena laughed again and said, "I'll get her. She can show you herself."

Owena turned to go, but Addolgar caught her arm, gently held it. "She didn't think she was welcome here."

"She was wrong. We never turn a Penarddun female away. Ever. But her father had other plans."

"Does she understand that?"

"She's learning. It'll take time. He . . . he made sure she felt completely alone."

"She's not alone," he said simply. "She has me."

Owena smiled, and gods, he saw Braith in that smile. "We'll make sure she learns that too."

"Well, don't be too pushy. You don't want to put her off me. But feel free to put in a good word."

Laughing again, Owena patted his shoulder and walked out of the chamber. But Addolgar didn't know what was so funny. He really wanted her to put in a good word for him.

Braith looked up as Owena walked into the chamber. They'd all eventually shifted to human so they could help with Addolgar since Owena said it would be quicker for Addolgar to heal that way.

"Should I assume from that smile he's going to be all right?" Braith asked, needing to hear something good.

"He'll be fine," Owena said on a laugh. "That boy is . . . entertaining to say the least." She dropped into a chair catty-corner from Braith, wiped her brow, and let out a long breath. "I hate artery work. Do the wrong thing and you could have the one you're trying to save bleeding out all over you."

"I'm so glad that didn't happen."

"Me, too. I've heard it's quite a mess when it does." Owena looked around. "Where's everyone else?"

"Went to town to get food and wine."

"Ahhh. To celebrate your return to the Penarddun fold."

"Have I returned?"

"Are you asking me because you're subtly telling me you're not? Or because you're seriously not sure?"

"Well, I'm not subtle."

Owena chuckled. "Nor was your mum."

"Why was she with him?" Braith asked.

"With your father?" Owena thought a moment. "Because she wanted you."

"She could have had me with anyone."

"Not every She-dragon finds a mate because not every She-dragon wants one. Your mother never wanted one. She liked fighting and she liked us. That was it. But she wanted you. She had you named when she was still a hatchling. But she needed a male to make that happen. The problem was finding a male willing to have an offspring outside of mating. When she couldn't, she turned to someone who wanted anything *but* his mate's love. Then she had a son . . . so she tried again. She had another son, so she tried again. Then she had you and she had what she wanted."

"And my father had what he wanted."

"Sons and a title." Owena rolled her eyes. "I always hated your father. Scum on a dying pond has more integrity than your father."

"Doesn't that lack of integrity taint me? Being his daughter?"

"You're not his daughter," Owena snapped, one finger pointing at her. "You're your *mum's* daughter. You're a Penarddun. Just like your mother and your mother's mother and her mother's mother. Going back a millennium. Your father was nothing more than a means to a very important end.

"But," Owena went on, leaning back in the chair, "it seems his time is over."

"He's betrayed the Queen."

"No. He betrayed Addiena. That's a fool's game." Owena studied her. "And she sent you to catch him?"

"It was either him or me." She glanced over at the chamber where Addolgar recovered. "If it wasn't for Addolgar and the Cadwaladr Clan, the Queen's Guard would be tossing my head off Devenallt Mountain as we speak." Braith ran her hands through her hair. "Is it true?" she asked. "Did my father really threaten to—"

"You know it's true, Braith."

"Do I?"

Owena leaned in. "You *know*. Penardduns don't lie. We hit. And we hit because we know we're stronger than most males. In fact, we're so strong it's hard for us to find males willing to put up with us. But you know, as a female, that if we could have, if we thought for a minute that your father wouldn't carry through with his vile threat—we would have come for you. We would have been there to lay your mum to rest. To perform all the rituals she was due. We *never* would have let you face that alone. Not the daughter of our dear sister. And definitely not a female of our line."

Braith finally had to ask, "What about the males of our line?"

Owena shrugged, flipped her hand casually. "We care for them. Love them. I have two of my own." Her flitting hand swept the air. "They're around somewhere. And I love them." Her lips pursed a bit, and Braith felt her heart tighten when she recognized the gesture as one her mother had often made. "They are a bit stupid, though."

The pain around Braith's heart lessened when she had to laugh. "Aunt Owena."

"They can't help it, you know. It happens in the egg," she reasoned. "As soon as they grow that genitalia, intelligence goes right out the window and we're left with this thing that just wants to stick it in any hole."

"*Aunt Owena!*"

"Oh, tell me I'm wrong!"

"Well," Braith admitted, "I don't know if I can do that."

"Of course you can't. But that's all right. We're Penard-duns, which means we accept males as they are. Handsome but stupid and useless without us."

"That is very giving of you," Braith teased.

But Owena said, in all seriousness, "I know."

Addolgar opened his eyes again and announced, "You're young again, Braith of the Darkness!"

Braith frowned. "What?"

"You're young again. I saw you much older and you were still astoundingly beautiful. But now you're young again . . . and you've multiplied."

"Multi . . ."

Braith looked over her shoulder and snarled at the additional versions of herself. "Don't you lot have something else to do?"

"Come on," one of the copies said to the others. "She's got her claws into this one."

"You need to learn to share, Braith of the Darkness," said another.

"You need to piss off, cousin."

One copy grabbed another copy's arm. "Come on, sister. She's attached to this one. You might as well give it up."

With some grumbling, the copies departed, leaving Addolgar alone with the original. The perfect, delicious original.

"How do you feel?" Braith asked him.

"Not bad. But I think that's because the Older You had me drink some ale that's completely wiped any and all pain from my system. I want to bring some of that home."

Braith dropped her head, but he could tell from the way her shoulders shook that she was laughing.

"Well," she finally said, "I'm glad you're all right. I was worried."

"So was I. But Older You took very good care of me."

"You should know, Addolgar, that Older Me is Owena. And I wouldn't call her Older anything, if I were you."

"Good idea. The lasses hate that."

"Yes. We lasses do."

Braith tucked the fur covering around Addolgar's body, but he pushed the covers off again.

"What are you doing?" she asked.

"Get in."

Braith's eyebrows went up. "Get in? Are you mad?"

"No. I need you to help me heal."

"Addolgar the Cheerful, you need no such thing!"

"Owena!" Addolgar yelled out as Braith desperately tried to cover his mouth. "Braith won't help me heal!"

"Gods, child!" Owena called from the other chamber. "Just get into bed with the big idiot. It's not like he can do anything with as much of your aunt's ale as I made him drink."

Addolgar grinned. "See? She agrees with me."

"Oh . . . fine!" Braith went around the other side of the bed they'd moved Addolgar to once Owena had used Magicks to force his body to shift to human, and got in next to him.

"Aren't you going to get naked?"

"No, I am not going to get naked!"

"Owena!" he called out. "Braith won't get naked!"

"Why are you making the poor lad work for it?" her aunt called back.

"I am not getting naked!" Braith yelled so everyone would hear it. "So just leave off!"

"Someone's no fun," one cousin announced.

"Poor Cadwaladr!" said another.

"Heard his father never had to work so hard," another piped in.

"There's truth to that!" admitted an aunt.

"I'll get naked!" offered another.

Pulling the covers up to cover both her and Addolgar, Braith settled into his side while yelling, "I swear by all the gods, if I have to come out there, there *will be* all hells to pay!"

There was finally silence from her kin after that announcement, and that's when Addolgar knew he'd been right. "Just like I said, Braith of the Darkness . . . you're finally home."

"And how do you know that, Addolgar the Cheerful?"

"Because your beautiful smile tells me so. Now cuddle me close so I can hold you while I sleep."

Braith did just that, placing her head against his chest and her arm around his waist. Addolgar wrapped his arms around Braith, sighed happily, and kissed the top of her head.

"I'm so glad you're here, Braith," he told her.

"So am I. Because clearly my kin can't be trusted around handsome dragons weak from blood loss."

And he adored the fact that she sounded a bit jealous when she said that.

Chapter 15

"Time to eat!" a voice bellowed, and Addolgar's eyes snapped open to see one of Braith's aunts standing over him. "You hungry, Cadwaladr?"

"Always," he admitted.

"Good." She motioned to a platter of meat she'd rested on a side table by the bed. "Owena wants you to eat. So eat."

"Yes, ma'am."

The She-dragon grunted and walked out of the chamber.

"Is she gone?" Braith whispered.

"Aye."

"Am I that loud?" she asked.

"Not at all. Braith, you barely speak."

"Why speak when you have little to say?"

"You have tons to say, you just think it instead. But what you're thinking shows on your face. And it's usually *scathing!*"

Braith giggled at that because they both knew he was right.

Braith sat up, the smell of fresh meat rousing her stomach. She hadn't had anything to eat or drink but Bercelak's jerky and lake water since they'd left the pub. Even nicer, someone had cooked the meat for them. Much easier for their human forms to digest, and she always enjoyed the smell of freshly cooked meat.

But before she dove headfirst into the platter of food, she studied Addolgar's face. His color was back, and he seemed stronger than he had the night before.

He returned her gaze before suddenly announcing, "You're so beautiful."

Braith let out a sigh. "Damn. I thought you were getting better."

"Sorry?"

"I thought you were getting better. But it seems you're still off from the loss of blood or my aunt's ale."

"Because I told you that you're beautiful?"

Braith frowned. Addolgar did sound . . . better. Stronger. More like himself.

"Well . . . I guess," she admitted. "I'm just not used to it."

"Get used to it. I hate having to constantly argue my point with you."

"I didn't think we were arguing."

"We would be if you kept not believing me when I tell you how beautiful you are."

Gods, she wished he'd stop saying it. It made her feel uncomfortable. Mostly because no one had ever said it to her before. Definitely not her father or brothers. And no other male dragon she'd spent time with before had said the things to her that Addolgar had said and continued to say.

Things that she had to admit—at least to herself—she loved to hear even while they made her uncomfortable.

"We still have to retrieve my father," Braith said, trying to change the subject.

"Trying to change the subject, I see," Addolgar announced. *Bastard.*

"Well, we do need to retrieve him."

"I know. And we will."

"You seem awfully confident about that."

"Your father has not decided to spend his life in the Northlands. I've been to the Northlands, Braith. It's nothing but snow and ice and miserable dragons and humans. Your father may be a miserable bastard, but he wants the Southlands. The Northlands is not what he wants, and he has to know he's not strong enough to ever get them. He couldn't even manage his own daughter much less a bloody Lightning Horde. So I have no doubts we'll find him. Now kiss me," he ordered.

"You are awfully surly this morning."

"The pain in my leg is brutal. My head hurts because I think I'm hungover from your aunt's blasted ale. And you haven't kissed me yet. So, aye, I *am* surly. *I'm allowed to be surly!*"

A sentiment bellowed at Braith. And one that made her giggle.

"What's so funny?" he grumbled.

"You're much more terrifying when you're cheerful. When you're surly, you just sound like a cranky hatchling." She thought a moment before adding, "Like Bercelak."

"There's no need to be so bloody rude, Braith of the Darkness!"

Her smile lit up the chamber and it brought Addolgar joy to see it. But he was feeling very cranky because he was in pain, so he refused to tell her any of that. Instead, he snapped, "You should have gone after your father yesterday while he was still on Outer Plains territory. Like I *told* you to."

"And left you to die?"

"If necessary."

"That would have been bloody stupid."

"The fact is that now we'll have to travel deep into Northland territory to retrieve your father."

"You said he wouldn't go there."

"I said he wouldn't stay there. I didn't say he wouldn't go there. But we can't wait for him to return here with a bloody Lightning Horde at his back."

"I don't know why you're getting angry at me. When we discussed this last night—"

"Last night I was drunk on that demon wine your aunts make! This morning I see everything quite clearly!"

"Well, you know what else you can see clearly?" she snarled. "My ass! *As I walk away!*"

Then she was off the bed and gone from the chamber, leaving him alone, in pain, and still cranky.

Surprisingly, yelling at her had not made him feel any better.

Braith walked until she'd found her way outside. Once she stood under the early morning suns, she took in a deep breath of the cool Outer Plains air and tried to stop herself from going back inside and pummeling Addolgar the Brainless. Because he deserved a right good pummeling!

"Good morn, cousin."

Braith turned and saw three of her cousins sunning themselves on boulders. Like lizards. Lizards in human form.

"What are you doing?" Braith asked.

"Enjoying the suns," replied one.

"It gives our scales a lovely bright hue," said another.

Braith blinked. "Except you're all in your human form. So how does that help your scales?"

They stared at her for several seconds before one stated, "You're a bit of a know-it-all, aren't you?"

"How is that . . ." Braith shook her head. She wouldn't go from arguing with one idiot to arguing with three.

When Braith didn't say anything, one of her cousins asked, "Do you think your father would have really killed you if our mums tried to contact you?"

"Yes," Braith said plainly. She'd accepted the truth of that late in the evening as Addolgar had slept beside her.

"That's so sad."

Braith shrugged. "Eh." She could no longer dig up the energy to care about what her father did, would do, or would like to do. If he'd had his chance, he probably would have strangled her as soon as she'd hatched, but he'd always been a bit terrified of her mum. With good reason. Her mother would have twisted his head around until it popped off his shoulders if he'd ever touched Braith.

"Well, uh . . ."

"Braith," Braith filled in for them.

"We remember. I think I remember playing with you when we were hatchlings. You're Braith, and I'm Caron, Crystin's eldest. This is Ffraid, Owena's middle daughter. And this is Delyth, Aledwen's eldest."

"We're glad you're here, cousin," Ffraid told Braith. "Our

mums worried over you constantly. So now maybe they'll shut up about you."

For some reason, the muttered words made Braith chuckle.

"And now that you're safe with us," Ffraid went on, "we can show your father what it really means to fuck with the House of Penarddun."

"Aye," Caron agreed. "Once we get your father back here, we'll deal with him."

"Get him back here?" Braith asked.

"Aye. Mum sent out Heledd—that's Aledwen's younger daughter you chatted with last night—and two of Ffraid's sisters. They're good trackers. They'll track him. And once we know where the bastard is, together we'll hunt him down and show him that Queen Addiena should be the least of his fears."

Braith stepped closer to her cousins. "Hunt him down . . . together?"

"Oh, luv," Caron said sadly, "do you still care about what happens to your father?"

"No," Braith said flatly. "I guess I'm just trying to understand. All of you will be coming with me and Addolgar . . . into Horde territory to help me bring in my father?"

The three She-dragons sat up and gazed at Braith.

"*Of course* that's what we mean," Delyth replied. "You're no longer in this alone, Braith of the Darkness. You're one of us."

"And that bastard father of yours no longer holds your safety over our heads," Ffraid added.

"But I wouldn't worry, cousin," Caron said, lifting her face up toward the sunlight and closing her eyes. "He'll be out of your life soon enough and then you can decide what you'll do next."

"Do next?"

"Like move here with us for training," Delyth said.

"Or spend your time with that hunk of Cadwaladr meat."

"Oh. Uh . . . yeah, uh . . ."

"Look!" Ffraid crowed. "She's blushing!"

"I am not!" Braith shot back.

"You are! It's so cute!"

"I am *not* cute!"

"Of course you're not, luv," Caron told her. "You're a Penarddun. No one will call us beautiful or heart-stopping—"

"Oh, no," Ffraid cut in. "They do call Penardduns heart *stoppers*."

When her cousins said nothing, "Get it?"

That's when they started laughing at a confused Ffraid. "What?" she asked. "Wait. Are you laughing at me or at my joke? Because my joke is quite witty."

Fed up with sitting around, feeling miserable and still cranky, Addolgar threw his legs over the side of the bed.

"What do you think you're doing?" Owena asked as she walked into the chamber with another jug of that cursed ale.

"I'm getting up. I can't sit around, doing nothing—"

"That's exactly what you're going to do until that leg heals."

Addolgar stood up, felt pain shoot through his leg and right into his back, making his head hurt even more. He ignored it. "My leg's healed enough," he lied.

Owena sighed and stepped back. "Oy!" she called out. "The Mountain is trying to walk on that leg."

Addolgar stopped, focused on Owena. "The Mountain?"

"What do you want us to call you?"

"By my name?"

"Eh," Owena said, sounding just like her niece.

Three more of Braith's aunts walked into the chamber.

"What's going on?" Crystin asked.

"I think he's trying to leave," Owena answered.

"Where are you trying to go, Mountain?"

"Stop calling me Mountain. We have to find Emyr. If you

hadn't realized, your niece's life depends on returning him to the Queen."

"Oh, for the sake of the gods," Crystin sighed out. "This is already being handled."

Addolgar, now hopping around on one leg trying to reach his travel bags and the human clothes within, asked, "Handled?"

"We have our best trackers hunting down that ponce as we speak. If they can't bring the idiot back themselves, we'll do it, kick him around a bit, and then pass him off to your precious Queen to finish him."

Resting his hands on a wooden chair, Addolgar looked over at the four She-dragons. Like Braith, they were all tall with strong shoulders and necks, powerful legs, and bright eyes, but, he sensed, there was an inherent lack of understanding among them that he hadn't had to worry about with Braith. She understood things quite clearly. But the She-dragons of the House of Penarddun as a whole . . .

Addolgar just didn't know. He knew little of royals, but the ones he'd had any dealings with were nothing like these females. The Penarddurs had no servants, wore mostly trousers when they were human, and liked to brawl. With each other. True, he really liked that about them, but it still had him very worried.

"The trackers you sent," he said, "they weren't your daughters, were they?"

"Of course they were. Our daughters are the best trackers you'll ever find."

Addolgar briefly dropped his head. When he was in a better mood, he'd probably handle this with more skill. But he was in pain and cranky.

"You let your *daughters* go into Northland territory? *Horde* territory? With Lightnings? The dragons who kidnap our females, cut off one of their wings, and force them to be their mates?"

Owena frowned. "I thought they didn't do that anymore."

"Of course they do!" Addolgar bellowed. "They just took Davon the Elegant from her kin's cave. And you lot sent your defenseless daughters to face them! *Alone!*"

"Ohhhh," Crystin said. "So we need big, strong males like you to protect us from big, strong males? Is that it?"

Addolgar wagged a finger at Crystin. "I have sisters, Lady Crystin. And you'll not trick me with that one."

Owena walked toward him. "Don't worry about our daughters, Mountain—"

"Please don't call me that."

"—they'll be just fine. They know how not to be seen. Especially by big, strong males of any species. So you can get back into bed."

"I've made up my mind," he insisted.

That's when all four females moved toward him until they surrounded him. Owena pointed at the bed.

"Get over there."

"No. You can't make me."

"Oh, dear boy," Crystin told him sadly. "Yes. We can."

Devouring several pieces of bacon she'd snatched from a plate on the table, Braith walked toward the chamber where Addolgar was resting. As she walked, she passed all her aunts and cousins heading in the opposite direction.

"Where are you all off to?" she asked.

"Going into town for a bit. Get a few supplies. Need anything?"

Braith shook her head. "I'm fine. Thanks. Did you check with Addolgar, though?"

Her Aunt Crystin stopped, blinked at her. "Uh-huh. He's fine."

"All right," Braith said around the delicious, chewy bacon in her mouth. She continued on. She wasn't in the mood for another fight with Addolgar, so she only planned to pass the chamber and glance in to make sure he was sleeping or, at the very least, hadn't rolled off the bed in a fit of Cadwaladr rage.

And, as planned, she glanced in and kept walking. . . .

Then Braith stopped, blinked, looked around, and, finally, took several steps back until she arrived at the chamber opening.

"Not a word," he growled. "Not a bloody word."

Taking another bite of bacon, Braith sauntered into the chamber until she reached the bed. She gazed down at Addolgar.

"Comfortable?" she asked.

"Leave off."

"Just want to make sure you're comfortable, Sergeant." She leaned over and carefully studied the chains that had his arms secured to the bed. "Oh, poor lad." She leaned back, shook her head sadly. "These aren't dwarven steel, I'm afraid. You could probably break through dwarven steel like *I* did." She bit the inside of her mouth to keep from laughing when Addolgar rolled his eyes. "This is Volcano dragon steel. Even a Penarddun can't break Volcano steel."

"You're enjoying this, aren't you?" he demanded.

"Of course not. I'm sure this was done in your best interest." She smirked. "Did you try to leave? Did you find out they sent my cousins into Northland territory?"

"Even you have to know that was foolish."

"They didn't ask me. But at least my cousins are not wounded. Can't fight anyone with that leg of yours."

"It's healing."

"I'm sure it is. But it'll be even better tomorrow."

Addolgar snarled, looking off.

"Don't be mad at me," Braith told him. "I didn't chain you up."

"But you would have."

"If it would allow you to heal properly so you can adequately back me up in a fight—damn right I would."

He glowered at her. "Did you know?"

She took another bite of bacon before asking, "Know what?"

"That your kin has started calling me The Mountain?"

The snort and the bacon she'd been chewing were out of her mouth before she could even think to stop them, so when both hit Addolgar full in the face, she could tell he was not happy about it.

"Get out," he ordered.

"Addolgar—"

"Just go."

"You're being unreasonable." She dropped the rest of the bacon on the plate of untouched meat Owena had placed on the side table earlier and wiped her hands off on her trousers.

"I know you're in pain," she said.

"I'm fine."

"And that you're anxious and miserable. I understand all that."

"You understand nothing, heartless female."

"But we're all just trying to take care of you."

"By tying me to the bed? Is that what Daughters of the House of Penarddun call taking care of the wounded?"

"They only did that to protect you."

"And you're full of massive shi—"

"Addolgar the Cheerful!" she barked, mostly so she wouldn't laugh. "Watch how you speak to me, Low Born!"

"Finally," he grumbled. "Signs that you *are*, actually, a bloody royal."

"I am a royal. Royal blood runs through my veins, and my aunts say that my mother left me a vast fortune that my father didn't know about. Now it's all mine. They've been saving it for me. A dragon's hoard of jewels and gold, just for me."

"What is your point in telling me this?"

"So you'll know that I'm a powerful royal now with all my gold."

"And?"

"You better be nice to me."

"Or what?" he challenged, his dark silver brows pulled low, his brown eyes annoyed. Addolgar the Cheerful was definitely a healer's nightmare. He was always in such good spirits that when he was truly wounded or ill, he just became an incorrigible baby.

A handsome, adorable, incorrigible baby.

Braith moved to the foot of the bed and using one finger, stroked it down the arch of Addolgar's foot, then using three fingers, she slipped her hand under the cover and stroked carefully across Addolgar's bandaged ankle and up his calf.

"What are you doing?" he asked as she, and her hand, moved forward.

"Amusing myself as powerful royals are allowed to do." She dragged her fingers up his inside thigh. "Are you, Low Born, saying I'm not allowed to amuse myself with you?"

Still frowning, Addolgar stared at her, clearly confused. Until the back of her hand brushed against his cock, and his entire body jerked in surprise. His frown slowly faded and he gazed at her with wide eyes.

"Well," she pushed, "am I not allowed to amuse myself with you?"

Addolgar cleared his throat, shook his head. "Of course you are . . . powerful royal. Amuse yourself all you'd like."

When had Braith become this brazen little wench who couldn't seem to stop smiling and touching his cock? Not that he minded her being a brazen little wench. He liked her a lot. Perhaps more than he should. But now he knew he'd been right all along. Braith *had been* missing something. But now, back with her kin, a part of them, she was whole once more. And being whole would make anyone happy.

And a happy Braith was a Braith who brazenly put her hand under his fur covering and stroked his cock.

Her fingers strong and firm, she smiled as she watched him.

"Unchain me, Braith," he ordered, desperate to get his hands on her. To drag her to the bed and take her, hard and fast.

But Braith's reply was a simple, "No."

"What do you mean no?"

"No," she said again, her hand still stroking him.

"Dammit, Braith, get these chains off me!"

"No."

"I'll tear this bed apart," he threatened.

"And then you'll have to answer to my aunts. They're very proud of this bed. Ripped some poor bloke's castle apart, stone by stone, to get it, too. Do *you* want to tell them what happened to their bed when they get back?"

Growling and seriously annoyed, Addolgar still had to admit, "No. I do not."

"That's what I thought."

Who knew Braith could be so bloody smug? So damn haughty? And gods in heaven, a hand had never felt so good before.

"Braith," he groaned out, unable to stay mad at her for long when she was doing such wonderful things to—

"Oy!" he snapped when she pulled her hand away. "Put your hand back there, female!"

"Calm yourself, Sergeant."

She grabbed the bottom of her green cotton shirt, a loan from one of her cousins. Clothes from a fellow female that actually fit Braith's shoulders, neck, and arms. She pulled the material over her head and tossed it aside.

"I'll be right back," she said before burrowing under the fur covering.

Addolgar leaned up to see what she was doing. "You'll be

right back? Braith of the Darkness, what exactly are you up—*gods!*"

Her hot mouth pressed against the side of his cock, her tongue teasing as it followed the veins to the tip.

Addolgar got even harder. As he was unable to see anything but her head moving under that fur covering, all he could do was feel and it felt bloody amazing.

He gripped the chains with his fingers, cursing the fact that Braith seemed to be right. Volcano dragon steel was impossible to break.

Braith now had the head of his cock in her mouth, and Addolgar was trying to focus on the crystals hanging from the cave ceiling. They sparkled, reflecting the light from the nearby pit fire.

No. That wasn't working. He didn't give a centaur's shit about crystals hanging from the ceiling. He didn't give a centaur's shit about anything at the moment except Braith, her mouth, and what they were both doing to his cock.

Addolgar really didn't think he could take much more, but then Braith did something no other female had ever done to him before—she released her flame.

Not a giant ball of it, meant to destroy or batter everything in her way. Just a bit of flame. Just enough, in fact, to almost have him coming right there.

"*Braith*," he snarled out between gritted teeth. "Braith, get up here now. *Now!*"

She crawled up his chest until her head came out from under the fur covering. "Too much?" she asked. Although the grin on her face told him she didn't care if it was.

"Get naked, Braith," he ordered. "And ride me. Now."

"But—"

"No more joking, Braith. Either you ride me now, hard, or I tear this bed apart and *you* will have to deal with your aunts. You."

She sat up, the fur covering falling away as she did. Her

nipples were hard, and she was breathing deep, her green eyes dark as she watched him.

"Fuck me, Braith of the Darkness," Addolgar told her. "Fuck me before I destroy everything just to get to you."

Braith couldn't get out of her boots and trousers fast enough. In fact, she still had her trousers hanging from one leg when she straddled his hips. She couldn't be bothered to take them off completely. Not when his cock was pointing right to the ceiling, hard and true, his face begging her to take what was hers.

Holding his cock between her fingers, she maneuvered over it, and then slowly lowered herself down. It filled her, so thick and long that Braith had to stretch her thighs farther apart. She took her hand away and let her weight do the rest.

When she finally rested against Addolgar's body, they were both panting. She'd never felt like this before. It was as if her entire body was alive, feeling everything, *wanting* to feel everything. She no longer missed her safe haven in the cave where she spent all her hours alone. Not when she could have this. And for the first time in her life, she felt she *could* have this. She could have it if she wanted it.

She began rocking her hips against Addolgar, using her muscles to squeeze his cock. His back arched, pushing himself deeper inside her, and Braith leaned forward, pressing one hand against his chest to hold her body up.

She gazed deep into his eyes and Addolgar stared right back.

"You are so beautiful," he said—and she believed him. She believed that *he* believed she was beautiful.

The hand braced against him slid up until she tightly gripped his shoulder. Her other hand, with her gaze still locked with his, slid down her stomach and between her thighs. With the tip of her middle finger, she circled her clit.

She wanted them to come together, and Addolgar's hands were currently . . . occupied.

Their groans filled the chamber, their bodies writhing on the bed as Braith did what Addolgar had ordered her to do and rode him harder and harder, until he came inside her, his body nearly lifting off the bed. Braith's own orgasm followed close behind, her thighs gripping him so tight she feared she'd broken his hips.

When her body had stopped shaking, Braith dropped down on Addolgar's chest, his still-hard cock buried inside her.

It took them long minutes to get their breath back. And when they finally did, Addolgar stated, "I am *so* hungry now. And I blame *you* for that, Braith of the Darkness."

And, yes, Braith did consider that a compliment.

Chapter 16

At some point, Braith had removed Addolgar's chains, but by then he'd had no desire to go anywhere. He was much too comfortable, too bloody happy, to even consider leaving this bed. Not when he had her asleep in his arms, one impossibly long leg wrapped around his waist, her silky hair sweeping across his chest.

He stroked her back and let her sleep until he heard the happy scream of returning hatchlings.

"Braith," he murmured softly. "Wake up, luv. Your kin are home."

She lifted her head, pushing her hair off her face. "Huh?"

"Your kin have returned."

Braith rested her arms on his chest and frowned into his face. "So? Oh. Did they call for me?"

"No, but—"

Owena walked in. "When you're up," she said to Braith, "come into the hall. We have something for you."

"Ooooh!" Braith cheered. "Gifts!"

Owena laughed and walked out. That's when Addolgar realized something. "They don't care, do they?"

"Don't care about what?"

"You, the long lost daughter of their sister, being with someone like me."

"Someone like you?"

"A Cadwaladr. A low born."

"Considering they sigh every time your father's name is mentioned, I'd have to say no, they don't care."

"For good or bad, there were few who escaped my father's attention before he mated with me mum. But it was never far from anyone's mind that he was and always would be a Cadwaladr. A battle dog that the royals use for protection."

"I like dogs," she softly mused. "Especially when they have a little extra fat and are well seasoned."

"Don't"—Addolgar closed his eyes and worked hard to not laugh—"ever say that to my mother. She has a fondness for dogs. Live, happy ones."

"Is that why there were all those dogs running around your—"

"Gods," he cut in, "you didn't eat one, did you?"

"No, no." Braith sat up. "I was too annoyed at you to eat much of anything while at your parents' home."

He chuckled. "Aye. You were."

"I'm going to go see what they got me," Braith told him, tossing off the fur covering. "I'll bring you some supper."

Addolgar sat up, stretching and yawning.

"What are you doing?"

"I'm getting up." He shook his head before she could argue that. "Don't worry. I'm not going anywhere. I just can't lie here anymore. Besides"—he smiled—"I want to see what they got you too."

"What is he doing up and about?" Owena demanded.

Braith, with Addolgar's arm over her shoulder so he could hop on his good leg, led the dragon to the big table in the middle of the hall chamber.

"Chair or table?" she asked him.

"Table."

She got him on the table and waited until he was comfortably situated before facing her aunt.

"What did you ask?"

"I asked what he was doing up?"

"Don't worry. He's not planning to make a run for it."

"He better not," Owena warned.

"So what did you get me from town?" Braith asked.

"Go on, Delyth. Show your cousin what you picked out for her."

Delyth, with her hands behind her back, walked up to Braith and, after a lengthy pause, brought both her arms around. She held out something cloth-covered and long. Braith pulled back the cloth and blinked.

"Oh," she said, staring at the steel and leather-covered hilt. "A sword. How nice."

"It's a good weight," Delyth replied. "A short sword to start you out."

"Right." Braith took the weapon from her cousin's outstretched hands. She hefted it a bit, held it up. "Lovely. Thank you."

"You're welcome."

Braith turned and showed Addolgar the weapon.

He stared at it for a long moment before he asked, "*That's* what you got her?"

"What does that mean?" Delyth snapped.

"That's a bloody toothpick."

Delyth marched around Braith until she faced Addolgar. "It's not for when she's dragon. It's for when she's human."

"As human she can break dwarven steel into pieces." He reached over and took the sword from Braith's hands. "It's a beautiful weapon. One my sister Ghleanna would adore. But this isn't for Braith."

"Then what *is* the right weapon for Braith, Lord Smarty Claws?"

Addolgar, his brow going up at the challenge from Delyth, slipped off the table Braith had just put him on and hopped back to their chamber.

"Addolgar!"

"I'm fine!"

Owena shook her head. "That leg will never heal if he keeps running around on it."

"I know."

A few seconds later, Addolgar returned with his oversized carrying bag. He hopped over to the table, tossed the bag on it, then sat down again. Once comfortable, he reached into his bag and pulled out a large-headed hammer.

"A hammer?" Delyth asked, hands on hips. "A sword, Cadwaladr, is elegant. A beautiful extension of a warrior's arm. But you want to give my *royal*-born cousin a thick, heavy, clumsy weapon like a hammer?"

Addolgar studied the weapon in his big hand, looked over at Braith, and threw it at her.

She caught it, easily. Swung it once, twice, then lifted it

with both hands. It felt right in her hands. Comfortable. The way, she assumed, a weapon was supposed to feel.

Braith grinned at Addolgar. A grin he returned.

Owena nodded. "He's right. She's a hammer dragon."

Disgusted, Delyth glowered at both Braith and Addolgar. "You know," she finally said, "you two certainly are perfect together. You're both bloody know-it-alls."

Addolgar sat on the table between Owena, Aledwen, and Crystin. Together, they watched and gave pointers to Braith while she became acquainted with his hammer.

Wait. That came out wrong.

Crystin poked Addolgar in the ribs and he had to grit his teeth from crying out. It seemed the Penarddun "poke" was equivalent to the Cadwaladr head-butt after a night of heavy drinking.

"Yes?" he asked Crystin, once he could do it without crying.

"That niece of ours," she said low, so only he and the other aunts could hear her, "she's a nice lass, isn't she?"

Addolgar thought on that for a moment. He didn't know if he'd call Braith "nice." Bunnies were nice. Braith was more . . . lusty! Yes. She was lusty. And beautiful. And adorable. And—

"You don't think she's nice?" Crystin demanded and that's when he realized Braith's aunts had been waiting for a response. When one hadn't come, they'd taken that as a bad thing.

"No," he replied honestly. "I don't think she's nice. She's anything but nice. And when you get to know her again, you'll also realize she's not nice." He looked over the three She-dragons in human form glowering at him. That's when he added, "Because nice is boring. And that's the last thing your niece is. So, no, my ladies, I don't think she's nice at all."

"You know," Braith said, unaware of the other conversations going on around her, "I think with some training, I could wield two of these at the same time. Oh!" She looked at Addolgar, her eyes wide with excitement. "Or an ax."

With a shrug, he reached into his bag and pulled out his ax. He tossed it at her, but Braith wasn't ready for it and she instinctively ducked. The weapon collided with her cousin Ffraid, who'd been standing behind her. Thankfully, the She-dragon was hit with the flat of the blade so it just knocked her on her pretty little ass.

Everyone stopped and stared at poor Ffraid stretched out on the ground, the ax resting on her chest.

Owena leaned over so she could look around Braith. She gazed down at her inert daughter. "You all right, Ffraid?" she called out.

Ffraid raised a hand but her only answer was a groan.

Owena leaned back, nodded. "She'll be fine."

Before Addolgar could dispute that—he had thrown that ax rather hard, knowing quite well that *Braith* could handle the power of it—Aledwen suddenly jumped off the table, her hand to her forehead.

"Sister?" Crystin asked. "What is it?"

"It's Heledd. She comes this way." She suddenly tore off her fur cloak. "She is not alone," she announced to the room.

Addolgar didn't really know what that meant, but based on the way everyone suddenly moved with purpose, he knew it couldn't be good.

It seemed to be a practiced thing. Several of the older offspring hustled the hatchlings, who were still too young to shift to human, to some other place inside the vast cave while the aunts and older cousins and sisters, retrieved weapons and shields.

Braith still held his hammer. "What's going on?" she asked.

Aledwen, now shifted to her dragon-form, faced her niece. "Your father sent Lightnings after Heledd and her cousins."

"How many?" Addolgar demanded, horrified any Southland male would set Lightnings upon the females of their kind.

Aledwen blinked, then answered, "She thinks . . . nearly a horde's worth."

Braith let out a breath and, in that instant, Addolgar saw her resolve. He knew what she would do.

"Braith, no."

"You stay here," she told him. "You're not fit enough to fight."

"Please," he said, grabbing Braith's arm. "Let me call to my kin."

"We don't have time, Addolgar," Crystin said. She looked at her niece. "But you should wait here, Braith."

"I won't."

"Braith . . . this isn't your fault."

"Perhaps. But you're my kin. I'm coming with you."

Crystin looked at her sisters and they all nodded. Not the reaction Addolgar had been hoping for.

While the aunts and cousins began to head out of the chamber, Addolgar shifted to his dragon-form, as did Braith.

"This is reckless, Braith," he warned her. "You're not a warrior. Not yet."

"I know that."

"The Lightnings, as much as I hate them, are fierce warriors. I trained for decades with me uncles before I was *ever* allowed to face them in battle. You've only been actively kicking ass for the last few *days*."

"I don't plan to be foolish, Addolgar. But I can't just let them go out there and face this alone."

"They're not alone. They're a crowd."

"Addolgar—"

"Your aunt is right. This isn't your fault."

"I never said it was. But I didn't have to bring you here. I did, and my father knew I would. He sent Lightnings *knowing* there would be mostly females here. Just what a

Lightning Horde would want to hear." She stepped closer, placed her claw on his forearm. "But I need you to stay here. You're still healing and, to be honest, Addolgar, I can't afford to lose you." She shrugged. "I've been swinging your hammer around and it hasn't bothered you once that I haven't grown tired. Most males I've known . . . that just makes them nervous."

He took his hammer from her, rammed the base on the rocky floor. It extended into a weapon that could only be held by a dragon in its natural form.

"That's remarkable," she said, smiling as he handed the weapon back to her.

"My sister and I got tired of needing two sets of weapons, one for when we were dragons and one for when we shifted to our human forms. So a Volcano blacksmith made this for us." He wrapped his claw over hers, looked deep into her eyes. "Use it well."

"I will."

She stepped back from him, and that's when Addolgar added, "Their natural weapon is lightning. When they open their maws, be prepared. That shit goes everywhere. Just like in a storm."

"Okay."

"And if they're in armor, well, their armor doesn't cover all their important bits. Feel free to attack the groin if necessary. Use your tail."

"It'll be fine," she tried to assure him. "Just please . . . stay here. Keep safe." She leaned into him, nuzzled her head against his. Then she was gone.

As Addolgar sat there, already missing her, Caron walked by, heading toward the exit. She smiled at him.

"Don't worry, Mountain, we'll take good care of our cousin."

Addolgar growled. "*Stop* calling me that."

Chapter 17

Braith had just reached the chamber where she'd met her cousins only a few days ago when Heledd flew in. She was going so fast that when she tried to touch down, she hit the ground hard, and turned into a rolling ball of blue scales and black claws until she hit the far wall.

Braith ran to her side just as her other two cousins followed Heledd in. This time, the aunts caught them, preventing them from ending up like Heledd.

Helping her cousin up, Braith asked, "Are you all right?"

"They're right behind us." Heledd looked over at the rest of the kin. "We need to move."

"You all know what to do," Crystin said. "Now go." And Braith's kin did, charging out of the cave and into the open. "You," Crystin barked at Braith. "Stay by my side. I don't want to face The Mountain if something happens to you."

Heledd patted Braith's shoulder before heading back out. Braith did as she was ordered and went to her aunt's side. Together they moved toward the exit, but before they reached it, Lightnings dropped from the skies. There were so many, Braith didn't even bother to count, concerned that she would let the number make her feel defeated before she even began.

And without a word, the Lightnings charged, attacking Braith's kin inside and outside of the cave. They had no intent to harm; they wanted to bring the females in alive and relatively healthy. So they were trying to disarm, which was exactly what two Lightnings did to Braith.

She'd barely raised her hammer before it was ripped from

her claws and tossed aside. Then the two males were on her, slamming her to the ground.

All she managed to hear was, "Get her wing!" before the panic set in.

He wanted to pace, but he didn't want to do it while hopping. He had no idea what was going on outside and he was completely and utterly not happy about it!

"Fuck it!" he finally muttered. "I'll just bloody hop."

But before Addolgar could move from his spot by the hall table, he scented what some would consider a thunderstorm. That scent of lightning in the air. But he knew there was no storm deep inside these cave walls.

Gods, he was definitely not at his best if he was forgetting the battle strategies of the Lightnings. Especially when it came to rounding up females. He'd always heard there was a lot of arguing about that strategy among the Lightnings. Most came head-on because they had a better chance of getting hold of the most hearty females. Those females not afraid to attack, although there was always the risk of mortally wounding them during battle. At the same time, other Lightnings would go in the back way, where they often found the ones too young to take, the old She-dragons—which could be ridiculously dangerous at those advanced ages, especially if they were the ones minding the hatchlings—and the weaker She-dragons too afraid to run. The weaker She-dragons were also the ones the Lightnings could make use of.

Addolgar knew that somewhere in this cave the Penard-duns had hidden the hatchlings. He may not be able to help Braith, but he wouldn't let anything happen to her young cousins while the Lightnings were searching for other females. Turning, he started to hop over to his ax when a flash of purple flashed by him. But it was too late. He was already flying across the chamber and crashing into the opposite wall.

"Look what we have here, lads!" he heard a Lightning announce. "A lonely little Fire Breather!"

One Lightning was holding her down while the other pulled out his ax. "Flip her over!"

Not liking the sound of that one gods-damn bit, Braith got one forearm out from under her attacker, bent it, and brought it up. Her elbow collided with the Lightning's jaw, stunning him, but he still wouldn't loosen his hold. So she brought her elbow across his snout again. That knocked him out and she pushed his body off her. She tried to scramble away, to get her hammer, but a claw grabbed her by the ankle, dragging her back.

"Oh, no you don't," a male said. He didn't seem to care what she'd done to his comrade.

Braith tried to grab something she could hold on to, but her talons tore through nothing but dirt and stone.

She was yanked back to the Lightning and, desperate, she kicked out, hitting him in the chest. With an "oof!" he flew back several feet, and Braith tried again to get to her claws.

"Get that one!" someone yelled, and Braith knew they were talking about her.

Addolgar slid down the wall and landed on his ass. He could already hear his father telling him this was his fault because he wasn't paying attention! And knowing the old bastard was right, yet again, did nothing but piss Addolgar off.

An ax head slipped under Addolgar's chin and lifted. "Hello there, darlin'," the Lightning taunted. "Those females leave you in here to protect you from the big, bad Northlanders?"

"Poor thing," another one tossed in as the ten or so Lightnings laughed. "What should we do with him?"

"Make it quick, I think. Wouldn't be right to let him linger in shame."

A clawed foot was placed against Addolgar's shoulder to keep him sitting up and the dragon pulled his ax back, readying to swing and remove Addolgar's head. A part of his body he was quite attached to.

"Give us your name, darlin'," the Lightning told him, "so we can tell the females we take that you died with your head up."

"Name's Addolgar the Cheerful," Addolgar replied over the hearty laughter of the Lightnings.

"What a lovely name. It'll look good on your funeral pyre."

Then Addolgar added, "Of the Cadwaladr Clan."

The ax, in mid-swing, stopped and the laughter died. The moment lasted no more than two, maybe three, seconds, but that was all Addolgar needed. He grabbed the claw pressed against his shoulder and yanked the Lightning down and close, their snouts inches from each other.

"Nice to meet ya, daaaaarlin'," Addolgar shot back, mimicking the Lightning's accent. Then he snatched the ax from the Lightning's claw and rammed the blade into his neck. Blood spurted and Addolgar got up, bringing the Lightning with him. The ax had only gone in halfway, so the Lightning was still putting up a bit of a fight, but it was easy enough to hold on to him, which Addolgar did.

"Now, let's be clear, shall we?" He pulled the ax out of the dragon he held in his claws, and placed the blood-covered weapon on the ground beside him. "There's only one way this can go, darlin's," Addolgar teased. "You know it. . . . I know it."

And to prove it, Addolgar put his claws into the wound and proceeded to tear the screaming head of the Lightning the rest of the way off until he stopped screaming.

Addolgar dropped the body and held the head in one claw while he grabbed the weapon with the other.

"So, darlin's . . . what's your pleasure?"

That's when they all charged Addolgar at once.

Braith scrambled a few feet away from the one who'd grabbed her leg and then dived the rest of the way to get her hammer.

She'd just wrapped her claws around the handle when her legs were grabbed again and she was dragged back. Once she stopped, Braith flipped onto her back and raised her hammer in time to block the sword trying to cut off her wing. She shoved, pushing the sword away from her, and rammed the head of her weapon into the Lightning's chest. He lurched back and looked down at what was now a concave pit where his ribs used to be.

He lifted his gaze to Braith and raised his claw. "Please—" he managed to squeak out, but Braith ignored his plea, running forward and bringing the hammer down on the Lightning's head. He dropped to his knees, his head flat, his neck compressed.

Panting, Braith sensed there were more Lightnings behind her and she spun around, now ready to fight. But it wasn't Lightnings; it was her three aunts, watching her while the cousins fought alongside their own daughters and nieces.

"Wait . . ." Braith took a breath, tried to understand. "You didn't help me?"

"We wanted to see if you could help yourself," Crystin explained. "And you did. Nice one, niece."

"Nice . . . ? Are you . . . ? You . . . you treacherous cows!"

"Where's the loyalty?"

"Shut up!"

"Oy!" a male voice called from outside the cavern. The sound of it was so disconcerting, all of Braith's kin and the Lightnings stopped fighting, and Braith and her aunts walked toward the cave opening.

An older Lightning who was missing the scales and skin on the left side of his face so it seemed like he was perpetually smiling, stood in front of the cave opening, his gaze hungrily examining Braith's kin.

"Southland females," he growled out, and that's when Braith realized he was also missing the scales and skin on the right side of his neck. The area was so damaged, his words seemed to be torn from his throat. "There is no need to fight us. To risk your lives. Come with us now of your own free will and we swear on our honor that we won't harm you. We'll take you to our land and treat you like the queens you are." His expression turned hard, even while it still looked like he smiled. "But fight us now—and your regret will be great."

"Take our wings, will you?" Owena asked him. "I thought you lot didn't do that anymore."

"We do what we must. Now come. Join us, so we can stop all this fighting. We'd hate to risk so much . . . beauty."

Owena looked around at her kin. "What do you say, Penardduns? Do we give ourselves to these Lightnings? Or stand our ground?"

Funny. Braith was tired of giving herself to dragons she didn't respect, like her father and the Queen. But she was also tired of being proud and standing her ground like a good little She-dragon.

So she did neither. Instead she ran. Using rage, annoyance, and outright viciousness, Braith of the Darkness ran out of the cave and right toward the Lightning leader. He saw her coming and smiled until she raised Addolgar's hammer. The leader reared back, but Braith just kept coming. She couldn't stop herself and, to be honest, she wouldn't. This felt . . . right. So very, very right.

As she neared the Lightning leader, Braith unleashed her wings and rose up in the air, bringing the hammer up and over with both front claws and then down until it collided with the Lightning leader's head. He let out a roar when the hammer hit him, but that's when Braith rammed her back claws into the Lightning's chest and forced him to the ground. She dug her talons past his scales and kept him pinned to the ground with the strength of her legs while she brought the hammer up and over, again and again and again, until she'd beaten the Lightning leader's already damaged head into a blood-and-bone pulp.

Covered in the Lightning's blood, she turned around and faced her kin.

Her aunts gawked at her, tears in their eyes, until Crystin said through barely held-back sobs, "Your mother . . . would be so *proud!*"

"Then let's do this in my mother's honor," Braith suggested. "And kill . . . *all of them!*"

Chapter 18

Braith liked Addolgar's hammer. She liked it a lot. It fit her somehow. Knives, swords . . . no. All that slashing steel and shoving pointy ends into things did nothing for her. But battering that hammer onto a Lightning's head gave her a perverse pleasure. She got hit a few times. A couple of cuts. But nothing she couldn't handle.

At one point she stopped and took a look around. Her aunts were mostly delegating. Ordering their daughters on which Lightnings to kill and, sometimes, how. Heledd walked among the bodies, looking at each one. Braith didn't know what her cousin was looking for until she saw her gaze move back to the cave opening.

"What is it?" Braith asked her cousin.

"There's some missing."

There were so many, Braith wondered how she knew. If she truly knew. "Are you sure?"

"I'm sure."

From what Braith understood, the Lightnings would have no interest in the hatchlings, even the female ones. They at least respected that particular boundary. But they were probably more than happy to come around and attack from behind . . . and yet they hadn't.

"Addolgar," she said, looking to Crystin. "Addolgar!"

Braith raced past her kin and back into the cave. She heard Crystin behind her, yelling at her daughters and Owena to follow. Braith didn't wait for them. She couldn't.

She charged down passage after passage, trying not to think too much about poor, defenseless Addolgar. She never should have left him. She never should have deserted him!

She finally hit the passage that would lead her to the main chamber, and ran full out around that last corner—where she stumbled to an awkward stop, her kin running into the back of her and nearly knocking her on her face.

Together, they stood and stared, watching Addolgar—on one leg only—swing his ax down, taking the head off some Lightning. Then using his wings to move, he spun, and swung his ax again, cutting into the side of another Lightning. He tore the blade out, swung again, this time into the Lightning's neck. Another Lightning came up behind him, but Addolgar threw his wings out, knocking his enemy into the wall. He turned, brought the ax up, tearing the stunned Lightning open from groin to belly. Addolgar yanked the blade out, and the Lightning's intestines fell to the floor in a nasty pile.

That left only one Lightning. A rather young one by the

looks of him. Addolgar faced him, hopped toward him on his good leg. He took his blood-covered ax and pressed the blunt head against the youngster's throat. He pushed until the Lightning was backed up against a wall.

"Cadwaladr trash," the youngster hissed, trying to hide the fact he was terrified.

"Go home, Lightning," Addolgar told him. "Go home and tell them what happened here today. They'll not only face the Penardduns if they are ever stupid enough to come back here, but they'll also face Cadwaladr *trash*. Now leave my sight, boy, before I get testy."

The Lightning slid against the wall, moving away from that ax head. Once he was far enough away, he turned, and ran out the way Braith assumed those Lightnings had all come in.

Owena sat back on her haunches, crossed her forearms over her chest and said, "You shouldn't be playing around on that bad leg, Mountain."

Addolgar's back tensed at Owena's words. "I'm *not* playing around on my leg, and *stop* calling me Mountain!"

Addolgar turned around, ready to tell Owena what she could do with her bloody nicknames when he saw Braith. She looked . . . happy. As happy as he'd ever seen her.

He grinned and announced, "Look at you, Braith of the Darkness, all covered in Lightning blood! My father would be so proud!"

"Thank you." Braith held up his hammer. "Can I keep this?"

"Absolutely," he said, hopping over to her. "You'll need it." He reached her and pulled her against his body, hugging her tight. He let out a breath at having her safe with him again. Even better . . . she hugged him back.

"I was so worried," she told him, "when Heledd told us we

hadn't gotten all of them. I realized they must have come in through another way."

"Lightnings like the sneak attack. Too bad for them, I love killing Lightnings, so it all worked in my favor."

"Good job, Mountain," Crystin praised. "Your father would be proud of you, too, I think."

"And I thought you knew my father."

Braith leaned her head back and looked up at Addolgar. "Wait, why do I *need* your hammer?"

"It's your hammer now. At least until we have one made for you. And you'll need it for when we go after your bastard father."

Braith broke out in another smile that warmed Addolgar's heart. She was whole now, wasn't she? Truly whole.

Crystin stepped up to them, placed her claw on Braith's shoulder. "We'll clean up this gods-damn mess, take care of the hatchlings, and head out tomorrow morning to find Emyr."

Braith studied her aunt. "You don't have to, Aunt Crystin. This is my fight."

"You're a Daughter of the House of Penarddun, Braith, which makes this *our* fight."

"Plus," Owena casually tossed in, "your bastard father's pissed us off for the last gods-damn time."

There was agreement from Braith's other aunts and cousins.

"He sent Lightnings after us like we're some bloody cattle to be auctioned off," Caron growled.

"Which is bad enough," Ffraid added. "But he also sent them after his own daughter. If my Da was here right now, he'd be losing his mind."

"Let's not involve your fathers," Owena said. "You know how they are when they get cranky."

"And they'll just blame us," Aledwen muttered.

"Besides, they're encamped closer to Dark Plains than they are the Outer Plains so it'll take them days to get here. And, to be honest"—Crystin studied her blood-and-brain-covered sword—"I am so very ready to *end* your father, Braith of the Darkness."

Braith looked at Addolgar, then her aunts and cousins. "Then that's what we'll do."

Chapter 19

Three days later, his wounded leg strong again, Addolgar stepped up behind Lady Katarina. She was still very pretty, but she was no match for his Braith.

"My lady?"

She didn't turn around, her focus on the field of flowers she stood in. "I really thought they'd leave you be if I made it look like I'd killed you. I had no idea they'd want to make sure you were dead."

"I'm a Cadwaladr, my lady. One would be foolish *not* to ensure a Cadwaladr is dead. We have a way of coming back again and again until we are."

"Well, I'm glad Lady Braith was there. I could tell by the way she looked at you during our trip that she'd make sure you survived."

"She did."

Katarina slowly faced him. She studied him for a long moment before she nodded her head in approval. "I see."

"I'm sure you do."

"Sergeant Addolgar . . . understand, my goal wasn't to betray the Queen. Or my kind."

"Then what are you doing, my lady?"

She sat back on her haunches, clutched her claws together. "What can I say? I fell in love."

Addolgar couldn't help but feel vaguely disgusted. "With Elder Emyr?"

Her eyes widened. "Oh, gods, no! No, no, no. Not Emyr. Herleif."

"Herleif?"

"Of the . . . uh . . ." She cleared her throat. "Torbjörn Horde."

"A Lightning?" Addolgar struggled to control his rarely seen anger. "You betrayed us all for a *Lightning*?"

"I betrayed no one, Sergeant. I swear that on the souls of my ancestors."

"But you sent them to raid the Penardduns' cave."

"That was not Herleif's Horde." She closed her eyes, brought the tips of her talons to her temples, and rubbed. "I was a fool, Addolgar."

"For trusting Emyr?"

"Aye." She opened her eyes, dropped her claws to her sides. "The deal was simple. Soldiers that were loyal to Emyr and his sons would escort me safely through the Northlands and into Torbjörn territory."

"In exchange for what?"

"Herleif's troops given to Emyr for him to command against the Queen."

"How is that not betrayal, m'lady?" When Katarina looked away, Addolgar guessed, "They were going to kill Emyr and his sons instead."

"I knew he was not someone the Queen would miss."

"Oh, well then . . ."

"I know you don't understand this, Addolgar. You're a Cadwaladr."

Perhaps 'twas true. Perhaps the Cadwaladrs would never plan such a thing because they weren't royal enough to justify such shitty behavior. Yet he could also say with absolute

certainty that the honor-bound Braith and her Penarddun kin
would never do such a thing either. And their blood was as
royal as Katarina's.

"But it turned out," she went on, unaware that Addolgar
saw her much differently now, "Emyr already had plans of
his own in place. He was going to hand me over to Olgeir
and his Horde and, in return . . ." She swallowed, continued
on, "In return, they were going to march around to the
borderlands between the Southlands and the Western
Mountains."

Addolgar blinked in surprise. "They were going to strike
your father."

"Aye. And then attack the Queen's troops from her weakest
point."

"Olgeir's smarter than I gave him credit for," Addolgar
grudgingly admitted.

"I couldn't let that happen," she said fiercely. "Not to *my*
father. I know he'd never allow me to mate a Northlander, but
he's still my father. I still love him."

Whatever. His sisters would never let anyone—not their
father, not even the Queen—get between them and the males
they loved. But they, like Braith, had a little something
called integrity and backbone. "The troops that attacked
Braith's kin?"

"A small local Horde whose territory Emyr had permis-
sion to travel through. But that's when I knew something was
very wrong. The Henriksson Horde is an enemy of Herleif's
people and *loathe* Southland dragons. They never would have
allowed us to travel through their territory unchallenged. But
they allowed us to travel through for Olgeir. When I realized
that . . . well, one night I went off to relieve myself, shifted
to human, and snuck back. That's when I heard Emyr's plan."
She frowned and noted, "Emyr had to repeat that plan several
times to his sons. They were quite stupid."

Addolgar thought on that comment a moment. "Were?"

Then he gawked at the royal. "Lady Katarina . . . what have you done?"

She gave a very small and dainty shrug. "What I had to."

"Oy. Mountain."

Annoyed by that nickname, Addolgar glared over his shoulder. Owena stood behind him and gave a short jerk of her head, as always ignoring his glare.

"Stay here a moment," he told Katarina before he went off after Owena. He followed the She-dragon until he reached a clearing. Braith and the rest of her kin stood waiting. Waiting and staring. He walked past them, not stopping until he reached Elder Emyr. The dragon sat slumped in front of the pit fire, remnants of drool and vomit dried on his chest scales, one of his eyes picked out by the crows that had planted themselves on all the bodies.

"She poisoned them all," Owena said low, as if afraid to wake the dead. "All of them."

Addolgar immediately turned and walked over to Braith. No matter how she might have felt about the dragon, Emyr had still been her father. He took her claw and led her a bit away from her kin and the rotting smell of death.

"Are you all right?" he asked when they stopped.

"It's not exactly what I expected. Not like this." She suddenly looked up. "Is Katarina still alive?"

"She is. I found her in a clearing."

"What happened?"

"She's in love. With a Lightning from the Torbjörn Horde."

Braith's eyes widened at that. "A royal of stature willingly going to a Lightning? That's something Addiena will never tolerate."

"I know. Katarina knew it, too."

"Why did she kill them?"

"For several reasons, it seems, but apparently I'm not royal enough to truly understand her logic."

Braith smirked. "My father double-crossed her, didn't he?"

"Exactly. And she reacted accordingly."

"Huh. Well, my father always underestimated females," Braith murmured, glancing over at the bodies again.

Addolgar squeezed her claws with his own and she looked away from the corpses.

"What do you want to do?" he asked her.

"About Katarina?"

"Aye. Do you want to take her back to the Queen?"

Braith thought on that a moment. Then she asked, "Do you believe her? About the Lightning she says she's in love with?"

"I do. And, in case you're wondering, the Horde that Emyr sent to your kin's cave was the Henriksson, not the Torbjörns. They had nothing to do with the raid, if it helps any."

"It does since we did kill all those males. I'm sure there are more left behind, but that Horde was probably gutted."

"Why does it matter?"

"If we let her go, we need a commitment that the Torbjörns will not try to cross the borders again to attack."

"They won't. They weren't planning to. Kill your father and brothers, though . . . that did seem to be on the agenda."

"So many wanted that dragon dead," she sighed out. "And yet, I feel nothing for his loss from this world." Braith briefly closed her eyes, then said, "Let her go. If for no other reason, she did help to save your life."

Addolgar smiled. "I guess we do owe her for that."

"Then it's decided. We let her go and tell the Queen Katarina had already escaped and we couldn't safely go farther into Northland territory. We'll also take my father and brothers back to the Queen. See if their bodies appease her at all."

"Are you comfortable with that?"

"Addolgar, this needs to end. For you. For your kin. For *my* kin."

"What are we doing?" Crystin asked from behind them.

Braith stepped around Addolgar. "We're taking my father and brothers back to the Queen."

"They're already dead," Crystin complained.

"I am aware of that, Aunt Crystin."

"So we've got to carry these bodies back all the way to Devenallt Mountain?"

"Addolgar and *I* need to get my father's remains back to Devenallt Mountain."

"You don't think we're coming with you?" Crystin snapped, suddenly appearing quite annoyed. "Do you really think we'd let you meet that Red bitch on your own?"

"Auntie Crystin—"

"Shut up. You ramble like your mother sometimes."

Braith looked up at him. "I ramble?"

"Not compared to my people," Addolgar admitted.

Crystin faced her sisters. "We need to get these three idiots back to Devenallt Mountain without breaking our backs in the process. Any suggestions?"

"Aye," Owena said. "I've got one." She held out her claw to Addolgar. "Give us your ax, yeah?"

Addolgar took a step back. "Owena . . . no."

"Just give us your ax. We'll take care of the rest."

Disgusted, but not seeing much option, he looked at Braith. "And are you all right with *that*?"

His She-dragon shrugged her shoulders and replied, "Eh."

Addolgar decided to take that as a yes.

Braith winced as Crystin tossed the bags holding the heads of her father and two brothers at the foot of Addiena's throne.

The Queen glared down at the remains for a long moment before she focused that glare on Crystin. "Really?"

"As requested, Your Majesty. The traitor Elder Emyr and his sons."

"I wanted them alive . . . and would you two *stop that!*" Addiena suddenly bellowed.

They all turned and watched Bercelak and Ghleanna pull apart. Blood dripped from Bercelak's snout, and one side of Ghleanna's jaw was swollen. It seemed that the siblings had been fighting since Braith and Addolgar had left, much to the Queen's annoyance—and Braith's perverse sense of justice. Perhaps Addiena would now be less inclined to take so many hostages after this.

Bercelak pointed a damning black talon at his sister. "She started it, Your Majesty."

"*I* started it?" Ghleanna screeched. "You're such a big baby!"

"*Your Majesty!*"

"*That is enough!*" Addiena roared. She pointed her claw at Ghleanna. "Over there!" she ordered the She-dragon, motioning across her hall.

"But, Your Majesty—"

"*Ghleanna! Move!*"

With a nasty snarl at her brother, Ghleanna stomped across the hall.

Addiena let out a very long and pain-filled breath.

After she seemed a tad calmer, she focused back on Braith, her kin, and Addolgar.

"Now where was I?" she asked.

"You said you wanted them alive," Brigida the Foul answered for Braith and the others as she slowly made her way across the hall. "But truth be told, Your Majesty, you actually agreed to dead or alive. And the Penardduns went with dead."

Addiena glowered at Brigida, but she couldn't argue something that everyone who'd been in the throne room that day had heard. Especially in front of the other Elders, who were watching Addiena closely to see how she handled this. Many of them had offspring of their own, and unlike Braith's father, they did not want to think that their actions could affect their children the way Emyr's had been impacting Braith.

Tapping one talon against her stone throne, the Queen eyed the group standing before her. Finally, she demanded, "And what of Lady Katarina? Her father is most worried about her."

"The—" Braith began, but Brigida, who now stood beside her, cut in quickly.

"Tragically, Your Majesty, she was taken. By the Lightnings," Brigida added with a sneer.

"The Lightnings? They took her? Are you saying she was used as a bargaining chip by Emyr?"

Brigida blinked and glanced at the Penardduns.

"Ripped from us, she was," Owena elaborated. "It was so sad, watching those bastards fly off with her. But we were too late to get her back."

"And who," Addiena demanded, her eyes narrowing dangerously, "took her?"

Brigida, holding on to her walking stick, leaned in and announced, "Olgeir, Your Majesty. Dragonlord of the Olgeirsson Horde."

Shocked, because Braith had no idea why the name of that bloody Horde was being used at this moment, Braith glanced at Addolgar. But he gave a very tiny shake of his head and they both kept silent.

The Queen's front claws dug into the stone of her throne. "First," she growled, "they take Davon the Gold. Then they have the gall to take Katarina the Gold as well?"

The Queen looked down, her claws still digging into her throne. She stayed like that for a long bit, but then, suddenly, she raised those blue eyes until she was looking right at Braith. And, in that moment, Braith understood. She understood that the Queen *knew* they were all lying. She knew it, and she didn't care. Because she was going to use this to her benefit.

With a blink, the Queen assumed her most put-upon expression as she looked over her court.

"This cannot be borne," she told them in her most queenly voice. "They cross borders to steal what is ours. And that is not something that we can tolerate. That we *will* tolerate." She briefly scanned the chamber until her eyes locked on Bercelak. "Captain Bercelak," she said, "you will lead my troops into the north and give the Olgeirsson Horde a taste of the Southland's wrath."

Bercelak nodded. "It will be my pleasure, Your Majesty."

"Your Majesty," one of the Elders interrupted, "you said it yourself, if we attack the Lightnings on their own territory, they will consider it an act of war."

"And what are we to consider their attacks on *us*? On our She-dragons? No, no," she said, raising her claw, the talons with bits of stone still clinging to them. "The time is perfect." She looked at Braith again, blue eyes so very cold. "Isn't it . . . Lady Braith?"

Braith knew what the cow was doing. Understood it quite clearly.

Now, with Emyr dead, Braith knew this would be the last concession she ever made. But she would have to make it. If she wanted to live.

"It is, Your Majesty. It is the right time to strike. To stop whatever my father may have put into motion."

The Queen relaxed back into her throne. She gestured to the heads on her floor. "Get that trash from my sight. And, Captain Bercelak, we will meet in one hour to discuss how we'll be moving forward. So have your battle plans ready."

"I always do, Your Majesty."

The Queen focused on Braith.

"Welcome home, Lady Braith, and"—the Queen smiled at this last bit—"good job."

Chapter 20

They landed on the top of Devenallt Mountain, which was now covered with even more Cadwaladrs than Braith had even realized there were in the world, much less in close range of Devenallt.

Pissed, Braith faced Brigida the Foul and her aunts. "What the holy hells was all that?" she demanded.

"What do you think that was?" Crystin asked. "Us covering your ass."

"And doing a damn fine job of it, if you ask me," Owena added.

"I didn't ask you. And what was all that centaur shit about the Olgeirsson Horde? Why are we bringing them into this?"

Crystin shrugged. "I have no idea."

Braith looked at the White Dragonwitch. "Brigida?"

"Why don't you mind your own and I'll mind my own."

"Why don't you tell me what's going on?"

"Her Majesty, lazy whore that she is—"

"Brigida!" one of the Cadwaladrs cried out.

"—would let the bloody Lightnings swarm this land if we let her. But we gave her a good solid reason to send some of our troops in there, which—once Bercelak does what he does best—will piss off the rest of the Hordes and we will finally make a stand with those purple-scaled bastards. Or," she went on, "would you rather just hand over our females to them now, Braith of the Darkness?"

"That wasn't an option either, but doing this . . . what if

Addiena finds out that we never even saw the Olgeirsson Horde?"

"And when do you expect that to happen?" Brigida asked, moving around her to an edge on the packed mountain where she could take off comfortably. "When Olgeir himself actually *writes* her a letter informing her of this? Because even if the big bastard could write, I don't think he would bother, which means you're safe."

"But—"

"Leave it be, Braith of the Darkness. This no longer has anything to do with you or that idiot father of yours." Brigida expanded her wings from her body. "Just be glad you get to live another day."

Brigida stepped off the mountain and her wings caught the air, sending her soaring off.

Braith closed her eyes and let out a breath. She had no idea how she'd lost control of this.

"It'll be all right," Addolgar told her, his claw brushing down her shoulder.

"I hope you're right."

"Hey, Mountain!" Owena called out, and Braith quickly caught Addolgar's wrist before he could do something stupid. "We're hungry."

Now it was Addolgar's time to close his eyes and let out a breath. "Of course," he finally said. "Mum already knows you're coming."

As a ridiculously large group, they flew to the area just outside the gates of Ailean's castle. There, the Cadwaladrs and the Penardduns landed, shifted to human, and put on clothes. The Cadwaladrs, although no longer needing to protect Braith or Ghleanna, had not returned to their own caves or castles because they all wanted to get their chance to hunt and kill Lightnings in the north. So until Bercelak decided which of the Queen's troops would be coming with him, the Cadwaladrs would be making good use of Ailean's territory.

The Penardduns, however, had a longer trip back home and invited themselves to stay at the castle for the night. Something Addolgar knew his father wouldn't mind . . . but Addolgar couldn't speak for his mother. She just thought they were coming for dinner.

They entered the courtyard and found his mother and father waiting for them on the steps.

Shalin grinned and clapped her hands together when she saw her offspring come through the gates. They always felt her love without her ever saying a word.

Their father, though, was always more . . . chatty.

"We're so glad you all have your heads!" he announced . . . loudly.

Addolgar stopped at the bottom of the stairs, gazed up at his father. "Gee . . . thanks, Da."

"Well, what do you want me to say?"

Braith's aunts pushed past Addolgar and Ghleanna so that they could leer up the stairs at Ailean.

"Ailean," Crystin called out. "Long time, old friend."

"Crystin. Owena. Aledwen. Good to see all of you again. As always, the Penarddun She-dragons look beautiful."

Braith's aunts grinned widely at the compliment—Owena may have even giggled—while Ailean's mate and offspring rolled their eyes. Especially Ghleanna, who appeared the most appalled.

"Well," Crystin said, "we'll be staying here at least the night so I hope you'll have time for dinner and a little chat about old . . ."

Crystin's words faded away as three male dragons in human form walked out of the Main Hall doors. Addolgar didn't recognize them, but Caron ran up the stairs and threw herself into one of the dragons' arms.

"Daddy!"

Crystin crossed her arms over her chest and gawked up the stairs at her mate. "What the hells are you lot doing here?"

"Oh," Shalin said, smiling, "when I heard from Addolgar that all of you were safe and coming back to the Southlands together, I sent out messengers to retrieve your mates since I knew they were part of the troops camped not too far from here. Isn't that fortuitous?"

"Aye," Crystin muttered. "So very fortuitous."

The three males glowered down the stairs at their mates and one of them demanded, "What idiocy did you idiotic lot get me lovely daughters into this time, ya daft cows?"

"Don't even start!" Aledwen barked back, stomping up the stairs to the Main Hall, her sisters stomping right behind her. The three couples bickered all the way into the castle, but the way the Penarddun offspring didn't seem to notice or care told Addolgar this was how things went among their parents.

Once the Penardduns had gone inside, Shalin opened her arms and Addolgar went up the stairs to hug her.

"I'm so glad you're all right." She pulled back. "How's your leg?"

When the Lightning had rammed that spear into his leg, Addolgar had done his best to block what was happening from his kin. But his mother always knew. Always.

"It's fine, Mum."

"Did you cry like a baby when that Lightning speared you?"

Addolgar scowled at his father. "No. I did not."

"But you weren't paying attention, were you, boy?" When Addolgar didn't reply, Ailean threw up his hands. "How many times must I remind you lot to *pay attention*? Do you think I've been training you since hatching just for my bloody health?"

Shalin pulled away from Addolgar and placed her small hands on Ailean's arm. "My love, why don't you go check on our guests? I'm sure Crystin would just love to relive old memories."

"Fine. You talk to the boy then."

Once his father had gone back inside, Addolgar said, "I'm leaving."

But he hadn't even managed to turn all the way around so he could walk down the stairs before his mother grabbed him by the hair and held on tight.

"Mum!"

"You're not going anywhere. You and your brothers know how your father is. You know why he does what he does. So why must we go through this over and over again?"

"But—"

"He loves you, Addolgar. He loves all of you. In his own . . . Ailean-like way. He would do anything for you. Never forget that. So do not be a prat and simply remember that *I* love you more than the suns."

Knowing there was no point in arguing with the female he loved so much, Addolgar just sighed out, "Thanks, Mum."

She released his hair, turned him around again so he faced her, and patted his cheek. "You're welcome, dear."

Braith, feeling uncomfortable just standing there behind Addolgar while he bickered with his parents, walked off, leaving them to it.

She wandered into one of the horse stalls. At first, she thought maybe these were horses for eating, but then she saw all the saddles and realized that these were horses for riding. Braith walked up to a stall with a large black stallion, resting her arms on the wood gate. It was so strange, wasn't it? Dragons riding horses to get around even though dragons had wings. But the Cadwaladrs were . . . unique.

"Sorry about that."

Braith looked over her shoulder at Ghleanna. "About what?"

"My brother and father."

She shrugged and focused on the horse in front of her. "Doesn't bother me. Besides . . . my father's head just got tossed off Devenallt Mountain—it's not like I have any room to judge how other families get along."

Ghleanna winced. "Sorry about that, too."

"It could have been my head." Braith let out a breath. "Ghleanna . . . ?"

"Mmmhm?"

"I'm worried."

"About?"

Braith let out another breath and admitted to Addolgar's sister, "Olgeirsson did not take Lady Katarina."

"Oh, I know." She waved all that away. "Addolgar already told me."

"Wait. You know?"

"Of course I know. My brothers hide nothing from me when it comes to our enemies."

"And it doesn't bother you that we may be starting a war based on a lie?"

"What's the lie? Olgeir may have not taken Katarina, but he took Davon. She's just as important."

"I know she is, but . . ."

"But . . . what?"

"Well"—Braith frowned, the realization suddenly hitting her—"if Davon didn't matter . . . why does Katarina? Because of her father?"

"Doubtful. It probably has more to do with the fact I reminded Addiena that with a war she wouldn't have to get approval from the Elders for a gods-damn thing."

Braith gawked at the She-dragon. "What in all the holy hells would make you tell her that for?"

"Brigida ordered me to." Ghleanna shrugged. "And I don't want to be a lizard. She can turn anyone into a lizard."

"I understand not wanting to be a lizard, Ghleanna, but still—"

"Look, a good war cleans out the weak." She tapped

Braith's chest. "You should come with us to battle. I heard what you did to those Lightnings."

"Your brother says I have a way with hammers."

"You should talk to our older brother Rhys then. His name *is* Rhys the Hammer. He only fights with hammers. He'd get you set up with a nice one." She pushed her short, black hair off her face. "You in love with my brother, Braith?"

"Rhys? I barely know him."

"Don't be a smart-ass, royal."

"Don't ask me personal questions, Low Born."

Ghleanna pointed a finger at Braith. "You better be in love with my brother."

"You're *ordering* me to love your brother?"

"I won't have his gods-damn heart broken because of you!"

Braith faced her. "Heart broken?" She straightened her back. "Over *me*?"

"Of course over you," Ghleanna barked, punctuating it by placing both hands against Braith's shoulders and shoving.

"Well, he never told *me*," Braith snapped and pushed back.

"Maybe you're just not paying attention, royal." Shove.

"And maybe you're just assuming, Low Born." Shove back.

Ghleanna stopped, sniffed the air. "Oh," she said, smiling, "my brother's coming this way. Maybe we'll just go ask—"

Braith didn't let her finish. She grabbed the She-dragon by her face and flung her toward the closed back doors of the horse stalls. Ghleanna's body rammed into and through the wooden doors, landing in the woods on the other side.

By the time Braith turned back around, Addolgar was walking into the stalls from the other open doors.

"There you are," he said. "Hungry? Food's on, but you'll have to move fast or miss out. The Cadwaladrs will descend on that table in a matter of minutes."

"All right."

Addolgar studied the damaged back doors. "What happened over there?"

"Got me."

Braith headed out, but as she crossed the courtyard, Addolgar caught up to her and took her hand into his.

"Addolgar?" she said as they neared the steps.

"Mhmm?"

Braith opened her mouth to tell him what she was feeling but quickly closed it again. She couldn't. Not without knowing how he really felt. She refused to make a fool of herself.

"What is it?" he pushed.

"My aunts," she decided to tell him, "want me to come back with them. For a little while. Get to know them and the cousins a bit."

"Good," he said. He smiled, his hand briefly squeezing hers. "It's become painfully obvious to me what you've been missing all these years is being with your Penarddun kin. You belong with them."

"I do." They reached the stairs, and Braith took the opportunity to pull her hand away. "And what about you?"

"Probably with Bercelak to fight the Lightnings. The three of us—me, Bercelak, and Ghleanna—fight well together."

"Excellent." She patted his shoulder before turning and walking up the stairs. As Braith entered the Main Hall, a cheer went up from her kin. Most likely because someone had broken out the ale.

"There she is!" Crystin announced, now comfortably situated on her mate's lap. "Ailean, you should have seen our girl. Fights just like her mum. Full of ruthless rage and uncontrollable brutality."

"Would have brought a tear to my eye . . . if I hadn't been bleeding from it at the time," Aledwen tossed in.

"Oh, look," Owena stated, waving toward the door. "It's The Mountain!"

Addolgar let out a sigh and, cringing, Braith looked up at him and mouthed, *Sorry.*

"He'll be coming with us tomorrow, too, Shalin," Crystin

said to Addolgar's mother. "But don't worry. We'll take care of him like he's one of our own."

"Hopefully not like one of your own *sons*," Shalin muttered.

"It's not like we kill the males at hatching, so I don't know why you're complaining," Owena snapped.

"And we know they're around somewhere," Crystin explained. "I'm sure our sons are fine . . . wherever they are."

"Don't worry," Crystin's mate explained, his big hand around a pint of ale. "There's always a male around to train them since the females have no interest."

Braith stepped up to the table and explained to her kin, "Actually, Addolgar's not coming with us. He's going with Bercelak into the Northlands."

Addolgar pulled out a chair and sat down. Braith began to do the same, but Addolgar's arm went around her waist and he pulled her onto his lap.

"It'll take a few weeks for Bercelak to get all the troops and supplies he'll need together," he told her. "Until then, I'll be with you."

"Oh. All right then."

This wasn't what Braith had expected. She'd wanted a clean ending. Not this lingering thing where she would only manage to get more and more attached until she wouldn't ever be able to let him go.

Unsure what to do, Braith did what she always did. She sort of folded in on herself. It was how she'd always handled her father when . . . well, whenever he was around. Pretending nothing bothered her was something Braith had always been good at, and she put those years of practice to excellent use now. But as she looked around the table of amiably chatting dragons, she noticed that Addolgar's mother was staring at her.

When she saw that Braith was looking her way, the She-dragon raised her brows. Braith frowned, confused. Shalin raised her brows again and then gestured to Addolgar with a tilt of her head. Still unclear what she was trying to tell her, Braith gave a small shake of her head.

That's when Shalin the Innocent, Tamer of Ailean the Slag, slammed her hands down on the table and barked, "Gods-dammit, Braith, say what you're actually thinking!"

The only time Addolgar could remember hearing his mother yell was when she'd discovered Ghleanna and Addol-gar holding a screaming and crying Bercelak over a small but active volcano they'd discovered deep in her cave.

"*What the bloody hells is wrong with you two?*" she'd bel-lowed at them while holding a sobbing and recently hatched Bercelak to her chest.

This time, however, she didn't sound mad as much as frustrated.

"*Mum,*" he lightly chastised.

"She's not saying what she's thinking, Addolgar." Shalin wagged a finger at Braith. "Your father's gone now, so there's absolutely no reason to keep what you're feeling to yourself. I can assure you from what I remember of your aunts . . . they won't."

Crystin nodded. "She's right."

"So you might as well start with my Addolgar," Shalin pushed.

Addolgar studied the She-dragon in his lap. "Braith?"

Braith turned on his lap so she could more easily look at him and announced, "*I don't know what the hells we're doing!*" Okay, that was much more a bellow, wasn't it?

"Well," Addolgar explained calmly, "um, I thought we'd stay here for the night. Go back with your aunts and I'd stay there until Bercelak calls me to battle. And before I go, I'd Claim you as my own and then your aunts would train you in weapons combat. Which, when you think about it, is the per-fect time, because there will be Lightnings trying to make their way over the Outer Plains' border into the Southlands, thinking those borders are undefended. You'll get some excellent training slaughtering that lot."

"He's right," Crystin agreed while reaching over and taking one of the ribs from the platter a servant had just placed on the table. "Nothing better than those fools swarming the border only to face the Daughters of the House of Penarddun. Bloody good training for my girls. Bloody good." Then she cleaned that rib of meat and marrow in seconds.

"So that's the plan," Addolgar told Braith. "Unless you want to do something else."

Braith stared at him, her mouth open. "What?" he asked her. "What's that look for?"

She looked over at his mother, and all Shalin could do was shake her head and say, "I know, dear. But you learn to love them despite it all."

Confused, Addolgar began, "I don't under—"

But before he could get his sentence out, Braith jumped off his lap, placed her travel bag over her shoulder, grabbed the neck of his chain-mail shirt, and yanked him out of the chair. Then, with a strength everyone in the universe should fear, she dragged him out of the dining hall, up the stairs, and to his room. She pushed him inside and slammed the door shut.

"Sit," she ordered, tossing her travel bag near the bed.

"Yeah, but—"

"Sit!"

Addolgar sat on the bed.

Braith walked up to him and asked, "You want to Claim me?"

"Of course I do." Addolgar thought a moment and then, his heart dropping, he asked, "You don't want me to? You don't love me?"

"I didn't say that."

"So you do love me?"

"I didn't say that either."

"Well, which is it, female?"

"Don't bark at me!"

"Well, don't play with my heart!"

"I'm not—"

Braith stopped, closed her eyes, took a breath.

After a few seconds, she said, her voice low, "I love you, Addolgar. And I can't imagine anything I want more than being Claimed by you."

Addolgar grinned. "See?"

"See?" Braith barked, glowering. "What should I see?"

"That we're perfect together. How can you not see that?"

"You're trying to drive me insane, aren't you, Addolgar?"

"I don't think so." He thought a moment. "No. I'm pretty sure I'm not."

Gods, what was she getting herself into with this dragon? Because he was big and ridiculous and some days just plain . . . goofy. But he was perfect for her, wasn't he?

Addolgar suddenly grabbed Braith around the waist and again pulled her onto his lap.

"I'm so in love with you, Braith," he told her, and she felt in her bones that he meant every word. "And do you know why?"

"I have no idea," she replied honestly.

"Because I am such an amazing dragon that I know I richly deserve a She-dragon as wonderful as you. See?" he asked, grinning at her. "How could I *not* love you when you're so clearly made for me?"

Aye, the big bastard would always be a handful. That she knew, too. But she didn't care. Because like his mother had said, Braith would love him despite all the rest of it.

"You know I'm right, don't you?" Addolgar guessed, winking at her and grinning. "I'm amazing. You're amazing. And we'll have amazing offspring. Strong and smart like their mum and able to take a good, solid head-butt like their da."

Braith ran her hands through her hair. "We're already having offspring?"

"Not right away. First you need to get proper battle training."

"And why do you think that's necessary?"

"Because you really enjoyed fighting those Lightnings, and you were really good at it. You can't waste skill like yours, Braith. Plus, to be honest, you do have a warrior's name. Braith of the Darkness. That's a warrior's name and you can't waste a good warrior's name."

"I guess I didn't understand the rules."

"But now you know."

Braith pushed Addolgar's arms aside so that she could turn around and get back on his lap, her legs around his waist, her arms around his neck.

"I do love you, Addolgar," she told him, loving how the words made his grin grow even wider. "More and more each day. It wasn't just my kin I was missing in my life, but you. One without the other would break my heart, and I thought my heart was dead a long time ago."

"Not dead, Braith." Addolgar pushed her hair off her shoulders. "Just hibernating. Like a bear."

She laughed and kissed Addolgar, the warmth of his mouth making her feel safe and loved. His hands clutched the back of her shirt as he deepened their kiss, his tongue exploring her mouth, reminding her why she enjoyed being human around Addolgar.

When the kiss ended, they were panting, Addolgar resting his forehead against hers.

"It will not be easy to leave you for the cold of the North-lands, luv."

"But think of it this way . . . while you're away, you won't have to hear my aunts call you The Mountain."

Addolgar rolled his eyes. "Is there *any* way we can get them to stop doing that?"

"Of course not."

He rested his head on her shoulder. "I thought that's what you'd say. . . ."

"No point in getting upset," Braith said, running her hands through his hair. "Especially since I brought something just for you in my travel bag."

Addolgar raised his head. "For me?"

"Uh-huh."

Glancing over, Addolgar saw the bag lying on the floor. He grabbed it and, with Braith still on his lap, he dug his hand inside.

His grin went from cheerful to leering as he pulled out her aunt's chains, cuffs, and collar.

Addolgar held them up. "And what are we going to do with all this, Braith of the Darkness?"

Pressing her hand against his chest, Braith shoved her mate flat against the bed, pinning him there, and snatched the chains from him. She grinned down into his suddenly panic-stricken face. "Guess."

Epilogue

During the Reign of Queen Rhiannon the White

Addolgar landed on the ground and immediately shifted to human. While he put clothes on, he tried not to listen to the complaining going on a few feet away from him.

He was a general in Her Majesty's army. A Cadwaladr.

And an extremely proud father of seven Daughters of the House of Penarddun. Yet, Addolgar was being forced to listen to so much gods-damn complaining!

His eyes narrowed on the blue hair shining in the sunlight while the complaining went on and on.

For Addolgar was just one simple dragon. So it was unfair for *anyone* to think he could tolerate this. Or that he *should* tolerate this. He deserved much better for all he'd sacrificed over the years.

So, picking up his hammer, Addolgar walked up behind all that to-the-ground-length blue hair and raised his weapon. With his left eye beginning to twitch, he brought the hammer down.

But before it crashed into the head, silencing all that complaining, a strong hand caught his arm—and held it. Only one being he knew of, besides his brothers and Ghleanna, could do that.

He looked down into the smiling human face of his mate. Braith of the Darkness, Daughter of the House of Penarddun, and mother of thirteen offspring—seven perfect daughters, and six idiot sons—shook her head at him.

"I. Can't. Stand. It. *Anymore*," he told her, glaring at all that blue hair that did not belong to anyone from the House of Penarddun, but adorned the big, fat head of one of Addolgar's many nephews.

Briefly chewing her lip so she didn't laugh out loud, Braith called out, "How are you, dearest Éibhear?"

Sighing—dramatically—something his ridiculous princely nephew, the son of his brother Bercelak, had managed to make into a bloody art form in his short, less-than-a-century-old life—the idiot boy didn't even turn around before he started complaining more!

"I've had better days, Auntie Braith."

"I'm sure you have." She tugged on Addolgar's arm, raised her eyebrows. *Lower it,* she mouthed at him.

I don't want to.

Do it anyway.

With much regret—he'd never have a chance like that again—Addolgar lowered his weapon just as the idiot boy faced them.

"I thought you were staying in Dark Plains for a little longer," Braith prompted Éibhear. She looked over her shoulder at the boy, and the way her cotton shirt was cut, Addolgar could see part of the Claiming brand that he'd placed on her upper chest all those years ago. Addolgar wore Braith's Claiming mark with pride on his entire right leg, from ass to foot.

"I did, too," Éibhear continued to complain. "But apparently my father had other ideas."

"It was either that," Addolgar shot back at the boy, "or let Bercelak cut off your head like he planned!"

Éibhear, human and dressed in chain mail and the surcoat of some long-dead army, put his hands on his hips. "Why? Because I didn't agree with the old bastard?"

"You're a soldier!" Addolgar yelled. "You don't agree. You don't disagree. *You follow orders!*"

The boy raised his hands in the air. "Well . . . I don't like following orders. How about that, Uncle?"

Addolgar went for the boy again, but Braith rammed her hand against his chest, stopping him before he got more than a few feet.

"Éibhear dear," Braith said, "why don't you go inside and see your cousins."

"I don't feel like seeing anybody," the idiot boy complained.

Now, it was one thing when Addolgar's demands weren't followed, but it was another when Braith's nicely put requests weren't.

Slowly, the She-dragon faced her nephew-by-mating. As always, she had two hammers secured to her back. One was once Addolgar's hammer. The other was one Addolgar had had made for her. She'd been fighting with those two weapons for centuries now, and dragon, human, and centaur feared her. Of course, Addolgar had been right . . . the hammer was the perfect weapon for her. Unlike the current queen, Rhiannon, Braith was not sharp-tongued. She was blunt in word and deed, and blunt weapons were perfect for her. Lack of an edge never stopped her from killing enemies with an enthusiasm that even her own kin respected . . . and feared.

"Nephew," she said, walking up to Éibhear. "Go inside and see your cousins."

"Was I not clear?" Éibhear snapped back. "I said I don't feel like it."

"Oh. I see."

Braith turned away from the idiot boy and with her eyes on Addolgar, she pulled out one of her hammers, hefted it between both hands, and spun, swinging the weapon.

The boy, to his credit, was quick, though; his time in his mother's army had enhanced his reflexes. He dropped low and the hammer zipped by, the head of it ramming into the ancient tree beside him—and tearing it out at the root. The tree tipped over and, with great noise, fell.

Horrified, Éibhear stared first at the fallen tree, then up at Braith from his still-crouched position.

"I said," Braith calmly repeated, "go inside and see your cousins."

"Yes, ma'am."

The idiot boy stood on shaky legs and stumbled quickly toward the Penarddun cave. Once he'd disappeared inside, Braith secured her weapon and again faced Addolgar.

After staring at each other for a long moment, they both burst out laughing.

"Gods, Addolgar—what the holy hells? What happened to my sweet Éibhear?"

"And if I have to hear that bloody question again from some besotted female . . . *I will end him*!"

She returned to Addolgar's side. "What happened? I

thought he was to stay in Dark Plains for the next two or three moons. At least. And I definitely didn't think he'd be going back to the Northlands with the Lightnings after what he did to that Northlander's cousin."

Refusing to think too much about the near-war the boy had almost started with their current Northland allies, Addolgar stepped close to his mate and said low, "I'm not taking him back to the Lightnings."

"Where are you taking him?"

Addolgar didn't answer right away, trying to think of the best way to say it.

"Addolgar?" Braith pushed.

Forget it. There was no best way to say it.

"I'm taking him into the Ice Lands."

Braith blinked, shocked. "What the battle-fuck for?"

"He's to become Mì-runach."

She gasped, hand clasping over her mouth. "Addolgar, no! No!"

Although the Mì-runach were rarely mentioned among the Southland dragons, everyone knew of them. They were nothing more than a brutal death squad made up of warriors who couldn't follow orders. Who were more a risk to their comrades than they were a help. And the training for those who joined the Mì-runach was brutal, heartless, just like the dragons who made up their ranks.

"We have no other option," Addolgar told his mate. "You see how he's acting."

"He's young. And obsessed with some human female with impossibly long legs. Give him time. He'll work through this."

"Not without some help." Not without the heartless training of the Mì-runach.

"Isn't that what kin is for, Addolgar? Leave him here with my aunts. They'll get him in line."

"Absolutely not. First off, this wasn't my decision or even

just Bercelak's. It was Rhiannon's. She made this decision, so there'll be no going back. And secondly, I'll not have my daughters around that idiot boy's bad influence."

Braith's lips pursed and she rested a hand on her hip. "What about your sons?"

"What about them?"

"Don't they matter?"

"If they did, you would have warned me long before we had them," he said, as he'd been saying ever since his first son had been hatched.

"This again?" she demanded.

"You should have warned me!"

"What would it have changed?"

"Everything."

"*Da!*" one of Addolgar's sons yelled from behind him, making Addolgar cringe. "*Hello, Da!*"

Addolgar turned, faced his middle son. The boy was standing right behind him in human form, eating a big wheel of cheese, and yelling at him even though Addolgar was less than four feet away.

"Hello, son."

"*You staying long, Da?*"

"Not on this trip. But when I come back this way, I'll be staying for a bit."

"*Good!*" the boy continued to yell.

"Why are you yelling?"

"*Was I?*" he yelled.

The sound of something heavy hitting rock had Addolgar stepping around his middle son, but that just showed him the tragic sight of his two youngest sons taking turns running and ramming their heads into the side of their mountain home. Over and over again.

It's what Braith hadn't warned him about, even though Owena had apparently warned her. That although the males of the Penarddun line were big and strong and good, solid fighters, they were, to put it bluntly, painfully dumb. Not like their sisters at all.

"*Cheese?*" his middle son yelled, shoving the half-eaten wheel under Addolgar's defenseless nose.

"No."

Braith patted their son's arm. "Why don't you lot go inside? Éibhear's here, but only for the night."

"*Éibhear's here?*" the boy yelled. He faced his still-ramming-into-the-mountain brothers and yelled, "*Oy! Éibhear's here!*"

"*Éibhear's here!*" the other two cheered in unison. Then they charged toward the cave opening, but as they neared it, the youngest shoved his older brother so that he missed the opening and ran snout-first into the cave wall.

The boy flew back, landed, sat up, shook his big, blue head, and laughing, got to his claws. "*Bastard!*" he yelled before charging after his brother. Now the two would batter each other all the way inside until their great aunts and older female cousins told them to cut it out.

Grinning, his mouth filled with cheese, Addolgar's middle son ambled back into the cave.

"They could be worse," Braith reminded Addolgar.

"They could be?"

"They could be like Éibhear."

Addolgar remembered his brother's face when Bercelak had ordered his youngest son from his sight while Addolgar, Ghleanna, and Bercelak's second oldest son, Briec, worked hard to hold the dragon back from murdering his own flesh and blood.

"You're right," Addolgar finally agreed. "It could be worse."

Braith slipped her arms around Addolgar's waist, hugged him. "I'm glad you're here."

"So am I." He pulled her close, kissed her temple. "I wish I didn't have to go, but this needs to be done."

"And Bercelak chose the one dragon he could trust to make sure Éibhear gets to the Ice Lands safely. But you can't keep trying to kill that boy with your ax. It'll put a strain on family dinners."

"Only with Rhiannon, since she really loves the nasty bastard. And it wasn't me ax, it was me hammer."

Braith laughed. "Oh. Well then."

Addolgar hugged Braith again, resting his head on her shoulder. "Do you think the idiots—"

"*Addolgar*," she softly chastised.

"Fine. Do you think our *sons* will keep Éibhear here for the night? You know, keep him busy?"

"I do. They love Éibhear and they're such cheery bastards, they overlook almost everyone's rude behavior."

"Then let's go to town. Spend the night at that pub there."

Braith lifted his head from her shoulder, kissed him. Centuries and her kiss still made him as weak as one of her fists to the face.

Panting, they pressed their foreheads together and gazed at each other.

"Aye," Braith breathlessly agreed. "Let's go to the pub. You can have breakfast with the rest of our brats in the morning, before you leave."

She stepped back and took his hand. They were grinning at each other when Éibhear stepped out of the cave and yelled, "Do I really have to stay here talking to these dragons?"

Addolgar was marching over there to tell the idiot boy *exactly* what he had to do and how to do it, but Braith, still holding his hand, pulled him back as his two eldest daughters in their human forms came out of the cave and cut in front of the boy. They blocked him and his eldest daughter raised her arm and pointed her finger, motioning back inside the cave.

"I don't report to you," the idiot boy snarled at her.

That's when Addolgar's second oldest daughter stepped

into her cousin and stared him in the eye. Not even an inch shorter than the very large Éibhear, she glared at him until three more of Addolgar's tall, powerfully built daughters came out as well . . . and surrounded the idiot boy. Without a word, they overpowered their cousin without raising a weapon or issuing a threat. Their presence alone *was* a threat. Understanding that, the idiot boy snarled but turned around and went back into the cave.

His daughters faced Addolgar and Braith, waved, and said together, "Hi, Daddy."

"My beautiful daughters."

"We'll keep an eye on Éibhear tonight," his eldest offered with a smile that she had clearly inherited from her mother. "If you and Mum need some time alone."

Giggling, his daughters went back inside and Addolgar looked at his mate, grinned.

"I don't think I've ever seen you look prouder," Braith noted.

"Because I have perfect daughters, just like their mum, and . . . sturdy, reliable sons."

She laughed. "Sturdy and reliable? If that's the best you can do for our sons."

"It is. But," he promised her, "I'm sure after several hours alone with me beautiful mate, I can come up with something much, much better."

Pulling him toward town, Braith teased, "Well, when you give me an offer like that, Addolgar the Cheerful, I don't see how any female with a passionate love of hammers can turn you down. . . ."

ABOUT THE AUTHOR

Originally from Long Island, *New York Times* bestselling author G.A. Aiken has resigned herself to West Coast living, which involves healthy food, mostly sunny days, and lots of guys not wearing shirts when they really should be. Writing as Shelly Laurenston, she is also the creator of the wickedly funny Pride series for Brava. For more info about G.A. Aiken's dangerously and arrogantly sexy dragons, go to www.gaaiken.com.